the Padre Predator

A MYSTERY NOVEL

DAVID HARRY

DEDICATION

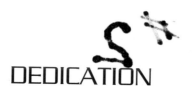

This book is dedicated to the men and women in uniform deployed throughout the world who work tirelessly 24/7 to keep us safe from scary things that could go boom in the night. A special thanks goes to the U.S. Coast Guard for their constant vigilance protecting our shores from all manner of assault. And it goes without saying that we all stand in awe, and in deep appreciation, of the Navy and Coast Guard SEALS who so willingly put their lives in jeopardy to protect our way of life. And to Navy Corpsman, Sebastian Gally, who has proudly served his country in Iraq and Afghanistan, I salute you. Thank you. Thank you. Thank you.

DISCLAIMER

Everything in this book, except for the establishments listed and a few local folks, is fictitious. The words spoken by any of the locals are, of course, also fictional. As I've said to anyone who will listen, South Padre Island is a gem in the sun. Despite its proximity to the drug-related turbulence now occurring in Mexico, SPI remains a safe and extremely friendly place to live or vacation.

Printed in the United States and published by Hotray LLC.

ISBN: 1461154014
ISBN-13: 9781461154013

SOUTH PADRE ISLAND AND PORT ISABEL ESTABLISHMENTS FREQUENTED BY JIMMY REDSTONE AND ANGELLA MARTINEZ

Beach House Vacation Rentals
Blue Marlin Supermarket
Boomerang Billy's at the Surf Motel
Cafe Kranzler
Coastal Current Weekly
D'Pizza Joint
Gabriella's Italian Grill & Pizzeria
Hilton Garden Inn
Isla Grand Beach Resort
Island Breeze
Island Market
Jim's Pier
K's Jewlery & Beads
Kelly's Irish Pub
Louie's Backyard
Marchan's Restaurant
Padre Island Brewing Company
Parade
Paragraphs On Padre
Port Isabel/South Padre Press
Schlitterbahn Beach Waterpark
Sea Ranch Restaurant
The Tiki
Tom and Jerry's Beach Club
Wal-Mart
Wanna-Wanna Beach Bar

Please don't forget to stop by and tell them Jimmy and Angella sent you. If by chance you're up for a drink you might want to follow in Jimmy's footsteps and try a Skinny Bones.

ONE

We were gathering at *Ted's* for breakfast. South Padre Island Police Chief William Duran had dispatched a text message to a few friends asking them to join him in welcoming me back to the island. Typical of him, the message was short and to the point.

Breakfast at Teds 7:30 welcome Redstone

From the reports I had read about him and the scuttlebutt among law enforcement people, it wasn't in Duran's character to hold breakfast meetings. He shunned social niceties, preferring to deal on an arm's-length basis with everyone. Something was bothering him. From what I had heard, when Duran was bothered he was certain to pass it along. That knowledge made me curious—and somewhat apprehensive.

I reminded myself that he had no direct control over me. But my boss, Lieutenant Miller Contentus, usually accommodated requests from police chiefs. Thus, the apprehension.

I suspected Angella Martinez had been invited. Angella was the rookie patrol officer Duran had assigned to work with me in the investigation of the murder of a Texas Ranger. That murder turned out to be the prelude to the smuggling of an atomic device into the country by way of South Padre Island. Also smuggled ashore had been a highly trained North Korean operative, a man named Tae-hyun, whose mission, as best we could figure it out, was to detonate the bomb somewhere in the United States.

That little caper had put me back in the hospital, but thanks to Angella, at least I'm alive to tell the tale.

I had come to the island to rehabilitate my left shoulder; the one torn up by a bullet from my partner's gun, when a Texas Ranger was found dead on the beach. That had been late spring. As it turns out, my rehab had mostly taken place across the street from Ted's at a gym called *Island Fitness* located on the second floor of a small strip mall directly above a favorite Winter Texan eatery called *Texas Moon*.

South Padre Island is a barrier island, less than a half-mile wide in most places and almost as far south as one can be along the western shore of the Gulf of Mexico and still remain in the United States. The weather, moderated by the relatively warm water of the gulf and the prevailing southerly winds, makes the island a summer vacation spot for Texans and a favorite winter home for people living in the north-central regions of the country. Winter Texans, as they are called, start arriving around the first of December and swell the population by several thousand. This being Thanksgiving week, only a relatively few had taken up residence. That meant that Ted's would have only a moderate waiting line.

I arrived at Ted's early and was surprised when Teran Hughes, the owner and head trainer of *Island Fitness*, came through the door. I didn't expect Duran to have invited Teran to breakfast, but one never knows with the Chief.

"Jimmy Redstone!" Teran shouted out from the door, his voice as upbeat as I remembered it. "You're looking great! You ready to get back in harness? Come over after breakfast and we'll get you started."

"Another week and the docs'll release me to full activity," I responded, postponing the inevitable. Working out was the last thing on my mind, at least just then. Truth was, to get re-instated as a Texas Ranger I'd have to pass the physical, and Teran held the key to that. He's the best trainer I've ever worked with. "Actually, I need to get back in shape," I confessed. "I'll get over there soon as I can." I'd been out of the hospital a month and my strength was finally returning.

"When you're ready, you know where to find us," Teran replied. "Actually, Angella still comes in several times a week. I was worried that with her promotion and all she would give up her training. But she's regular as always. By the way," he added, "what really happened to you out there? She's not saying, that's for sure."

"Got my neck cut." I showed him the scar. It was healing well with little discomfort. The doctors had done a magnificent job of repairing me. The trick had been keeping me alive long enough to be airlifted to the operating room. Angella had seen to that part of it.

Angella had called me almost every day. She had visited me regularly in the hospital in Brownsville, and then when I was transferred to my home in Austin she drove up several times to visit. The woman was a fast learner and showed every promise of becoming a major asset to the SPI police force. I hadn't heard about her promotion and assumed it had just happened. I was surprised she hadn't told me and wondered what else she was holding back. A detective's mind never sleeps — or at least that's what I believed.

Karen, the owner of *Ted's*, came over. "I presume you're here for your usual," she said, addressing Teran while nodding toward a cup of orange juice she held in her hand. "Or are you staying for breakfast?"

"Just the OJ," he answered. "Got one of the Thanksgiving regulars from Dallas coming in. Broke her ankle back in the spring. Trying to get back into shape — if you know what I mean." This last was obviously directed at me.

"I'll get there soon as I'm released," I said.

"Okay," Teran replied. "Just go easy on the pecan pancakes."

"You're not good for business," Karen chided. "Here's your juice," she said, handing him the glass she held. "Drink it and go. No charge today. Just don't drive away business."

"I'm out of here," Teran called. "Thanks for the juice. Great seeing you, Jimmy. I'll be there when you're ready. Hey, by the way, you interested in listening to some music? A bunch of us are getting together over at *Steamers* Friday night. What can be bad about music on Black Friday? A client's granddaughter from Dallas, goes by the name of Kat, is playing bass. Kid's good! Be great fun. Join us." He turned toward the door. "Speaking of the devil! Angella! You doing okay today?"

"Doing just fine," Angella answered, a trace of surprise forming at the corner of her lips.

"Just leaving," Teran said. "Guess it's rendezvous time? I'll leave you two alone."

Angella's face colored slightly. "Chief Duran's idea."

"If that's your story, stick to it. Have a great day. See you both in the gym."

I hugged Angella, perhaps a bit too tightly and a bit too long. But it felt good — and natural. She was not in uniform and looked trim and fit.

"You're looking much better," she commented when I finally released her. "How you feeling?"

"Like my old self. For better or worse, I suppose. Now all I need do is convince the doc." I studied Angella to see if she was withholding information about this meeting. I saw nothing. But that proved nothing. She had been promoted and hadn't yet told me.

"It'll come soon enough. I'm glad to see you looking yourself." She looked around the tiny restaurant. "Duran's not here. That's unusual, he's always early. If you show up at seven for a seven o'clock meeting he considers you late."

Her smile was even brighter than I had anticipated and her eyes twinkled. Or was that a reflection of the bright sun flooding through the high windows? Before I could respond to her comments about the Chief, the man himself came through the door. "Redstone," he called, "glad you're back. Welcome to the island! You're looking well."

"Good to be back," I responded, momentarily puzzled by his cheerleader persona. "Fact is, it's good to be anyplace."

"Thought we lost you out there. Touch and go for a while."

"I made it. Thanks to Angella, with help from a few SEALS, and a bunch of doctors."

"And half the U.S. Coast Guard," Duran added. "They had more patrol boats in the bay than I could count."

We were seated at a small table in the corner. Angella and I each ordered pecan pancakes and the Chief a bowl of oatmeal.

"Wife put me on a diet," he explained. "Says I can't chase crooks with the weight I've gained." Neither of us commented. He continued. "I was going to invite your friend, Lieutenant Mark Cruses and his fiancée, Trich, but it turns out he's still under house arrest." Duran glanced toward the door. "Shame on the Coast Guard," he added, his voice low enough so that only Angella and I could hear him.

"That boss of his, Captain Boyle, is...is a bit over the top," I added, not sure how far I should take this.

Duran again looked toward the door. "Better be careful. I invited the good Captain to join us. Sort of a peace offering, if you will."

Duran was referring to Mark Cruses's immediate commander, Captain Ernest Boyle. Mark had been the head of the SPI Coast Guard Station when a gang of Mexican drug runners smuggled the North Korean and his suitcase A-bomb, onto the island. The gang's leader, Roberto Alterez Santiago, was the one who had slit my throat. He also happened to be the father of Mark's fiancée, Trich.

Boyle and I had exchanged harsh words and had almost come to blows over files that Mark had hidden away. While we ultimately did work together, I'm not ready to say the animosity is gone. There seemed something odd about the man. "You don't really think Boyle will come, do you?" I asked Duran.

"Never know. We do work together. Have to coordinate operations while he's here. He's settled down a bit. Seemed good if we could patch things between the two of you. Man's certainly... well, let's just say...different."

Now it was my turn to watch the door. I wasn't anxious to confront Boyle, and if it got physical I'd be a pushover in my condition. I made a mental resolve to start up again with Teran as soon as I could.

The door opened, but, to my relief, it was not Boyle but two locals—Griff and Joni. They owned *Paragraphs on Padre,* the SPI bookstore where one of the murder suspects had been rumored to have worked. Angella's interview had determined the rumor to have been false. Angella had included Griff and Joni's pictures in the interview summary file that I had read, which is why I so readily recognized them. I was speculating on why Duran would invite them to breakfast when my question was resolved. They sat at a table for two under the window across the room.

"After breakfast," Duran said, "I want you both to come back to my office. Some things have been bothering me about that whole business. There are just too many loose ends. I have the feeling...well, just a feeling that more is going to go down."

"Anything specific?" I asked.

"Can't talk here." He glanced around, again lowered his voice and said, "First of all, Mark did nothing improper, but yet he's been relieved of duty." Duran lowered his voice even further, "And they sent Santiago back to Mexico. Something's not—"

My cell rang.

I ignored it.

"—not right. I hear things I don't like. I think..."

"Think what?" I asked Duran.

"Not here. Said too much already. Finish your pancakes and we'll take it up in my office."

His cell signaled a text message. So did Angella's.

My cell rang again. I glanced at the screen. Same caller.

Duran studied his message and then nodded for me to answer my phone.

TWO

"Is this Jimmy Redstone?" the male voice at the other end of the line inquired.

I couldn't identify the voice. I didn't recognize the number and the used car salesman tone didn't do anything to reduce my annoyance at being interrupted during breakfast. "Who the hell you think would be answering his phone?" I snarled, trying my best to annoy the caller as much as he had annoyed me.

"I'm sorry if I woke you, Mr. Redstone, but I thought you'd like to hear about the award first hand."

"For starters, you didn't wake me. And what the hell are you talking about? What award? Who the hell is this, anyway?" I excused myself from the table and walked outside.

"Name's Billy Ray Jenkins. Name won't mean anything to you. I'm head of public relations for the Texas Rangers."

"Baseball? What the—"

"You pulling my leg? Your organization."

Typical self-important desk jockey calling with a feel-good story idea. "You bothering me about some Ranger of the Month story?" That didn't actually make sense, since the details of my being hauled off the South Padre Island marsh were classified. And most likely always would be. I couldn't imagine the Feds allowing the public to know that an atomic bomb, or bombs, had been smuggled into the country. The fact that one had been recovered made matters worse. Besides the general panic, Washington would log-jam with investigations.

My life had been saved when Angella held my wound closed until a SEAL dropped out of the sky four feet away and field-sealed it. It had been touch-and-go for the next week, but without that SEAL and the corpsmen who came in behind him, I would have died twenty-five miles north of where I was now standing. Actually, I wanted to go back there with Angella so that I could stand over what could have been my grave and thank her properly. Perhaps, some day.

"If this is some kind of hero story you're working on, you got the wrong guy," I answered. "The hero was the Seal and those medics. And don't forget Angella Martinez; she's the real hero here. I'm just lucky to be alive. But, hey, that's all been classified. You print anything about what took place and you'll disappear from the face of the earth."

Disregarding my outburst, he calmly replied, "Nobody's being overlooked. And nothing's being printed. The military folks were doing what they've been trained for. Besides, I'm not calling for *Employee of the Month* or any of that bullshit. I'm talking about the President's award for *Duty Above and Beyond*. At the White House."

"President's award? Like, in Mr. President? In Washington?" I was blabbering.

"That's who I'm talking about. Only president we got."

"What about the others? Angella, Chief Duran, those folks?"

Billy Ray responded, "I can't speak for what's going on, but I have indications that others are included as well."

"Never heard of such an award!" I was in no mood to be paraded around. Having your neck sliced open and watching your own blood pour into the sand changes your perspective on a lot of things. I was ready to accept my pension and find some other endeavor to keep me occupied.

"That's just it. It's private. Since the public isn't being told about the bombs, the ceremony is private. It'll be held in the Oval Office and there'll be no record of attendance. It's a big thing, but just not public."

Public was the last thing I wanted at this time, so that suited me just fine. But this had been a major operation involving Homeland Security, the Coast Guard, the Navy and who knows how many other agencies, all run by a retired tough-as-nails four-star general, name of Maxwell Jamison. It wasn't the first time that Jamison had been called out of retirement to handle national security operations such as the one I found myself in the middle of. For all I knew, the operation was still ongoing. We had tracked down one of the bombs, but there were indications at the time that there were at least two others.

"In the scheme of what's going on I played a minor role," I protested. "I don't deserve to be singled out. I hope this is not a bullshit Ranger grab for PR. You're playing with fire you think you can make hay out of this one."

"Truth is, Ranger Redstone, you don't have much choice. The President has invited you. Your boss, Lt. Contentus, has approved. That's the end of it."

"The hell you say! I'm still recuperating. Tell them doctor's orders, can't travel, or some such bullshit. You guys are good at that stuff."

"Everything's settled," Jenkins replied, his voice maintaining an irritating smoothness. "You'll be escorted to D.C.. State's sparing no expense."

"And just when is this fiasco scheduled?"

"You'll be picked up momentarily. Allowing for the time change and transit time, you'll be there for the ceremony at five. Actual flight time will be under three hours, I'm told."

"Today! You got to be kidding! You mean now?"

"I mean now. Car's on the way. Plane leaves from Brownsville as soon as you're on board."

"What the hell am I supposed to wear? This is bullshit! You positive Contentus is aware of this?" I've never known the man to book bullshit.

"He'll be on the plane with you."

"Who the hell else will be on that plane?"

"That's all I know, sorry. I was told to tell you to wear a suit, preferably with a white shirt and tie."

That sounded like it came from Contentus. My usual dress code called for jeans and a pullover. The only good news in all this is that my conditioning training with Teran, together with the hospital stay, had been good to my waistline. I would easily fit into my only suit. Only problem was, the suit was in Austin and I was on South Padre Island, several hundred miles away.

As if he read my mind, Jenkins said, "Arrangements have been made for everything you need. As I said, the state is sparing no expense."

"Don't forget cuffs on the shirt and a set of links." I might as well get something out of this. "Collar 13, arm length, hell I don't know. Whatever's average for a six-foot guy."

"We have your measurements, sir. Anything else I can do for you?"

"How long has Contentus known about this?" I was preparing myself for getting on my boss's case for keeping it from me.

"He's being briefed as you are. I believe he spoke to the General once or twice, but this was all worked out between the White House and the Governor. I'm just the messenger."

Aren't we all, I thought, aren't we all.

THREE

What puzzled me was the time frame. Why was the President moving this award along so fast? It wasn't as though this was going to be made public, so why the big hurry?

I'm naturally suspicious, making me good at what I do. Hunt down bad folks. This whole operation smelled rotten. In my job nothing ever turns out the way it started, and I had no evidence that this would be any different.

The story had not yet leaked. The captured North Korean, Tae-hyun, presented a problem, however. What were they planning to do with him? Couldn't put him on trial, not unless they wanted the bomb story out. That's why they let Santiago, the Mexican drug lord, go back home to his ranch. Locking him or Tae-hyun away at Gitmo was politically, and possibly legally, impossible. The solution was far above my pay grade, but it did seem that arranging for them to show up dead would have been a better alternative.

I'm on leave, so I'm not authorized to carry a weapon. The Secret Service frowns on bringing weapons into the Oval Office anyway. I could see the headline. TEXAS RANGER ARRESTED FOR ATTEMPTED ASSASSINATION. Not a good career move, assuming I had any career remaining.

Make that EX-TEXAS RANGER ARRESTED.

No actually, the headline would read: TEXAS GOVERNOR DENIES EXISTENCE OF TEXAS RANGER.

I pushed the door open to rejoin Angella and Chief Duran, and found both of them walking toward me. Seems the welcome-back-Jimmy-Redstone party had run its course.

Once outside, Duran said, "Suppose you were told about D.C.? I'm not happy, don't like surprises."

"Don't blame me, Chief. I just found out about it myself. But why are you unhappy?"

"Seems I'm going also."

"As am I," Angella added.

"Car'll be by for us in fifteen minutes. Told them to come by headquarters. See you both in my office." He moved quickly to his personal car and shot off down the street.

"He's pissed," Angella volunteered as soon as he was safely out of hearing. "He's never this wound-up about anything."

"What's it to him if he takes an all-expenses-paid trip back east?"

"Don't know the full story. But I can tell you, he's been agitated lately. He's been getting into it lately with that INS guy, Greenspar. Not like him to let anybody get under his skin."

"Greenspar?"

"You remember. During the raid when we flushed Tae-hyun. Greenspar was the big guy arguing with the Chief."

"Oh, right, him," I nodded. "Chief almost shot the bastard."

“Not as bad as that. Anyway, Chief’s been picking up street vibes. Seems some illegal aliens have been coming onto the island and the Chief believes it’s happening with the blessing of INS. And possibly the Coast Guard. I got to snoop around. Didn’t get much.”

“What exactly what were you doing?”

“Duran’s certain INS has another safe house on the island. I was assigned to find it.”

“And?”

“Actually, I thought I found the house. Asked for 24/7 surveillance. Got it and...”

“And?”

Angella’s lips pressed together and she looked away.

I waited.

“Listen, Jimmy. We’re friends, but I shouldn’t be talking to you about SPI business. If you want, I’ll see if Duran will let me brief you.”

“I respect that,” I said, knowing enough about Angella to know that pressing her would not work. “Let’s get over to Duran’s office before he busts a gut.”

FOUR

"We only have a few minutes before the car arrives," Duran barked. "I called Contentus and he's not called back. I hope to hell your boss knows what's going down because I certainly don't."

"I called him also," I replied. "Same result." Usually, when Contentus doesn't get right back to me, that means something's up and he's working it. But I was on medical leave, so there was really no reason for him to respond quickly — or at all. I still hadn't become accustomed to being out in the cold, and it didn't sit well.

"Listen, Redstone, I'm not positive we've seen the end of the bomb issue. You and Angella stopped Tae-hyun. The bomb's in custody. But... but as you deduced, there's more than likely others."

I waited for him to continue. Telling me what I already knew was not his style. I glanced in Angella's direction to see if she'd shed light on what was going on. Her attention was focused on

Duran. I concluded she was purposefully avoiding eye contact with me.

Duran remained silent a full minute, during which time the soft swish of the slow moving over-head fan blade grew louder and louder. Finally, he decided to continue. "I'm also troubled that the detonator key was never found. There seems to have been a lot of activity in the last few days and I think it's related to the key."

"Activity?" I commented. "What exactly?"

"Illegals coming across the beach. Angella, tell Redstone what you found."

"I overheard a conversation between an illegal staying at a safe house and one of the facilitators. Seems as though they were asking about an *llave de contacto,* an ignition key. Could have been for a car, but in the context of the discussion it seemed to me that *llave de contacto* was hidden, or in the possession of someone in Mexico.

"What was the context of the discussion?"

Angella looked toward Duran who nodded. "The facilitator asked the illegal if he had brought the ignition key."

"What was his response?" I asked, wondering why Angella and Duran were feeding this to me with an eye dropper.

Again Duran nodded and Angella replied, "He didn't have it, but he had heard a rumor that a Korean guy was coming to Mexico to meet up with someone who had the key."

"Did you get a name—or a location?

Again a nod from Duran.

"Not exactly, but I did come away thinking it was a woman who had the key."

At last, a compound answer. Progress.

"Was this person – this woman – Mexican?"

"Definitely not Mexican. He referred to a *burro extranjeros*, meaning 'foreign donkey.'"

"Was this conversation at the safe house?"

"Yes."

Duran, who had been looking out of his window during the exchange, announced, "Car's here. Say nothing from this point on. Too many ears. And let me caution you both. If Homeland Security's involved, and I think they are, then all of the ears won't be attached to humans."

FIVE

Thirty minutes later we arrived at Brownsville International Airport, one of the sleepiest airports in the country. I was sitting beside the driver with Angella and Chief Duran in back. My several attempts to engage in conversation with the Chief went for naught. I didn't know the man well, and from the little interaction I had had with him, I found him tough minded, but fair. His demeanor was that of a person under control, in command of the situation. Today I found him distracted and seemingly uncomfortable. The one comment he had made was to the effect that this was my show at the White House and he had no desire to be there.

The driver passed up the main terminal and I asked, "So where are we headed?"

He remained silent. My answer came a few seconds later. The car veered to the right, traveled about a hundred feet on a narrow gravel road, more like a bike path, coming to a stop beside a small wooden hut desperately in need of paint—or a push-over.

A sign read, OFFICIAL VEHICLES ONLY BEYOND THIS POINT. The driver rolled down his window, held his badge out for the guard to examine. From what I could see, the badge looked to be Texas State Police. The guard retreated inside and made a phone call. A moment later he stepped out and pointed toward a building about five hundred feet away and instructed the driver to proceed in that direction.

Pulling up next to the building, the driver spoke to us for the first time. "Here you are," he said, his voice flat and terse. "You can get out now."

I wanted to ask him what we had done to deserve such behavior, but thought better of it. The guy was a jerk, and jerks, for the most part, are best allowed to lie dormant.

Before we were fully out of the car, a door at the side of the building opened and two uniformed TSA officers stepped forward. One of them said, "We've been waiting for you. Chief Duran, Detective Martinez, and Mr. Redstone. Right this way, please."

I did not feel the need to inform him that my official rank was Lieutenant. Lieutenant, J.G., to be exact. For now, Mr. would do.

I brought up the rear as we passed through a scanner.

The TSA guy said, "The other gentleman's already on the plane. Arrived a few minutes ago." He motioned for us to follow and led us back outside through a door on the far side of the building. A Learjet Sixty was parked a few feet away, the flag of Texas painted on the fuselage.

We were ushered up the steps. This time I was in the lead.

"Fancy meeting you here," my boss, Lt. Miller Contentus, said by way of greeting even before my eyes adjusted to the soft light inside the plane.

Startled, I replied, "Funny, that's what I was just about to say. What the hell's this about?"

"I'm as clueless as you are. General Jamison won't say. That man can be a horse's ass sometimes." He looked over my shoulder. "I see you brought company. Angella," he said, his lips curling upward on his otherwise solemn face. "And Chief Duran! Gang's all here! You have a clue what's going on?"

"I was hoping you would tell us," Duran replied.

A shapely young woman made an appearance from somewhere in the back of the plane. "Sit where you want, folks," she told us, her eyes alive, obviously enjoying her role as hostess. "We'll be taking off in a moment or two. I'll be back for drink orders when we're in the air. You want something to eat? I'll get it for you. We're pretty well stocked."

When she retreated, I said to Contentus, "If that woman works for the State, then I'm filing a complaint about the women you hire."

"When you pay thirteen million, or whatever this bugger costs, the women are thrown in." He reddened, something I had never seen before. "Hey, don't ever say I said that. Have a grievance filed against me sure thing."

"You owe me one," I replied, not half kidding. "I feel like a pampered drug dealer."

"What about a rock star?" Duran said, "You got drugs on your mind, Redstone."

"Dealers actually fly in smaller planes," Angella commented, obviously much more comfortable around her boss than when we were last together. "This would call too much attention to their movements."

The door to the cockpit opened and the pilot stepped into the cabin, wearing an officially pleasant smile. "Welcome aboard," he announced in an up-beat tone. "I'm Colonel Harrison Kopski. I'll be your pilot to and from the District. I'll be assisted in the cockpit by Major Donald Forsythe. Master Sergeant Nancy Walker, I believe you've met her, will see that you have everything you require. This is a Lear Jet Sixty XR and today we'll be cruising at four hundred fifty-five knots. I'm expecting a tail wind, so our flight time will be approximately two and a half hours. One hundred fifty five minutes to be exact. For most of the flight we will be at forty-one thousand feet and I don't expect we'll encounter turbulence. We'll be landing at Potomac Airfield, a few miles from the Capital." Without pausing, he continued. "I'll be delivering you to a specially equipped hanger where you each will have private facilities to freshen up, shower, shave, sleep, have your hair done, whatever you wish. You'll have about two, two and a-half, maybe even three hours to yourselves before you'll be picked up for the short drive to the White House. Timing will depend on the President's schedule, so don't worry if the car is a bit late. You won't be keeping the Commander-In-Chief waiting. Nobody does that."

"Any questions?"

Contentus commented, "I thought this was a State plane. Your uniform confuses me."

"Air Force. You're flying on orders from the President. Lend-lease from the Governor, you might say. On the ground this appears to be a civilian flight. In the air we're military all the way. Changes the vectoring and the priorities." He studied each of us a moment and then added, "One other thing. If you forgot anything, anything at all, shaving cream, razors," he glanced at Angella, "make-up, comb, hairbrush, that sort of thing, just tell Sergeant Walker and it will be there waiting for you. Oh, yes, suits, shirts, ties will be there as well." He smiled. "One of you ordered cufflinks. You got 'em. Hope you like 'em."

When no one responded, he said, "If there are no more questions, I'll move on back up front and we'll be on our way."

The others looked puzzled at the reference to the suits, ties, shirts and cufflinks.

"What about the cuff links?" Contentus pressed. "I told them you probably didn't have a clean shirt, but I didn't mention links."

"Okay, I 'fess up. I don't have the appropriate clothes for the White House. So they volunteered to supply everything I needed. On a whim I figured if the Government is offering, I'll accept. Got to look good for the Big Boss."

Duran saved me when he confessed, "I also told them I could use a Presidential-looking tie."

"Am I the only person who's got it together?" Contentus responded, finally breaking a smile.

"If this is confession time," Angella chimed in, "then I told them I didn't have a proper White House dress. Didn't think jeans and a tee would cut it."

Sergeant Walker appeared, pulled the door closed, checked our seat belts and took a seat herself. The plane began to taxi. She said, "Colonel doesn't waste time. He has priority clearance and he uses it. He'll have us in the air in a minute or two. Sit back, relax, enjoy the ride. As soon as we're up, I'll get you what you—"

The plane's engines ran up, cutting off the end of her sentence. The Lear surged forward and was soon streaking down a runway, or maybe with the jockey we had in the cockpit, he was using a taxiway. We were airborne in less than a minute.

A few minutes later, Walker stood facing us. "Drinks of choice, gentleman and lady," she inquired, "What'll it be?"

"It's still early, I'll take a beer," I replied. "Anything you have will work."

She turned to Angella.

"Orange juice, please."

"Orange juice!" I exclaimed, in mock surprise. "You're out of uniform, it's okay."

"What's that supposed to mean?" Duran asked, puzzled by my comment and searching Angella's face for a clue.

Angella twisted in her seat to face me. I could see her eyes narrow, hopefully in mock anger.

"Just a private joke," I replied, adding, "She refused to drink alcohol while we worked on the investigation. Claimed she was in uniform."

Walker then took the drink orders for the two bosses. Before disappearing to the back, she announced, "I have either steak or grilled chicken sandwiches for lunch. What's your choice?"

All four of us ordered steak. Two medium for the bosses and two medium rare for Angella and myself.

We had plenty of room. Four separate seats were arranged in a large square grouping with two on either side of the plane. Three seats were lined up facing the center across from the door. I had the impression those could be removed to make a small office or possibly a galley.

Angella and I sat across from each other behind Contentus and Duran. She turned to me and said, "You're looking fit. The bandage on your neck is much smaller than it was the last time I saw you."

"Actually, if the President hadn't interfered, I was scheduled to see the doc today. Most likely he'd take it off for good. It's healing nicely. Plastic surgeon did a great job. Says it'll heal with only a small line."

"Thank God for that."

"I don't know so much about God's role, but I'll drink to that SEAL." I said. Thinking back to the events surrounding Santiago slicing my neck, my vivid memory is not so much about my dying (I had resigned myself to that fate the moment he drew the razor-sharp blade across my neck) but rather the overwhelming peace that came over me when the SEAL's parachute sailed out of the dark horizon and filled my already blurred vision. I never heard the drop plane, and how long he was in the air I have no idea. All I know is that the most wonderful sight in my life was seeing him land not twenty feet from where I lay, my head in Angella's lap as she fought to hold back the blood.

"Believe me, I already have," Angella answered, her eyes saying more than the words. "For your information, it wasn't just one. There were six who landed and a medevac helicopter came in just behind them. Jamison, or whoever was in charge, did it right."

Duran turned in his seat to face us. "Go ahead, Angella, tell him your news. I had asked her to keep it to herself until she could tell you in person."

Her eyes came alive and she said, "I was saving it for later, but okay. I no longer have a uniform. I mean one that I need to wear to work every day." She paused for effect. "I was promoted to detective!"

"She's a natural," Duran injected. "Just don't let it get to your head young lady. Arrogance has done in more than one investigator."

"If that was directed at me then I protest," I replied, smiling. I pretended surprise, but Teran, who always knew everything on SPI, had already told me.

"If the shoe fits," Contentus added. He started to say more but the drinks came followed by the sandwiches. The conversation ceased. Angella selected a magazine from the supply on the bulkhead and lost herself in it, or so she pretended.

I finished my steak, drained a second beer and closed my eyes.

A hard thud woke me from a dream in which Angella and I were sitting in the weeds watching the boat with the terrorist pull away. We were helpless to stop him.

The plane slowed and taxied toward a large shed-like structure a good distance away from a small terminal building. The doors of the building slid open and the plane rolled to a stop inside. The doors closed behind us.

Colonel Kopski appeared in the cabin. "Welcome to the Nation's Capital. Hope you enjoyed your flight. When you disembark you will each be shown to your respective rooms. Please remain in your assigned room until you are called for. This is a secure facility and we must insist on your cooperation in remaining inside your room until the appropriate time. Everything you might require is already there, including the items you requested, Miss Martinez. Hope you all have a pleasant visit at the White House and I'll be here for your return flight home."

"What time do you expect that to be?" Contentus asked.

"I would guess around eight-thirty or so. But truthfully, I don't know. Might be earlier, might be later. The Boss is not always predictable. We'll be ready whenever it is. Have a good visit." He threw a salute and returned to the cockpit.

SIX

The room assigned to me belied the fact that we were in a hanger. The furnishings gave the appearance of an upscale hotel. Two double beds, sofa, two large-screen TVs, a desk, and even a fully stocked snack bar. The bathroom was laid out with a new tube of toothpaste, a fresh, still-in-the-box toothbrush, razors and blades, a comb and a brush, and a whole host of soaps, crèmes, shampoos, conditioners and body scrubbers.

I had just been jarred awake from a two-hour nap and was not the least bit tired, so I started pacing the room. I tried the TV, but mindlessly watching TV was not my normal activity. On a whim, I decided to take the pile of magazines I found on the desk and read them while soaking my still sore body in hot bath water.

I couldn't remember the last time I had done this, and to tell the truth, it felt good when I finally dragged my pruny body from the tub. I took my time dressing, managing to try on all three of the shirts I found hanging in the closet.

The suit was dark blue with faint vertical lines. I had to hand it to the person in charge. The suit fit perfectly—actually, too perfectly. I preferred to look the part of a slightly rumpled detective, as opposed to the professional lawyer appearance I now sported. Looking in the mirror, I got my *the chase is on* feeling when I saw my image.

I carefully removed the bandage from my neck. The wound was healing nicely; the angry red line had turned pink. I had been assured that by next summer it would be mostly white.

The shirt hid part of the damage. I selected the one with a hint of a vertical line to match the suit. There were five tie choices, and that decision proved to be the hardest. All the ties worked perfectly. Finally, I did a *eeny meeny miny mo* routine.

I was ready to go. How long I would have to wait was what I didn't know.

On came the TV. The Fox channel filled the room with noise, and as usual the hosts were bashing the President. This had been going on non-stop since his election. Not that I was a fan of his, but give the man a break already. No one could be as inept as their portrayal would lead a fan to believe.

I changed the channel and found an old John Wayne movie. *She Wore A Yellow Ribbon*. Lots of horses. Lots of Indians. Lots of bar fights. It was good to see someone else getting beat up. Once again proving accurate the old saying about misery.

About a third of the way into the movie, a loud knock sounded. Initially I thought it was the TV, but the second time convinced me otherwise. It was as though someone was trying to kick the door in.

I turned off the TV and opened the door.

Contentus and Duran were standing behind a mountain of a man. He must have weighed three-fifty and stood close to seven feet.

"You deaf? Been knocking on your door," the large guy said, glaring at me as if he would rather shoot me than speak to me.

"Watching TV. We ready to go? Where's Angella?"

"Back here," she called, moving out from behind the giant. "We were worried about you."

The black dress she was wearing was gorgeous. Or perhaps the right way to say it is: Angella was stunning! Her hair was combed out and her eyes gleamed. "You look sensational!" I blurted. "That dress is perfect on you."

"Thanks. It's easy when you have a private hair stylist and a professional make-up artist."

"Needs the raw material. You certainly have that to spare."

"Okay, you two, that's enough," Contentus barked. "You're coworkers, not lovers. Don't forget what brought us here."

"Compliments gone out of style?" I replied "I'm just telling her she looks gorgeous."

"Enough's enough," Duran broke in. "Our ride's waiting."

The big guy led us to a limo parked off to the side within the hanger. I looked around and at first couldn't find the jet that had brought us. Then I realized it had been moved to the side and a cover had been draped over it, rendering the logo of the great state of Texas invisible. My guess was that they were expecting other guests and didn't want questions raised about Texas.

Once we were all seated in the limo, the hanger door opened and the car rolled out. The time was exactly six p.m..

The big guy, who turned out to be our driver, spoke over the intercom. "You can relax. It's sixteen miles and it'll take us about thirty minutes. We'll be at the White House in time for your visit with the President. He's running a bit late, so not to worry. We'll enter under the West Wing and you're all pre-cleared. You'll find picture IDs for you back there. No need to check in. Please wear your ID so that it can be seen at all times. You will pass through the metal detector in the garage and then take the elevator directly up to the Oval Office. When you exit the elevator, you will be in a small area. You will not be going through the usual process, so no one will escort you and you will not be logged in. Wait there until the green light comes on over the door. That means the President is ready for you. Simply walk in. Any questions?"

When none of us responded, he continued. "Okay. Next thing, if any of you brought your weapons I suggest you leave them in this car along with all ammunition. Not a good idea to tangle with the gentlemen running the scanner. No sense of humor whatsoever. I suppose I don't have to remind you that knives, anything sharp, must remain in the car."

Nobody said anything, so he again continued, "Men—and lady—of few words. That's good. Means you understand. When you're finished up there, just take the elevator down to the garage and I'll be there for your return to the airfield. Be sure to take the elevator and not walk out through the door next to it. That door leads to the front controlled access. That won't be good."

We sat in silence for several minutes until Angella quipped, "The only thing missing from this ride is the body. We're sitting here in silence like pallbearers in search of a funeral."

"Be careful what you wish for?" I replied. "Don't give these guys any ideas."

"You referring to us?" Contentus asked. He was not comfortable being in a situation he did not himself script. The man wrote the book on control, and right now he was anything but in control.

"Present company excluded. I was thinking about your four-star general friend Maxwell Jamison. I got the feeling he would just as soon shoot you as talk to you."

"He's a tough old bird, all right. But good people under all that gruff. Been through a lot, keeps a steady hand."

We again fell silent and rode the rest of the way without further comment. I had to admit Angella was right. We did appear to be attending a funeral.

Even before we crossed the Potomac, the lighted Washington Monument focused my attention on the fact that we were going to the White House. Washington seemed more alive, more vibrant than it had the last time I was here many years back.

It was hard to believe twenty years had passed since we, my former wife and I, had brought our son Les here for his thirteenth birthday. We had dutifully climbed the steps to the Lincoln Memorial and read the carved stone aloud. Where had the time gone? How had I slipped so far from my son that we hardly now ever spoke? Was it my bad behavior that had caused the love between his mother and I to die? Or had my behavior occurred as a result of the lost love? The questions were numerous and easy. Only the answers were difficult.

"Okay, show time," the intercom voice announced, breaking into my nostalgia. "President's ready."

Passing through security was easier than I thought. No frisking, no emptying of pockets or purses, just a quick pass through the metal detector. We were ushered into the tiny elevator and deposited in a waiting area smaller than I thought it would be. I guessed that there was a traditional waiting room somewhere else. We had bypassed that procedure, meaning, I supposed, that no one knew we were here.

The green light flashed on and Contentus said, "Like the man said, it's show time. Be on your best behavior, Redstone."

I chose to ignore the jab.

The President was sitting on one of the two small sofas in the oval room. Across from him sat General Jamison. A gas-log fireplace warmed the room.

Both men stood when we entered. The President's famous smile was even more prominent in person. One could feel his presence.

Jamison shook hands with Contentus and patted his back. Contentus introduced Chief Duran, Angella, and then myself to Jamison.

Jamison then turned and introduced the four of us to the President in the same order, with me last.

"Sit, please," the President directed, his smile still as gracious and genuine as when we first entered. "First, I want to thank you folks for coming on such short notice. As you will see from what I am about to say, this is important. Second, I want to thank you personally, all four of you, for the great job you did eliminating the immediate threat." He turned to Angella and said, "Please don't take this the wrong way, but I had no idea beautiful women such as yourself are involved in such, shall we say, dangerous, work."

"Thank you, Mr. President," Angella answered, her face coloring despite the makeup.

Turning to me, he said, "I've seen footage of the scene and have been briefed on what led up to the confrontation. You both did a sensational job out there. Thank God you survived, Lieutenant Redstone."

"Thank you, Mr. President. In all honesty, the SEALS had a bigger hand in that than the good Lord though."

"You can thank General Jamison for that. Let me get to the point. You intercepted one of the bombs. But as important as that is, and I don't make light of it, even more important, you and Angella figured out exactly how the terrorists planned to introduce them into the country. Because of that, they were neutralized—at least temporarily giving us some breathing room. Thank God you did or there's no telling what would have happened. Your work disrupted them, at least for the moment. But we still believe the threat is real. Jamison will brief you further. The short form of this is that we need your help."

Here was the President of the United States calling four of us to the White House to ask for our help. It made no sense. Long ago, a mentor drilled into me that when things made no sense I didn't have all the facts. Or, to say it another way, the second shoe had not yet dropped.

Actually, I doubted if the first shoe had yet hit the ground.

The President stood as if to leave. "Lieutenant Redstone, a man as skilled as you, and with the distinguished record you have as a Texas Ranger, must be thinking, 'What's this about?' I very much appreciate your courtesy in not grilling me. Let me level with you as best as I can under the circumstances. This all happened because of a security breach at the very top. I believe the breach is at Homeland Security, but it must go deeper than that or none of this would have been possible. So far, we know of one person who infiltrated the Coast Guard. That person had to have been helped—from the inside—and he's dead. He certainly was not the leader. What we don't know is how many others there are and who managed it in the first place. Despite all our efforts, the person, or persons, at the top have avoided detection."

The President paused as if finished. But clearly he wasn't. He would not have brought us all the way here to tell us what we already had figured out. It served no purpose to tell outsiders about a traitor, possibly more, at the highest level of government.

"Lieutenant Redstone, you must be saying to yourself, 'So why tell us?' Well, here it is. I'm asking you—and Ms. Martinez—to track down the traitor, or traitors. I assume that warrants your trip to Washington."

"That does change the character of why we're here, Mr. President. I'll say that much," I responded, forcing sarcasm out of my tone.

"Then I'll count on you to make it right." He extended his hand and all four of us shook it before he turned to leave. "Thank you all for coming. General Jamison will brief you. You both will report directly to him."

The President then slipped out a side door and disappeared into the Rose Garden, leaving us alone with the general.

SEVEN

"Jamison," Contentus began, skipping formality with his old friend and going straight to the issue, "this is indeed most unusual. What the President has in mind is a job for the Feds, the FBI, possibly even the CIA. Not for a Texas Ranger, or for that matter, pardon me Angella, a South Padre Island rookie detective. So what gives?"

"I'll give it to you straight," Jamison responded, his jaw set as hard as always. "The atomic bomb landing on our soil frightened the bejeebers out of the President. Everybody knows there's been infiltration at the top. FBI is unable to confirm or deny high-level internal involvement. Frankly, he doesn't buy it. And what's more, he's convinced that if you hadn't put the puzzle together, the terrorists would have succeeded. Put it another way, he lost faith in the operation being run from Washington."

"General," I said, "I thought you ran the operation?"

"I do. But I'm no better than the structure working for me. The military is only as good as its intelligence. If there's a top-level security breach, then I'm receiving bad info. If so, I can't trust anything I get."

Contentus pressed him. "Then how in the hell do you expect two people from the outside, far outside I might add, to run this to ground? From an investigative perspective, it's not practical."

"Practical—or even possible—is not the issue. Something's rotten and we must get to the bottom of it. I don't have to tell you what would have happened if that bomb had gone off? We were given a second chance. We must move now."

"A Texas Ranger, a wounded Ranger on medical leave at that, and a rookie cop! You got to be nuts!" Contentus pressed.

"Nuts or not, that's our mission. The FBI has failed him. You know what that means? It means he can't trust anyone. He can't run the country that way. Bringing these two in changes the dynamic. Throws them off guard if you will. It's something they hadn't counted on."

"Any thoughts on where we begin this journey?" I asked.

"That's your department. You have full rein here," the General said, focusing his attention on me directly. "But I warn you of one thing. At all costs, this can't be made public. You understand me Redstone?"

"It's not a matter of me understanding. It's a matter of other circumstances." I was determined to not back down. But this man's burning intensity made it difficult. He was not accustomed to people questioning him.

"You have something in mind, say it!" Jamison demanded, his eyes burning into me with an intensity I had rarely ever seen outside of a prison. This man was not one for small talk.

"What are you going to do with the Korean? Santiago. The others? You can't hold them and you can't try them. Even the bomb itself presents a problem. It's leaking radiation and can't just be hidden in some warehouse."

"I'd shoot 'em if it was up to me. That's not your issue. You have two missions. First, determine if a second, or even a third, bomb is running loose. If they exist, find them. Second, find who the traitor—or traitors—are so we can eliminate them."

I had enough presence of mind not to ask what he meant by eliminating them, so I responded, "We can try to do the first, find the bombs, if they exist. But how in the hell do we even begin knowing anything about the internal workings of Homeland Security, or the Coast Guard? Or of any other department that might be involved in this thing? Neither of us has investigative authority over federal agencies. Besides, the FBI will go nuts when we try."

"Leave the military out of this!" Jamison snapped. "I'll handle them. I can deal with the service. You take care of the bureaucrats!"

I protested. "I have no ability to get inside information on federal departments. My God, that's a massive undertaking, even if I had authority, which I don't! I don't run in their circles. I'm in Austin, and they're in Washington and—"

"Excuses! I don't book excuses young man! Just get on with it! Your driver is your contact. He'll arrange anything you desire."

Contentus broke in before I could respond. "Seems you've worked this all through. There's a piece—or pieces—missing. Mind telling us the whole plan?"

"Redstone and Martinez will come onto Homeland Security payroll in an investigative capacity reporting directly to the head. For public consumption, their job will be to form an investigative division to ensure public money is being properly spent. They will each be given weapon-carrying authority and the ability to speak with anyone at anytime about anything. I will personally see they have top-level cooperation from all, and I do mean all, agencies."

"But," I said, "we're from Texas, not even close to here."

"As of now, you live here. Both of you."

Duran, having remained quiet through all this, asked, "And just who will Angella work for? I mean, who pays her expenses and all that?"

"As of midnight tonight, both Redstone and Martinez are federal employees. They will remain federal employees until this is over. At such time I expect they will return to their respective organizations."

"That's bull shit!" Contentus responded. "And just who agreed to that?"

"This has all been worked out between the White House and the Governor. Done deal. Get on with it."

That got my attention. "You're saying I'm no longer a Texas Ranger! Is that what I'm to understand?"

"That's exactly what I'm saying, Son. You two now work for me. Like it or not, that's the drill." He checked his watch. "Well, technically, not for another four hours, but who's counting."

Contentus grabbed his cell phone and started scrolling through the directory. I assumed he was calling Austin.

After a false start, someone on the other end answered and Contentus moved to a far wall of the Oval Office and said, "Sorry to bother you, Governor—"

He said nothing further and listened to the voice at the other end. In a few moments he flipped the phone closed. "He's on board all right. You two have been cut loose. You're on your own. The Governor wishes you both good luck."

Jamison said, "I know this is sudden, but we don't have time for polite negotiations and goodbye celebrations. This mission is critical. We must find any other bombs, if they exist, and we must find the mole. I don't need to explain to you why time is of the essence? We don't have the luxury to pussyfoot around." When I nodded, he continued, "Contentus, you and Duran can leave us. Go back to the hanger and the plane will take you both back to Texas. Redstone and Martinez will catch a later flight. They have work to do here first."

"I suppose we've been dismissed," Contentus said.

"You have. And one more thing. Both of you. While they work for me you both are to keep hands off. To be sure you understand, that includes no reporting or debriefing."

"Governor just explained that to me in no uncertain terms. I can't say as though I'm pleased. But orders are orders." Contentus looked in my direction. "My hands are tied. I can be a resource, but nothing more." He turned to Angella, who was standing off to the side, stunned at how fast her life had changed. "Good luck to both of you and may God bless our great country."

I couldn't tell if he was genuine or sarcastic. I suppose it made no difference which. Angella and I were into this over our heads with little real hope of digging our way out.

Duran, before taking his leave, shook my hand and hugged Angella. The events of the past few hours had me off balance, but my *this picture isn't right* alert sounded. Her body seemed to be pressed too tightly against his for a typical boss/employee relationship. I chalked it up to the image of Angella dressed up. She was certainly one hot, and to me, highly desirable, woman.

Duran then followed my boss—or should I say, former boss—out of the Oval Office.

Angella's earlier comment about us in need of a funeral hung heavy on my mind.

EIGHT

Jamison checked his watch. "I must make an appearance at the dinner the President is hosting, so we don't have much time. Here's what we have on this. The man you caught, the Korean, is what we are calling the igniter. He carries the ignition piece. In essence, it's a key that must be inserted in the bomb before it can be activated. I believe you know as much. Thanks to your work, we believe we've caught the other three igniters. Sandy Hook, Seattle, and San Diego. No other bombs have been recovered. However, there is strong evidence the other three were decoys. But, it seems the igniter key, or as some call it, the detonation key, from Tae-hyun is missing as well."

Men in Jamison's position and with his background and training are impossible to read. Yet I was picking up a vibe. I bit the bullet, so to speak. "What is it you're not telling me?"

"Intelligence from the CIA on the subject of atomic weapons is notoriously poor. Years ago we lost track of the so-called suitcase atomic weapons on their watch, and that might have been deliberately arranged by a rogue operator. I've had our people retrace everything known about the situation and we've turned up nothing." He paused to think about what he was going to say. "That's not exactly right. We found out nothing more about the missing weapons, but we did uncover... what should I call it...a suspicious pattern of missing and or deceased people who supposedly could have shed light on the subject."

"Do you have names, a lead? Some beginning point?"

"Nothing of any use, I'm afraid. All dead ends. Suggests to me a multi-department operation. But that's not my field of expertise."

"Where do we begin?"

"We'll set you up with offices, titles, that sort of stuff. Then my plan is to let you do your thing. I like the way you think and you two make a great team. Just get to it and find the bombs and the traitors. And do it quickly. You have the whole government at your disposal. Use the resources." Jamison studied us both for a moment and then added, "We can't very well set this operation up as a hunt for atomic bombs. So this must be accomplished with no publicity whatsoever. The reporters in this town have everything and everybody wired, so if we followed normal channels it would be a matter of days before a leak occurred. That's where you two come in. But remember, the President is a political animal, and if someone high up has turned, he wants him out, and the sooner the better. This is a political mess in the making. Even if the bombs don't go off, this can ruin his legacy."

"First you tell us to use the resources and now you're saying that if we do so our mission will leak. What is it to be?"

"Welcome to Washington, Mr. Redstone. I have every confidence you'll find a way."

I dropped the subject. "When will you announce our new positions?" I wanted to know how much time we had to get the operation underway before any news was out.

"Tomorrow. I want you two to set up housekeeping here in D.C.. I don't know your sleeping arrangements and frankly that's not my concern. You two want to take an apartment together, be my guest. You want separate pads, that's fine also. Just do it and do it fast. Tiny, that's your driver, will get you anything you require. That man can move mountains, so to speak. The government is picking up all costs and expenses. Tiny will work all that out for you. You're a field operator, I expect you in the field. That means moving back and forth quickly between D.C. and the Valley. That's where I come in, military transportation. Tiny will arrange it. Take advantage."

"Tiny work for you?"

"No one works for me. I'm officially retired. Tiny is Secret Service. You think just anybody can drive into the West Wing garage?" He pulled a device the size of an iPod from his pocket and turned it on.

Instantly the image of Contentus and Duran sitting in the car filled the screen. They looked solemn. Contentus was speaking. "Those two are being set up, for what I don't know. Redstone is good, but what the hell they think he'll accomplish snooping around Homeland Security I don't get. President's covering his ass is all I can figure."

"Jamison's your friend," Chief Duran replied. "He and I tangled earlier on this. Coast Guard's in it up to their gunnels, you ask me. I don't trust that asshole Captain Boyle. He's the guy took over the SPI Coast Guard station after Lieutenant Cruses ended up in a coma. I knew young Cruses well. Good guy. He and I worked together. He ran the Station well. Men loved him.

Boyle comes along, there's no talking to him. Guy'll do anything to protect his ass."

Jamison flipped the machine off.

"Got to be careful what you say when you're on government property. Big brother is most likely listening—and watching."

"Is that a threat?" I asked, figuring we had just been warned to keep our noses clean.

"Just letting you know we have ways of finding out what's going on. This is a national emergency by anyone's definition. Even got a code for the operation. Domestic. Operation Domestic. Don't know who comes up with these names, but that's what it is. Highest security alert. President, hear that to mean me, has unlimited authority to do what he deems best on this one, no holds barred. Just do your job and all will be well."

"I wouldn't dream of doing anything but my job. That go for you also, Angella?"

"Nothing but," she replied. "Glad to be of service."

Jamison opened the door to the hall and rang for the elevator.

The door opened and he said, "Tiny will meet you in the garage. You folks can work out the details."

"Thanks. And we'll not discuss anything relevant in the car, so you needn't bother wasting your time monitoring us."

"I had no intention of doing so. I have a dinner party to attend."

The door to the Oval Office swung closed and I was positive I would never again be ushered through those doors.

NINE

Kelvin "Tiny" Jurald was indeed waiting for us when we arrived in the garage. He introduced himself saying, "I understand I'm now working with you both. I was briefed while you were upstairs. This is not to my liking, but if the President asks, I obey. Simple as that. The only thing I promise is that when you're with me you'll be safe. Away from me you're on your own. Kapish?"

I could understand why he was assigned to the President. It would take a cannon to knock him down. "How about we go get dinner," I said, not wanting to talk in the garage or in the car. "That okay with you?"

He patted his ample girth. "You think I ever pass on a meal? Get in."

"For starters, how about turning off the video cam and the sound track?"

"Done already. First thing I did when I got the assignment, sweep the car."

"Can we trust you, or are you setting us up?" It was the first Angella had spoken, other than a few perfunctory words, since we had been given this assignment. It was good to know she was thinking clearly.

"It's a fair question—this one time. When I work with someone, I work with them. I got your back and I'm the best there is in the business. Period. Trust is paramount with what we do. And that's a two-way street. Kapish?"

"Kapish," I answered, not exactly sure what the word meant, but guessing it meant some form of *understand*.

Tiny took us to a small Italian restaurant somewhere in Georgetown. It smelled of Chianti; a hint of rosemary hung in the air. I assumed they knew him, because we were immediately ushered into a private room.

"The pasta here is excellent," Tiny informed me. "Homemade. Actually, everything on the menu is excellent. Beats the steak sandwiches you had on the plane."

I wondered if these people ever allowed anything to chance. Snooping into private conversations, monitoring what you ate, who you slept with, seemed to be a way of life for them. I said nothing.

After we ordered, he asked, "A couple of housekeeping chores. I made an executive decision for you. I sent the plane back to Texas with those stiffs you came with. Boss types if ever there were any. I can arrange another plane back tonight if you insist, but I thought it would be better to get the apartment situation straightened out sooner rather than later."

Angella and I glanced at each other.

Tiny missed nothing. "While you were upstairs, they played me the tape of the capture down there on South Padre Island. I also saw the way you looked at Angella when you came out of your room at the hanger. There's definitely chemistry between you."

"You saw that yourself?" Angella asked, skepticism in her voice. "Or did they brief you? And who is the *they* anyway?"

"You're firing too fast. I'm trained to read faces, and most importantly, eyes. We have less than a second to determine if a movement is a threat to the President. And, need I tell you, we must get it right. Trust me, I know how to get it right. You were sitting in that marsh with his head on your lap literally holding the blood back. I heard the professional calmness in your voice on the radio to Duran. But I saw the emotional involvement in your eyes when you thought you'd lost him. Need I say more?"

Angella was quiet for a long moment, her eyes focused on her lap. Moisture formed at the corners of her eyes. "He passed out just before the SEAL took over. I thought he was gone. That's what you saw."

"Let's not quibble over this. The point is, you two are connected. You want to share an apartment, I'm told its okay. Look, there are plenty of two-bedroom apartments available. Get a three-bedroom one if you want. Sharing an apartment doesn't mean sharing a bed. But it's no skin off my nose if you do. You want company, get a three-bedroom unit and I'll take one of the rooms. Give us more time to work together when you're in town. I actually prefer that idea."

Angella looked at me. "My divorce is now final. Jimmy, you set the ground rules. 'No involvement with a partner' is what you said. I'm taking you at your word. Does sharing an apartment work for you? I mean the room part, not the bed part."

"Only if you behave yourself," I quipped.

"It's not me I'm worried about," she responded. "I think I'm going to regret this, but let's take a three-bedroom unit. I kinda like the idea of having a chaperone. You married, Tiny?"

"Happily so. For fifteen years. Have two sons and a daughter." He smiled. "But I'm not a chaperone. People do what people do. I make no judgments."

"What will your wife say about our sleeping arrangements?"

"As long as I remain in my room there's no problem. This is one of the tamer arrangements I've been involved with. The job comes first."

"I'm okay with it, for now," Angella said, "but I retain the option to move out if it gets, shall we say, uncomfortable."

"I'll get something lined up first thing in the morning. The Service has a list of available places. Concentrate on a furnished unit. We can go see the choices in the morning. Then I'll take you shopping. You like, we can get an Xbox and some games. By noon we should be ready to rock and roll."

"Sounds like a dorm room at college. I hope we have better things to do than play games," Angella answered, agitation showing on her face. "Let's think this thing through."

I jumped in. "Before we start laying out our course of action, I need to know the ground rules." I turned to face Tiny. "What's your function in all this? Are you part of the team? I mean, do you go with us in the field, or what?"

Tiny turned serious. "I'm a resource. You tell me what you need, I get it done. You need an introduction, someone to run interference for you, I'm your man. You need facts looked up in a database, on line, from any agency of government, I'll get them for you. You want to run theories past me, that's fine. I'll listen, tell you what I think. But I'm not a detective. I don't extrapolate one fact to the next. FBI does that, not Secret Service. Kapish?"

"Not entirely. Just what do you want from us? You said you wanted to be in the loop, to be informed."

"That's right. I need to know where you are at all times. You got a suspect, I want to know. Treat me as you would your boss. I want to know what's going down. And I need to know it in real time. Kapish?"

"Let's get back to who you report to," Angella chimed in. "Start with who briefed you."

"Jamison is running this personally. He plays everything close. Man's wearing four stars. Nobody in government says no to him. You can literally hear people's heels clicking when he comes close. He has one person, and only one person, he trusts. Former military, also a former general."

"What's his name?"

"Not a him. A her. Gen. Lucinda Westminster McNaughton. Retired. You think Jamison is a son of a bitch. You ain't seen nothing! McNaughton is hell on wheels. She's some piece of work. You cross her, your ass is dead meat. Nobody, and I mean nobody, will lift a hand to help you if she gets on your case."

"What gives her so much power?" I asked.

"Comes from a well-connected family. Old line." He pulled out his cell and tapped the screen several times. Finally he found what he wanted and held it up for me to see.

It was an article in the *Statesman*, the Austin newspaper. Actually, it was an article that was scheduled to appear in tomorrow's paper. The headline read, *Injured Texas Ranger Retiring.* The subheadline read *Boating Accident Almost Severs Artery.* The article went on to talk about my length of service and praised the doctors for their precise work in a four-hour operation for sewing my carotid artery back together. It also prominently mentioned that

I had recently been reinstated from a suspension because I fatally wounded Badman Tex under suspicious circumstances.

I said to Tiny, "You're showing me this because—"

"Because she wrote it." He turned to Angella and asked, "You want to see the *Breeze*—or the Parade? Or perhaps the *Port Isabel and South Padre Island Press?* It'll run in all of them."

"Might as well. At least I'll know the party line."

Tiny touched the screen a few more times and held the phone up for Angella to see.

Local Cop Resigns, was the headline. The story told how Angella had been promoted prematurely to detective, leading to speculation that there was an improper relationship with the Chief of Police. An internal investigation turned up nothing definitive, but Angella elected to resign. There was a hint of insubordination on her part, but no real facts. A digital image of her sitting with the Chief at the *Wanna-Wanna Beach Bar* appeared below the article.

Angella's face turned bright red and her eyes narrowed. I was reading from behind her and placed my hand on her shoulder. She pushed it away.

"This is bull shit!" she said, loud enough for the wait staff to hear. "My career is ruined!"

"You think they care about your career or even your reputation?" Tiny replied. "They now own you and the sooner you understand that the better this will all work. I'm surprised they didn't charge you with some impropriety, such as sleeping with Duran."

"What makes you—"

"They could have used the picture of Duran saying goodbye to you in the Oval Office. That picture tells a story."

Angella glared at Tiny across the table. "Ass holes! They think that'll make me work harder, they're mistaken!"

Tiny looked at her, his eyes calm, his face in perfect control. "They don't need pictures for that. This mission is highly dangerous because you have no idea who your enemy is, internal or external. You'll do your best, if not for your country, but just to remain alive. I'll do my best to protect you, but truth is, I'm one guy swimming upstream alone. I didn't sign on to baby sit a couple of Texas cowboys on an atomic bomb hunt working for the Wild Witch of the East. But here we are. So we'll all suck it up and do what has to be done."

Angella continued to glare at him.

"Get over it, Angella! I told you, I don't give a rat's butt who you're sleeping with or not sleeping with. I just care about keeping you alive and getting you what you need to do your job. Kapish?"

Her eyes softened slightly. Then she smiled. "Kapish, Big Guy. Kapish."

"Before you put that phone away," I said to Tiny, "bring up a picture of McNaughton. I want to see who I'm working for."

In a moment we were looking at a woman in her mid-sixties, who, if Tiny hadn't said anything, I would have taken for a model. She looked to be about five ten, maybe even six feet. There simply was no other word to describe her, other than to say she was gorgeous. The intensity of her expression made her exotic.

"Not at all who I would have picked as a general. What branch?"

"Marines."

"Marines!" I exclaimed. "She for real? When was this taken?"

"Tonight. I thought you might ask. And yes, she's very much for real. Still works out and, I venture to say, could kick your butt."

My hand involuntarily went to the scar on my neck. "What else need we know about McNaughton?"

"She is absolutely tied to Jamison. He trusts her beyond question. She's been known to run her own operations, but he supports her unconditionally no matter what she does. They are tighter than my high school jeans."

"My take from what you've just said is that their sleeping arrangements are not entirely separate."

"Been lovers for over twenty-five years. Still going strong."

"And what does Mrs. General Maxwell Jamison have to say about all this?"

"She smiles and holds his arm when at official dinners. The rest of the time she's either heavily under the influence or partying on her own. That's just the way it is."

TEN

"You can't stay the night at the hanger. So I took the liberty of booking two rooms at the Crystal City Marriot. Everything from the hanger has been moved over."

"You don't miss a trick," I said, wondering how much of this had been prearranged.

My tone must have communicated my displeasure with him meddling in our lives, because he replied, "Just doing my job. I'm no more happy about this than you are, believe me. But I'm on assignment so my game face is on. I suggest you do the same. Kapish?"

"Kapish," I replied. He was right. We could piss and moan about the crap we had landed in, or we could use our energy for constructive purposes. "Kapish."

"The rooms are in your street names. Didn't see any reason to use aliases, not yet anyway," Tiny told us when he stopped in the circular drive in front of the Marriott. "Don't suppose you will need this, but for your information, the Metro line to D.C.

runs below this plaza. Just go downstairs and walk a few blocks in the tunnel. Also, there is shopping down there, and a few nice restaurants in case you need anything. See you two in the morning. Is nine too late?"

"Nine works for me," I answered. "Okay by you?" I asked Angella.

"Works," she replied, her tone conveying annoyance.

Once in the lobby, I said to her: "I'm guessing your annoyance is over the situation and not the wake-up time."

"I'm still too angry to sleep," she replied, "so let's plan our lives. My room or yours?"

"Mine's fine," I said.

When we were settled, Angella asked, "Where do we start in all this? I haven't a clue."

"I liken it to opening a ball of twine. You find a loose end and start pulling. We start by listing what we do know?"

Angella thought for a moment before replying, "Certainly nothing about the Homeland Security part of this. And very little else."

"That's not entirely accurate. On the Homeland Security side, we know that a radioman was assigned to the SPI Coast Guard station. We know he was a plant. Coast Guard is now part of Homeland Security. For that to happen, the permanent radioman had to be taken out, and the new one put in. One twine-end is to follow the plant's history back in time, see where that leads. Another thing we know is that someone in a position of authority had to arrange to have the replacement in place."

Angella dug out her cell phone and began entering notes.

"Number two, actually, number one, part C, is to find out who makes the actual station assignments and work schedules.

Must be some command chain this goes through. We can talk with Mark, and find out what he knows about all this."

"They're hanging poor Mark out to dry, and he had nothing to do with this," Angella commented, momentarily looking up from her note taking.

"I agree, except that he was engaged to the daughter of Santiago, the man who organized the infiltration. It was her brother, Alterez, who actually killed the Ranger as well as the replacement boat operator. Alterez is dying of radiation poisoning and Santiago's under house custody in his own house. I feel sorry for her, losing a brother and having a father all but incarcerated."

"And possibly her fiancée, Mark," I added.

Angella's eyes narrowed as they did when she was on to a lead. "You just said something that triggered a thought. Alterez was dosed with radiation. He's dying in a contamination ward in a hospital somewhere. That means whoever else came into contact with a bomb may also be radiation contaminated."

"They took the protective shield off the one they floated into SPI to lighten it. They probably didn't do that with the others, but it does make sense to check hospitals for radiation anyway."

Angella entered information into her browser. In a few minutes, she said, "It's called Acute Radiation Syndrome (ARS)."

While she was busy with the keyboard, I said, "Hospitals would have made it public if a bunch of people had ARS. What are the symptoms?"

"Looks like nausea, vomiting, headache, fatigue, hair loss. Could also be diarrhea, bloody vomit or stools."

"We can start by rounding up hospital reports of people with those symptoms. See what turns up."

"How the hell we going to do that?"

"That's Tiny's problem, not ours."

"Two threads down, a zillion to go," Angella quipped, her spirits seemingly rising. "So what's the next thread?"

"Been thinking of that. We create our own by letting the Korean go. They can't try him. They can't really hold him very much longer before some press weasel gets his nose in the tent. We let him go and watch him run. He either hooks up with the ignition key, or hooks up with someone who leads us to a key—or to a bomb."

"Or he just leaves the country never to be seen again! That's too far out of the box. They'll never allow it."

"Like I said, he can't be put on trial, and he can't be held. They'll agree, if for no other reason than to shoot him as an escaped prisoner. You heard Jamison say just that."

"Actually, you're right. Jamison will have him shot."

"That's not our problem. Hey, this has been a long day and I'm still not back to my old self, whatever that really was. Say goodnight, Gracie."

"What the hell's that supposed to mean?" Angella asked, her brow rolling up in puzzlement.

"You're too young to remember the George Burns, Gracie Allen show. That's how they ended each episode."

"You kicking me out?"

"I'd prefer you to stay, don't get me wrong. But barring that I'm going to get some sleep. We'll be house hunting in the morning and I need to be fresh for the important decisions."

"Important decisions?"

"Like picking out new undies and socks. The exciting stuff."

"So what's my exit line?"

"Goodnight."

ELEVEN

By noon we had finished clothes shopping and were already looking at our fifth apartment. This one was actually in Arlington, less than a mile from Crystal City where we were staying, and was also connected to the Metro by a tunnel accessible from the underground garage. It was a six-floor modern building and appeared to be all aluminum and glass. The owner was in Europe on an extended Secret Service assignment.

The furnishings, even to my relatively untrained eye, were sensational. The place had three bedrooms and a spacious kitchen. The complex had a pool and the obligatory exercise room.

Tiny chimed in. He had been relatively quiet all morning, dutifully driving us all over the area. "Service says you'd be doing them a favor if you took this one."

"Why does the Service care?"

"The owner is on government assignment and the Service is already paying the bills. If you take it, it won't cost them anything.

Always a good deal, especially when we want other things from them."

"Like what?"

"A car, perhaps. The Metro works for getting in and out of the city, but you'll need wheels to move around outside the area."

I glanced at Angella and the answer was clear. She was prowling through the pantry and had several expensive looking cooking utensils out on the counter. "Looks as though you're planning a dinner party," I called over to her. The smile on her face and lightness in her movements said it all.

"It would be fun, wouldn't it? I've always dreamed of a kitchen like this. We'll have to make some friends just so I can throw a party."

"You can cook for me if that pleases you." Tiny called to her.

I was thinking of something romantic, just the two of us, followed by some wine, soft music. The living room fireplace would add just the right touch. I was starting to think three bedrooms was one, or possibly two, more than we actually required.

I glanced at Angella and was certain she was reading my mind. Or had I been talking out loud?

"What ever it is you're thinking, don't say it," Angella said to me, a twinkle in her eye that I had not seen before. There certainly was chemistry between us.

"We'll take this one," I unnecessarily said to Tiny. He had already known the answer.

"I've already checked. I'm told you can move your stuff in later today. Need to sign a few papers with the Service. You won't steal stuff, you'll move out when asked, that sort of stuff. Papers will be ready at three today. That's perfect 'cause our next stop is to install you two in your offices. That one was a bit tricky, but you're going to report to the National Cyber Security Center as Special Investigative Officers."

"What the hell is that?"

"That's the point. You'll fly under the radar. Everyone'll think you're a couple of geeks searching the Internet for other geeks."

"Last thing in the world I'd be mistaken for is a geek," I said. "Hope you guys know how to go undercover better than that."

"Your offices are being set up as we speak. Let's get some lunch and then go do the admin bullshit; pick up your business cards, get IDs and badges, fingerprints, all the normal first day crap."

"What about pay? Who pays us and how does that all work?" I didn't want to sound mercenary, but getting paid is important. "Life in Washington is expensive, or so I've heard."

"It's being worked out now. McNaughton is charged with running the traps. That's good for you, 'cause when it comes to money, she's not in touch. I won't promise, but I'd be surprised if she doesn't slot you in somewhere between GS twelve and GS fifteen."

"Translate, please," Angella said.

"GS twelve is about seventy-five K and fifteen is about a hundred twenty, something in that order."

"Wow!" Angella exclaimed. Ever the practical one, she asked, "Will they be deducting for this pad?"

"I don't expect they will," Tiny replied, "but one never knows about the government. Keep Lucinda on your side and nice things will happen."

I was beginning to like this gig. Even with colossal overtime I had never made more then the GS twelve numbers. My guess is that Angella made less than thirty thousand a year. Hell, her boss didn't make eighty thousand.

TWELVE

Three hours later, I was standing outside my new office watching through the doorway as a small army of people hung pictures, ran cords, opened supply boxes and stowed everything in the desk and credenza that had just arrived. The desk alone appeared larger than my office back in Austin.

The only things missing were chairs for the round conference table. I was told they would be in place by late afternoon.

Angella's office was across the hall, and the only difference I could discern was her conference table was smaller than mine. Everything else seemed identical.

An energetic well-traveled woman who looked to be in her mid-sixties, but was one of those types who are ageless, was directing the operation. When the action slowed a bit, she came over. "I hope you like the picture selection, Mr. Redstone. Please feel free to bring in any of your personal artwork and we'll exchange what's on the wall."

"They'll be fine for now," I replied. "You folks know how to make a person feel right at home."

"Plenty of practice," she replied, gesturing to show a worker where to place the chairs. All's ready for you now. If you'll sit in your chair, they'll log you on the network and set up your pass codes. Then you'll be set to go."

"Thank you," I replied, caught up in the efficiency of the operation.

"I'm here to help. Used to be called secretary. Now the fashionable term is Assistant. Whatever you require, I'll obtain for you. My name's Woody, Lisa Woods to be formal. You are free to contact me twenty-four seven. All my contact info is in your desk drawer. If you look up Woody on the system, it's there as well. Please don't hesitate."

The logon procedure was a bit complicated, but I mastered it on the third try. The last of the workers was finally gone and I surfed the Internet, getting comfortable in my new digs. I expected to be spending a lot of time in this office trying to ferret out the traitor.

I looked up just as Lucinda McNaughton came through the door. There was no mistaking her. In person she was even more stunning than in the video. All legs and arms. Model slender. She appeared taller than her lover Jamison. Hard to think of her as a Marine General.

She thrust out her hand. "I'm Lucinda McNaughton," she announced. "I suppose you already know as much. Tiny doesn't miss a trick. Bet he showed you pictures. Friends call me Cindy. They tell me you're the best there is—at least in Texas. We'll see about that soon enough, now won't we, Cowboy? I've assigned you to a GS fourteen rating. I doubt you deserve that kind of money, but consider it compensation for what you've gone through. Actually, that was my idea. Need some new blood in Washington. I like your idea of letting the Korean run. You solved a host of problems with that suggestion. Hope to hell it doesn't backfire. But we're playing with fire here anyway."

"Better than shooting him in his cell."

"Actually, Max suggested shooting him while he tried to escape. I like your plan better. Max may yet get his wish."

"I'm happy to accommodate. If my plan goes afoul then the General's wish may be granted."

"I like the way you think, Cowboy. Not afraid to go out on a limb. Around here there's a high chance someone will cut it off behind you. I've given the order that will free the Korean on your command. Do so when you're ready. Justice Department signed off. Between the two of us, they're happy to be off the hook. You never heard such a loud sigh of relief when I told the AG what you planned to do."

"I thought I'd have a fight on my hands. You move fast."

"If that Korean fell off the face of the earth, no one would care. But truth is, it pays to have the president behind you. He owes you for intercepting the WMD. In the political world, you are either in or out. Right now, you're in. Keep it that way. Trust me. You won't do well being out."

"From what I've been told, you're only as good as your last mission."

"True enough. But loyalty counts. Stay with the program and you'll be just fine. As far as I'm concerned, this job's yours for as long as I'm around, not just for this one mission. So settle in. You watch my back, I'll watch yours. Do I make myself clear?"

Her back was certainly not hard to watch. But I didn't think it appropriate to express such a thought. "Thanks for the vote of confidence," was all I could manage. My mind was otherwise occupied by trying to calculate how much a GS fourteen made.

"That's one hundred twenty thousand a year, case you didn't know. Your co-worker is at GS thirteen, an even hundred. Not a bad promotion for her. Your job is to train her. From what I've been told, she's a natural. Don't ruin her. But I don't want her running wild either." A hint of a twinkle flashed across her face and was gone in an instant.

"What's that supposed to mean?"

"You know damn well what I'm talking about, Cowboy. Damn well! That bullshit with the bank robber! You shot him in cold blood plain and simple. Your partner saved your ass from a murder charge. Taking a bullet in the shoulder is a small price to pay for staying out of jail. I'm sure you're fully aware what kind of hell it is for a cop to be in prison? Don't screw up on my watch, Cowboy. The President takes the heat when that happens. And I'm here to tell you you'll have to go through me first!" Her eyes turned stone cold. "On my watch, that bullet would have gone through your brain, not your shoulder! And don't ever make the mistake of thinking I don't mean what I say!"

"I'm certain you do," I responded. I'd seen a lot of tough people in my day, and General Lucinda Westminster McNaughton ranked right up there with psychopathic killers in focusing on the mission. She and General Jamison were certainly a matched set. I wondered who was in charge in their private lives. Bet she was.

"Good," she replied. "We understand each other then." The ice melted as fast as it had appeared. "You play it smart and all will be fine in your little world. You dare hold back on Tiny, or me, and I promise you the world will fall around you. Tiny reports directly to me, and if I get even a sniff you're going rogue,

I'll end it immediately. And it wont be pretty. We on the same page, Cowboy?"

"Investigation of this nature is difficult. It's not always possible to telegraph the plays. It's never linear. Part of my job is to locate the traitor. The fewer who know what I'm about, the better for all of us."

"Unless you think I'm the traitor—or in league with the traitor—then there can't be any harm in keeping me in the loop. Tiny's the best we got. He's been vetted every way from Thursday. Man can be trusted without question. So don't hold back, you understand?"

Aye, Aye, sir, is what I wanted to say. But thinking better of it, I forced a smile. "I look forward to serving with you. I'll play by the rules." I hoped I'd be able to keep that commitment, but an investigation of criminal activity has a life of its own, and one never knows exactly where it will ultimately lead. God help us all if this one led back to retired General Lucinda McNaughton—or even worse, to her longtime lover, General Maxwell Jamison.

THIRTEEN

Monday night, after arranging our few possessions in our new digs, we decided to allow the government to buy us another festive dinner, washing it all down with two bottles of wine. Even Angella had allowed herself to partake. She was glowing by the time we returned to the apartment. I hinted to her to join me in my room.

"I thought you had to get your beauty sleep," she teased. "Besides, I'm uncomfortable with Tiny in the next room. Better to keep our business between the two of us." I couldn't argue with her logic. At least she wasn't still angry with me for not pursuing her the night before with more vigor. A good sign.

In the morning we ate a quick breakfast and Tiny drove us to the airfield, which was only twenty minutes from our apartment. With Tiny at the wheel, we didn't seem to stop once. This time we flew on an unmarked government jet that I had reason to believe belonged to the Secret Service. We could never pin Tiny down on that. All he would say was, "I'm just the ordering clerk. Jamison is in charge of transportation. Ask him if you're concerned."

We flew first to Austin so I could get my things, including my Beretta, and then on to Brownsville. We were on the ground slightly after seven PM.

The last time I worked on the island I stayed at the Tiki. This time, Tiny arranged for me to stay at the newly-opened Hilton Garden Inn just north of The Tiki, across from the Convention Center.

Thankfully, Tiny agreed to remain in Washington and watch our backs from the relative safety of his office. That was just fine for me. Tae-hyun was being detained at the Border Patrol detention center just west of South Padre Island and less than ten miles from where we had captured him.

I expected the process to take a few days before he was released. Once he was freed, I also expected him to lay low getting his bearings and possibly instructions. My plan was to remain close to my room during that time and study the data Tiny provided on the assignments we had given him.

Tiny had arranged for a car to meet our plane and drive us to SPI. Angella still had a house in Port Isabel, but had to pick up her car at police headquarters on SPI. The car dropped us both at the police station, and she drove me north about three miles to the motel. My plan was to have her spend the night. Since we had not been free to talk openly, no plan had been established.

"Nice place they got for you this time," she said when I told her where I was staying. "Beats the Tiki," she exclaimed as she glided to a stop in the hotel parking lot. "You're right on the beach. Get out your fishing rod and you might even get lucky."

I studied her to see if there was a hidden meaning in her words. I again felt the attraction. "Come in for a drink," I said. "Then we can explore the view together."

"Love to. Thought you'd never ask."

I checked in. We went to my room. And dutifully we both admired the view of the beach, the waves rolling endlessly over the sand.

"I love to watch the sandpipers at the water's edge work the sand," Angella commented, her head leaning back against my shoulder. "Want to get something to eat?"

"Not a bad idea. Any suggestions?"

"*Gabriella's* Italian Grill. My favorite."

"*Gabriella's* it is then."

As it turned out, *Gabriella's* was closed the week of Thanksgiving. So we drove up-island about a mile to *Cafe Kranzler*, a newly-opened intimate restaurant. The hostess led us to a table next to the window off to the side. We ordered dinner and the waiter suggested a wine he claimed would go perfectly with the red snapper we had ordered. Angella nodded agreement.

The dinner was excellent. The wine was even better. Angella, while not dressed the way she had been when we met the President, glowed. She said it was the hair stylist and makeup instructions she had received. I knew better.

We walked out of the restaurant just past eleven and, instead of going directly to the hotel, Angella suggested a walk on the beach. "Kind of like coming full circle," she suggested, recalling how we had met.

I wanted to add that when we met there was a dead body involved. But I was trying not to spoil the glow of the wine and the softness of her eyes, so I simply smiled and said, "Perfect idea."

We parked at the end of White Sands street, between the Tiki and a pink four-unit condo. This was the same beach access where I first walked onto the beach months earlier. The tide was in and the water was almost to the street, leaving very little room to walk. We carried our shoes and walked hand-in-hand along the top of the beach, the surprisingly warm water occasionally washing over our toes.

"I remember years ago," Angella said, breaking the silence, "catching crabs in this very spot. Too bad the water is so high or we could catch some ourselves."

I pulled her close and she lifted her face, her eyes intently focused on mine. We kissed and she pulled me against her. We stood that way for several minutes, sinking further into the sand with every wave that rolled over our feet.

I felt her phone buzz against my leg, but neither of us made any motion to respond.

Another eternity, perhaps a minute, passed and Angella, pulling back slightly, said, "If there were people on the beach I'm sure one of them would be thinking, *get a room.*"

"Got a room. Let's go."

"Shame the water is so high tonight. This would be perfect."

Angella's wild side was showing. A good sign.

We walked slowly back to her car, stopping several times to kiss and hold each other. I was finally in the moment, enjoying the present, allowing the future to take care of itself.

We dried our feet as best we could, brushing most of the sand onto the street. As careful as we were, sand began to accumulate on the floor mats. "Small price to pay," Angella commented. "That's what vacuum's are for."

A few minutes later we were back in the Hilton Inn parking lot. Angella reached for her phone. "Pardon me, this thing keeps vibrating. Someone is insistent." She studied the phone a moment. "It's Duran. Wants to talk to me."

"Now?"

"Says it's urgent. Go in, get settled. I'll be back."

I threw a mock pout, but reluctantly climbed out of the car.

"If the situation was reversed," Angella called, "you'd go. So ease up."

"Before you run off," I replied, "take a minute to check the tracking device. Need to be certain it's working before we spring Tae-hyun." The detention center was on the mainland less than ten miles from where we now were. "The transponder they implanted in him has a twenty-mile range, so we should pick the signal up here." I nodded toward her bag. "First we should get it calibrated."

Angella checked her watch. "It's almost midnight. We need to do the calibration quickly, so I can get over to see the Chief."

It was clear her mind was not on Tae-hyun at the moment. I leaned into her car while she dug the tracker out of her bag. She was clearly agitated and I reached across the front seat to calm her.

She absently brushed my hand away as she held up a device about the size of a cell phone. The screen displayed a map of the area. A solid red dot in the center slowly faded from bright to dim, repeating the sequence every few seconds. The latitude and longitude appeared along the bottom of the display. An outline of a map appeared faintly across the screen. "Looks like he's where he's supposed to be. How accurate is this thing anyway?"

"Tiny says the hand-held devices have an accuracy of about a hundred feet. The recon plane can track him almost to the yard. This device will pick up the recon feeds if you want. The plane's not up there now; no sense in trying."

"What time will he be set free? That will set our schedule."

"Let me check." I pulled out my cell, scrolled through several text messages and then said, "Tiny says between eight and noon tomorrow."

"Why so soon? Didn't you say we'd have a few days?"

"I signed the papers before we took off this morning. Figured the Feds couldn't get out of their own way. Take them a week or two to process the paperwork."

"Apparently not when your friend Cindy Long Legs is involved."

"My friend?"

"Oh, Cowboy, you're just the greatest detective ever walked the scorched Texas earth." Angella replied, mocking Cindy. She laughed, but her message was clear.

I leaned my head into the car. "Do I detect a bit of…shall I call it, jealousy?"

"Just stating a fact."

"The only fact you got right is the long legs part. Nothing—"

If I hadn't stepped back quickly, the rear wheels would have run me over.

A few feet away she slammed on the brakes. I started toward the car.

But she had only stopped long enough to close the passenger door. That accomplished, the tires came alive and she spun out of the parking lot.

FOURTEEN

I fell asleep waiting for Angella to return. But obviously she hadn't, because I was still sleeping when the phone rang at seven the next morning. It was Angella and it wasn't good news.

"Duran's in the hospital!" she announced. She sounded as though she hadn't slept, and her voice held a strange quality, almost as if I was a stranger. This certainly wasn't the voice of the woman who had planned to share my bed less than eight hours earlier.

"What happened?"

"He's in the hospital in critical condition." She was struggling to keep the emotion from taking control. "I went to his office last night, and when he wasn't there I texted him several times and received no response. That worried me because he was waiting to visit with me. Oh, my God, Jimmy it was awful. Is it always this way?"

"Hold on a moment. Slow down. What happened?"

"I went to his house and his garage door was open. The light was on in his car and I could see he was sitting there. Actually, not really sitting but leaning forward, leaning on the steering wheel. I thought he had a heart attack so I ran over to him. Oh, God, it was simply awful."

This time I just waited for her to continue.

"Someone had shot him in the head, just above his ear. I reached in to sit him upright, stupidly asking him if he was okay. When I saw his eyes I knew he was dead, or near death. I called it in."

"From what you said, I assume he's still alive."

"On a respirator. I can't talk now. I'll pick you up on the way over there. Be out front in five minutes."

Angella's car sped into the parking lot three minutes later. I was standing out front. I jumped in beside her, and before the door was even closed she hit the accelerator. "Take it easy," I said as she raced back toward the center of town, where the speed limit is 30 MPH. "You want to go this fast you would do well to ask for an escort."

"Sorry," she replied. "I'm worried about the Chief."

That was the first she had spoken. No, *sorry for standing you up last night*. No, *how are you?* No, *how about a rain check?* It was as if there had been nothing between us, as if last night hadn't existed. We had been within minutes of making love. Now we were almost total strangers.

I reached across and laid my hand on her leg. She didn't push it away, but she didn't place hers over mine or respond in any manner. "What's the latest condition?" I asked, respecting her mood.

"Don't know."

"I'm sure you've checked."

"Of course. Wouldn't give me the time of day. They've been keeping me at arms length. I'm *persona non grata* since that article Mommy Long Legs concocted appeared in the local papers."

Angella was certainly off her game. I hoped it would pass soon. I didn't like the tension between us.

The remainder of the drive to Brownsville was in silence. For my part, I was thinking of all the trips to this hospital we had made when Mark Cruses was hospitalized with a severe concussion. This was also the hospital where Mark's fiancée, Trich, worked. To state the obvious, I did not have pleasant memories of this place and I had the distinct impression that my memories were about to get even worse.

We were met at the Chief's door by a burly man with shoulders that looked as though they belonged in front of an ox cart. He introduced himself as Lieutenant Jose Garcia and informed us that he was acting chief now that Duran was incapacitated.

"I've been expecting you two. Come with me. We need to talk in private." We followed him down the hall to an empty room. The door closed behind us and he said, "None of this is public yet. I'm talking to you because you're working for the Feds. Chief told me about your visit to Washington. I also know he wanted to speak with you, Angella. Did you ever get to him?"

Angella's fingers scratching the side of her leg told me she was uncomfortable. "How do you know he wanted to talk with me?"

"From his cell phone. The text message he sent you is still on the phone. It shows you received it at midnight."

"Modern electronics at its best," Angella joked. Her fingertips continued working against her leg. "I missed him. Sent him several texts. Got no response."

Garcia thought about that for a moment and then said, "He was shot about one, maybe a little earlier, won't know for sure until the report's back. You called in at one-twelve. So we're putting the time at about twelve-fifty."

"Any leads?" I asked.

"Nothing definite yet. Could be an intruder hiding in his garage. Could be a friend. Gun's not out. No defensive marks, nothing to indicate he saw it coming. Wife's being questioned. There's some talk he was having domestic trouble." He cleared his throat. "That newspaper article about you, Angella, didn't help one bit. Stop by headquarters later so we can complete your statement. I know they talked with you last night, but I want to get a definite time frame from you starting, let's say, at eleven."

"He was happily married," Angella replied. "That article was pure bullshit!"

"Hildy, that's Duran's wife Hildegard, claims to have been in bed sleeping. Can't verify."

"You really think his wife was involved?" I asked, puzzled that Garcia would have been taken in by Cindy's plant.

"Even before the article there were rumors of the Chief having domestic difficulty." He paused, considered his next words, then making up his mind, said, "Actually, it was over Angella. The article in the paper stirred it up, but, in fact, ever since Angella's promotion there's been talk."

"You mean about Angella and the Chief getting crosswise?"

"Not that part. The...the sexual part. I understand Hildy thinks Angella slept her way to detective. We think someone on the force fed the fire."

"That's nonsense!" Angella proclaimed, more animated than I had ever seen her. "A man gets promoted, it's on merit. A woman does a good job, gets promoted, right away everyone assumes the worst!"

"Calm down." Garcia scolded, "I'm just telling you what's going down. But you should know that Duran passed over several men more qualified than you for the job. And a few of them are causing mischief."

"There was absolutely nothing between us and I resent the implication! If you must know, it was a recommendation from Redstone's boss, and perhaps even some pressure from General Jamison, that did it."

"Why would they do that?"

"Could it be that I saved a Texas Ranger's life? Or maybe that I helped save the country from an atomic bomb attack?"

"Duly noted," Garcia responded, not getting drawn into arguing with Angella. "I heard you were at the station last evening. What was that about?"

"Following up on his text."

"Did you see him?"

Angella hesitated slightly too long before responding, "No I did not. I texted him and he did not respond."

"What did you do then?"

Again the hesitation. "Went to his house. He never answered his text, so I went to see what he wanted."

Garcia thought about what he had just heard and said, "You texted him?"

"Yes, several times."

"To his cell?"

"Yes."

"I didn't see any incoming texts from your cell. I'll check the log again, but I'm pretty convinced I'm correct."

"Maybe he erased them."

"What time did you text?"

"When I left the hotel, the Hilton Inn where Redstone's staying. That was sometime after midnight. From then until about one."

One thing I knew for certain, Angella did not text from the hotel parking lot. Not the way she had been burning rubber. Maybe she stopped along the way, but the Chief's office is a two minute drive.

"I suppose he could have erased your messages," Garcia conceded. "But why erase only yours? Other calls were on there."

"Around the same time?"

"Ten to two."

"What was the nature of the messages?"

"No messages. Just incoming calls. Actually, just one number, several calls."

"You know who they came from?"

"Homer Greenspar."

"The INS guy?" I asked, wondering why he was calling so late at night.

"He and the Chief get into it all the time. There's always some undercover operation going on. Only tells us about it when its going bad. Says we have too many leaks in the Department. Only guy I know Chief can't get along with."

"I saw that during the raid when we smoked out Tae-hyun. Chief and he got into it big time."

"I forgot about that. Ya, if the Chief had given the word, I'd have shot the son-of-a-bitch!"

"It's strange he'd be calling the chief. That wasn't his style. Never told the Chief anything," Angella responded, agitation sounding in her voice. Changing the subject, she asked, "You find the weapon?"

"Not yet." He studied Angella a long while. Started to say something, changed his mind and said, "Gotta get back to the room."

When Garcia was out of hearing, I said to Angella, "What the hell's going on? You couldn't have sent a text. Not the way you were driving."

"What do you mean?"

"You damn near ran me over. Remember?"

"I was playing with you."

"Where there's smoke kind of thing. Wife thinks you're having an affair, he must have given her some reason. You know what that could have been?"

"Shit, not you also!"

"Just answer the question. Any reason why his wife would suspect you two? I mean, other than you got an early promotion?"

"Nothing! I'm not screwing the Chief! That what you want to hear?"

"If it's the truth."

"It's the truth! I can't believe you'd even question that."

There was no percentage pursuing that thread. I also wanted to understand why she hadn't come back to my room. Something was amiss. I needed a safe subject. I thought of Tae-hyun. "Where's that gadget? The transponder. Korean's about to be released."

She pulled out the transponder, her hand still trembling. "Shit!" she exclaimed a moment later. "If this thing's accurate, he's on the island! See."

She held the device so I could see the display. There, big as life was the long slender outline of SPI with a red blinking light near the south end. "That's the camp ground, is it not? Or is that Schlitterbahn?"

"I hadn't thought about Schlitterbahn. That's exactly where this is pointing. How the hell did he get there so fast?"

I checked my watch and it was just past nine. "The earliest he was to be released was eight."

Angella took the monitor and hit a few buttons. "That's strange," she exclaimed, "If I'm reading this right, he's been there for hours, possibly all night."

"I thought it kept a full log."

"It shows he's been there since about three this morning. Track from the jail starts just before midnight."

"Get the Warden on the line, see what's up."

A few minutes later she handed the phone to me, saying, "Warden wants to speak directly to you."

"Warden? This is Jimmy Redstone. Can you tell me exactly who the order to release Tae-hyun early came from? I was under the impression he was not to be released until this morning."

I jotted his answer into my notebook, but there was really no need to do so. "What time was that?" I asked. I wrote the time next to the name.

We spoke a while longer but nothing useful came of it. He promised to inform me if any further facts came to his attention.

Turning to Angella, I said, "Korean was released at ten last night on orders from…" I needlessly looked down at my notes. "Kelvin Jurald!"

Our handler, Tiny, had freed him last night and had not told us!

FIFTEEN

"What the hell are you doing releasing the Korean early?" I barked into the phone as soon as Tiny answered. "The least you could have done was let us know!"

"What the hell you talking about?" Tiny shot back. "I did no such thing!" His deep voice rattled my phone.

"You called the Warden at the County Detention Center and instructed him to release the Igniter at…let's see…ten last night!"

"I did no such thing!" Tiny was insistent.

"Then we have a major problem. Hold while I get the Warden back on the line."

When the connection was made and all three of us were conferenced together, I said, "Warden, I'm going to have Mr. Kelvin Jurald speak to you. Please tell us if this is the same person you spoke with last night concerning the release of Tae-hyun."

Tiny proceeded to say, "Warden, my name is Kelvin Jurald. I'm with the United States Secret Service. Did I speak to you last night for any purpose?"

The warden responded immediately, "Someone using your name called me. But it was not the same voice. The man I spoke with had a much higher pitch."

"Any doubt?"

"None," the warden replied. "The person on the line now is not the same person I spoke with last night."

I didn't feel it was the time or place, nor was I the right person, to interrogate him further. Something must have convinced him he was doing the right thing last night. I'll leave that for the FBI, or whatever agency the Feds use to investigate such lapses. "Warden," I said, "I assume you have a recording of that call."

"We certainly do. All such calls are recorded."

"Is it digital?"

"Most certainly. Easier for playing in court and getting transcribed."

"Send a copy to myself and a copy to Tiny... Mr. Jurald... immediately." We each provided email addresses. "Also, send me a copy of the detainee's entire file, including any visitor information and anything else you might have. We must speak with anyone who spoke to him when he was with you."

"I can answer that last question. He spoke to no one."

"No one came to see him? No phone calls? Nothing?"

"All affirmative, I can assure you."

"Okay, send what you have anyway."

His tone turned sharp, patience wearing thin. "Is there anything else you will require from us, Mr. Redstone?"

"Nothing for now. Just don't destroy any records."

"Wouldn't ever dream of it. Goodbye, Mr. Redstone and happy hunting."

Tiny said, "Redstone, stay on the line." The warden clicked off and Tiny said, "I have the hospital reports for you. As you guessed, Brownsville, Harlingen and McAllen all reported people with radioactive poisoning symptoms. Mind, they're not kept as radioactive poisoning, but we checked for the individual symptom combinations. That's it. Nothing in New Jersey, New York, California or Seattle. This is inconclusive. Those symptoms can be from other causes. Getting back to Texas, though, we had some hits from Hildago, Kenedy and Bexar counties. Anything strike you as strange?"

"For starters, it seems that a lot of folks came near the weapon. Another, the spread. I understand the lower Rio Grande counties. But Bexar. That's San Antone! That's about one hundred fifty, maybe even more, miles, away!"

"That's what doesn't make sense. I can understand a bunch of Valley people involved in getting the weapon ashore. Maybe some of the folks who were involved in the rescue operation. But no one was from San Antonio that we know of. By the way. Forgot to ask. How's Duran?"

"Holding for now. But doesn't sound good." I decided not to say anything about Angella's squirrelly behavior. "It'll be touch and go for a while. I'm planning on tracking down Trich Santiago. That's Mark Cruses' fiancée."

"Good idea. Talk with you later."

"Did you locate Trich?" I asked Angella when I rejoined her.

"She's waiting to talk to us. I suggested the cafeteria. Unless you feel that's too public."

"No, let's go."

Angella sent a message to Trich asking her to meet us. When she entered the room, she was a different person from the bubbly woman we had last spoken with. Her eyes were puffy, her hair not as well groomed as before, and she had lost weight. A lot of weight, to the point where she looked malnourished. She smiled a quick, almost forced, smile when she spotted me. She threw her arms around my body and pressed tightly against me. I could feel her sobbing.

In a moment she pulled away and said hello to Angella. Then, turning back to me, said, "Oh, God. I knew it was too good to last. Have you seen Mark? They won't let me see or speak to him. No calls or anything. I hope he's okay. They won't tell me anything."

"I don't know much either, but Angella and I will visit him either today or tomorrow."

"What'll they do with him? What's a court-martial?"

I explained to her what the procedure was. The more I spoke the more devastated she became. I tried several times to cheer her up, but nothing worked. Finally, I said, "After we see him I'll call you."

"Thank you for doing that for me. You are so nice. Mark said nice things about you. You are a nice man. I talk to his mother every day and she also does not hear from him. She's so worried."

"I'll call Nora also."

"She will like that. I will tell her you will call."

"Are you still living at home?"

"Yes." Trich looked down and it was several seconds before her eyes returned to my face. Something was bothering her.

"Tell me about your family," I said, opening the door to finding out what she knew and didn't know. Out of the corner of my eye I could see Angella focusing on her facial expression. From past discussions with Trich, we both knew she was without guile. Her eyes told us everything we needed to know.

"Father is home."

"How's that going?"

"Not so well. He stays in his office. Hasn't left, except to eat and sleep. He doesn't even go out to the fields or to the horses. Many meals he eats alone."

"No visitors?"

"Mostly." She glanced away.

"What is it Trich? We need to know. Your father is...well, let's just say...important to us."

"One visitor comes to see him."

"Who is it?"

"Don't know his name."

"Describe him." Thinking about her father's other life from South Padre Island where he seemed to be married to a woman named Joy Malcolm, I added, "Or is it a woman?"

"No, not a woman! A man. An American. A tall American."

"Please describe this man?"

"I should not be talking about Father."

"This is important to Mark."

Tears again filled her eyes and she brushed moisture from her right cheek. "I am never close to him when he comes. I see him only from a distance. Usually it is dark, so it is hard to know what he looks like."

"Anything stand out other than being tall?"

"Hair. He has...how do I say it?...big hair."

"Do you mean his hair stands up above his head?" Angella asked. "Or does it puff out at the sides?"

"Out at the sides. Full."

"What else can you tell us about this tall American with the full hair?" Angella followed up.

"Only that the workers say he has mean eyes. When he comes to the front gate, they are scared. No one likes this man."

"Do you know his name?" Name probably made no difference. It would be rare indeed if anyone we were interested in used his or her real name. But it was good to get a base line. Often the alias names were in a database.

"He does not speak with anyone but my father."

"When he comes to the gate, how do the men know what he wants?"

"They know. He does not speak."

It was clear Trich's agitation level had reached its limit. We had pushed her about as far as it was smart to push. "If you learn anything more about this man please let us know." Trich nodded, but I wasn't sure her heart was in it.

Angella, sensing my dilemma, asked, "Trich, have you seen your brother?" Her question sounded genuine, an inquiry from a friend. The last time we had spoken with her, Alterez had not been home in months. Trich had no way to know that we knew about his sickness, nor did she know that it came from the massive radiation he had received when he transported the unshielded radioactive bomb across the island.

The tears came again, this time accompanied by deep anguish. She cried for several minutes. Angella comforted her by first taking her hand and then by pulling her close.

Finally, Trich managed, "He's deathly sick. Father called Juan Roberto home from his studies to be with him. Alterez is in the *Centro Medico Internacional* hospital. His hair is gone and his body is burned. He was hit by lightening. Mother won't leave his room. When I go, he pushes me away."

Her deep sobbing drowned out the rest of what she was saying. I felt sorry for her, but if it hadn't been for Angella's excellent work, I'd have been the one dead on the beach at the hand of her father. She had no way to know that. And truthfully, it was not her business to know. She was innocent in this, but she was about to lose a brother she loved. My heart went out to her, but there was nothing any of us could do.

When Trich gained control of herself, Angella calmly asked, “Is there a message you want us to take to Mark? Anything you want us to say?”

She blushed, her eyes focused on the floor. “Please tell him I am thinking of him every minute. Tell him I love him. I want to see him.”

Angella put her arm around Trich and replied, “We’ll tell him for you. Now you take care of yourself. Everything will be alright.”

SIXTEEN

A few minutes later, we were in the hospital parking lot about to head to Mark's apartment on SPI. I was still convinced the Coast Guard was somehow in the middle of this, which meant that an operation was ongoing. Why else would Mark still be on house arrest? Angella had no other explanation for the confusing behavior of his chain of command.

"Want me to clear our visit with the Coast Guard?" Angella asked, cell phone in hand. "Protocol says we should. Mark's on house arrest. We show up and things can get ugly for all of us. And especially for Mark."

Absentmindedly, I nodded my agreement, then thought better of it. "Let's not telegraph our plays."

"What if they have a guard posted?"

"It'll give us a chance to see how our newly-minted Homeland Security badges work. Same agency. Should be interesting. Jamison said we have unlimited access to whom ever. I'm taking him at his word."

Angella looked at me as if I'd gone over the edge. Nonetheless, she dutifully hit the END button and threw the phone in her bag.

"You thinking what I'm thinking?" I asked Angella.

"About?"

"About the tall American."

"Fits the description of Greenspar. I was wondering why the INS is visiting a Mexican who is on the quarantine list."

"A bigger question," I said, "was what the hell was the INS doing in the same house with the Korean in the first place?"

Angella, after obviously playing back in her mind an earlier conversation, responded, "I recall he told Duran he was running undercover operatives."

"Undercover operatives in the same place as a smuggled Korean? Need to understand that operation better."

"I just thought of something." She dug into her bag for the tracker device. "He's still there. See, he's over by Schlitterbahn."

"You're obviously ahead of me. That's where he was earlier. He hasn't moved."

"I was recalling the first time we came across him."

It took me a few seconds and then it came to me. We had chased him onto the beach in his underwear. He then hijacked a garbage truck. The truck was found abandoned near Schlitterbahn. "Good thinking!" I exclaimed. "There must be a place down there where he holes up. We can use the device to find the hole. Let's go."

Just then both Angella's and my phone beeped simultaneously.

Text message from Tiny: **Plane waiting at Brownsville. See you in DC at 16h. Important you both be here. Leave Igniter. Surveillance will track him.**

SEVENTEEN

"Is this what it's going to be like working for the Feds?" Angella asked. "I feel I'm tethered to a bungee cord. If so, I don't think I'll last very long."

"That's what the pay check gets you; travel and constant meetings. Always coordinating. It's no wonder it takes them so long to get anything accomplished."

The airport was less than three miles from the hospital and we were approaching the parking lot.

"I suppose someone will meet us," Angella commented. "I have no idea how to find the plane. It most certainly won't be listed on the arrivals/departure board."

"Got an idea," I replied. I had turned into the small parking lot, but instead of finding an empty space, I drove out the other side, circled around and found the gravel path we had used a few days earlier. A tall slender man stepped out of the guard house and motioned for me to roll down the window.

I did so and handed him my Homeland Security ID. He studied it briefly and then asked to see Angella's credentials. He satisfied himself we were who we said we were and then motioned us toward the same building we had gone to before.

As before, the TSA guard studied our IDs and nodded. He said, "Park your car next to the building and leave the keys inside. We'll park it in the front lot for you. Keys will be inside at the TSA office." He then told us our plane was waiting on the other side of the building and that we could pass through the waiting room or walk around. Our choice.

We decided to go into the building. Once inside, we could see a dual-prop plane parked on the tarmac, a boarding ladder extending from the open door.

Angella asked, "Suppose that's our ride?"

"Can't be. That puppy can't get us to Washington in three hours. Lucky to do it in three days from the looks of it!"

No other plane was visible on the airfield. I didn't even see a hanger where a plane could be hidden.

We waited fifteen minutes, and when no other plane appeared, I said, "Time to see where this leads." We headed out toward the ladder and found an envelope taped to the rail. On the outside of the envelope, printed in block letters, it read: WELCOME ABOARD REDSTONE/MARTINEZ INSTRUCTIONS ARE INSIDE

Angella ripped open the envelope and read the note. "The pilot has been instructed to maintain a locked door for security reasons. When you board the plane, please push the "door" button located by the entrance. The pilot will take off when the door closes. When you land, again push the button to open the door. Don't worry about the time, the meeting will be delayed until you arrive. Enjoy your flight." Angella looked up from the paper and said, "I don't like this one bit. Government might be trying to save a few dollars, but flying this thing to D.C. is insane. We'd be better off going back inside and catching the next Continental flight."

"Tiny can cool his ass. Let's go," I replied. One thing I learned about Angella is that she has a keen sense of right and wrong. Not that I don't, mind you, but I'm a bit more goal driven and tend to force things toward that end. I started toward the steps.

"Hold up a moment, Jimmy. I'm texting Tiny for confirmation."

A few minutes later she held up her cell phone. I read Tiny's terse but explicit reply: FOLLOW INSTRUCTIONS. MEETING WILL WAIT FOR YOU. NO JET AVAILABLE. DON'T GO COMMERCIAL. MEET YOU AT AIRPORT.

I reached up and pushed the door button.

"Wish you hadn't done that so fast," Angella scolded, "I'm inclined to fly commercial. Who's he to tell us how to move around?"

I pushed the button again, but the steps continued to recede into the plane. "Maybe the steps must come all the way up before they go back down," I said.

When the steps were fully retracted I hit the button once again, but instead of them going back down, the door folded upward behind them, sealing us inside.

I operated the door button once again.

"I guess we're committed," Angella commented when the door remained closed.

Within a few seconds the engine was running and we were moving away from the terminal, gaining speed as we went. Then we were airborne and out over the Gulf of Mexico. The small plane hung suspended between the dark-blue of the water below us and the light-blue of the sky above. If it weren't for the throbbing of the engines, this would be a perfect flying day.

Angella leaned close. "I do have to say, Jimmy, you are a gentleman."

"What brought that on?"

"My behavior last night. Totally unprofessional. You didn't bring it up."

I wasn't certain if she was referring to her tantrum about Cindy or not coming back to the room. "Nothing to say." I had thought about what I would say to her, but quite frankly nothing felt right. Was it jealousy on her part? If so, bringing it up would just make it worse. If she was referring to not coming back, I didn't like her decision, but I understood it. When her meeting with Duran went south the way it did any thought of the evening's romance was long gone. Great chemistry had been soundly trumped.

"I feel foolish. Don't know what got into me. I'm sorry. The way you seemed to be responding to her. She had you eating out of her hand. That's not like you at all."

"No apology necessary. For the record, I wasn't *eating out of her hand*. I was...getting accustomed to her. Never met anyone on this side of the bars with as much pure drive in their demeanor as that woman."

"You like strong women, it's clear."

"Suppose I do. Never thought about it. You're not suggesting..."

"I'm not suggesting anything. You're a free man."

"Out with it, Angella. Your eyes are not matching your tone."

"Is this what life with a detective leads to? It doesn't matter what I say, you hear what you want?" Without waiting for me to reply, she continued, "I guess I've been thinking about that chemistry comment Tiny made. He's right. I felt it last night. In fact I feel it now. But it's so soon after my divorce. I need time to find myself."

I started to say something like, *I understand. Take your time.* Or, *hey, we're partners. Partners don't get involved.* But the truth was, I wanted this woman more than anyone I had ever met. But then I thought of Chief Duran and the lingering hug in the Oval office. And the timing of his shooting. The hair on the back of my neck bristled. So I simply said, "Time will work out all things."

Angella noticed my hesitation and sat straighter in her seat. The tender moment, if indeed this had been a tender moment, was over.

I studied the water below us. I hadn't flown on a prop plane for years, but it seemed to me we hadn't gained much altitude. I could see the waves breaking below us, their white tops curling forward. A large pod of dolphins was visible. At any other time I would have been thrilled to see them frolicking about, but something was not right. We should have been flying north, following the Gulf Coast as it swept north and then curving to the east. Instead, we were ever so slowly turning south.

A moment later the coastline was on our right. I tapped Angella on the shoulder and said, "Isn't that Mexico?"

She leaned over me and studied the shore-line. Sitting back up, she announced, "That certainly is! We're heading south. I flew over this area about three months ago, and—"

I waited for her to finish, but she said nothing further.

"So what were you doing flying down here?"

"Training."

"What kind of training does a South Padre Island cop need in an airplane over Mexican waters?"

"Why do I always feel I'm being interrogated? Chief Duran wanted all his officers to realize first hand just how easy it is for smugglers to move people and drugs north."

I made a mental note to check that out. Drug movement is traditionally a federal responsibility. Goodness knows, we have enough organizations chartered to stop it. "So, where are we?"

"Don't know exactly. But we are definitely heading south."

We followed the coast for about an hour and then turned west, losing what little altitude we had as we moved toward the shore. We passed over a sand spit separated from the mainland by a body of water. A bay or a river, I couldn't tell which.

"Judging from the light color of the water, I would say that the water below us is relatively shallow," Angella informed me.

Then the forest took over and we flew south-west as best I could judge, barely above the tree tops. The only thing below us was jungle. Every now and again a narrow dirt road became visible, only to be lost a moment later.

Angella pointed off to the right where smoke snaked up through the dense covering. Probably a distillery for illegal booze—or worse, a meth lab.

Angella tried several times to communicate on her phone, but apparently could not get a signal. She studied the phone's display, I assume hoping to catch an indication of a cellular network.

Judging from her expression, I was certain she had no luck.

"Fleeting signal," She advised me after a few minutes. "In and out. Not enough for talking. I was hoping for a text to get through, but so far nothing."

"Doesn't text take a special network?"

"I'm trying everything I know. It's nasty down there. We're in the middle of drug country and I'm afraid this isn't going to end well."

"Power of positive thinking," I advised. "This is, after all, a United States airplane." I was trying for positive spin.

Before Angella could respond, we banked hard to the right, made a full circle and slid down between an opening in the trees I had not noticed. We bumped hard across what looked to be a hastily created dirt track that was rock-strewn and pitted. The plane came to a blessed stop not far from what appeared to be a small river.

The cockpit door remained locked and not a word came over the intercom. We had no idea what nationality our pilot was, nor the gender.

The opening surrounding the plane seemed deserted. Nothing man-made was visible. Light barely penetrated the dense covering and I wondered how in the world the pilot got us in here. I had no doubt that we could not be seen by satellite tracking.

Neither of us moved to open the door. I was determined to force their hand and make the pilot come out of the cockpit to face us directly. I drew my Beretta and Angella did the same.

I motioned for Angella to position herself on the other side of the cockpit door. My plan was to jump anyone who came out. Killing the pilot would only exacerbate our situation. I wanted this cat-and-mouse bullshit to end. And the sooner the better.

It was stifling hot in the plane, and perspiration had already soaked through my shirt. Angella's face glistened and she waved her left hand slowly to create air movement.

The standoff continued. We heard no sound from the cockpit and nothing moved on the ground.

Suddenly, Angella motioned for me to look out of the window. Approaching the plane from the woods was a solitary female figure wearing the brown uniform of the United States Immigration Service.

With relief, I pressed the door button and said to Angella, "Hope you brought your passport; these folks have no sense of humor." I started down the steps.

Angella was a few steps behind and cut her reply short when several men rushed from the trees, automatic weapons in their hands.

"Hands up!" one of the men shouted in Spanish-influenced English.

He then switched to Spanish and yelled something to the others. Angella translated, saying the men had been instructed to shoot us if we so much as sneezed. The woman wearing the INS uniform disappeared into the jungle.

"Follow them," Angella said from behind me. "They want us off the steps. Drop your gun." I looked at her as if to say, *not on your life*.

Reading my look correctly, she said, "They have orders to shoot if you don't immediately drop your weapon." Angella proceeded to drop hers.

I took another step down, still holding mine. Three semi-automatic pistols moved in unison in my direction. Some Spanish was shouted and Angella said, "Drop it Jimmy, they are about to shoot."

Not seeing much choice, I let my gun fall and walked down the last few steps. When my feet hit the ground, two men rushed forward and took my arms. I was force-marched off to the side of the opening. Behind me, two men pushed Angella along in the same direction I was moving.

The plane then began to taxi across the opening back in the direction it had landed. Once at the far end of the opening, the plane slowly turned and, gathering speed, lifted off the ground.

Within a few seconds the plane was lost in the trees. The only evidence that it had ever existed was a faint droning of the engine. Soon, all we could hear was silence.

Angella and I were now standing next to each other with armed guards on either side. Another man, who seemed to be the leader, walked over to us and without saying a word patted me down. Angella was then subject to the same pat-down.

The leader then motioned for us to get down. At first I thought he wanted us to sit in the grass, but then I noticed that several of his men were squatting on their heels. I did likewise and Angella followed my lead.

We stayed that way for what seemed an eternity but was most likely less than an hour. My knees were beyond hurting and I wondered if I'd ever get them straight again. That position didn't seem to bother the Mexicans who were guarding us.

The leader barked orders and all the men, except for the two who were closest to Angella and I, disappeared into the forest.

A moment later, the faint sound of a plane could be heard. Was our plane returning? Angella apparently had heard it also. She looked at me with a questioning expression. I shrugged my shoulders, causing my guard to hit me in the ribs with his elbow.

The plane engine grew louder, and a moment later I saw a flash of light as the sun momentarily reflected from some surface. Then a plane appeared through the trees and came across the opening in our direction.

It stopped almost in the same spot where our plane had stopped. This plane was identical to the one that brought us here except that it had a red stripe on the wing. The one we came in on had a blue stripe. These guys seemed to have a small air force.

A look of deep concern flashed across Angella's face and she pulled her bag tightly against her body. I guessed her cell phone had gone off, but with the engine noise I heard nothing.

The door to the plane opened and several men appeared from the jungle, assault rifles in hand, and rushed up the steps and into the plane. A few minutes later they emerged, pushing a small man in front of them.

Angella leaned close. "No wonder the alarm went off." She had realized what was happening a split second ahead of me. The guard pushed her away from me and said something to her in Spanish. My interpretation is that he told her to shut up. Only his language was not so polite.

Walking down the steps from the aircraft, wearing the same ripped shirt and dirt-stained pants as the last time we had met, was none other than Tae-hyun, the fugitive Korean. He also wore the same puzzled expression I had last seen. His eyes darted non-stop back and forth among those gathered at the base of the steps.

When he saw Angella and I his eyes froze for an instant, but only for an instant. The expression he wore never flinched.

EIGHTEEN

The Korean was immediately ushered in the direction taken by the fake INS woman. Ten minutes later, Angella and I were pulled to our feet and pushed along the same path. I was having trouble walking, my knees refusing to cooperate. Every time I stumbled, the guard pushed his rifle into my ribs. I was certain I could overpower the guard, but there were too many of them behind him. One guy in particular, judging from the way the barrels of his sawed-off shotgun never wavered from the side of my head, seemed anxious to blast away. I hoped he didn't trip along the way and *accidentally* discharge his weapon.

We were taken to another clearing that had three thatch huts forming a semi-circle, with what looked to be a fire pit in the center. We were directed to the hut at the far end of the group. Both of us were pushed inside.

The hut consisted of a single room with a lone light bulb hanging from the center. I had not seen any power lines coming into the camp and I guessed that any electricity we might have would come from a generator. There were no appliances in the room, not even a sink or a toilet.

There was, however, a nasty-looking bucket off to one side. It didn't take much imagination to know what its function was. How it was to be emptied was yet to be determined. My immediate concern was how we would fill it.

Our captors shouted commands through a door formed by what looked to be banana fronds tied together. Their Spanish was too quick for me to understand. The tone conveyed their message. We were in deep trouble.

Between their shouting and gesturing, Angella managed to ask questions in Spanish. Their replies sounded nasty.

"They say we'll be safe if we listen to what they tell us," Angella said when the shouting died away. "They are divided on what to do with us, but the leader says he has no intention of harming us if we follow his orders. He says we are not to leave this hut for any reason at any time. He says the men will shoot us if we are outside."

I looked toward the bucket. "What about—"

"When the bucket is full, we are to slide it outside. We are not to put our heads out. It will be emptied. They will bring food twice a day and water as well. They won't hesitate to shoot us if we try to escape."

"Do they know we are government agents?"

"That's what's keeping us alive. They don't want trouble with the U.S. Government. One of them said he'd try to find something soft for us to sleep on."

"I believe there are six of them," I said. "How many did you count?"

"Same," Angella answered. "But some of them are with the Korean, so there may be less watching us. He's in the far hut."

“Even if we escaped, we’d never find our way out of this jungle. You have any idea where we are?”

“Best guess, near Nuevo León. About fifty, maybe seventy, miles inland from the Gulf. Almost due south of Brownsville. This area is thought to be one of the centers of the drug trade. From something I read while you were in the hospital, Santiago is—or was—the leader in this region.”

“So this is Padre Territory,” I said, referring to the name his son had called him just before the old man had sliced my neck. “He’s confined to his house. Trich said he pretty much lives in his office. I wonder if someone else has taken over. Or maybe they’re fighting over control.”

“That could explain the hostility of the men. They clearly are agitated about not shooting us.”

“A wounded leader—that’s what Padre is right now, wounded—always breeds distrust. Until a new clear leader emerges, nothing is predictable.”

“That’s actually how Santiago’s referred to among his followers. Means Father. They think of him that way as well. He keeps these folks out of poverty. They owe everything to him. It will be hard to replace him while he’s alive, even though he’s confined.”

“So let me get this straight. We’re brought to the headquarters of a drug gang by a United States INS plane at the direction of our friend Tiny of the Secret Service. Smell a rat?”

“Stinks, you ask me.”

I started to discuss my thoughts, but thought better of it. I lowered my voice to a soft whisper. “This may be the middle of Shitsville, but if this is a U.S. operation they’ll have this place bugged. Either we whisper, or hold anything important until we get out.” I wanted to add, “Assuming we get out,” but that was stating the obvious.

"Any thoughts how we're going to arrange the potty?" Angella asked.

I had been wondering how long it would take her to react to our primitive surroundings.

"Have to do it like they do on boats without a head. When either of us moves into that area, the other faces away. That's my best solution, sorry. I'm all ears if you have a better answer."

"Speaking of chemistry. If this doesn't kill it, nothing will." She managed a weak smile. "We'll make it work. At least we're alive. Let's keep it that way."

One thing I had noticed about Angella when I first began working with her was her positive attitude. The more I thought about her shooting Duran, the less sense it made. But, and here's where the rub comes, it is fundamental that in order for a con to be a con he—or she—must be good at the con. Over the years I've tracked—and sometimes apprehended—the very best. Seems Texas is full of them, especially around the oil patch. If Angella was pulling off a con, then she'd rate right up there with the best of them. I wasn't ready to commit one way or the other.

Together, we examined the small hut, inspecting the construction. I wanted to know if there was another way out other than the single door. We found nothing.

"At least the floor and walls are clean," Angella commented. "Don't see evidence of insect infestation."

I found an area I liked and sat facing the door, my back against the wall. Angella did the same a few feet away.

An hour passed, and then a second hour. I was getting hungry. I was also becoming uncomfortable, not wanting to be the first to use the makeshift potty.

I finally gave in and walked over to the bucket. Angella dutifully turned to face the wall while I relieved myself.

When I returned to my corner, she said, "Thanks for going first. I'm about to burst."

I faced the wall. "Hopefully, they'll bring toilet paper, or napkins or something when they bring lunch." I commented.

"Do we receive overseas combat pay for this?" she quipped. "Maybe lack of modesty pay as well?" Angella returned to her place against the wall and said, "I have sanitizer in my bag. That will work until it runs out."

"Wonder what's in the other huts? You say the Korean is in the far one? Is the middle one empty? If it is, think about asking them to move you over there. Give you privacy."

"As uncomfortable as this is going to get, I mean with you and me living like animals in this room together, I wouldn't want to be alone out here with them. Who in the hell knows what they might do? I've already heard them say something about a prostitute. Actually, the phrase was 'an available woman.' I'm certain they're referring to me."

Footsteps sounded outside. I tensed, not knowing what to expect. Angella's face showed a steely resolve, which, in a strange sort of way, was comforting.

There was movement at the doorway as the palm fronds flexed inward. A cardboard box was thrust through the opening, but no one came in behind it.

A meal had been served. But in truth, to call what they gave us a meal is an undeserved dignity. Two chunks of mostly green bread, some type of rotten fruit and a piece of meat neither of us would touch. A blob of what looked like cheese, but had jungle ants swarming on it, was also in the box. Two bottles of water rounded out our diet.

I broke the bread into pieces, being careful to eliminate the mold as best I could. Angella tackled the cheese in the same manner, using the side of the box to scrape the insects away. She also salvaged some of the fruit.

We ate in silence, savoring the water. Angella commented that she planned to save some of the water for hygiene purposes, and I decided to do the same.

Then back to our respective spaces to await the next event. We sat in silence for several more hours as the forest grew dark and the indigenous sounds increased.

At some point, a generator started up not far away. The light bulb fluttered on. A big event in our closed little world. The noise of the machine allowed us to talk more freely. I asked, "Have you been able to hear what they've been saying?" I had heard mumbles, but since I only have a limited Spanish listening vocabulary and only if the words are spoken slowly, it all sounded like background noise to me. Note to self: learn Spanish.

"Bits and pieces. It's as we suspected. They are unhappy watching us. They are frightened the U.S. will send in the Marines to rescue us. They want out of here, and the sooner the better. I did hear them refer to Padre several times, but I can't determine if he's still in charge or if they are fighting."

Somewhat later another box was pushed through the opening. The food was not much improved, except there were two candy bars and some napkins. "They are listening to our conversation," I whispered to Angella. "I'm sure the napkins are for other purposes."

"Maybe whoever put them in there is just being kind. Some people are you know."

"Not usually in this situation. But point well taken. I'll keep an open mind."

A few minutes later the generator stopped and the hut went totally dark. It was impossible to see my fingers in front of my eyes.

I could not find a comfortable position to sleep and I sat awake most of the night, possibly dozing from time to time. I kept imagining the noises were coming closer and that at any minute a large animal would burst through the door, its mouth open ready to rip us apart. Every movement of the fronds caused me to come alert, ready to fend off an attacker. At one point something ran across the roof, followed almost immediately by something chasing it.

Then it went quiet. Too quiet.

I tried to determine if the guards were still outside, but there were no human noises. A thought struck me and I inched over toward Angella. I couldn't determine if she was awake or not, so I sat beside her waiting.

A few minutes later she raised her head. "That you Jimmy?" she asked, her voice barely a whisper.

"I had a thought," I began, keeping my voice as low as I could. "They didn't bother with our cell phones. That means there's no signal here."

"Lotta good that'll do us."

"Not the cell phone. The tracker. Works off the satellite."

"It's working. When the plane landed it went off. Good thing the guard didn't hear it."

"I thought your cell phone had gone off. Didn't think about the tracker. Lucky a guard didn't see you."

Angella dug into her bag. A light flashed on.

"Blank screen," she announced. "Satellite doesn't work inside."

"Worked inside on the island," I replied.

"Tiny said when it's indoors it's supplemented by cellular something."

"Then we'll try it outside. You follow me out when I take the potty out. Hold it so they won't see it. We'll do it at first light in the morning. It's worth a try. Now try to get some sleep, I'll sit guard."

"This is a Thanksgiving I'll never forget," Angella whispered.

"I forgot. You're right. Don't suppose they'll be serving turkey."

"Be lucky to get another candy bar. We get out of here I'll cook you a turkey with all the trimmings. You like candied sweet potatoes?"

"Anything you make will be wonderful. I'll bake my famous pumpkin pie."

"What makes it famous?"

"The fact that I make it. Tell me what you have in mind about the trimmings."

"Gravy, mashed potatoes, green—"

"Not those trimmings. I was thinking more like a rain check on the other night."

"We'll have to let that play out."

I couldn't see her face so I didn't know if her answer had a wink attached or not. But I chose to think it did.

"I mean it about the dinner," Angella said, putting her hand on my knee. "We'll organize the *trimmings* at the appropriate time."

"No more *food* talk, I'm starving," I replied, taking the squeeze of my knee as the wink I was craving.

"Good idea on all counts. I'll try to sleep a bit. Wake me so you can have a turn, before we venture out."

Angella fell asleep almost instantly. I sat there next to her listening to her steady breathing. We were in the middle of God only knew where, being held prisoners by people who behaved as if they had little regard for human life, and I was comforted by a simple hand on my leg.

I must have dozed off because when I next realized where we were, I could see the fingers of my outstretched hand.

NINETEEN

It was time to get started on our adventure into the jungle. I treated myself to the candy bar and a sip of the precious water. Then I woke Angella.

It was still silent outside, except for the jungle sounds, which had gradually settled down as the night wore on. Or was it just that I was becoming accustomed to our surroundings?

I retrieved the bucket and moved to the doorway. Angella followed behind me, the tracker held at her hip. I stuck my head outside, bracing for a club—or worse.

Nothing.

In fact, as best as I could determine, no one was out there. I motioned for Angella to follow and moved as far from the building as I dared go. Angella was only a few inches from me as we moved. She whispered, "It's coming up."

Suddenly, I heard voices coming from the direction of the path. The light was still dim and the brush too dense to see movement. I strained to be sure the sounds were human and not some animal rummaging around.

Angella's body went rigid, her eyes concentrating on the same spot as mine. She tapped my arm and motioned for me to follow her as she retreated to our hut.

We were back inside when she whispered, "They're talking about the Korean. Seems he's supposed to lead them to a meeting place for the key. He's refusing. Says he wants to be sent home. They beat him, but he won't tell them where the meeting place is. Claims he knows nothing about meeting anyone for a key. They're arguing over whether to shoot him."

"What did they say about a meeting?"

"From what I gather, someone has the key. They believe he's to meet with that someone. He says he doesn't know where the key is."

"What did they say about us?"

"They need clarification of our status. The men want to shoot us, but the head guy says the heat is on over the last American lawman they killed. They're still afraid of an all-out retaliation. They're planning for us to be here months."

"Months!"

"Calm down, Jimmy. They can hear everything you say."

"Well, fuck them then."

"Calm down! We'll work through this."

"When I get my hands on Tiny I'll wring his neck."

"Hate to break this to you, but you can barely reach his neck."

"Then I'll shoot his legs off so I can reach his neck!"

"You think he's the plant?"

"He got the Korean out early. Maybe to kill Duran. He lured us onto the plane. Adds up. We'll see."

"Warden says it wasn't Tiny," she reminded me.

"Voices can be disguised. He got us on the plane. You sent him a text. He answered. Shit, what more do we need? But what I can't figure is why we're here."

"At first when I saw Tae-hyun I thought it had something to do with the key. But based on what you said, that's not right. I agree with you, Jimmy, why us? If the key is missing, why bring us down here with Tae-hyun?"

"Could be two different operations."

"Why the same location then?" Angella asked, not buying the distinct operation theory.

"Coincidence of timing. Also, could be this is all they have available," I replied, grasping at theories and drawing a blank.

"The key is what I don't understand," Angella replied. "Think about it."

I drew a blank. "If Tae-hyun had the key out on the marsh then where did it go? You and I were out there on the boat with him."

"And so were a hundred other people," Angella was quick to point out. "After they airlifted you, Coast Guard, Navy, INS, Border Patrol, ATF, Homeland Security, FBI and even at one point, the Fish and Wildlife Service. Who the hell knows where the key went—or even if Tae-hyun had it in the first place?"

The fronds were pushed aside and one of the guards appeared in the doorway, his arms heavy with two blankets. Throwing the blankets on the floor, he barked, *"Algunos de cama. Todo lo que podía conseguir. Mantenga esto a ti misma!"*

"*Muchas gracias*!" Angella responded.

The man nodded and slipped back outside.

"He smuggled these to us and is afraid of what the others will do if they find out it was him."

"At least they're not all corrupt. Did the tracker work?"

She retrieved the device and turned the display on. In the short time we had been outside, it had captured and stored the image of where we were. A river leading to a town was visible. The rest was green. A red light was flashing in the center of the green area.

"At least it's working. That's a start. Turn it off to conserve the battery."

The fronds opened and closed and our bucket was sitting in the opening. The waste was gone, but the smell remained. I quickly moved it to the far corner.

Footsteps and voices were now all around us. "What I'm thinking," I whispered to Angella, "is that they're not standing guard at night. With the tracker, we should be able to make our way to the river and follow it to the town."

"There's a reason why they aren't guarding at night. You sure you want to be out there? Might run into something worse."

"An animal? Maybe eaten by a jack rabbit," I responded, trying to lighten her up a bit.

"Getting killed by a jaguar or bobcat can't be blamed on them," Angella replied, her sense of humor gone. "What's one or two tourists who wander off by themselves got to do with anything? Happens all the time."

"Remember, more people are killed by snakes and insects than by big animals."

Angella wasn't buying it. "That's a lot of comfort. So we die by snake bite or eaten by a crocodile, that doesn't help matters. In fact, we need to be careful they don't throw one of them creatures in here."

I thought about what Angella was saying and noticed something move under the blanket next to her leg. I pushed her back and jumped on the blanket with all my weight. I didn't feel anything, but to be on the safe side I lifted the blanket and shook it toward the wall.

Nothing fell out.

I held it up as high as I could and motioned for Angella to look on the other side. She did so and then said, "All clear. Nothing."

I checked the second blanket and nothing turned up. "Better safe than sorry," I sheepishly said. "You're right about them planting something here. Better be on the safe side."

I slumped against the wall, preparing myself for a long day of waiting.

Angella slid over next to me. "Jimmy," she whispered, her voice unsteady as if she were unsure of what she was about to say, "in the short time I've been with you I've come face-to-face with more violence than I could have imagined."

"You opted into police work. Your husband—former husband—is a cop. You knew what you were getting into."

"But when it's...personal, like you getting your neck slashed and Duran getting shot, it's ...well, different. What I'm saying is... well, to be frank, I don't know if I'm cut out for this. Seeing people who you care about die—or almost die—and knowing you're the only person who can save them. I mean, one false move and—"

Now it was my turn to put my hand on her knee. "Focus on the positive, Angella. You saved my life. If you hadn't followed your hunch that Duran needed to talk to you, he'd probably be dead now."

"But that's just it. I almost came back to you at the hotel. That's what I wanted to do—more than you can ever know—but I didn't. But what if I had and Duran died? How do you know what is right?"

Funny how when your lives are on the line, as ours were now, morality issues float to the surface. I didn't pretend to know the answers. "When the moment comes to act, you do what feels right at that instant. You sort it out later."

"How do I know what's right?"

"Good people know right from wrong. It's the people we chase who don't know the difference. You're a good person. You do what feels right at the time."

"Is that what you do?"

"Adrenalin takes over. Sometimes I don't do exactly what the textbook says."

Later. Much later, a food box was shoved through the door. The moldy bread and fruit had been replaced by four candy bars.

"Someone likes us," Angella said as she again scraped the cheese against the side of the box to get rid of the ants. "Bet it was the guy who brought the blankets." She stopped scraping and peered intently into the filthy box. "Something's in here. It's now covered with these ants, or whatever they are." Using her thumb and forefinger, she gingerly lifted a crumpled scrap of paper and knocked the insects off. She then unfolded it and found writing on the inside. She translated, "Be careful. Cameras are watching at all times. They know you were out. Don't do it again. These are dangerous men."

I moved close to Angella while we were eating and said, "I'm thinking we need to get out of here and the sooner the better."

"Is that smart? They'll hunt us down and kill us. It's easy for them; they know this area. We don't."

"What have you eaten since we got here?"

"Same as you. A few pieces of bread and some cheese, or whatever that stuff is. I'm living on the candy bars."

"That's my point. In a few days we'll be too weak to do anything. Something goes wrong out there, they'll kill us. One way or another, it won't end well if we do nothing. We're here for a reason and waiting plays to them. We need to change the dynamic."

"I was thinking about why we're here," Angella said. "It may be as simple as the fact that we're tasked with finding the traitor. Someone, Tiny, or whomever he's working for or with, doesn't want us getting even close to the trail. So they detour us to Mexico."

"Possible," I answered. "All the more reason to get out. I say we leave around midnight, make our way to the river and follow it to the town. We should get there by morning. We can find the local police and have them call Cindy—or someone."

"If the idea is to get us off the traitor's trail, then you're right. They'll eliminate us sooner or later." She thought for a moment before adding, "Maybe they're using us to track Tae-hyun. When he gets the key, they let him go and we follow him with the tracker."

Angella was onto something. "That works if...if there's another bomb and they don't know exactly where it is. They want us to follow him and lead them to the bomb. And then... then what?"

"Then they eliminate us and go forward with their plan," she replied.

"Too complicated. This is about pinning the operation on us—or on at least one of us."

"Do you believe I had nothing to do with the Chief being shot?"

"I never thought otherwise."

She studied my face without comment, clearly making up her mind if she believed me.

I broke the silence. "Let's sleep as much now as we can. It's going to be a long night. Who knows when it'll end after that."

Angella cheered up. "Maybe with these blankets it'll be better than last night. I barely slept."

"Want company?" I asked.

"It's not Thanksgiving *trimmings* time, if that's what you're asking. There are two blankets. We can each have one. Share and share alike."

TWENTY

Angella and I managed to sleep on and off most of the day. When we weren't sleeping, we sat quietly talking, mostly about our past lives. The few times I steered the conversation close to Angella's marriage, she veered away. I can't say that I was more forthcoming, but we did discuss my almost non-existent relationship with my thirty-three year old son, Lester. He moved to Alaska six years ago, to, as he put it, "live the life humans were meant to live." By that I think he meant scavenge the earth for food and sit huddled in a cold log cabin trying to keep the elements at bay. I don't know who is winning, he or the elements. But since I find myself periodically on the sending end of a money gram, I don't believe it is him.

"After listening to you describe your son's reasons for escaping to Alaska," Angella commented when I fell silent, "you might want to consider following his lead."

"Meaning?"

"Aren't we *scavenging the earth for food and sitting huddled in a hot cabin trying to keep the elements at bay?* Not much difference from what your son is doing from what I can tell."

"Look to the bright side. At least we get paid for this fun."

"Lot of good that'll do when we're..." She paused. "I know, power of positive thinking."

"Any time people are shooting at you it's the same. All it takes is one bullet and lights out. If you dwell on it, it'll eat you alive. So positive is the only way. Or you get out. Hang up your badge."

"You know, Jimmy, you're a hard person to figure out."

She waited for me to respond, but when I just sat there, my back pressed against the hard wall, saying nothing, she continued, "I know you don't want to discuss this, but it's troubling me. Duran showed me his file on you—or at least a part of his file. The part about how Badman Tex died."

"Please, Angella, that's a closed subject. I don't—"

"Hear me out. It's important to me to get the facts straight. It's troubling me." I remained quiet and she raced on. "What I've pieced together is that you and your partner, Lonnie Turner, if I recall correctly, apprehended Tex just after he robbed a bank. He was shot in the head by a bullet from your gun. Am I right so far?"

"So far, you have an A going for you. You might want to stop while you're ahead."

"You testified that Tex shot you in the shoulder."

"Check."

"You also testified that the bullet hitting your shoulder caused your gun to discharge. The bullet hit Tex."

"Keep going. You're on a roll."

"The ballistics expert testified that the trajectories are wrong. He said the bullet that went through your shoulder came from where your partner Lonnie was standing and not from where Tex was located."

"That's what the expert said. So where're you going with this?"

Ignoring my comment, Angella continued, "And Tex's gun, or so one expert said, did not appear to have been discharged until after he died."

"Okay."

"Any comment?"

"I told you, case closed. Both then and now."

"I'm your partner."

"Experts can say lots of things."

"But trajectories don't lie."

"But positions can change. Time of death is never an exact science. A few seconds either way, a few inches either way. FBI investigated. Rangers investigated. I'm not in jail."

"You haven't answered my question. You talked about following your gut. Doing what feels right. Did it feel right to shoot Tex? Did you deliberately pull the trigger?"

Some things are best left as they are. "The walls have ears," I replied, not wishing to elaborate. For that matter, Angella had ears.

"Maybe this isn't a good time. But you've dedicated your life to tracking criminals and enforcing the law. Then, or so the experts testified, you crossed the line. How do you justify what you did? I need to know. I really need to know."

When Angella had begun this line of questioning, I thought she was on a fishing expedition to satisfy a curiosity. But watching her face, and particularly, her troubled eyes, I began to understand that my behavior with Tex was deeply troubling to her. Coupled with her earlier questions about her own involvement with death and how she would react, I realized she was struggling to understand herself.

But Tex had indeed provoked me. Not so much by his gun, but by what his eyes had said to me. Silently screaming, "I'll kill as many people as I want and you can't stop me!" Taunting me to stop him, to save other lives.

How much should I tell Angella? If she was to trust me with her life, which is what being a law enforcement partner boils down to, then she deserved to know what I was about. But the Badman Tex situation was—and still is—too close to my core. I knew one thing for certain. If I dwelled on it, I'd not be able to carry a shield.

I finally said, "Assume that the ballistics expert was accurate. Assume I was shot by Lonnie and that Tex's gun was shot after he died. Assume all that. My question is: Then what? What comes of it?"

Now it was Angella's turn to fall silent. She got to her feet and walked across the room. My first thought was that it was a strange time to use the bucket. I mean, in the middle of a conversation. But that was not where Angella was going. She paced back and forth along the opposite wall. Several minutes went by before she returned to stand in front of me. "If I do as you say and assume the expert was right, then I'm left with the conclusion that either you or Lonnie shot Tex. If Lonnie had done it there'd be no reason to shoot you. So my conclusion is that you shot Badman Tex and your partner shot you."

"Now that you've gone through the mental gymnastics, where does it leave you?"

"Actually, feeling better about myself — and you. You're human. I know you like to see life black and white. A person is either bad or good. But you broke the law and that is bad. Yet you believe you're good. This must have shaken you because it proves there are shades. Humans are not perfect. That's what I've been struggling with. What if I'm not always perfect?"

"Sounds like I tuned to the Sunday night church hour. Only thing missing is the collection basket."

"And confession," Angella added. "Don't forget confession."

TWENTY-ONE

Several hours later, with the philosophical talk behind us, it was time for action. I had not heard any voices or guard movements for a long while. The night sounds of the jungle were in full throttle, however, and the place seemed alive with creatures on the ground and in the trees.

I took the bucket out as an excuse to be outside. Nothing was moving. Crouching as low as I could I waited, my body pressed against the building. When I first ventured outside, the jungle grew quieter. As I waited in the darkness, the sounds gradually came back to what I had begun to realize was normal. I slipped back inside.

"All seems clear," I whispered to Angella, who had been waiting just inside the opening. "Let's give it, say, another half-hour and then go."

"I'm following your lead in this," she whispered back. "Just give the signal."

I crawled back outside and sat on the ground, focusing my attention on the terrain at the perimeter of the clearing. I had studied the tracker map and was trying to visualize our course from here to the river. There were several pathways leading out into the jungle and I thought I could make out the one we were led in on. But I wasn't positive.

A hand came over my shoulder and clamped against my mouth. I froze in anticipation of another knife to my throat. Or a club to the head.

Neither happened.

It was Angella warning me to be quiet. I turned toward her and she removed her hand. She leaned close, her lips pressed against my ear. "There's something out there. Listen. Not the normal jungle sounds."

I heard nothing unusual. She moved quietly back into the hut and, staying low to the ground, I followed her lead.

She again pressed her lips against my ear, her voice barely audible. "There's someone out there. I'm certain."

I continued straining my ears, but nothing registered. I lay on the floor in order to see under the fronds.

Nothing moved.

Then I saw a slight movement on the path I had been studying. Could be a monkey moving in the trees. Could be anything.

We waited.

Then a voice said something in Spanish. I did not know *what* was said, but I knew *who* was saying it.

Angella whispered, "He said, 'He's close by here. In one of these buildings. Give the tracker a moment and we'll know for sure.' They must be looking for Tae-hyun."

I pulled back from the door and sat upright facing Angella. "That's Padre himself," I said. "What the hell's he doing here? Trich said he never left the house."

Angella moved next to me so that we could talk even softer. "She probably doesn't know what he does at night. I feel sorry for her."

When Padre and I last met, he had almost killed me. Had he come to finish the job? Our Government had deported him to his home in Mexico in order to avoid a trial they could never hold. But he was confined to his ranch. So much for house arrest.

"He's a drug lord, is he not?" Angella said, answering my rhetorical question. "This is drug country. Two plus two."

"I doubt if he could be here without our government knowing. I was told he was wearing an ankle monitor." Then the thought struck me that maybe Angella and I knew too much also. Maybe putting us in Homeland Security was the beginning of a Government plan to eliminate us with no questions asked. More importantly, no investigation by Contentus or Duran. And no trial.

The more I thought about that scenario, the more it made sense. Tiny then was just acting on orders from above. Eliminate all those who knew that an A-bomb had been smuggled into the country. Chief Duran lay dying in the hospital, Angella and I—and even Tae-hyun—were captive in a Mexican jungle. How very neat. Almost all the people who knew about the atomic weapon were out here. In fact, the only person missing was Contentus. I strained even harder to listen for his voice.

Angella broke through my thoughts. "He's tracking something—or someone. If he were responsible for us or Tae-hyun being here, he'd know exactly where we'd be."

"Could be us," I responded, following up on my thoughts. "He could be tracking us."

"Not unless someone implanted a transmitter in one or both of us."

"I suppose that's possible."

"It's the Korean," she said. "They just found him in the far hut. He's been beaten and they are afraid he doesn't have the stamina to walk. They're preparing to carry him out."

"First break we got. Assuming they don't come for us, we'll follow them out. We can track the Korean with *our* tracker. We don't even need to keep them in sight."

A moment later, figures receded into the jungle. All human sounds ceased and the normal screeching had again begun to build.

"Ready to move out? You have Tae-hyun on the tracker?"

"Moving toward the river," Angella announced, pointing toward the screen.

"Let's go. No more talking. Watch your step."

We crept forward slowly, soundlessly. I half expected a gang of angry drug-runners to open fire on us from the middle hut. But nothing moved. We knew there were men in the jungle ahead of us, but we could not see or hear any human sounds.

Angella tapped me on the shoulder. I stopped and turned to face her. She was studying the tracker and pointed to the flashing dot. It was stationary ahead.

We waited also. Then the dot began to move and we resumed our trek.

We turned a corner and froze. Standing in the middle of the path just in front of us was the largest bobcat I had ever seen.

Lucky for us, it was watching the men in front of us and had not yet picked up our scent.

We had no knives or guns. There wasn't time to find a stick or a rock. We were totally vulnerable to the predator.

The bobcat was chewing lazily. I recalled a story an old-time Texas Ranger had once told about how drugs were fed to wild animals by drug dealers to calm them. That way they could avoid shooting them when the sound of a rifle would give away their positions. Apparently, that's what we had just witnessed, because when the bobcat finished chewing, it turned, saw us standing less than twenty feet away and, instead of attacking, it ambled off into the forest without an apparent care in the world.

I just hoped he didn't have kinfolk hanging around.

"What the hell just happened?" Angella whispered.

I put my finger to my lips, making a mental note to tell her later.

When we arrived at the river, we saw two boats paddling silently downstream away from the town. I pointed up river, away from their direction. I figured they had a boat waiting for them out in the bay, and if we followed, we'd end up stranded with no ability to go forward. We needed to find the town and civilization if we had any hope of getting out of this alive. "Use the tracker, try to figure out how far the town is," I instructed Angella.

"Now that we're in the open the satellite has a good view. It has painted in a lot of detail that we didn't have before. The town is less than ten miles from here. The river bends a bit, but not too bad."

"If we make good time it'll take about five hours." I checked my watch. "That'll put us there around first light. Let's make tracks."

And make tracks we did.

For three hours the going was relatively easy. There was just enough moonlight reflecting from the river to allow us to pick our way without too much trouble. I guessed we had been moving at a pace of about two-and-a-half miles an hour. That would leave us between two and three miles to go.

Then the banks of the river grew steep and we had to move inland. The travel time slowed to a crawl. And then stopped entirely when my right foot caught the edge of rock and my toe wedged underneath. The heel of my left foot lost traction and I fell backward, my toe still trapped under the rock. Something snapped. Pain shot up my leg and I was certain I had either broken my ankle or snapped a tendon.

Putting any amount of weight on it was impossible. Pain shot through my body when I moved my toes. "It's either a very bad sprain or it's broke," I told Angella. "Either way, I'm can't move very fast." I pulled down my sock and the ankle was already the size of an orange. It throbbed like hell.

"We can't just sit here," Angella said. "When they realize we're gone, they'll get here in no time. I'm going on ahead. Crawl into the brush and hide yourself."

I started to protest, but knew she was right. Saving my life was becoming a habit. "Don't risk your life for me," I said, trying to sound more altruistic than I felt. "If you can't find someone reliable, don't come back."

"I'll be back," Angella promised. "I'll be back."

"You sound like MacArthur in the Pacific. Just don't take unnecessary chances."

"Who's MacArthur?"

"Forget it."

"I can take care of myself," Angella said, showing the same resolve she always did when things got tough. You do the same." She helped me crawl into the brush. I went in as far as I could go, found a tree and propped myself against it in a sitting position. Angella gathered brush and piled it on me. "I'll be back as soon as I can." She bent and kissed my forehead.

"Is that all I get?"

"It'll have to do. If I do more I may never leave. See you in a few hours."

TWENTY-TWO

I spent the next several hours dozing, but mostly trying to find a position to ease the pain in my ankle. Nothing seemed to work. At some point, I must have passed out, because when I opened my eyes it was full daylight. Judging from the sun's position, it was after noon.

No Angella.

I was stiff. Just dragging myself closer to the tree so that I could sit straighter caused excruciating pain to shoot up my leg.

Possibly I had been dreaming, but I recalled that earlier, how much earlier I don't know, there had been commotion on the trail. People were shouting in Spanish.

I dug out my last candy bar, ate half of it and saved the rest for later. I again tried to move, but the pain came in waves. I considered walking back to the river and swimming downstream, but it would take most of a day to get to where I could climb down the steep bank.

The thought of spending another night out here didn't make me any too happy. Not being able to move made me helpless prey for any animal, large or small. I recalled the bobcat and assumed it would be ravenous when the drugs wore off. Thinking of animals made me think that they would likely smell the candy. So I ate the last of the bar as I imagined a man sentenced to death might eat—alone—and wishing to see just one more morning sky.

Instead, I saw the evening sky.

Then the night sky.

Animal sounds came from every direction. Things moving. Things calling other things. Things eating things. Me struggling to remain awake, while at the same time expecting to be attacked and ripped apart at any moment. I knew I would never hear my attacker coming. Noisy animals would go hungry in the wild.

Thinking is not always a good thing. I began to wonder if the bobcat would kill me first, or just start eating. What part would he go for first? The most tender, I imagined. That would be my stomach, since my back was against the tree. I tightened my stomach muscles and thought of Teran and all the hours in his gym. But that had been months ago. I was now out of shape—and easy prey.

I tightened my abs again and soon realized that I couldn't sit for more than a few seconds sucking it up. With every movement of the leaves above me, I foolishly sucked in my stomach.

My mouth was dry and my lips cracked. Aside from the quick drink of water Angella and I had taken before we came inland from the river, I had had nothing to drink since leaving the compound almost twenty-four hours ago.

I heard a sound. To be accurate, I felt the vibration of the jungle floor. I tensed my stomach.

The movement grew more pronounced before I could make out any actual sound. Whatever it was, it was large. I didn't think bears lived this far south, but I wasn't positive. After hours spent thinking about being eaten alive, I was determined to put up as much of a fight as I could, broken ankle or not.

I forced myself to roll over onto my stomach so that my knees were below me. This allowed me to crawl away from the sound and move deeper into the jungle. It was better than being ripped apart by some mammoth beast of prey.

I felt it rather than saw it. Something had my good ankle and I struggled to work it free. I couldn't see what it was, but the harder I pulled, the harder it pulled back. Slowly, I ran my hand down my leg, trying to feel what it could be. My fingers touched something firm and slippery and my hand involuntarily pulled back.

Snake, I concluded. A snake had wrapped itself around my foot and was crushing my toes. I touched it again and this time it felt solid, but still slippery. I felt around for something to beat it off with. My hand closed on a broken branch. I got a good grip on the thick twig and smashed it against my foot, at the same time pulling my leg upward as hard as I could.

My foot moved a few inches and then locked tight.

I swatted again and again, but my foot was held tight, the pressure increasing.

The thrashing did nothing for releasing my foot, but it did call attention to my position. The vibrations were getting stronger and the sounds I heard were now clearly distinguishable as human voices. Angry sounding Spanish with just a trace of English mixed in.

I slapped at my captor once again and succeeded only in opening a wound on my shin. My foot was locked in place and now I had no movement at all.

Several flashlights moved slowly in my direction. I gathered as much vegetation as I could and pulled it around me. I lay perfectly still, not daring to even turn my head. I could see shadows through the debris as lights moved closer.

Then someone said something in Spanish and the lights started to move at an angle away from me.

A moment later the lights were beyond my head, off to the side about ten feet. I slowly let my breath out.

At that same instant something, a human foot I later learned, landed directly on my bad ankle, catching me off-guard. I let out an involuntary scream and the lights immediately focused directly on my half-buried face.

TWENTY-THREE

"Jimmy Redstone, I presume," the deep voice boomed. "Fancy meeting you here."

The light was in my eyes, but the voice belonged to Tiny. Not a particularly comforting realization, since he was the person responsible for me being in this hell-hole to begin with. I tried to sit up, but the pressure on my ankle generated a deep grunt instead.

"Careful there. Stay where you are, we'll immobilize the ankle before we move you out of here."

"Get the damn snake off my other foot! It's numb already."

The lights moved down my leg and Tiny laughed.

"What's so friggin' funny, you sadistic asshole?" I yelled. "I'm half dead on account of you!"

"It's not a snake! Your foot's caught in a vine." He pulled a large knife from his waist holder. In an instant my foot was free. "Don't try to get up. That ankle looks nasty. And this foot is bruised. Looks like something's been beating on it."

I didn't ask about Angella because I didn't know if he was aware she had gone into town for help. The less he knew, the better chance she had of getting out of Mexico alive.

Two men bent down next to me, one of them wrapped something around my bad ankle. I felt it getting tighter. I suppose they were inflating something. Almost instantly, the pain cut back. One of the men wrapped a bandage around the foot I had beat upon. Then they lifted me by the armpits and draped my arms over their shoulders. We started to make our way back to the path.

It was slow going. The pain was not as severe as I had expected. One of the men said, "Let me know if you need something for the pain, but I'd rather not shoot you up if we can avoid it. It's best if you have your wits about you."

"I'll manage," I said. "The pain's not bad now."

"At least that's a good sign," Tiny commented. "For now."

When we got to the main path, the group turned away from town, back toward the direction Angella and I had come. I asked, "Where the hell we going? Town's the other way."

Tiny replied, "Back where you belong."

I didn't ask any more questions and Tiny said nothing more as we slowly made our way back down river. In about two miles we turned away from the river and moved into the jungle. I had given up hope of breaking free of these men. There simply was no way I could outrun them. One thing I did know was that I did not want to spend another night propped against a tree waiting to be eaten. I would rather take my chances with madmen than with animals in the wild.

As we moved deeper into the trees, the vegetation again grew thicker and I could only imagine what fate lay in store for me at the end of this journey.

We walked for what I judged to be fifteen minutes. Tiny then said, "We wait here. Take a load off."

The men all sat. Water was passed around, followed by high protein energy bars.

After eating my fill, I said to Tiny, "You have a lot of explaining to do."

He replied, "From where I sit, it would seem it's the other way around. This is not a good place to speak."

I didn't know what he meant, but it was clear he wasn't about to tell me anything. So I fell silent. I was concerned about Angella. But until I understood the situation, I continued to hold my tongue. I wanted to give her every chance to escape. We were up against a group of people who were obviously well financed and well organized.

Someone had known that the Korean had a chip in him and had tracked him using the same tracker we had. That suggested Tiny, or whatever organization Tiny really worked for. The fact that Tiny was a member of the Secret Service, charged with preserving the President's life, made it all the harder to fathom. If Tiny was compromised, then the President's life was in danger. Was that what this was all about? But the President trusted him. Or did he? I wouldn't be involved if the President had faith in everyone around him.

How far did this extend? Was the President's confidant and go-to person in times of crises, General Maxwell Jamison, involved? It has never happened in the history of the United States that a four-star general was found to be a traitor. But there is always a first time.

What about his friend, Lucinda McNaughton? With all her money and connections it was possible, but not likely. But where then did it stop? Was the plan to eliminate Angella and I, as I had thought earlier? That certainly would explain the large pay checks. They didn't expect to pay much out. If the plan was to kill the President, then me dying in the Mexican jungle would suit their purposes better than saving me. Especially if I were being set up as the assassin.

That brought me to the conclusion that they were not, in fact, trying to save me.

If they weren't saving me, where was Angella? Could she be working with them? If she had killed Duran, then she was a highly trained operative with the emotions of a machine. That could explain her divorce. But then what explains the chemistry? And the chemistry was real—I could sill feel it.

I had learned over my many years investigating difficult crimes that it is easy to suspect everyone. The hard part is separating out the guilty. Right now, Tiny was at the top of the list. I had difficulty even thinking of Angella in that same context.

But she could work for him. Or maybe the other way around?

The longer we sat, the more active my mind became and the more possibilities I conjured up. This I knew to be dangerous when all the facts are not available. But all the facts are never available.

Tiny checked his watch and said to the man sitting next to him, "First light is an hour away. Let's get this show on the road, Captain." The man stood, signaled to the others, and several men followed him into the jungle.

They were not more than twenty feet away, but I could no longer see them. They did not speak, but I could hear sounds of movement. After a while, one of the men came over to the man called Captain and said in broken English, "We're ready."

The captain walked over to Tiny and said, "On your command, we'll light'em. You got exactly five minutes from that point."

"Understood,"Tiny responded. "I've worked with these guys before. Never known them to be off by more than thirty, forty, seconds at most. They never come in early. Lives depend on their accurate timing." He studied his watch for a few more minutes and then said, "Get Redstone over to the clearing. He'll need more time than usual."

My two escorts immediately lifted me and I hobbled down the path in the direction the men had been working. It was starting to get light, but I could still not see more than a few feet ahead.

Tiny put his hand up and we all stopped. He checked his watch again and held up five fingers.

A minute later four fingers.

We were on a count down, but I could not figure out what we were counting down.

One finger went into the air and the captain moved next to Tiny. His head came up to Tiny's stomach.

"Time,"Tiny said softly.

"Close your eyes, now!" the captain barked the command in a way that caused my eyes to close without thought. He then shouted, "Go!" into a small radio.

Even through closed eyes, the light was blinding. There was no noise, just sudden daylight.

We moved forward a few more feet to a clearing that was glowing. Slowly my eyes adjusted. Ahead of me was a small flat area of grass. It was a makeshift landing area, and I wasn't sure if it was the same one we came in on or a different one. This one seemed much smaller though. But the lighting could be playing tricks.

Tiny leaned down to me and said, "If all goes well we'll be out of here and on our way home in four minutes."

I didn't understand what was going to happen until I heard the unmistakable sound of a helicopter low over the trees.

Within two minutes the helicopter was a few feet off the ground and two Marines in jungle attire jumped to the ground and raced across the opening to where I had been positioned. They lifted me and ran back toward the hovering Blackhawk. The big chopper touched down, the door flew open and I was carried up the steps and deposited on the floor. A strap was drawn around my waist.

Glancing up, I saw Tiny, bent over and making his way to where I was sitting. The doors were already closed and we were moving forward and up.

Tiny said, "Exactly three minutes. These guys are good. That's critical if there's enemy fire."

"That's about the only thing we haven't seen," I replied, looking out through the small window across from me to make certain they weren't firing at us. I needn't have worried. The lights were already out and the clearing empty. The men had blended back into the jungle and were invisible from above.

"Where are we headed?" I asked Tiny, not expecting a straight answer.

"Where else? Brownsville. Got to get you cleaned up. God you stink! Then on to D.C.."

"My ankle needs medical attention," I replied, probing to see where this was all leading.

"In Brownsville. We'll get it fixed up, some fresh clothes. Lot more comfortable there than down here. Let's hold the questions until we're in a proper forum. There's a lot of debriefing ahead."

"So what's the story with Angella?" I broke down and asked. "We leaving her back there or what?"

“We’ll discuss everything when we’re in a proper environment. We’ll be there shortly. Relax and get some sleep; you can use it. I know I can.” He closed his eyes and either fell into instant sleep—or he was a really good actor.

I was betting on the actor.

TWENTY-FOUR

The Blackhawk landed at a far corner of the Brownsville airport next to a jet having no markings. Tiny jumped out and told me to stay put, as though I was capable of going anywhere on my own.

A few minutes later he was back. "Slight change of plans. We're going straight on to Washington. Got medical folks on board. Using a Medevac plane for this leg." Sarcastically he added, "Only the best for our agents."

Before I had a chance to ask him how I was supposed to change planes, the two Marines who had carried onto the helicopter now carried me off.

Ten minutes later I was seated in the jet and someone, I assume a doctor, came by, looked at my ankle, flexed it, wanted to know where it hurt. I told him the inside. He then announced, "Don't believe it's broken, but to be on the safe side we'll take some pictures when we're airborne. We can do what we need to do at that time. Get you fixed up in no time." He disappeared into the back of the plane.

I said to Tiny, "What now?"

"One passenger missing. Be along any minute. Then we're off."

He had no sooner finished telling me about what we were going to have for dinner when Angella appeared. She was limping a bit and had what appeared to be a nasty cut across her forehead. Blood was caked around it.

Seeing me, she exclaimed, "Oh, thank goodness you're alive! They refused to tell me anything about what happened to you. Are you okay? How's your ankle? How did you get here?"

"Time for debriefing is later," Tiny broke in. "We need to do it on the record. Sorry. No private discussions. Kapish?"

"Can I at least hug him? He's my partner."

"Do what you need to and then fasten your belt. We're about to take off."

She threw her arms around me. "Thank goodness you made it out! I was so worried. I'll be happy if I never go south of the border again."

"That wasn't exactly a tourist trip," I quipped. "Stay on the path, you'll be fine."

"You sound like an advertisement by the Mexican Chamber of Commerce."

"Enough!" Tiny said. "There'll be time enough later. I can't have you two talking business or I'll have to separate you like school children."

"Sounds as though we're under some sort of arrest," I responded, dismayed at his attitude.

"That's premature. But unless you can adequately explain what you were doing in Mexico at a compound run by the drug mob, you most likely will be."

"And to whom must we make this explanation?" It took all my will power to remain in my seat. Tiny was on the verge of losing a few teeth, never mind that he outweighed me by over a hundred pounds. Never mind that I couldn't stand up if I wanted to.

"Ultimately, to General Jamison. But that goes through me. So it will be me who handles your debriefing."

I was ticked at his presumption. "Unless I'm mistaken, I'm at a higher grade level than you are. So how does it add up that I need to explain anything to you?"

"You've been on the government team less than a week and you're telling me who reports to whom! For your information, it's not grade that counts. It's reporting structure. And you report through me, and don't forget that."

"With you reminding me once or twice a day there's little chance of forgetting," I shot back, getting angrier all the time.

"Gentlemen," Angella counseled, "this is not the time or place to be arguing. We have a mission to accomplish and we're going backward. You two need to play nice. We'll get to the bottom of this. But I must say Tiny, you sure have let us down."

Neither of us responded. The plane lurched forward, taxied a little distance and then began rolling in earnest. In less than five minutes we were out over the Gulf of Mexico. This time we actually did turn northeast. At least we were finally going in the right direction.

The plane leveled off and two orderlies appeared from the rear of the plane and escorted me to a fully equipped mini-hospital located in the back of the plane through a double door. I was told to lie down on an examining table. I did so and they promptly wheeled me under some sort of expensive-looking machine and proceeded to take a dozen or so pictures at every conceivable angle.

When they were finished, one of them said, "The doctor will read these and be with you shortly."

It was not as if there was a whole waiting line ahead of me—or maybe there was. I had no way to know. I suppose waiting is all part of the medical routine.

I rejoined the others up front and was relieved to see that Angella's wound, which had looked nasty when I first saw it, had been cleaned. It was superficial and didn't require a bandage.

In less than ten minutes, the same man who had spoken to me earlier came into the room. "I'm Major Kincaid," he announced in the manner most doctors take. "I'm an MD, just so you know. The pictures confirmed my suspicion. Your ankle is severely sprained, but not broken. You have what is called a level-two eversion sprain. The deltoid ligament is stretched and may be partially torn. That is both good and bad. The bad part is that there is little I can do to make it heal faster. The typical treatment is RICE, which stands for rest, ice, compression and elevation. You're now past the RI part, so all I can do is compress it and ask you to keep it elevated as much as possible. I'll fit you with a walking boot and, so long as you keep pressure off it, nature will perform its natural miracles. But I caution you, running and side pressures will make it worse and delay healing. If it rips, surgery will be necessary."

I was grateful it didn't need pins and plates and screws and six months on my back. I had work to do, and from the way this investigation had started, there would be little chance of getting done what needed to get done if I had to rehab my ankle.

While the doctor worked to stabilize my ankle and fit me with a walking boot, I thought of what had happened and why. And the more I thought about it, the more confused and angry I became. It was clear that the Korean had been kidnapped like we had been and taken to the hideout. It was also clear that he had been rescued from the kidnapers by the drug leader Santiago using tracking equipment similar to ours. That meant someone other than us had the Korean's code. That could only have come from a high source in the U.S. Government.

And then we have Tiny, who just happened to know exactly where I could be found in the jungle. It was no coincidence that he was out there. The rescue operation had been well planned and coordinated. General Jamison had to be involved in that operation.

The confusing part was that if Tiny had kidnapped Angella and me as well as the Korean, then he would not have required tracking equipment to find the Korean. And why take us both to the same place?

"Okay, young man," the doctor was saying, "You're good to join your friends. Later I'll bring you Oxycodone, but my advice is not to use it unless absolutely necessary. The swelling will go down slowly and the less you're on your feet, the better. Good luck."

I hobbled to the front of the plane, my right ankle again throbbing. It was packed tightly in the boot, and I quickly sat down and elevated it by placing it on the seat across from me.

"Tiny, we need to talk," I said, trying to keep the agitation from my voice. From the look Angella shot me I took it I had not succeeded. "You have some explaining to do and the sooner we get this out in the open the better we'll all be."

"You have it backward," the big guy responded. "You're the ones who need to explain your actions. The words I've heard associated with you two are traitors and treason. I have authority to arrest you both, but I decided I'd wait until after we hear your stories."

“What the hell you talking about?” I said, beating Angella to the punch.

“Making off to Mexico with the Korean for starters. I could have left you both for the Mexican government to deal with. That would have been the end of it. They don’t take kindly to smuggling people into their country. The other way around is the natural order of the universe. People and drugs flow north. Money flows south. They get agitated if you reverse the formula.”

“You know damn well that’s not true!”

“What’s not true? The order of things?”

“You. You’re the one who ordered us to get on that plane.”

“I did nothing of the sort! What I do know is that I tracked you by using Santiago. If we hadn’t put that bug in the Korean, God only knows how far you’d have gone.”

“Even assuming we ran off with the Korean, what the hell good would that have done us—or anybody?”

“The bomb is gone. We have reason to believe you know where it is. That’s why you were meeting Tae-hyun. To regroup and set it up again.”

“The bomb’s gone!” I repeated. “What the hell you mean the bomb’s gone? I thought the military—”

“It was being stored in an arsenal waiting for the go-ahead to dismantle it. They have to dispose of the fusion material—or whatever the hell makes those babies hot—and of course no one could agree on what to do. They moved it from the arsenal in Harlingen to the Corpus Christi Coast Guard station. When inspectors went in to secure the fusion material, the bomb was gone.”

“If the bomb, Tae-hyun and the detonator key all come together, we’re right back in hell.”

Angella broke in, her eyes on fire. “You know full well we didn’t run to Mexico with the Korean. You calling us traitors!”

"If the shoe fits—"

If my foot hadn't become wedged in the chair, there would have been a fight. I might have lost, but Tiny wouldn't still have all his natural teeth.

As it was, Angella leaped to her feet. "You're the one who set this up! We followed your orders and damn near lost our lives! You're the one who needs to explain himself, not us."

Now Tiny was out of his seat, his head slightly bent forward to avoid touching the ceiling. "I gave no such orders! What the hell you talking about?"

"You most certainly did." She dug into her purse and pulled out her phone. "Shit, the battery's dead or I'd show you the text you sent." She turned to me, "Yours working? You received the text also."

"Lost in the jungle somewhere, I'm afraid. But I received it and read it. Came from you without question."

Tiny glared at both of us. "Let me get this straight. You two ran off to Mexico with the Korean on my orders?" He studied us both and then said, "I must warn you, we're being monitored from D.C. and everything you say will be held against you. As you well know, it's a crime to give a false statement to a federal agent in an investigation. This is now an official investigation."

I managed to free my boot and stood to face him. "That's a two-way street. So whatever you say will be held against you as well." We were now playing our own version of liar's poker. Or as we called it in high school, chicken. "For the precious record, you did not instruct us to bring Tae-hyun."

"So you did that on your own," Tiny said, sitting down in his seat.

"Have no idea who brought him. I only know it wasn't Angella or I."

"So what's your story?" Tiny demanded. "Didn't the doctor say to stay off your foot and keep it elevated? Sit down both of you and let's talk through this."

"You know, Tiny," I said, "You're a first-class rat. I take it back. You're a rat without any class! You think for one moment Angella and I would work against our country? I nearly lost my life finding that bomb in the first place. If it hadn't been for me the damn thing would have gone off by now. What the hell's wrong with you?"

"Facts are facts. I only know you ran off to Mexico with the Korean knowing full well we wanted to confine him to this country. That's what we know."

"Then you know exactly nothing! That's what comes of being a desk jockey. You think you know something from a few random facts? You know nothing."

Before Tiny could respond, a TV screen folded down from the bulkhead. General Jamison's face took shape in front of us.

"Enough gentlemen! And lady! I've heard enough to know we have a problem. Start at the beginning, Mr. Redstone and tell us everything that happened from the time you landed in Port Isabel from D.C.. Leave out nothing. Ms. Martinez, be sure to listen carefully and fill in any time gaps in the story. It's all being recorded, so be sure it's accurate. You both will be bound by what you say. I don't have time for games. You get one chance to tell your story. If it doesn't check out perfectly, then God help you."

"Isn't this the time I ask for a lawyer before I say anything?" I quipped.

"That's certainly your prerogative," the General responded, his face set even harder than before. His eyes burned into the screen and an artery throbbed in his neck. But despite his obvious agitation, his voice was controlled. “I would never step on the Constitution I’ve taken an oath to protect. However, it is my prerogative to put you both in the brig. That plane you’re flying on can just as easily land in Guantanamo as in Washington. You get my drift, Redstone?”

TWENTY-FIVE

Surprisingly, the general listened to our statements without interruption. When we were both finished speaking, he said, "I'm again advising you both that everything you've just said has been witnessed and recorded. Do you both understand that?"

We looked at each other and then answered that we did. "You both understand you have just given this statement to me as a federal investigator under a criminal investigation. Is that correct?"

Again we both said we understood.

"Is there anything either of you desire to change or add?"

Both of us said no.

"Do you both swear that the statement you just gave is the full truth as you know it to be?"

"Yes," I said.

"It is," Angella replied, clearly tired of this routine.

"Okay, then. What happens to you from this point onward will depend upon whether the facts you presented are accurate or not. It's clear from what you just said that Tiny, I guess for the record I should say Kelvin Jurald, issued the order to release the Korean, Tae-hyun, early. For your information, at one time Tae-hyun held the rank of Sojua, or Major, in the North Korean army. We don't know if he's still in the army, but we believe not. But this makes the man highly dangerous and not to be taken lightly. Judging from how he's played us, I suppose you already know this."

I didn't know if Jamison was asking a rhetorical question or not, but at the risk of sounding the fool, I replied, "He does seem to know his way around. I suppose he understands English and may even be able to speak the language. Do we know where he is now?"

"Never mind that for now," Jamison said, "You're not cleared for any information until we resolve where we are. Back to the business at hand." He studied papers that had been placed in front of him. Then he looked back at the camera. "We just retrieved copies of the text messages that you two referred to. Before we go there, I want Jurald on the record."

"You believe their story?" Tiny stammered. "You think I'm behind this?" Tiny's demeanor had gone from cock of the hill to belligerent.

"I'm making no assumptions," Jamison shot back. "Just swear to tell the truth and get on with it. I remind you you're under oath and we are on the record. Now tell us your side of this and leave out the editorial comments! Do you understand?"

"That's bull shit!" Tiny said.

"Yes or no!" Jamison demanded, what little patience he had exhibited earlier was gone. "Do you or do you not understand that your answers are being recorded?"

"Yes." Tiny said through clenched teeth. Tiny glanced at both of us, his expression one of a man caught in the wrong place. If this had been my investigation, I would have him down for the prime suspect. I'm sure Jamison was thinking the same thoughts.

When Tiny finally spoke, it was with resolve and very slowly. He denied speaking with the warden and denied sending us text messages asking us to go to Brownsville to take a flight anywhere. He also denied sending us messages confirming that we were to board the prop plane to D.C..

However, he did admit that when he saw on his tracker that Tae-hyun was in Mexico, he commissioned Santiago to go get him and bring him back to the United States. He also admitted that he went to Nuevo León to be close to the operation. "I wanted to make sure nothing got screwed up. At that time I had no idea that Redstone and Martinez were also down there. All I knew was that they had disappeared—actually gone silent."

"So how did you know where Redstone was? It's clear to all of us you were tracking him."

"I was in the Police Station, in the back room, when Angella came in. I arranged for her to be brought out of the country and then called you to coordinate his evacuation."

Tiny then detailed the rescue operation and Jamison patiently waited for him to finish. Tiny was walked through the routine of verifying the accuracy of his statement just as Angella and I had been. Clearly, Jamison was not leaving anything to chance. I had no doubt that the man was serious. Since we were not military, he had no authority to hold us for court-martial, but I doubt if that would have stopped him. By the time the Justice Department sorted it all out, there was no telling what hell we would have gone through.

Tiny appeared uncomfortable, tugging on his collar. Small beads of perspiration formed on his forehead.

General Jamison again concentrated on several additional papers an aide put in front of him. After what seemed an eternity, he said, "It's inconclusive, at best. Most of what all of you say checks out. But it's not making sense to me. Because you are under Presidential directive, Redstone and Martinez, I'll accept your stories. Tiny, just so you know, there are several text messages from you; one to the warden instructing him to release Taehyun and one to Redstone and one to Martinez telling them to come back to D.C.. The confirmation messages you sent them also are confirmed."

"I never sent any such messages!" Tiny protested. His face turned deep red in anger.

"Keep your powder dry, Jurald! These messages were definitely sent from a telephone number registered to you. But, and this plays in your favor, it's a number you've never used for any other purpose. My communications technician believes someone other than you set this cell up. That's a matter for the FBI. Until we have the answer, I'll allow you to continue your role with Redstone and Martinez. But we'll continue to monitor each of you closely. My suggestion going forward, agree on a code word for any message sent among you. Might keep you alive."

"I have a question," I said before Jamison cut us off.

"Make it good, I have things to do here."

"When the bomb was found, I mean out there in the marsh, its radiation-protective cover had been removed. I assume the cover is back in place."

"Correct. In fact, we recovered the shield in the Gulf about a quarter mile offshore. We had a new cover fabricated. Foot thick solid lead. I'm told no radiation will leak from that. The bomb is now shielded by both covers. Sucker now weighs upwards of seventy-five tons, maybe even over a hundred."

"From what I've been told, it's gone missing."

"Correct."

"Any idea where it is?"

"That's your job. But keep in mind we can't just broadcast an APB. Justice has been notified and a limited search has been conducted. I don't have to tell you, but this is classified as Top Secret. I've arranged for special treatment for you and Martinez, since neither of you hold a clearance. Tiny has clearance in any event.

Big of him. I didn't care to debate with Jamison just how the hell I was supposed to find a top secret bomb if we didn't have full access to the system. I changed the conversation. "I assume it disappeared between Harlingen and Corpus."

"Correct."

"How was it being transported?"

"By truck."

"Armed guard?"

"INS."

"INS? Why not military?"

"Nothing you have a need to know. You finished interrogating me?"

Responding to his mood, I replied, "For now I am."

"Listen Redstone. We got some political problems here. Don't make them worse. According to the nuclear non-proliferation treaty, we need to report its presence in the United States. But the President refuses to go public. That would set off a panic. Need to get rid of it, but the question is how? That's not my concern. It's been booted to the Secretary of State and Attorney General to work out. Atomic material, especially weapons, come under civilian control is all I can say about it now. If you have nothing further, I'll get on with my day."

"Okay, Tiny," I said, when the picture faded, "We still being taped?"

"I think it's smart to assume anything you ever say is subject to being recorded."

"I suppose that's why government employees always talk gibberish."

Angella responded, "That's not the reason at all."

"You got a better explanation?"

"Try stupid."

"Now, now," Tiny responded, "Give us credit."

"If the shoe fits."

I turned to face Tiny. "Do you know how the bomb was moved to the Coast Guard station?"

"No reason to know that. I was told it was missing."

"That might explain some of the radiation illnesses we had seen creeping across Texas," I said.

Angella had been sitting quietly taking everything in. She leaned forward. "The bomb disappearing from the Coast Guard station also might explain Captain Boyle's behavior and why Mark is still under house arrest."

"Good point. Put Boyle on our list."

"Remember, Jamison specifically said to leave the military to him."

"Coast Guard is Homeland Security. I'm treating his statement as ambiguous."

"From what I see," Angella said, "ambiguous is not a concept Jamison understands. You get him after you and there's no telling what the outcome will be."

"Got to do what we think best. Keep Boyle in our sights." I directed my attention back to Tiny. "So, where's Tae-hyun now that you rescued him from the bad guys?"

"In Brownsville."

"Let him go. I still want to see which way he runs."

Tiny's eyebrows went up. But when I didn't back down he went to a terminal on the bulkhead, logged in, and typed something on the keypad. A few minutes later he was back. "He should be freed within the hour. I'll set the tracker to display on the plane's monitors. Be interesting to see where he heads."

Dinner was served. As we had experienced on our first flight to the district, the food and service were excellent, rivaling the best restaurant experience I could remember.

Angella fell silent, and the several times I tried to engage her in conversation, she seemed agitated. When I asked her about it, she simply said, "We'll speak later, in private."

Tiny bristled at her comment, but refrained from saying anything. In fact, no one spoke for the remainder of the trip.

Near Washington, I asked, "We landing at the hangar or at National?"

"I assume Andrews, since this is a military flight, but not certain. If it makes a difference I can check."

"Don't bother, just curious."

"We'll be on the ground in less then fifteen minutes," Tiny informed us, "anything you need?"

Angella said, "Can we get an update on the radiation treatment from medical facilities across the country? That might give us some more leads. Maybe a pattern or something."

Tiny went to the terminal, again typed in commands. In a few minutes, he said. "System's been closed for landing. We'll get the printout when we're on the ground. Fasten your belts."

The captain came on the speaker and gave us the standard landing routine. The only added piece of information was that we were landing at Andrews and a car would meet us at the plane.

“Convenient,” Angella quipped.

“Also, there’s no record of us coming or going. I’m not sure if that’s good or bad.”

“Depends upon why anyone would want to know.” I answered, a vague discomfort settling around me. Nothing good ever came from that feeling.

TWENTY-SIX

Angella sat quietly in the limo studying the reports we had been handed when the plane landed. For my part, I was content to relax and gather my thoughts during the short ride to our apartment.

Tiny, sensing the tension, remained silent until the driver stopped the car in front of the apartment. Instead of getting out when we did, he said, "I think it best if I went home tonight. Hopefully, time will heal the gap between us. I'm sorry for doubting you both, but it comes with the territory."

"I suppose," I replied, grateful that he was leaving us. It was clear to him that he had lost our trust and I was not yet ready to apologize. In point of fact, I was not ready to accept the story that someone else had taken a cell phone in his name. I was thinking of asking Cindy to find someone else to be our liaison, but to do so I needed to discuss what I had in mind with Angella. This in itself presented a slight dilemma, because I had no desire to go through the *Cowboy* routine with Angella anytime soon.

Inside the apartment, I said to Angella, "I'm not comfortable talking here. Let's catch the Metro and visit our offices. We can at least pretend we really have day jobs."

"I was thinking the same thing. We have to talk."

Outside, she said, "There's a problem. The radiation sickness is slowly making its way from Texas east."

"How far east?"

"Almost to where we are. Remember, it lags several days and not all doctors report all symptoms. But if we're to put any credence on the reports, it's definitely moving in this direction. The last cluster was yesterday in Pittsburgh."

"What do you suppose is causing the migration?"

Angella's face set hard. "I'm speculating here, pure speculation. But if the bomb was inside all that lead any leakage would be minimal. Certainly it wouldn't be enough to cause radiation symptoms in humans."

"So, what's your take?"

"Could someone be stupid enough to have removed the lead shield? If so, then the bomb is headed in this direction."

"That's certainly a possibility. But only a fool would do that! Everyone around would be dead in a matter of weeks. We'd be able to track it with radiation detectors. I'm betting on it being in its original case, or a small one like it. Make it easy to transport."

"Now it's critical to track Tae-hyun. If he moves in this direction, we'll know for certain the bomb is east."

Angella looked off into the distance for a long moment and then said, "What if he's a decoy? What if the real detonator, or igniter, or whatever they're calling him, is already here?"

"Then we'll most likely not stop the bomb from being activated. It's small, but it could wipe out the Capital!"

"Then we need to get moving," Angella said. "At the office we can regroup. We both need new firearms anyway."

TWENTY-SEVEN

I found Woody sitting behind my desk reading a novel. The office was now neatly arranged and actually appeared as though someone was working here. I stood in the doorway for a moment waiting for her to look up. But she was obviously engrossed, turning pages rather quickly as she went.

"Hello there, Woody," I finally called. "Hate to disturb you." It was Saturday and I hadn't expected anyone to be around.

Startled, Woody dropped the book and stood. I stand at an even six feet. I judged her to be about five-ten. Life had not been kind to her and if she had had good looks in her youth, age had wiped it all away. Today she wore a red sweater with a scarf around her neck. The slacks she had been wearing when she directed traffic during the set-up of our offices had been replaced by a skirt. She held out her hand. "I was expecting you later today. You got here sooner than I thought."

"Made good time. Do you have an office—or a desk?"

She pointed to the empty desk positioned just outside the door to my office. "I'm your Executive Assistant. Now don't be getting me confused with a secretary who does your typing and filing, that sort of stuff. I don't do any of that. I'm here to make appointments, keep your calendar, arrange your travel, get files, run traps, that sort of thing. But not typing." She glanced at my black boot. "I heard you had injured your foot. How bad is it?"

"Category two. Rest and elevation, neither of which it will receive. Nothing broken. Slow me up for a while, but hey, it goes with the territory."

"You should take it easy. It'll heal faster."

Ignoring her advice, I said, "Give me examples of what I would give you to do. I'm new to this secre…assistant…thing."

"Anything you need in your life. Think of me as a concierge. You need it done, I'll get it done. If it's a government charge, I'll get it paid. If it's a personal charge, I'll need your credit card. Don't worry, I'm trustworthy. Want references?"

"Not necessary. Here's my card. I catch you cheating on it, I'll shoot you. That clear enough?"

"Don't need to be dramatic. Been around you types my whole life and I'm not dead yet. I do my job well. Never had a problem."

"You can start by getting me a weapon and ammunition. Angella Martinez will want one also. I'm partial to Berettas."

"Look in your top drawer."

I slid the drawer open and found a Px4 Storm SD. Behind it was a PX4 leather holster with a thumb break. The drawer below it held several magazines of .45 caliber ammunition.

I looked at her and started to say I had a preference for 9mm.

She cut me off. "I know what you prefer, but this is Beretta's newest model. Comes with excellent credentials. The muzzle velocity of this one is lower than the 9mm, but that is more than made up for by the greater mass of the bullet. All in all, this gives you slightly greater stopping power and more accuracy."

I was impressed. I had no idea who this woman was, or where she had obtained her knowledge of weapons. But it was clear she knew her way around. I wouldn't make the mistake of underestimating her again. I was glad she had my back.

"I have vests on the way. I rounded up a couple of the new ones for you to try out. Lightweight, will stop just about anything. Anything else I can do for you?"

"Angella has a set of medical reports on radiation treatment. I want to see them. Also, let's get a U.S. map up on the wall with some colored pins."

"It'll take a few minutes for the reports, but charts and pins are out. That's old line. Frankly, too much latency. Here. Let me show you what I mean."

She came around to my side of the desk, slid out a panel from the top of the knee space and said, "We've gone electronic. This control pod handles a bank of monitors as well as the overhead projectors." She pushed a few buttons and a panel on the far wall opened, revealing a white reflective screen flanked by six flat-screen monitors, three on either side of the white screen. "You want a map of the United States you dial it up, thus." She proceeded to type in *map of the United States*.

Immediately, on the screen the United States appeared. "If you look down here," she continued, pointing to the control pod, "you'll see a miniature screen showing what is displayed over there. Take a stylus, or a pencil, or your pinky if you like, and touch any part of the little screen. A color marker will appear on the main screen. You can select any color you desire by simply touching the point and then touching the color button along the bottom. The good part about this system is that it will remember each display by name so you can mark this one and then call up any other data you want. You assign the data to the color and then the system will automatically update the dots. When you want this back you can bring it back. I'll name it *radiation*. You can move data from the white screen to any monitor."

"I'll take forever to learn how to use this," I said, only half-kidding.

"No need to. I have a control pod at my desk as well. Same goes for your computer. It's duplicated on mine. Just call out what you want and I'll put it up on the screen. While you're playing with your new toy, you can call up the report you want. Tiny sent you a copy, so find it in your email, move the attachment over to the icon of the display system and it'll be up there for you."

Woody looked over my shoulder and guided me through the log-in process. Moving the report attachment was straightforward. Immediately the data spread across the map. A note appeared asking what color I wanted to assign to it. I typed in blue, which seemed a fitting color for radiation.

Woody disappeared out of my office and said she would be gone for about five minutes. I took the time to search the remaining drawers to uncover the other surprises she had in store for me.

In the center drawer I found a new cell phone, identical to the one I had lost. I searched the other drawers and found nothing other than the standard issue paper, pens, pencils and paperclips. A very typical desk.

Woody came back, saw me fumbling in the desk and said, "Other than the phone, there's only standard issue stuff in there. The real material is in your computer. I loaded files of the agency, including the Coast Guard. I also loaded your friend Mark's files as well."

I looked at her long and hard. "Is there anything about me you don't know?"

"I shouldn't think so. It's my job to keep you alive and to do that job I need to know everything about you. I've been around a while, and with your clearance I can get almost anything you need."

"I don't doubt that," I said. "Not for a moment do I doubt you."

"I would hope not. I'll leave you to your work." She started for the door. "By the way, the cell phone number is the same. Called a friend at Verizon. I took the liberty of upgrading your data plan to unlimited. Save the Government money that way."

It didn't take very long to see the radiation pattern. The trail was moving across the country. At one spot, just outside Houston, there was a major cluster. "Woody," I called out. "Can you show the date and time each patient first reported symptoms?"

The information came up within a few seconds and confirmed what I had anticipated. There was a large cluster in South Texas around the time the bomb was discovered unshielded. These lasted for three weeks. All in South Texas hospitals with new cases reported every day. I assumed that was when the second cover went into place.

Then there were sporadic reports for two weeks, moving up toward Corpus Christi. I surmised that was when the bomb was being relocated to the Coast Guard station.

But a major cluster appeared a week later in and around Kenedy and King counties in South Texas. These were serious cases, and the reports were identical to those earlier from Harlingen and Brownsville.

The conclusion I reached was that Angella had been right on. The lead shield had been removed somewhere along the way.

The last report came in early this morning from a hospital not far from our apartment. That could imply the bomb was already in the Washington vicinity.

"Do we have the tracking data on Tae-hyun?" I called to Woody.

The track showed up and, in response to the color question, I selected red.

A red dot appeared in Brownsville and another on South Padre Island. Woody had joined me at the console. "How do I blow up this section?" feeling helpless and a bit overwhelmed by the technology. This was a far cry from the vu-graphs I grew up with.

"Looks like he's back at the same place, as before. South end of the island, near Schlitterbahn." The voice belonged to Angella. How long she had been standing in the doorway I didn't know.

"He's there for a reason," I said. "Meeting somebody, or something. He's parked for now, but we don't know for how long. While he's cooling his heels, or whatever Korean's cool, let's try to find out who orchestrated the hijacking of the bomb. One thing we know, it wasn't the Korean."

"Where do we start?" Angella asked. "This is where I need mentoring."

I glanced toward Woody, who took the hint and left the office, closing the door behind her. "Follow the money," I stalled, "is what Mark's father always said." Markus Cruses, my first partner and legendary Texas Ranger, drilled it into me. Follow the money! "His corollary was: follow the goods. We now can assume the bomb was repackaged into a new container, and because the lead shield is not around it, we have to think it is rather small. Being transported in a small vehicle."

"Military or civilian, only two choices. Should be easy to find if it's federal issue," Angella volunteered.

"To be on the safe side, I think we should confirm the bomb's not in the lead shield." I called Jamison's number. When he didn't answer, I left a message asking him to confirm that the lead shield is still at the station in Corpus.

I opened the door and asked Woody to see what she could dig up on a military vehicle coming to D.C. from South Texas.

"I'll get on it. Should have something for you quickly. Can't very easily hide a truck." She disappeared around the corner.

Angella gave me the, *what the hell was that all about*? look.

I simply shrugged and said, "Tell you later."

Angella nodded. "I suppose we also need to know who fabricated the new cover; who installed it; who loaded it; who drove the truck."

"You're on the right trail. Give the list to Woody, let's see the extent of her ability." I lowered my voice. "The woman's been around. I'm guessing she worked an FBI desk for a while."

"As an agent or administrative support?"

"That, my dear partner, is the sixty-four dollar question."

TWENTY-EIGHT

We did what cops are asked to do when they have spare time on their hands. Go to a firing range and practice. This is critical when using a weapon for the first time. Woody was going to take some time to perform her magic, so Angella and I went to the basement firing range. To say this was a state-of-the-art facility is an understatement. It was also enormous, and was attached to a full exercise facility with two Olympic-size pools attached. The unmistakable smell of chlorine permeated the air.

"I never expected this!" Angella exclaimed. "And it's full of people. Don't these people have work to do?"

"It's Saturday. They're on their own time. I'm impressed." I recalled from an organization chart I had seen that a large percentage of the people in Homeland Security carried a weapon. They had to be in excellent physical condition to handle the tasks they were assigned.

A large group of what appeared to be trainees were being instructed on the technique of dropping to one knee and concurrently firing. They were still expected to hit a moving target in the chest. The drill master, a woman wearing a ball cap with a pony tail extending out through the back loop, had them do it over and over until every one of them did it right.

I was long beyond that rigor, boot or no boot.

We waited for a range to become available and watched as several men and a handful of women practiced their target-shooting skills. Their scores were electronically posted above the targets, and not one of them scored as low as my average score back when I was at my peak. And I was considered a good shot. They were all in the range of Angella, who Contentus had told me was one of the two highest in Cameron County, Texas, where she trained and maintained proficiency. To be one of the best shooters in South Texas is a statement in itself.

"These folks are good," Angella commented. "Remind me not to challenge them."

"Hopefully, the enemy is outside," I responded, only half-joking.

Angella gave me one of her long looks that communicated far more than any words she would have used. As if to say, *Have you not been paying attention? It is precisely the inside they're afraid of!*

When it was finally my turn, I took my time and lined up each shot. As careful as I was, my score was just above my normal average. They were far below anything I had seen by the others. Angella, on the other hand, scored higher then her normal. "It's the weapon," she announced, allowing a slight smile to form. "It's better balanced than anything I've ever shot with before. Woody knows what she's about."

"So's this one. But it didn't improve my score."

"Sorry. You'll just have to spend more time down here. That's all it takes, repetitions, repetitions, repetitions. That's the key."

"Maybe for you." I fired off several more rounds, and gradually my score rose.

"See," she said, "improvement already. Keep at it."

An hour later I was in what I chose to call the acceptable zone. It was far above any score I had ever achieved. High as it was, I was still not in league with Angella.

Woody was waiting for us when we finally surfaced. She had laid out several piles of documents. Within fifteen minutes we had a viable reconstruction of what must have taken place with the bomb. "We're going to have to personally interview several of the people you have here. That means more travel. These folks are still in the hospital. Different hospitals. The two I want to speak with are in San Antone and Houston. They seem to be the key folks."

"You can use the FBI to take the interviews," Woody suggested. "I can get it set up. They'll have the reports for you later today if you want."

"I prefer to do my own interrogation, thanks. Can you arrange transportation?"

"How about I arrange for a video conference. You can interview from your office and see their reactions yourself."

"Those things are grainy," I said. But then I recalled the conversation from the airplane with General Jamison. There had been nothing grainy about that. He seemed to be in the room with us. "Okay," I relented, "if you can get good clear video, go for it."

"I'll get right on it. But it probably won't be 'til morning 'til I get it all set up. Oh, by the way, you're to attend a reception at the White House tonight at seven."

That was the first I had heard of any such reception, and frankly, I was surprised. "What kind of reception?" I asked, puzzled as to why someone so new to the organization would be on anyone's invite list, especially to the White House. "I…I don't have the proper…attire."

"A tux and the trimmings will be delivered to your condo. As to the why, that's easy. White House asked for people above a certain level who are veterans. Your name popped up. I'm just the messenger; don't shoot me."

"I'm not a veteran," Angella was quick to point out.

"I am well aware of that fact, my dear. That's why you won't be attending."

TWENTY-NINE

No sooner had Angella and I returned to our apartment in Arlington than my cell went off. It was Tiny reporting that unusual activity in and around Tae-hyun had been observed on South Padre Island. He suggested that we both get down there and stay close to the target.

Angella had stormed off to her room the moment she entered the condo, obviously still miffed at being excluded from the White House reception. Several times I told her I would skip it, but she shrugged me off. I wanted to see for myself exactly where Tae-hyun was located, but she had the tracker.

I knocked on her door and received no answer. I knocked again with the same result. Then I called to her, my loud voice reflecting my displeasure with her behavior. "Angella. I need the tracker. Please come out here."

A moment later the door opened a crack and Angella, her body hidden behind the door, held out the tracker. Her arm was wet and I guess she had been in the shower. "Anything else you want, or can I continue my bath?"

"Don't drown," I replied. "I don't know how I'd explain that to the powers that be."

The door slammed.

I studied the tracker and then said to Tiny, "Target is where he's been. What's the nature of the unusual activity?"

"Don't really know," Tiny answered. "Just know you two need to be down there as soon as possible. I booked you on a commercial flight from National. Leaves in an hour. There's a car on the way for you. Be at your place in about five minutes."

"I can't go. Command performance at the White House tonight. I'll blow it off if you want."

"Shit! I forgot about that. You need to be there. Get Angella out of the tub and send her alone. I'll have a ride ready for you after you're finished tonight."

"Easier said than done," I said, referring to Angella and her recent attitude.

"Just do it. Have her on the plane." The line went dead.

I again knocked on Angella's door. To my surprise she called, "Come in, Cowboy."

I opened the door expecting, or more accurately, hoping, to find Angella soaking in the bathtub. Male imaginations are not to be believed sometimes—and this was one of those times.

Angella was fully dressed in jeans and a sweatshirt, and I could see the outline of her gun on her right side.

I quickly explained the situation to her and before I finished, she said, "I suppose I'm going down alone? When do I leave?"

"How about right now? Car's waiting. I'll join you as soon as I can get there."

"Take your time. I'll be fine. You can tell me all about it, Cowboy."

"Is this about Cindy?" I asked, finally understanding her behavior.

Without a word, she turned, threw a few things in her bag and left the apartment.

"Stay safe," I called after her.

I hadn't expected a response and didn't receive one.

- - - - - -

I napped until five, took a long hot shower and dressed. I hadn't worn formal attire in so many years and I felt awkward and a bit silly. But I had to admit, there is nothing like a tux to dress a man up. I wished Angella was going with me. Not having her at my side made me feel...well, naked and vulnerable.

At seven sharp I climbed out of a cab, approached the Secret Service check post that seemed to be two blocks from the White House and presented my identification. The uniformed woman in the guard stand pointed in the general direction of a group of people standing a few feet away and motioned for me to join them. I recognized one of the men from the shooting range and nodded in his direction. He did not nod in return.

The last time I had approached this place was from the other side and underground. It could have been on Mars for all the resemblance that visit had to this one. I was convinced a mistake had been made and that I didn't belong here this evening. I fully expected to be turned away.

A group of six people arrived and, following the same routine, ended up being ushered to our cluster. One man stood out because of his bulk. He towered above the others and seemed to stand a few feet behind them. He had arrived alone and clearly wanted to remain apart.

It took me a while before I recalled that his name was Homer Greenspar. He was the INS assistant director and the person Chief Duran could not get along with. Thinking of Duran, I wondered how he was doing. My first thought was that no news was good news. Given everything that had been going on, especially getting valid information from Tiny, I concluded that no news is simply that: no news.

I was about to introduce myself to Greenspar when, to my surprise, my name was called. I was given a card with my name on it and told to proceed along the walkway to the White House. An escort would meet me at the door.

Once inside, I was shown to a long snaking receiving line leading to where the President and First Lady stood shaking hands and graciously greeting guests. Just before I approached the President, my card was taken by a somber man. When I reached my hand out to grasp the President's, I noticed that the somber gentlemen read my name from the card and whispered something into a lapel microphone. I assume he was announcing me to the President.

The President, instead of immediately releasing his grip, pulled me close. I had noticed that he had done this with a number of people ahead of me. When his lips were close to my ear, he said, "At precisely eight-twenty, please be in the China Room, alone. The Marine guard at the door to the East Room will show you the way. Tell no one." He then released my hand and immediately turned his attention to the next person in line.

A moment later I entered the East Room, where I spotted General Jamison. Next to the general, her arm draped over his, was a stunning blond. I guessed she was the good general's wife. Hovering, not far away, was his second in command, Lucinda Westminster McNaughton, holding forth with a group of men who were listening rather than interacting.

The people in this room presumably held high government rank and yet, in the presence of Cindy, they were like students around the master, hanging on to her every word.

Jamison spotted me and motioned for me to join his group. When I did, he said, "Jimmy Redstone. Please meet my wife, Nancy. Nancy, Jimmy recently joined our team from Texas. He's here to help keep the country safe. You remember Miller Contentus. Redstone worked for him."

"Oh, a Texas Ranger then," she beamed. "Glad to meet you." She held my hand a second too long, adding meaning to the toothy smile. She moved closer to me. Too close for comfort.

The general hadn't seemed to pay any attention. But I was mistaken. His power of observation was as keen as ever. "Jimmy, please excuse us. I must speak with some folks." With that, he steered his wife across the room.

"I see you met the lovely Mrs. Jamison," Lucinda said, slipping in beside me when Jamison was gone. "She's a piece of work."

"Not a good idea talking about my boss's spouse," I replied. "Not a good career move. So I'll refrain from comment."

"You'd be the only one then," Lucinda replied. "Truth is, she beds everything in pants, except perhaps her own husband." She looked directly at me. "Case you're interested, Cowboy, I hear she's not bad either."

I long ago learned it's not good form to talk about employers or their family, so I said, "I'm new to this town. Just learning my way around. I'll pass on activities of that nature."

Her wink was ambiguous, but before I could put my foot further down my throat, Cindy said, "Have it your way, Cowboy. Come, I want to introduce you to someone."

Before she led me away, I said to her, "Can you look into something for me? This is a bit off target, but not far."

"Make it quick."

"Mark Cruses. Lt. Markus Cruses. Can you—"

"He's the commander of the Coast Guard station on South Padre. What about him?"

"He's on house arrest. It was his protection of the video file that broke the case. I've known him since he was a boy. He's a credit to the service."

"You left out the part about you being his godfather."

I was dealing with one sharp person. She had just politely reminded me of that fact. "Indeed I am. And proud of it! Can you review his situation? Something's not right."

"I'll see what I can do. Anything else you desire, Cowboy?"

"Can't think of a thing." Actually, I could, but not without ending up dead—or worse. Either from the general or from Angella.

"Okay, then. Follow me." She took my hand and led me directly to Homer Greenspar. Homer's handclasp nearly broke the bones in my right hand. His actual title was Director of Immigration and Naturalization. I realized I was already playing the Beltway power game when I noted that his position was a few levels above mine.

"Didn't I see you on SPI several months back?" he asked. "During an ill-conceived raid. That's when the Korean got away—in his underwear. You and a good-looking young cop chased him onto the beach and lost him."

"Good memory," I replied, noting that he either didn't have all the facts or chose to play his hand close. "Names Tae-hyun."

"I know his name." Greenspar then lowered his voice. "I'm privy to the file. Know what he did as well. Also know you're the guy who busted him. Good piece of work."

"Thanks," I responded, not wishing to prolong this conversation. "For the record, it was Angella and I who busted him."

"You're also the folks who ordered him released." His frown telegraphed his thoughts on that decision. There was no ambiguity as to where he stood.

"I did," I replied, confirming what he already knew.

"Not a smart idea, Redstone. No telling what those cockroaches will do! Hope you got someone covering your ass."

Landing a blow to his chin would feel good about now. I wondered how many years in the brig that would get me. Be worth it.

But I refrained. At least I had gained something from my anger management schooling. Instead, I replied, "It's under control. We'll be fine." I said this with little conviction, knowing what he didn't yet know. The bomb was coming closer. The only good news was that the last I had checked our Korean was still in South Texas. My assumption was that not until the two merged would we be in danger.

Thinking of Tae-hyun, Angella should be on scene by now. I suppose no news is good news. I again corrected myself. No news is *no news*. Period.

"I hope you're right, Redstone. I hope you're right. My experience is otherwise."

My watch read eight-fifteen. I had no idea how long it would take me to get to the China room. Walking with the boot definitely threw off my timing. I excused myself with the tried and true, "Would you folks please excuse me, I have to find a men's room."

I hobbled out of the East Room and immediately found a Marine Guard. He snapped to attention when I approached. I asked him to point me to the China room. "Follow me, Sir," he snapped, before turning smartly to his left. My guess is that the President often used the China room for quick private meetings during formal receptions.

I entered the empty room and immediately felt small. The china displayed from an earlier era was presented in front of a red wall-covering casting an inviting warm glow across the room. The warmth of the room, however, did nothing to settle the flood of anxiety that swept over me.

My watch indicated that it was now three minutes beyond the meeting time. A few minutes in the life of the President is insignificant, unless of course those were the minutes just preceding the detonation of the North Korean bomb.

Another ten minutes went by and the warmth of the room yielded to emptiness. I began to associate with the antiques; good for decorative purposes only.

It was now eight-forty. The President was twenty minutes late. Perhaps my watch was off, causing me to arrive a few minutes late and missing him. Quiet panic followed closely on the heels of the doubt.

At precisely eight forty-five the door opened and closed.

I was alone in the China room with the President of the United States.

THIRTY

The President was taller than I remembered from our last meeting. He walked directly over to me and without formality, reached out his hand. "I apologize for being late," he began, "but I can't be away more than a few minutes so let me get to the point. I orchestrated this private meeting because I am now convinced more than ever we have a major breach of security at the very top of Homeland Security. I trust Jamison with my life, but truth is, something's wrong. This would normally be a Secret Service and Bureau operation, but I have reason to believe they may be compromised as well."

"Pardon me for asking, but why me, Mr. President?" I asked, sensing he wanted to tell me more. "I'm not plugged in one bit."

"That's just the point. You're from outside the beltway. I've great admiration for the Texas Rangers and you come highly recommended. My thought is that if I randomly pick the person, then the chance of him—or her—being compromised is reduced. You're not entirely random, but close enough. So, you're it.

These folks will stop at nothing to bring down the Government. We have secret papers being leaked to the media almost daily. My friends on the right tell me it's the far left. The left are convinced it's coming from the right. It's destructive, and getting worse."

"I'm not convinced it's political. Someone, or some group, wants to bring down the country. That's beyond politics. If you don't mind me saying, I think…I think someone has a personal grudge."

"Against the country?"

"Or against you? Or just against freedom in general."

"Just find them and we'll deal with them in whatever manner we can." He paused, studied me a moment and then said, "I just wanted to tell you personally that you have my blessing—and permission—to do whatever you need to do to find and stop the traitor—or traitors." He reached in his pocket and gave me a card with a phone number. "Use that number if you need emergency help. It will get to me, or to someone I trust. Tell them what you need and you'll receive it, no questions asked. Just be right! Use the code, Padre. Any message without that code will be ignored. The phone will be answered with a simple hello. Just speak the code and the message. The line will go dead. Trust that it will work. You can also use that number and code for progress reports if you want to avoid Jamison. Do that sparingly or he'll get onto it and there'll be hell to pay."

"Yes, I understand. Mr. President, you can count on me keeping your trust." I knew it sounded trite, but I could think of nothing else to respond with. In hind sight, there are a million things I could have said, but that's what Monday mornings are for.

"I already know that. But I wanted you to know that should the bomb go off, we're poised to eradicate North Korea. We can't do that without significant collateral damage, especially to our own troops on the border. South Korea, China, Japan and even

Russia will react violently, as will most of the rest of the world. But I refuse to stand silent if an atomic bomb is unleashed in our country. Our retaliation will be immediate and certain, whether or not I, or even any member of my cabinet, survives. At this very moment carriers are being deployed to the area, ostensibly to practice war games with the Japanese. Our nuclear subs already have their orders. The pump is primed, as Jamison likes to say."

"Mr. President, I don't mean to interfere in State matters, but could you not let the North Korean government know of your proposed action so that they can recall this mission? Tae-hyun can be ordered home. Now that we're onto their plans, certainly they are not foolish enough to risk destruction."

The President glared at me for a moment clearly letting me know he was displeased that I had overstepped my bounds. But instead of taking me to task, he calmly replied, "We have ongoing back-channel discussions with them, as well as with several of their neighbors. They steadfastly refuse to acknowledge any involvement. For them to call it off now would be an acknowledgement on their part. They're positive we'd retaliate anyway. So for them it is a lose-lose proposition. That is the problem with brinksmanship as a deterrent. Ultimately, it is mutually destructive. Anyway, we are well past that possibility now. You must, at all costs, stop the bomb from being detonated. It is no longer only a domestic concern."

"I'll do my best," I replied lamely. "I'll do my best."

"Let's just pray that's enough," he said, momentarily allowing his shoulders to slump. "I've mounted an all out campaign to stop this attack and to find the traitors. So far the only success we've had was your interception of the one bomb. If there are others..." Regaining command, he said, "Let's focus on the positive. You will stop them. Period. There is no margin for error."

THIRTY-ONE

Shortly after our meeting, the President and First Lady excused themselves and left the reception. I made my way to the door, intending to slip out unnoticed. I didn't belong here. Dressing me in a fancy tux didn't change the fact that I saw myself as an apple slice in a cherry pie. Actually, more on the order of a hemlock seed.

A woman intercepted me at the door. She was wearing a press credential tag with Washington Post at the bottom. Thrusting a card into my hand, she announced her name as Abby Johnson. The card read, *Abigail Johnson*. And below her name the title *Homeland Security Desk* was engraved in bold lettering. "We can talk here," she said, "or would you prefer somewhere a bit more private?" A confident smile illuminated her otherwise bland face. "This is important."

My immediate thought was to say nothing and flee the White House. But that thought made me feel like a criminal—the kind with their shirts pulled over their heads when the TV cameras go on.

My hesitation gave Johnson the opportunity to say, “I know your instinct is to not speak to the press. I respect that. But two things you should know. First, I get paid to produce, and I intend to produce—with your cooperation or without it. Second, I’m willing, at least for now, to talk with you off the record. Nothing we discuss will appear in print.”

“What makes you believe I have something to talk about?”

“For starters, you have an impressive corner office at Homeland Security on the floor reserved for investigations.” She bent down her first finger and started on the second. “Couple that with the fact that you just met privately with POTUS.” Another finger was bent over. “And third, you’ve been seen with Tiny Jurald. Tiny’s good at what he does, but one thing he’s not good at is being incognito. Hard to think of him as a spook. Man his size gets noticed.”

“I have nothing to say.” Frankly, I didn’t know what the protocol was, never having been in this situation. On my turf, I called the shots. The few times I spoke to the press it was at the request of the Rangers.

“You think there’s anything I don’t know you’re fooling yourselves. Now, as I said, we can talk off the record or I can print half a story.”

“What half? What are you talking about?” I asked, wanting to know what she had and trying not to give anything away.

“Something’s up. When a man with your record suddenly resigns from the Texas Rangers and shows up in Washington with a rookie cop as a partner, something’s up. Distinguished Texas Ranger I’m told.”

“I’m just here, was invited, because I am a veteran.”

"I call bullshit! Don't take me for a fool, Mr. Redstone." A heavy scowl replaced the broad smile, the lines extending upward from the corners of her lips. "I'm not a backwoods journalist anxious to print handouts. There's a story here and I intend to find it."

"Excuse me, I have nothing to say to the press." I pushed past her and started through the door.

Johnson let me take two steps and then said, "You think I don't know about the bombs and how close we came to disaster, you're fooling yourself. Coincidentally, the President's calling for a conference on nuclear waste material control. For years our government refused to address the issue. Intercepting those bombs shook him to the core. Just because we went along and buried the story doesn't mean it will remain that way. You and that rookie played a major role. You want to talk or continue to bullshit me? I won't let another story slide, believe me."

"What is it you want?"

"For background. I want to know exactly what happened down there."

"Don't have time now. I'll do it next time I'm in town."

"Tell you what. I'll give you one week. I'm still checking facts, so the time table will work. But I want the story directly from you on an exclusive basis."

"And if I say no?"

"I'll print it all. Name, rank, serial number. Might not be a hundred percent accurate, but it'll be close enough."

"I won't be blackmailed, so this conversation is ended."

"Don't wait too long, Redstone. Others won't."

"Should I care?"

"Only if you don't want to be hung out to dry. *Twist in the wind*, I believe the phrase is."

THIRTY-TWO

"You and the President are becoming real buds," Angella quipped an hour later when I called her from my office. I had explained that we had met privately in the China Room but refrained from discussing what he had said. On the positive side, I noted the snippiness was gone from her tone. She sounded relaxed and in command.

"He's concerned," I replied, trying not to give away anything on the unsecured phone. "I'll brief you in person when I get down there."

"If the President didn't have faith that he could talk to you in private on the phone," Angella was saying, "and had to go to the trouble of inviting you to a reception and then sneaking off for a private talk, then God help the country. So where does that leave us?"

"The only thing I know for certain is that if we don't figure this out, and do it soon, all hell's going to break loose. President is clearly worried."

"Not enough to stop his politicking. Didn't you just say he's going to Dallas tomorrow for a fund raising lunch? Ask me, he should stay home until this is resolved."

"That's what politicians do. They politic. Can no more stop that than I can turn off snooping."

"Speaking of snooping, how's your foot?" Angella inquired, neatly changing the subject. "Sorry, I should have asked earlier."

"Throbs. Walking around the White House didn't help matters."

"The doctor told you to stay off it. You're not a good patient."

"Doctors tell you lots of things. Wonder if he'd write a note saying, *please excuse little Jimmy from failing to stop the atomic bomb from wiping out Washington because he had to sit with his foot up his ass?*"

"You made your point."

"I'll elevate it on the plane ride."

Changing the subject, Angella said, "Well, we know where Tae-hyun is. He hasn't moved since he holed up down here. I've treated myself to a room at the Isla Grand Beach Resort, less than a mile from him current position. Great room. Double bed. Bathtub and all."

Sounded like an invite to me. "Tiny arranged a flight down. Actually, I'm hitchhiking with a Secret Service detail going to Dallas in advance of the President. They'll drop me at Brownsville. Leaves in an hour. Landing by one, two at the latest. Leave a light on."

I stood to leave and realized someone was in Angella's office. I quietly moved across the waiting room separating our respective offices, keeping as close to the wall as possible so as not to throw shadows. Through the smoked glass of the door I could see the outline of a body hunched over Angella's desk.

I pushed the door open and moved inside, quickly stepping to my right to change the angle of attack. I have found out the hard way that you are particularly vulnerable when you surprise an intruder. It is impossible for one person to open a door and cover all angles at the same time. This is one of those times when I miss a partner.

As soon as the door was fully open, it was clear who the intruder was. What was not clear was what she was doing in Angella's office at nine-thirty.

"Oh," Woody said, her head swiveling in my direction. "You startled me. Goodness gracious, I could have had a heart attack!"

"And just what are you doing here so late?" I demanded, moving close to her so that I could see what she had been concentrating on so intently before my interruption.

"Just fixing things up for you," Woody replied, her voice eventoned. "I retrieved the files you wanted and set video appointments for early in the morning. I sent both of you e-mails to that effect. I wanted to get you background information on each of the people you're going to talk with."

"Left my Blackberry in the apartment," I said. "Didn't see your e-mails yet."

"You should carry the Blackberry at all times. Never know when I'll have to get to you." I made a mental note that Woody was taking the offense, just as a trained agent caught in a compromising position would have been trained to do.

"Mind showing me the files?" I asked, not being sidetracked.

Woody pulled open the middle desk drawer and retrieved a large stack of neatly labeled files. These were the files of the people we wanted to speak with. Another stack held the names of several high-ranking Department of Homeland Security personnel.

"And what are these for?" I asked, pointing to the personnel files.

"I thought they would be helpful. Seems to me someone at the top is monitoring everything you two are doing. I found the copy trace, but I can't find where it goes."

"What's a copy trace?" I asked, puzzled that she would have gone to so much effort without instructions.

"Whenever a document is pulled, or when any data goes in or out of a government database, it is possible to have automatic copies made and forwarded to a separate file. That's called a copy trace. I noticed that was happening so I called a friend and found that a trace was placed on all your material. Except, it came from the top and the destination is not available. The material goes into a separate file and those with coded access can view the file."

"Can we override the trace?"

"With the Secretary's approval."

"Of course that presupposes it's not her," I quipped.

"One way to find out. Ask her. You can have your friend General Jamison do it. Or even better yet, Lucinda and the Secretary are buds. She can ask for you."

"Does everyone know everyone in Washington?" I asked.

"Pretty much. Government works that way. Scratch my back sort of thing. You're dead in the water, you have no friends. Here, it's not what you know, but who you know."

"Lucinda knows everyone, from what I can tell."

"That's for sure. What are you doing here at nine-thirty? You should still be at the White House." Woody asked, slipping the question in casually. A bit too casually. "And, just how was the reception?"

"Reception went well. Boring actually. President made an appearance and then left. I left right after he did. I came here to get ready for the interviews." I wasn't sure whether I was angry—concerned is a better word—with her being here this time of night, or thankful for her dedication.

A text message from Tiny appeared on my cell interrupting my train of thought. **PLANE LEAVING FROM ANDREWS AT 10:45. BE AT FRONT GATE BY 10:15.**

I turned back to Woody. "Got to go. I'll take the files with me."

I started to gather them, but she said, "I'll put them in a carry bag for you. Give me a moment." She took the files I was holding and put them with files she picked up from Angella's desk. She then carried the stack out to her station. A few minutes later she handed me two carry bags. "Here, this will make it easier. Here's the log out cards. Give them to the guard on your way out. Have a safe flight."

In the cab I replayed my conversation with Woody. Only then did I realize that I had not told her I was taking a flight. She either had been listening to my conversation with Angella, or she had a separate source. Either way, she made me uncomfortable. Mental note: Get Woody's background.

THIRTY-THREE

Once on the plane, I spread out the files and went through them one by one, starting with the ones marked, I suppose by Woody, **Homeland Security Top Gun**. I was impressed with the caliber and qualifications of the people the government had recruited to head the various departments. I was also impressed with the breadth of their responsibilities, which included agencies such as: the National Guard, the Federal Emergency Management Agency, the Coast Guard, Customs and Border Protection, Immigration and Customs Enforcement, Citizenship and Immigration Services, the Secret Service, the Transportation Security Administration, and Civil Air Patrol.

I began by concentrating on three agencies: the Coast Guard, Customs and Border Patrol, and INS. I selected these three because of their operation in intercepting—actually failing to intercept—the bomb and Tae-hyun in the first instance. While the Secret Service could be involved—the actions of Tiny came to mind — it didn't seem likely. Thinking of INS brought to mind the involvement of the big guy, Homer Greenspar.

Every one of the top people were well qualified, professional, and came with impeccable credentials. Woody had included the most recent security checks obtained from the FBI. I didn't know how she had managed to obtain copies of secret files, and I'm not sure I wanted to know. I doubted she would tell me even if I asked. The FBI had spent considerable time re-checking backgrounds and their investigations had been exhaustive.

The files showed nothing suspicious, just as the President had said.

I put the files away and then noticed a yellow pad in the bag and pulled it out. It was filled with what looked to be computer address strings and arrows pointing from one to another. It looked like some misplaced child's game and made no sense to me.

I studied it a while longer and concluded that the addresses seemed to belong to people who had access to the files. It also appeared that the person—or persons—getting access worked at hiding their tracks, because intermediary addresses were used. But in every case, the arrows pointed to one of two addresses.

But the good news was that whoever was going into the files had not employed professionals, because if they had I wouldn't have been able to decipher what they had done. My only real conclusion was that it had to be someone with high-level password access.

I also concluded that the person behind this knew who we were going to interview in the morning. So much for security.

I had planned to catch a nap on the flight to Brownsville, but by the time I finished with the files we were low over the Gulf of Mexico. A few moments later I could see the pulsating beacon from the Brownsville airport.

Within five minutes we were rolling to a stop away from the terminal. A car was waiting, its yellow roof light casting rotary shadows on the otherwise dark tarmac.

My cell came alive. **Target on the move. I'm following. Call when you land.** The message had come in from Angella's phone slightly before midnight and contained the agreed-upon code word. I checked my watch. The message had been sent almost two hours ago. But I had forgotten to change my watch to an hour earlier. That meant Angella's message was only forty-five minutes old.

Let's see, thirty minutes to the Island and I'd only be an hour and fifteen minutes behind her. I hit the speed dial button.

No answer.

I sent a text: **Landed Brnsvlle on island by 1:30 Where RU**

Route 48 was empty and the driver pushed the government issue car full out. We drove through Port Isabel and sailed onto the deserted causeway bridge at one-eighteen. Halfway across the bridge the unmistakable red and blue pulsating lights signifying an emergency operation became visible ahead and off to the right.

I recalled Angella's tracker screen and visualized the position of the red flashing dot showing where Tae-hyun had gone to ground. From memory that red dot coincided exactly to where the red/blue lights were now flashing.

I leaned forward and said to the driver, "What's going down over there? You picking anything up on the government radio?"

"No idea," came the gruff reply. "I'm Coast Guard. That's civilian. Not my business."

"It is now, Son. That's where we're now heading."

"My orders are to take you to the Coast Guard Station."

"Son, you have new orders. Need I call Captain Boyle directly?" I held my cell phone up so that he could see it.

"Those lights are on the way to the station. I can't help it if you jump out on the way."

"Just slow down. Jumping with this boot won't do."

THIRTY-FOUR

Acting Police Chief Jose Garcia walked over to me as I hobbled across Schlitterbahn's vast parking lot. "Glad you're here. Maybe you can make sense of this."

"What do you have?" I asked. "And where's Angella?"

"She's part of it. She called in around midnight and said Taehyun's gone. She told us about an old guard hut off to the side. That's it over there. Apparently he was using it. There's a mattress and not much else. She also said there was blood on the mattress. We arrived a few minutes later but Angella was gone."

"What about the blood?"

"Don't know what to make of it. Not much. It was smeared around."

"Any sign of violence? Anything unusual?"

"Nothing. I had the lab guys take samples of the blood. But there's not enough to establish that a crime has even been committed. The only possible violation I see is someone sleeping in this hut without a CO. Schlitterbahn says it's not theirs. Not even a B&E."

"Mind if I look?"

"Be my guest." Garcia lead the way across the lot to the small hut. My guess is that this was used during construction of the park and was just never torn down.

"How's Chief Duran doing?" I asked as we walked toward the hut.

"Not well," came the terse reply. "Keep him in your prayers. Doctors won't predict."

"Is he conscious?"

"Comes and goes. Doesn't look good, I'm afraid."

Garcia had described the scene inside the hut well. The only thing I could add was that the blood seemed to be smeared in two distinct locations. But he was accurate, nobody died, or was seriously injured, from this minute amount of blood loss. I doubted if this even came from a knife wound.

Back in the lot I said to Garcia, "Mind dropping me at the Isla Grand?"

A few minutes later I was checked in and went up to my room. Angella had been right; the room was upscale from what I had become accustomed to. In this regard, I liked my new life.

A text message arrived. **TARGET SECURE BACK AT HOTEL IN FIFTEEN MINUTES**

I replied: **IN ROOM 410**

I took a quick shower and was pulling on my jeans when the door opened. Angella had managed to obtain a key from the front desk.

I looked to Angella, who, seemingly reading my mind, but most likely seeing my wide eyes, said, "Things are heating up, we have to talk." She put her finger across her lips. Without saying a word she motioned for me to take off my shirt.

I didn't think it was prudent to thwart her advances, not if I ever wanted to advance beyond where we were.

Then my jeans. This was getting interesting.

Angella then walked over close to me and spun me around so that I was facing the bed. She pushed me toward it. Push is perhaps a misleading word. I all but ran and leaped into the bed.

She then had me turn on my side so that I was facing away from her. When I did so, she sat on the other side of the bed. I could hear her pulling off her jeans. I wasn't certain, but from the sounds I heard I visualized her pulling her sweater over her head.

I was ready. More than ready, actually.

She then slipped in under the covers and snuggled against my body from behind. She pressed her mouth to my ear, much as the President had done in the receiving line.

"Listen closely," she began in a voice barely audible, even at such close range, "and don't say a thing. It may not seem this way, but I'm not seducing you. We'll save that for another time. They know our every move because our clothes have been bugged. I found a label stuck into my PJs that contains, as best as I can tell, a microphone. I went through the rest of my clothes and almost every blouse, and even my bras, have a similar label. I'll bet your clothes have the same label."

I tried to respond and she again cautioned me to be quiet.

"Whoever is monitoring us is sophisticated, so we can't talk for long without the mikes. Just monitoring our breathing tells them what's going on. Until we work out how to get around this, I suggest we wear the mikes and write to each other. In the morning we can buy new clothes."

I nodded my agreement.

"Keep your head turned until I get my bra and sweater back on. Let's not give them more than we already have." Angella then climbed out of bed and a moment later my jeans and shirt landed on my head.

I next heard the bathroom door close. I sat up and reluctantly got dressed.

By the time I was tightening my belt, she was back in the room. "Sorry," she said, pushing the door closed behind her, "but I had to use the facilities."

"You were going to fill me in on what's been going on," I said, playing the male lead in this seemingly never-ending play. "I was over to Schlitterbahn and saw the empty hut, blood and all. Hope you were tracking the target."

"Most certainly was. I found him in *The Blue Marlin Supermarket*. Stocking up on food. I suppose he took the Shuttle. We can check the cabbies, but I'd be surprised."

"What did he buy?"

"No way of knowing, short of asking the store. I caught up to him as he crossed the sidewalk. He then proceeded to Jim's Pier on the bay. Walked north along the boardwalk. Then he turned east a block. There's a small motel, five or six rooms. That's where he is right now." Angella then produced the tracker and showed me the red flashing dot. "If he moves more than a hundred feet I'll receive an alarm."

"Does he know he's being followed?"

"I'd say he has a suspicion. Kept looking back. I had to remain pretty far away. Boardwalk is well-lighted, so I couldn't get onto the walk until I was certain he had turned the corner and was not doubling back."

"Okay," I said. "Didn't get any sleep on the plane. I'm turning in. We need to be ready for the interviews in the morning. If I'm not mistaken, police headquarters has a TV link."

"They do. But I don't know who knows how to work it."

"That's Woody's problem. I'll text her to get it set up." I wanted to tell Angella about my suspicions of our administrative assistant, but thought better of it until we were free of the bugs.

"I got some sleep earlier," Angella said. "Seems like yesterday. I'm planning to get up early and head across the bridge to Wal-Mart for some clothes shopping. I left most everything back in Arlington."

"Good thought. I'm out of clean clothes. I'm down to my last pair of shorts. I need time to wash some things out."

After Angella left, I took off my boxers and sure enough, glued to the inside of the waistband was a small tag that said, "Made in China." The tag was thicker than normal and felt solid to the touch. I curbed my desire to rip it out.

In an abundance of caution, I checked my weapon and found a "made in China" label stuck to the inside of the holster. I carefully peeled it off and stuck it to the base of the lamp next to my bed. The activities of the next room occupant would be recorded and duly noted in the voluminous records of Homeland Security—or whoever was listening.

If it hadn't already been obvious it was now clear, this operation was being masterminded at the top level—and by experts.

THIRTY-FIVE

By pre-arrangement, I met Angella in the lobby at six, after sleeping less than two hours. Shopping Wal-Mart at that time of day took no time and we were back on the island before seven.

I had Angella pull into a service station and I used the lone pay phone, a dying breed, to call my former boss. I trusted Contentus with my life.

I briefly filled him in on what we had found. Then I asked the critical and highly sensitive question. The question I knew he would bristle over. "Can we trust Jamison?"

The answer was immediate. "Absolutely! You know his story. The man was a POW and broke free of the North Vietnamese. He came back for the rest of us. He didn't have to do that, but he did. I owe my life to him and he's never once given anyone cause to doubt him." In all the years I worked for him, I had never heard Contentus, a man who never trusted anything, so adamant.

I protested, "But that's the perfect profile of a person who could get high in the government and turn from the inside." I hadn't told him about the President's concerns, and perhaps I should have.

"You're barking up the wrong tree, Redstone! The man bleeds red, white and blue!"

"Someone high up is behind this," I replied, sounding lame.

"Find someone else. Jamison is not your man!"

"Find out for me if I can trust Tiny. He seems to have his footprint in this as well."

"I already spoke to Jamison about him. I was briefed on that unexplained trip you two took to Mexico. Someone is using phone numbers in Tiny's name. The man's been checked every which way from Sunday. He's clean. I have Jamison's assurance on that."

"How did you know about us being in Mexico?"

"We secure on this line?" Contentus asked.

"As secure as a random payphone can be."

"Let's just say we have a Ranger working down where you were. Leave it at that for now."

I thought about the blankets and candy bar; about the warnings we had received concerning us being monitored; about the fact we weren't shot. I then realized we had more going for us than simple luck. "Okay, thanks. Whoever is behind this has also been checked thoroughly by the FBI—and by military security. Nothing comes up. Something's not right. I don't know the good guys from the bad guys."

"Stay with it. You'll find a thread. Count on Jamison being a good guy. If I'm wrong, neither you nor anyone else will save this country. Remember, no one said this was going to be easy."

I next called Tiny, who came on the line like I'd always imagined a bear would behave when a rival got into its food supply.

"Where the hell are you?" he demanded. "Neither of you are answering your cells! You're not in your rooms. What gives?"

"Hold on a moment," I replied, throwing a quizzical look toward Angella. "Just how do you know we're not in the hotel?"

"Woody called and said you're gone."

"How the hell would she know?"

"Says she tried to call you this morning when she found out the Korean's gone. She's coordinating the interviews."

"For reasons I'll tell you later, we're not talking on the cells unless we have to. We have reason to believe everything we say is tapped."

"Not surprised. What do you need? You called me."

"Get us full background information on the following people." I read him a list from my notes of the ones Woody had given us. "Get these from your own trusted sources and whatever you do, don't use Woody or even let her know you're doing this."

"You suspect her?"

"Everyone's fair game. I need to know everything about those folks, and I mean everything! When will you have it gathered?"

"I have no idea."

"We'll check back later. No texting, no messages."

Angella stood quietly taking it all in. When I hung up, she asked, "And just what do you expect from a rehash of the personnel files? I'm sure they'll be the same as Woody gave us."

"If that's so, that may be good news as far as Woody's concerned. But if she slipped a few things out then we know she's in league with the perp. Not elegant, but we need to cross-check anything and everything we got. I figure the FBI and the military have gone over these folks with a fine-tooth comb. We need to come at it from the back door."

THIRTY-SIX

We hung up from Tiny and proceeded to police headquarters. Woody had done her job. The interview room was set up and the TV monitor was working perfectly. The video links were up and running and the connection was perfect. My assumption was that we were using military channels relayed by satellite, but I didn't need to know the technical details.

By noon we were finished interviewing everyone on the list. From the facial and other expressions, the folks we spoke with were telling the truth—at least as far as they knew it. Two of the men we spoke with were on the truck from Harlingen. A third helped form the lead shield.

"So what did you make of the interviews?" Angella asked.

I consulted my notes. "The lead shield was made at the site where the bomb was initially held. Our guy was given a wooden box to insert within the shield. Presumably the bomb was within the wood box. He got radiation poisoning from his exposure, but has no idea why he's sick. Doctors don't expect any lasting side effects."

I added, "Then the shield—presumably with the bomb inside—was transported to Corpus, to the Coast Guard station up there."

Angella consulted her notes and then said, "I made note of his comment about the inspection checkpoint. I thought that was interesting." Angella glanced at me to see if I agreed with her. I nodded. "Seems at the checkpoint they directed the truck into a barn for what they called a thorough inspection."

"What checkpoint is he talking about?" I asked. "You were nodding when he spoke, so I didn't follow up. Didn't want to call attention to the checkpoint."

"On highway 77, going north from Brownsville, about a hundred miles north, all traffic passes through a border-type check."

"You mean even if I, a U.S. citizen, were to be driving north, I'd be stopped at a checkpoint within the U.S.?" In all the years I had traveled the highways of Texas I had never driven north on 77. I suppose that was because my territory was the interior of Texas mostly from Austin north and west.

"Been there for years," Angella commented.

Pieces were coming together. "So at this checkpoint the truck was run through a barn? I suppose he meant a shed, for inspection. Then the trip north to Corpus resumed."

Angella's eyes came alive. "Oh, shit! I see where you're going! Without the bomb! They went from the checkpoint north without the bomb."

I checked my notes before I continued. "It fits! This other guy, Joey Dawson, says he was commissioned to drive a SUV from Sarita, Texas, to Houston. That SUV had the bomb in it. Bet if we find the SUV, it'll set off the radiation detectors."

"Sarita is where the checkpoint is located," Angella commented. "And this poor guy'll pay for this with his life. His radiation was bad."

"My assumption is that the wooden box was leaking radiation and that some other shield was added in Houston, or somewhere along the way. That's why the folks we've tracked further north only have mild side effects."

"I'm also guessing that the shield they added in Houston was not lead but some material not big and bulky and something that doesn't weigh what lead weighs. That way they can use a station wagon or even a regular car. No need for a large truck." I thought for a moment and then sent a text to Woody asking her to find out who authorized the use of the shed at the Sarita checkpoint. I also instructed her to see if government money was used to buy or fabricate lead, or any other radiation shield in or around Houston, and who authorized it.

The tracker in Angella's purse went off. Tae-hyun was on the move once again.

"We have a cross-roads here," I said to Angella. "Follow the bomb, or spend time ferreting out the traitor." But the President's priority had clearly been stopping the bomb over finding the traitor. "We need to stay with Tae-hyun. He'll lead us to the bomb."

"That was the original plan. When he gets close to the bomb we can pick him up any time we want."

"That's the good side," I replied. "But what if there's another bomb that we don't know about? He could get to it before we can react."

"What if we lose him?" Angella asked.

"Good point. Let's be certain Jamison's folks are following him as well."

It took less than five minutes to get Jamison on the line. He sounded distracted. I visualized him orchestrating the attack on North Korea, getting all the so-called assets in place.

"The latest intel on the target," Jamison's crisp voice barked, "was that he was on the move. Going toward Harlingen. Reported ten minutes ago."

I fed him what little information we had gathered on the bomb movement. He then said, "Way ahead of you on this one, Redstone! We've been tracking the radiation leakage since Houston. Got a team keeping close tabs on the vehicle."

"At least you could have told me," I replied, agitated that he was running his own operation, keeping us outside the loop.

"I'll tell you what you need to know!" he barked. "You deal with the people, I'll deal with the weapons! You're insane if you think for one moment I'd allow this country to be solely at your mercy! There are any number of agencies working on this matter." The line went dead.

So much for mutual trust.

I called Tiny to see if we could set up a visual contact on Taehyun. I wanted someone within a hundred feet of him twenty-four-seven. "He's not to know they're there," I instructed Tiny. "But we need to know every contact he makes, in person or electronically. And I mean every contact! Send it live to Angella as the info becomes available. If he gets within a hundred miles of Washington, arrest him." At Angella's suggestion, I didn't inform Tiny of my disturbing conversation with Jamison.

Tiny responded by telling us he had already initiated such surveillance at the request of Jamison.

"When did he order that?"

"About five minutes ago. It'll take us several hours before we can be in place. Told that to Jamison and he damn near took my head off. He said he could invade a bleep'n country in that amount of time."

An hour later Woody responded with the information pertaining to who authorized the use of the shed at the checkpoint. Turns out it was Tiny himself.

He was sure one busy guy.

THIRTY-SEVEN

We were walking out of SPI police headquarters when the tracker went off again. Tae-hyun seemed to be heading toward the Harlingen airport. "Let's go," I said to Angella. "Arrange for a police escort, at least until we get close to him."

A few blocks south on Padre Boulevard, a fast-moving police car, its red and blue lights flashing, passed us and pulled directly in front.

"That's our escort," Angella said. "They'll take us across the bridge and hand us to Port Isabel. The cities will play tag all the way to Harlingen if need be until we catch him."

Angella pulled out the tracker. "He's almost at the airport. It'll take us about thirty minutes to catch him, even at this speed."

We were five minutes from the airport when Tiny called to report that the target had bought a one-way ticket to Dallas. Plane leaves in ten minutes. Border Patrol is holding him, pending our instructions.

"Put someone on the plane with him." I instructed Tiny. "Secret Service or Marshal Service. Hell, even Border Patrol. Anybody will do."

Tiny put me on hold and when he came back said, "We're in luck. There's a federal marshal available in Houston. The plane makes a stop there on the way to Dallas."

"Have him go along. He's to follow Tae-hyun when he leaves the plane in Dallas. We need to know who he's meeting."

"Got it."

"Beats shit out of me!" I exclaimed. "Tiny, got any thoughts on what this is about?"

"Dallas is off track from the District. He's got ID, which makes it easy for us to track. They may even know about the tracker. They know we're following and don't seem to care."

"Hell!" I exclaimed, finally seeing the picture. "He's a hare!"

Angella glanced at me.

"Hare, as in hounds and hares," I said. "The dogs chase the hares, but never can catch them. Go round in circles. That explains our little excursion to Mexico as well."

"Keep going, Jimmy. I'm not on your page yet," Angella said.

"They're distracting us. It's brilliant actually."

Tiny broke in. "Sending people on wild goose chases is as old as—"

"It's not us so much, Tiny," I replied. "It's you, Jamison, the whole friggin' government is busy tracking us, extracting us from Mexico, now dragging us up to Dallas. Something else is going down. Everyone's looking right and the action's on the left."

Tiny spoke up. "I take it then you're not going to Dallas. I set up a Navy jet. Have you there before Tae-hyun. We can divert his plane if need be."

"Cancel the ride! That's what they want. We're going back to the island."

Angella snapped open her cell phone. A moment later the cop car in front of us did a U-turn and waited for us on the other side of the road. Angella fell in behind them and we roared off in the direction we had come.

Tiny asked, "Want me to join you down there?"

"Good idea. When can you get here?"

"Four hours, maybe sooner."

"Make it sooner rather than later," I said.

"Cancel the police escort," I said to Angella. "No need to wear out our welcome. A few minutes won't make any difference at this point."

- - - - - -

Once back on the island we stopped for a late lunch at Tom and Jerry's Beach Club. We both had burgers and washed it all down with a couple of beers.

After lunch, we went back to my room to get the files.

Mindful of the microphone I had stuck to the lamp, I turned on the TV to cover over our voices. CNN was playing in the background while I again examined every page of every file. Angella took each file when I was finished with it and repeated the procedure.

Nothing turned up.

I studied Angella while we worked. Her lips were clenched into tight lines, a result of her concentration. I wanted more than anything else to soften those lips using my own.

She looked up. "What now? What am I doing to invoke that... oh, no, don't even go there. Jimmy, this is not the ..." Remembering the bugs, she stopped talking and blew me a kiss. At the same time she mouthed the word, *later*. Before I returned back to work I once again told myself she was one gorgeous woman.

Over her shoulder, barely registering, CNN was showing a picture of the President's plane landing in Dallas. I listened to the commentator explaining that the President had landed earlier in the day at Dallas Love Field. They were filling air time while they waited for him to take off back to Andrews Air Force base. The commentator then went on to remind the audience that Dallas Love Field was where President John F. Kennedy had landed in 1963 only hours before he was assassinated.

"Holly crap!" I shouted, jumping up from my chair. "We're idiots!"

"What's going on?" Angella replied, reacting to my actions by also jumping to her feet and turning to face the TV. "I don't under—"

"He's going to assassinate the President! When does Tae-hyun's plane land?"

Angella grabbed her cell, called Southwest Air, identified herself as Homeland Security and was put through to a supervisor. She turned and announced, "Plane was delayed, but will arrive in thirty minutes."

"Find out when the President will be back to his plane."

"Says it will be at least an hour. Nothing is permitted to land or take off when the President is at the airport."

I called Jamison, who immediately bridged on the head of Secret Service as well as the Dallas command center.

"I don't believe it's a coincidence that Tae-hyun will land in Dallas a few minutes before the President comes back to his plane." The line remained silent as the agents took it all in.

"There's a federal marshal on the plane keeping an eye on him," I continued. "Can you contact him and have him take the target off the plane. I want the target unharmed if possible."

A command voice broke the silence on the other side. "Why this guy's running free is not my business, but he's not getting close to the President, or even to Air Force One for that matter. I'm diverting the Southwest flight to Oklahoma!"

"Don't do that," I said. "He's our only lead to a …a critical piece of equipment. This operation is being undertaken at the President's direct request, so we need him to run free. I need you to keep him from the President and nothing more."

"Don't tell me how to run—"

"Sorry, Craig, but I'm with Redstone on this one." It was Jamison. "May not be the best plan, but it's what we have."

"If that's an order, I'll abide," the voice belonging to Craig replied. "But note that I don't approve. Okay, Dallas, take him off the plane. You know the plan. Delay landing until you're ready and everyone's in place."

"Put the operation on a video feed," Jamison said. "Will that present a problem?"

"We'll accommodate, Sir."

"How about feeding it to us as well?" I said.

"That will be difficult for–"

"We'll handle Redstone's feed from this end," Jamison barked. "Listen, the man passed through security. He doesn't have a weapon. There's a marshal on him. Keep the Southwest plane away from Air Force One. We'll be fine."

"Yes, Sir. We'll handle it, Sir. No problem."

"Anything further?" Jamison asked.

"Nothing from me, Sir." Craig replied.

"Redstone?"

"Clear here."

"Okay, gentleman. We have a plan. Redstone, we'll call you with instructions for the video."

The line clicked off. Jamison, it seems, has an aversion for saying goodbye. Come to think of it, he doesn't say hello either.

A few minutes later my cell rang. The technician on the other end wanted to know the brand name of the TV. When I gave it to him he said, "That'll work. I've already checked with the hotel and we're in touch with the cable company. We need to run a few checks. I'll text you what channel to use."

While we were waiting, Angella said, "I thought Tae-hyun being in Dallas was a decoy. You abandon that idea?"

"What makes you ask that?"

"Because you alerted Jamison."

"Can't take chances when the Commander In Chief's involved."

"Then according to your theory, they know we'll pick him up. Surely, they don't for a moment believe he'll get to the President. So what do we do?"

"What we should have done hours ago," I replied.

"And that is?" Angella asked.

"If Tae-hyun is a decoy, then there's another guy heading north. Assume Tae-hyun Jr. started from down here. We can start by checking for stolen vehicles."

"Could have started anywhere," Angella volunteered.

"Can't deal with *anywhere* right now. Can only deal with what we know. Issue a request for anyone fitting his description, also for any stolen cars from SPI or Port Isabel."

"You think he—" Angella began.

"I frankly don't know what to think. But I've never been good at sitting on my hands." I pulled off the boot. My ankle throbbed even harder.

"What ever happened to patience? Isn't that what you taught me?"

"You're seeing me at my patient best. It's not getting us anywhere. Time to force aggressive. I can feel grass growing on my ass."

THIRTY-EIGHT

The text arrived: **CHANNEL 287**

Angella tuned the TV to channel 287. Black and white dots filled the screen. The dots began to dance around, forming images that faded in and out.

"Southwest flight 43 lands in five minutes," a voice boomed. "Give us another few minutes and we'll have a video feed. Flight wing Delta Baker from the Dallas Naval Air Station has just launched. AWAC is in place. Dallas air space is now closed to everything except military. Nothing can get to the President from the air."

"Hope to hell you're right, my friend. Hope you're right."

"No more chatter," Jamison broke in. "Run the operation!"

The air went silent.

As promised, the black dots began assembling into blurry patterns. Suddenly, an image of a plane taxiing directly toward us filled the screen. The camera panned upward, revealing the unmistakable insignia of Southwest Airlines. The camera continued its tour, and several people dressed in black could be seen crouching behind a portable barrier. There was a roof over the barrier so passengers in the terminal and passengers in the plane could not see the armed warriors. A ladder-stand was positioned in front of the barrier. The plan apparently was to stop the plane short of the jet-bridge and have armed agents board from the rear door. They would remove Tae-hyun before anybody was released from their seats. The good news is that there was a low probability of the target having a weapon other than his fist. I had participated in this exercise in a training program, but had never done it live.

In theory, the take-out would be over before the passengers even realized the plane had been boarded.

That's theory.

This is for real. And we know from painful first-hand experience, Tae-hyun has a way of escaping the tightest of situations. The man had been highly trained by top professionals and was not known for going down easily. One wrong move and an entire planeload of innocent people would be in danger.

This operation had the makings for disaster. At least it could be explained in terms of Presidential safety. From my limited experience with the D.C. crowd, explanations were paramount.

Angella asked, "Why don't they just allow the passengers to deplane normally and jump him at the bottom of the ramp?"

"Normally, they would isolate him as he deplaned and then quietly move him into a private room. But the President's life is at risk and they're taking no chance that he can escape."

"Even if it means putting innocent people at risk?"

"When it comes to protecting the President, there are no innocent people."

That remark got Angella's attention. "That's a bit extreme, is it not?"

"Not politically correct, I suppose. But accurate."

The plane rolled to a stop. In my mind's eye I visualized what was going on inside the passenger compartment. The attendants would have been given the passenger extraction code by the pilot. The marshal would have been identified. He would be in communication with the command headquarters throughout the operation. The Chief Attendant would also have been given Tae-hyun's name, physical description and seat assignment. It was his or her job to stand just in front of the row where Tae-hyun was sitting. The passengers would already have been told the plane was going to stop short of the jet-bridge and to remain in their seats with their seat belts fastened. God help any fool who jumped up to retrieve a bag early.

Realizing Angella had no way of knowing what was going on, I explained the drill to her.

On the monitor we could see the steps being rolled into place at the rear of the aircraft.

"Why is nothing happening?" Angella asked.

"They've now told the pilot that the boarding force is ready. The pilot is relaying the information to the flight crew. The attendants from the back of the plane are moving forward of Tae-hyun. When they're in position, the pilot will be notified and then you will see one person walk up the steps. That person will be wearing regular civilian cloths with a concealed vest. The door will open and that person will enter the plane. If all is in order, the others will enter the plane behind that person.

"The door is opening!" Angella exclaimed. "A woman is half-way up the steps."

The camera was now focused on the plane and we could see people sitting quietly in their seats, looking forward, unaware of the action behind them.

The door opened fully and the woman proceeded up the remaining steps and disappeared into the plane.

The voice then said, "Hold. Hold."

The woman reappeared in the doorway.

The voice said, "Ready."

The woman's right thumb pointed upward and she disappeared back into the plane.

The voice said, "Go!"

On the screen a shadow flowed up the steps. The instant the shadow entered the aircraft the interior lights went out.

A moment later, a voice said, "Got him. He's sedated."

Then silence for another moment."

"Out of the aircraft. Target's secure."

The lights in the plane came back on.

The door closed and the airplane moved the last few feet to the jet-bridge. The woman we had seen enter the plane apparently remained onboard. We had no way of knowing how many other agents also remained on board with her, because we could only see Tae-hyun and two other figures come out through the door. The others may have preceded them, but if so, they moved so quickly they were invisible on the small screen. Another possibility is that the camera purposely avoided them.

Before I could react, Angella directed my attention to the TV screen. They were now in a small room and Tae-hyun was slumped in a chair. Angella's eyes were wide.

I said to her, "What the hell's got you so worked up?"

"Tae-hyun. There's..."

Angella's hand moved toward her holster.

"You can't shoot him through the TV," I commented, "no matter how hard you concentrate."

"...there's something wrong!" she said, peering intently at the screen. "If I didn't know better, I'd say they took the wrong man off the plane!"

I studied the image a while longer, then said, "Maybe it's because he's sedated?"

"That's what I thought at first. But look, he's too tall. I tied him up in that boat, so I know how big he is. This is wrong."

I called Jamison. "We think you have the wrong person. Have him ID'd."

"We have the man who boarded the plane with the Target's identity," a voice immediately replied. "We have the right man."

"Print him!" Jamison commanded. "And do it now!"

A moment later someone stepped forward with an electronic device that looked like a cell phone. I knew it to be a mobile finger print reader connected wirelessly to the FBI's fingerprint database, or IAFIS, the largest biometric database in the world. Normally, it would take ten minutes to process the prints. But for terrorist alerts the expected time was measured in seconds.

A full minute passed. Then two. Followed by a third.

I said, "Angella, you're dead on. If they had Tae-hyun it would have come back instantly. He's in our terrorist database for certain. This guy is an imposter. From the looks of it, he's new to the country."

A moment later a voice said, "No match! We took the right man off the plane. Don't understand."

"Stand him up! Put the camera on his face!" I shouted into my cell. Jamison repeated my request, but without the emotion.

As soon as that was accomplished we knew for certain Tae-hyun was not in Dallas. "Arrest him," Jamison said. "Keep him in a secure area away from anyone. Find out what you can from him." He then turned to someone standing beside him but off-camera. "Open the air space. Recall the squadron. Brian, the operation is yours. Carry on." To me he said, "Redstone, I don't know what the hell's going on, but you're being played. For that matter, we're all being played and I don't like the feel of this. Find that asshole before it's too late!"

The audio went dead, the video turned to white and black dots and I said to Angella, "Man's a cut-out. Won't lead us anywhere."

Angella sat on the corner of the bed, her head cocked to the side, an expression on her face I hadn't seen before. She sat that way for a moment, her lower jaw moving slightly, before she asked, "Why go to such an elaborate plan? They couldn't be serious about him getting to the President. The decoy was wearing a transponder! As you said, they had to know we'd stop him."

"They wanted us to follow. That would have put us up in Dallas away from the real Tae-hyun." Now it was my turn to stand mute for a few minutes reviewing the pieces that we had.

"Oh, shit!" I exclaimed, all semblance of professionalism gone, "it was right in front of us and neither of us saw it!"

"What was?" Angella asked, her eyes following my every movement.

"The blood on the mattress. They switched the transducer from Tae-hyun to an imposter. I was right earlier. Tae-hyun's on the loose."

Angella looked at me as if I had lost it. "That was evident the moment we identified the imposter in Dallas as not being Tae-hyun."

"But that's not the point. The point is: where are all these North Koreans coming from? Especially one who, at least from a distance, can pass for Tae-hyun?"

"What's your conclusion?"

"He's the second igniter. My guess—and it's only a wild guess—they lost the second bomb. Now they're improvising."

"And in the process," Angella added, "discrediting us."

"Discredited or not, Tae-hyun is now running free. This little diversion gave him at least a five-hour lead and possibly even more."

"More like seventeen hours," Angella corrected me.

THIRTY-NINE

"Captain Boyle's on my cell," Angella announced. "Demands to speak to you directly."

Angella and I were walking on the beach. The weather was glorious. The fact that it was after Thanksgiving made it all the nicer. We had wanted to talk freely and were pretty confident our clothes were now free of microphones, but uncertain about either of our rooms. In a juvenile fit of anger I had flushed the lamp microphone down the toilet, exclaiming. "Let those bastards listen to their cousins—the cockroaches!"

Angella had rolled her eyes, but wisely refrained from further comment.

Now Boyle was on the line. He was Mark Cruses' commander and had taken over command of the local Coast Guard station when Mark had been knocked unconscious. Boyle and I had had some words, and while we eventually spent some time together being briefed, the tension had not dissipated. I was itching to get him in an interrogation room. There were enough unexplained *coincidences* involving the local Coast Guard. Actually, it wasn't so much the enlisted men. They all performed their thankless tasks day in and day out with excellence. But it was their commander I had a bone to pick with. Even the bomb had disappeared on their watch. Well, not exactly on their watch, if my theory of a transfer at the checkpoint proved to be accurate.

Enough conjecture. I reached for Angella's phone. I could not imagine what he wanted from me at this point.

"This is Redstone," I said into Angella's phone, raising my voice to be heard over the wind and surf.

"Redstone," Boyle's voice boomed from the phone, "you really screwed up this time!" I backed the receiver away from my ear. "We had that son of a bitch and you let him go! Whole country's now on red alert! Jamison's blaming me for allowing another Korean into the country! Get your ass over to the station immediately. We need a plan."

My instinct was to tell him to kiss off. I didn't work for him and never would. But I did report to Jamison and apparently so did he, at least unofficially. The Coast Guard being part of Homeland Security, I didn't think it prudent to play hardball. These guys have a nasty way of winning. So I said, "Angella and I will be there in a half-hour."

"Can't hear you, Redstone! Lot of background noise. Is that surf I hear? Where the hell are you?"

"Make that an hour," I said, my voice loud enough for him to hear even without modern electronics.

"You say half-hour?"

"One hour!" I said, snapping the phone closed. He works for Jamison, so he's accustomed to the line going dead. Let him cool his heels.

A moment later the cell rang again. Angella answered and immediately handed it to me. My ear about burst. "...the hell you think we're running here? A kid's day camp? There's a car on the way. Where the hell are you? Get your asses over here now! Got that?"

"Beach access five," I said, again slamming the phone closed.

- - - - - -

Angella and I were ushered by a young man in a crisp white uniform into the same command room at the Coast Guard station where we had viewed the video file Mark Cruses had managed to save. The video showed how Tae-hyun had been smuggled into the country on a Coast Guard vessel. The video had also shown the throat being cut of the undercover Texas Ranger working with a Mexican drug lord. I had the impression at the time that Captain Boyle did not want that file to be seen, probably because it cast the Guard in a bad light. Or maybe, just maybe, a military expert would examine it and determine that a Guard officer, perhaps Boyle himself, was behind what had happened.

"This room seems so different this time," I said to Angella.

"For one thing, General Jamison was on the screen the last time."

"Be careful what you say," I cautioned her, "we're most likely being monitored."

"Thanks for the reminder. Don't lose sight that it was the video Mark hid that was the key to us intercepting the bomb and capturing Tae-hyun."

"But the powers that be can't get past the fact that Mark had been the station commander, coupled with his fiancée being the daughter of the drug lord who orchestrated the smuggling. Until they get to the bottom of that mess, I'm afraid Mark's off-limits."

I didn't know what to expect from Boyle. On the phone he had sounded agitated, yet Jamison certainly had told him about the bomb being hijacked before it had arrived at the Corpus station. Had the hijacking occurred while the bomb was on site, Boyle would be under arrest—or worse.

During the short drive to the station, Angella had whispered, "Jimmy, you have a strange look on your face. I'm guessing it has to do with Boyle. Pardon me for telling you how to act, but don't for a moment forget that at the station Boyle is king. Throw-away-the-key kind of king."

Angella had been exactly right on. I was ready for anything he had to dish out. I heard his footsteps even before the door opened. My whole body tensed.

"I have a surprise for you Redstone," Boyle announced, even before he was completely through the door.

I had had enough of his surprises. Without thinking, my body assumed its battle-ready stance. My feet were spread, my knees loose. My arms hung at my sides ready for whatever came. The fact that I was wobbly in my boot was forgotten. There was no disguising my dislike for this man.

That was all before I saw the smile, or what passed for a smile, pasted on his face. Boyle's hand was out in greeting and I reluctantly grasped it.

He then turned to Angella. "Good to see you again, Ms. Martinez." They shook hands as well.

"Sit, the both of you. Redstone, you look like you're ready to pounce. With your ankle I would have thought you'd give up the macho, at least until the boot is off. You're going to hurt yourself, you keep that up."

He had called my bluff and I felt foolish. The man was right. He had done nothing to provoke me and it was clear from my action that I was looking to pick a fight. I followed Angella into a chair, having been properly dressed down.

Boyle took a seat across the table directly opposite me. The smile was still there, but it seemed forced. He cleared his throat as if he did not know where to begin. Angella and I waited. I was following Angella's advice. We were in his house. It was his show.

"First," Boyle began, "I must say allowing that cockroach to run free was a bad move. Lots of people are calling for your resignations." He paused to see our reactions. Seeing nothing, Boyle continued. "You have a powerful sponsor, but even that gets old with screw-ups of this magnitude."

Under the table, Angella put her hand on my thigh. Her timing was fast enough to save me from a physical encounter that I was bound to lose. I relaxed back into my seat and replied, "You all but declare a national emergency, send a car for us, just to repeat what you already told me on the phone? I'm sure you have more on your plate than wasting time on this." Angella's pressure on my leg increased. I heeded her silent warning and instead of telling him that if he had been doing his job properly in the first place the bomb would not have landed and we wouldn't be in this situation now, I swallowed hard and said, "Let's just get to why you brought us to the station. Get it all on the table. We don't need to beat around the deck—or whatever the Coast Guard saying is."

Boyle's eyes momentarily flared. His chin set hard. I knew that look. He was ready to come after me. Since the feeling was mutual I hoped he would. But he held his ground.

Gradually he relaxed. He surprised me by saying, "I do owe you an apology, Redstone. Actually, more of a thank you." He again cleared his throat. "When the bomb was found missing from the Corpus station Jamison came down on me. Thought he was going to strip me of my command, he was so angry. But then you figured out the transfer had taken place over in Sarita while the truck was being guarded by INS officers. That got me off the hook. So a thank you is in order."

Actually, that was not entirely true. Jamison, or someone reporting to him, had figured it out before I had. But for some reason Jamison was down on Boyle. I decided to stay out of that for now, except to note that Boyle was on Jamison's target list. He was on ours as well. I also made a mental note to remember that the Feds were going all out on this. They were using every agency they had, and that included the FBI, the Secret Service and perhaps even military intelligence. It was a wonder we were not tripping over each other. Or maybe we were.

"Second, we have a mutual problem to solve. I understand the tracking sender, or whatever it's called, was switched from Tae-hyun to a decoy. We know the decoy came in through New York and flew down here using a phony ID. Don't think we'll get any useful information from that channel."

"I agree," I replied, staying non-committal until I knew where this was going. "He's a cut-out."

"Look, Redstone, I'm a seaman, not a detective. But I've put together a few facts. First, someone with some medical knowledge had to remove and re-implant that sender. From what I understand, it's inserted rather deeply into the buttocks. Isn't possible to dig it out yourself the way they implant it."

"That's what we've been told," Angella said. "But don't know first-hand how it all works."

"I've been assured that's a fact," Boyle said. "Second, our medic, Seaman First Class Thomas Delaney, did not report for work this morning. He's a good kid, been with this station over a year and never yet missed a day."

It would have been nice to have had this information earlier in the day, but crying and spilt milk came to mind, so I kept my mouth closed.

Angella obviously had the same thought. She said, "It adds up. It wasn't until we identified the decoy in Dallas that I realized the sender had been switched."

"Any idea where Delaney might be?" I asked, pushing aside the other comments and questions I had.

"We checked his apartment. Lives alone. Nobody's seen him."

"What's his address?" Angella asked. She was clearly acting as a shield between Boyle and myself.

Boyle consulted a file and read the address. Angella copied it into her phone.

"Is this the surprise you promised?" I asked. I wondered why he hadn't told me over the phone. Sending a car seemed over the top—even for him.

He glared at me.

I glared back.

Angella tensed, but did not reach out to restrain me.

"Redstone," he began, "you're right. I didn't bring you down here for what I've told you so far. Before I give you the news, however, I must say if you worked for me I'd have you in the frig-gin' brig! I have my reasons for keeping Mark isolated. Too much doesn't add up around him, what with his girlfriend being the daughter of that…that *asesino a sueldo.* You went over my head and

I don't like it one bit! This won't be the end of it." He pushed his chair back and stood.

Angella's hand was on my leg again and this time she was applying pressure. I remained seated. To my surprise, and I'm certain to Angella's as well, I responded by saying nothing. She was right, this was Boyle's show, let him choreograph the acts.

Boyle, getting no rise from me, continued, "I've been ordered, ordered mind you, to reinstate Mark Cruses. He'll resume his duties as before. All restrictions have been removed."

I suppose that meant he's also free to resume his relationship with Trich. I thought better of asking.

"You can coordinate directly with him. As of eighteen hundred," he made a show of checking his watch, "that's a half-hour from now, he's in charge. He'll still report to me, but I've been ordered back to Corpus. One screw-up and I'll have his head. And yours as well!"

The door slammed behind him.

FORTY

To wait for Mark to arrive or not wait for Mark, that was the debate. I wanted to wait. Angella suggested that we had to give him space to get re-oriented to his command. While we dithered, my cell sounded. I didn't recognize the number so I ignored it. Angella said, "You get so few calls, I think it wise to get it."

"Redstone, here," I said, not sure I had caught it in time. Silence greeted me, and I repeated, "Redstone, here."

Almost immediately a voice said, "Jimmy Redstone, code Padre. Hold for the President."

The line went silent and remained that way for several minutes. I explained to Angella what was happening and she shrugged her shoulders. "He's your buddy. Maybe he just wants a fishing buddy."

Another several minutes went by while the line remained silent. Angella pointed out the window and I walked over to see what she was gesturing about.

Less than a hundred yards away a helicopter's blades were spinning, kicking up small gusts of sand and shells. Captain Boyle walked briskly toward the chopper carrying a brief case in one hand and talking on a cell phone with the other. Behind him marched a seaman dressed in jeans and a blue shirt carrying a large duffle.

I placed my hand over the cell phone and said, "Boyle's moving out. Good riddance."

That had to be the moment the President chose to come on the line. "What is that you're saying, Jimmy? Didn't catch it all. Good riddance for what?"

"Sorry, Mr. President. I was commenting to Angella, Ms. Martinez."

"Tell her hello for me. Thank you for taking my call. I just wanted to thank you personally for alerting us in Dallas to a potential threat. Never want to take any of those for granted. Can't afford an incident. You caught this one early enough so we had no real danger. Good job."

"Thank you, Mr. President." I didn't feel right telling him there never had been a threat, it had all been staged to make Angella and I chase north.

"And please pass on my thanks to Ms. Martinez. You two make a good team. Do you need anything from me at this point?"

"No, Sir. Thank you for asking."

"My advisors inform me that as of this date there is no imminent danger. Is that correct from your vantage point?"

I had no earthly idea of what to expect. All I knew was that I was getting my butt run all over Texas, with a side excursion to Mexico, and not one bit closer to the bomb—or the traitor. But the President's question called for a yes or no answer, not a thesis. "It is indeed correct, Mr. President."

"Well then goodbye, and good luck. God bless us all." The line went dead.

Mark drove into the station parking lot just as we emerged from the building. He waved for us to wait for him. "I suppose you heard the news," he said, smiling broadly. "I have to get inside and be briefed, but how about us getting together, say for dinner? I'm meeting Trich at the *Sea Ranch* at seven. Almost next door to the station. Great food. Great views. Please join us."

"We'd love—"

"Maybe tomorrow or the next day," Angella interrupted my response. "You two need time to be alone. We saw her a few days ago and she's lost without you. You have a wonderful fiancée and she's frightened."

"Angella's right, of course," I hastened to add. "And your mother's beside herself."

"I know, I know," Mark replied. "I already spoke to Mother and she's coming down day after tomorrow. Good idea. We can all get together then." The smile faded. "I've been thinking about what's been going on. One thing I can assure you, the Coast Guard is not involved in the smuggling. That much I know. These are good people. These kids put their lives on the line every day. Someone outside the service is manipulating things."

I had never seen Mark so intense. I hesitated to ask the next question, but this was the perfect opportunity. "Tell me this, off the record, what about Boyle? He seems to be at the center of everything that's happening."

Without a moment's hesitation, Mark replied, "Under it all, he's solid. I've seen the man in action and he's a good officer and a good person as well. This all looks bad for him, but I'd trust him."

"Even considering how he's treated you?" I replied.

"It's his way. He's doing what he believes is best. I disobeyed his orders with the file. Things happened on my watch. He's an old-line guy, takes no prisoners, so to speak. But he's solid."

I was surprised by Mark's assessment and wondered if this was one military man protecting another. But I've known Mark all his life and never known him to do or say anything dishonest.

We said our goodbyes and he hurried inside.

It may have been wishful thinking on my part, but the guard at the door seemed to stand a bit taller and salute a bit sharper when Mark passed him.

No Coast Guard car was designated to take us back to the hotel. Instead, we walked across the street and over the dunes to the gulf beach. The water slides of Schlitterbahn were visible off to our left as we walked. We judged the hotel to be about a mile, maybe a mile and half, north along the beach. The wind was at our backs and the air was warm.

"Let's begin by visiting the medic's apartment," I said to Angella. "Probably another dead end, but at least it's a place to start."

"A thread end," she absently commented.

"What's on your mind?" I asked, responding to Angella's mood.

"Just thinking back over everything. Remember Joy Malcolm?"

"How could I forget her?" Joy had been *married* to Padre. Actually, they weren't married. But it's possible —likely—Joy hadn't known that her *husband* John had a wife and children in Mexico. Joy was still under investigation by the FBI, and as far as we knew nothing positive had turned up. Perhaps the FBI was allowing her to run, just as we were allowing Tae-hyun to run, to see where she would lead them. "What about her?" I asked.

"Just wondering what she might know about all this. Another thread end is all."

I called Woody and asked her to abstract the FBI file on Malcolm. She said it would take her about an hour. Actually, she sent it before we reached our hotel.

We walked most of the way back to the hotel with no further discussion. I broke the silence by asking, "What do you make of Mark's response to my question about Boyle?"

"Funny, I was just about to ask you the same thing."

"You first."

"I think he's genuine. This isn't a military problem. If it was, military intelligence would have ferreted it out long before now. No, I'm betting on someone, or a few someones, in or near the top of some other agency masterminding this."

"I don't disagree," I replied, feeling comfortable with Angella's assessment. "I would add the observation that had this been a military-planned mission, it would have been concise and well-timed. This operation has been disrupted by us intercepting the bomb. They are now playing catch up and not getting it right. Diverting us to Mexico and then not shooting us was an ill-conceived plan at best."

"Not so ill-conceived as you might think," Angella replied, expressing a different view. "They succeeded in diverting attention away from the bomb while Tiny and others were focused on us. During that time they hijacked the bomb while everyone was looking south."

"But letting us live was not smart."

"Tiny caught them by surprise in his rescue operation of Taehyun and you."

"The clumsy attempt in Dallas is what has my focus. There never was any chance of them doing anything with the President."

"Just another diversion," Angella replied, following her thread. "The fact that the President was in Dallas was a coincidence that played to their advantage. The imposter had no weapon he could use and no possible access to the President or to Air Force One."

"From what? What was the diversion about? What did they do while we were looking north? Had they flown the imposter to any other airport, we'd still be chasing him across country thinking we were on the trail of Tae-hyun."

"Maybe that gave them all the time they required?"

"For what?" I asked again. Angella was on a roll and I was prepared to go with it.

"Bobbin's empty," she said. "Need to refill. No more threads to follow. I just know it was a diversion. Too stupid to be anything else."

We were back at the hotel and went up to my room to read Joy Malcolm's file.

After going through it, I commented to Angella, "Inconclusive. Preliminary report is that she didn't know about John's double life. But they're watching her for drug trafficking. She's definitely a user."

"She hung out at *Louie's Backyard,*" Angella reminded me. She checked her watch, and said, "This is about her time. You thinking of heading over there?"

"Can't hurt. A Bones would work well right about now."

"A what?"

"Spiced rum and diet Coke. Everyone knows what a Bones is."

"I've been hanging at all the wrong places. Never heard of it. Let's go."

FORTY-ONE

Some things seem to never change. We walked into *Louie's* and there she was. Same friends, same glass in her hand, same loud voice. Drunk, high on drugs or acting. Joy Malcolm was holding court. Also, as before, she didn't miss a thing that happened around her.

No sooner were we through the door than she spotted us. "There's our cop friends. Jimmy Redstone. I was hoping to see you, see how you're doing. Heard from Teran you were on the island. Says you're looking good. Missed you in the gym this morning. I got up early for no avail." She glanced at Angella and then back to me. "I suppose you have better things to do in the morning than spend time in the stinking gym!"

I didn't know how much Joy had been told about what went down. Public story was I fell off a horse and cut my neck on a rock. The fact that there are almost no rocks out in the marsh hadn't deterred the Feds from their cover story. Another Washington spin that made little sense. "I've been grounded from riding horses for a while," I called over to her. "Other than that, I'm fine."

"You don't look so fine in that boot. Get that from falling off a curb—or kicking some butt?" A few of her drinking buddies joined her in laughter.

"Got it caught in a tree root. Wasn't looking where I was going. So how about you?"

"Never been better!" She turned to her friends. "Right?"

"Never been better," the aging blonde on her left dutifully replied. "Now that your husband's out of your hair. Never been better."

I leaned in past Joy and ordered a Bones.

Angella said, "Make that two. I have to see what this is about."

"A Bones!" Joy repeated, "What the hell's a Bones?"

Angella elbowed me in the side, as if to say, "*See, I'm not the only one!*"

The bartender, a woman with as much hanging out of her blouse as inside, replied, "Real name's Skinny Bones. Captain Morgan spiced, Diet Coke, a touch of limejuice. A waist watcher special." She winked and trotted off, but not before Joy called out, "Make that three! Any other takers?"

The blonde's hand went up.

"Joy, her voice many decibels higher than necessary, called to the retreating bartender, "Make that four Skinny Bones!" The emphasis being on skinny.

Not missing a nuance, Joy leaned close, put her arm over my shoulder, and stage whispered, "Bren's hitting on you. But don't take it to heart. She'll flirt with anything that moves—and I mean *anything*."

"Don't start," Joy's blonde friend injected. "The last time it didn't end so well for you."

"Speaking of not ending well, suppose you know, John's gone?" she said. "I was getting ready to dump him. Man beat me to the punch. Just walked out one day. No one's seen or heard from him since." She held up her glass. "Drink to him. Good riddance, I say."

"Here, here," a few buddies said. The others had turned away, apparently bored with Joy's antics.

"So, you here for R&R? Or are you still tracking the serial killer?"

"There's no serial killer," her friend said. "One guy got his neck cut. Your friend died of an OD. Don't go off on that serial killer thing again. Heard enough of that nonsense! You're making a fool of yourself."

Joy turned to her friend. "Every time I see these two, someone dies." She swiveled back in my direction. "Who is it this time? Anyone I know?"

"You know everyone, my dear," her friend said, "so how's he going to answer? And besides, if anyone on this island so much as thinks about dying, you know about it."

"Hey, let the man answer," Joy said, cutting them off. "Someone dead or not? We want to know."

"Not that I know," I responded. "Angella, you know of any dead bodies?"

"Haven't checked the beach today, but other than what might be out there, none that I can think of," Angella answered, keeping it light.

"What about Chief Duran?" Joy said, "He was shot! Hey, that's why you're here, isn't it? Trying to find his killer."

"Chief Duran's not dead!" Angella exclaimed. "You need to watch what you say." Now it was my turn to calm Angella. Both of our anger management skills needed work.

"Now you've gone and done it, Girl," the blonde said. "Leave these nice people alone. Let them have their drinks in peace. You keep bothering them, next thing you know they'll go to *Boomerang Billy's* or to *Kelly's Irish Pub* for happy hour."

"I'm not stopping them from anything. Just saying hello to old friends is all. Someone shot the Chief. He was a nice man, didn't book a lot of crap from people, but he was fair. Who knows who we'll get next. Take a while to break the replacement in. Just saying."

Angella and I found a small table across from the bar. From where we sat we could look out over the bay. I was faced south and Angella north. Halfway through my Bones Angella said, "Don't turn now, but Jim's Pier just lit up."

"So?"

"Red and blue."

"More than one?"

"I'd say six or seven. More on the way."

My cell sounded. Mark Cruses was calling. "Hi, Mark," I said when I answered. "Aren't you having dinner with Trich?"

"Had to postpone. I'm on my way to Jim's Pier."

"You and every official car on the island. What's going down?"

He told me what he had heard. I flipped the cell closed and said to Angella. "Finish your drink; we're meeting Mark."

"What's up?"

"The missing medic. He's not missing any longer."

FORTY-TWO

Actually, we couldn't get on the pier, so we parked and walked three blocks. The pier was cordoned off with yellow tape and about ten police cars were parked at random angles for a full block around the pier. A coroner van was snaking its way through the mess.

I remembered the pier from this summer when I sat, a beer in my hands, watching the Friday night fireworks being launched from a barge anchored on the bay. I had first seen the fireworks display from *Louie's* with Joy commenting on each explosion with an *ooh* or an *aah*. She seemed to be partial to the red and white star bursts; those would receive several *oohs* and *aahs.* Since we were now past Labor Day, the fireworks were in hibernation. But the red and blue flashing lights around the pier more than made up for the otherwise tranquility of the island.

We flashed our badges to get past the several uniformed guards who were busy keeping looky-lous out. The body had been found on a private fishing boat by the owner. That much

Mark had told me. And that pretty much exhausted his knowledge of what had happened. He did comment on the fact that the medic was a good guy.

If this had been a motel shooting, I'd put my money on drugs or some form of sexual misbehavior. Sometimes it was as simple as a wife walking in with a shotgun and blasting the goodies off an errant husband. But not with boats. It was rare when the police were called to investigate a murder on a boat, especially one tied to a dock.

Mark caught up to us midway across the parking area. We shook hands and he thanked me several times for getting him the command back. I finally told him I had nothing to do with it.

"Not what I hear. All restrictions have been removed. I called Trich and she told me how sick her brother was and that her father was under house arrest. I haven't had time to read the file, but I bet you had something to do with that as well."

"We can talk later," I said. We approached the boat and I asked a uniformed cop to brief us.

"White male, about thirty-eight, single shot to the back of the head from close range. DOA."

I called Tiny. His flight had been delayed, but he was now on the ground in Brownsville and would be here in about twenty minutes. He said, "If you're at the pier, then you know about the killing. Look for our agent, a man about six-foot-two, bald, glasses. Name's Pierre Defly. Answers to Pete. He should find you. I sent him your picture. He can be trusted."

Before Tiny finished his thought, a man fitting the description walked over. Angella positioned herself between us and I nodded to her that it was okay.

I hung up with Tiny and the agent said, "Name's Pete. Tiny told me to find you. A single bullet to the brain. You ask me, it was professional all the way."

"Any chance of a suicide?"

Mark replied, "Not if it's Delaney our medic. He's rock solid. A good guy."

"Suicides don't use silencers," Pete commented. "Also, I doubt if he was killed on the boat. My take, the perp dropped him off."

"Connected to our target?" I asked, knowing the answer.

"Can't imagine otherwise. Someone removes the target's transponder and the next day a medic is found with a bullet to the back of the head. Connected all the way."

"Do we have his name? Any other info on him?"

"They're not releasing anything," Pete informed us. "Want me to get it?"

"Name's Thomas Delaney," Mark said. "He's a medic with the Coast Guard."

"Has there been positive identification?" I asked.

"That's why I'm here," Mark answered.

I asked the nearest cop. "Who's in charge?"

He pointed to a woman, about my age, with skin that appeared to come from a tannery.

"Name?"

"Lt. Malone. She's Assistant Chief. Lt. Garcia's off island tonight."

I walked over to Malone and introduced myself.

"What does Homeland Security have to do with a dead guy in a boat?" she asked, her mouth set as tough as her skin. "There's a lot of uninvited people showing up on this here pier. Angella, I wouldn't think you'd want to get involved, seeing as how you're …" Malone cut herself short. Then said, "I'm about to throw them all out of here."

"Don't know for sure, but we lost an asset on the island last night. Too much of a coincidence."

"We're not releasing anything until we know what we have. Sorry, you'll have to wait your turn." She turned to walk off.

"Pardon me, Lieutenant, but I'm asking nice this time. One phone call and you'll be told what to do. Let's not go there."

She turned instantly, and now her eyes were really burning. This woman was accustomed to getting what she wanted. "No one threatens me! You understand that? Now get you sorry ass out of here before I have you physically thrown out."

Angella had been listening to the exchange and was already on the line to Acting Chief Garcia. Within five minutes, Malone was reaching for her cell phone. I saw her nodding several times before she shoved the phone into her bag. She glared in our direction and then charged directly at us. If she had horns, even the clowns would not have saved me.

"Okay, you win! This round is yours! Don't know where you guys get the pull, but got my ass chewed right proper. You happy now? Who's this guy?" She nodded in the direction of agent Pete.

"Name's Pierre Defly, Special Agent with the Secret Service."

"Special Agent? What the hell's this about?"

"Tell you later. This is not the time or place."

Malone studied us for a long moment. Then said, "Haven't identified him yet. Died instantly from a single bullet to the brain. We ruled out suicide. Left no prints. No gun. TOD appears to be about three AM last night."

"I'm here to identify him," Mark spoke up.

"You from the Coast Guard?" Malone asked, extending her hand. "Come with me."

We all trailed along. I could tell by the sick look on Mark's face that he instantly recognized the dead guy. "Name's Thomas Delaney. Seaman First Class Thomas Delaney. He is—was—our medic at the station."

I nodded to Angella, who stepped forward and snapped a picture of the dead guy.

"Send it to Tiny. He can put it in the database."

"What database?" Malone asked. "What the hell's going on here? Why's Homeland Security, the Secret Service, here?"

"I can't tell you."

"Can't, or won't?"

"Won't. Giving you the same cooperation you gave me. See if you can make *my* phone ring."

Malone stomped off. Angella said, "Take it easy, Jimmy. These are friends. I worked with these folks and they're good people. There's no call for being rude. Malone's okay."

"I'm tired of having to pull rank every time I need something from the locals. Tell your friends to cooperate."

"I suppose that goes two ways. How much cooperation you think the Feds give these folks? Guess what you'll get if you ever need her help?" Angella was wound up. "You'll get chuffed to a chair. And that'll be the good part."

Angella's text alert went off.

The good news was the dead man was who Mark said he was. The bad news was that neither the time of death nor the location of death were official.

The most important news was that Tae-hyun still had not been located.

FORTY-THREE

The tech team was finishing up. Only it wasn't the locals who were doing the work. Lt. Malone had been ordered to stand down and allow the FBI exclusive access to the pier. They also took over the Schlitterbahn investigation. Needless to say, both Malone and her boss Garcia were pissed.

The preliminary indication from Schlitterbahn was that the blood in Tae-hyun's room belonged to Tae-hyun as well as to someone else. These statements always say 'preliminary'. In this case, it was a certainty—about Tae-hyun. The FBI had an absolute match. The uncertainty was the other person.

A car passed through the police barricade and rolled to a stop in the parking lot. Tiny climbed out of the back seat. He looked as though he had been sleeping in his suit for a week. His usual smile was back. We exchanged greetings.

I excused myself and called Lt. Contentus in Austin. He came on the line immediately. "I've found nothing important you can use," he announced. "Except that an Immigration official had to approve the use of the shed at the check point, even though your Secret Service handler Jurald requested it."

"So, who ultimately approved it?"

"They won't release that information. You'll have to get it from the INS. My contact says the Assistant Deputy is the only one who can authorize it."

"That would be a man named Homer Greenspar. A big man, same build as Tiny. At first I thought they were brothers."

"Greenspar? I know him. He was involved in that raid when you guys flushed the Korean on SPI. Duran made a note that Greenspar's operative was working the Island without Duran's knowledge. When we were flying back from Washington after meeting the President he mentioned it again. Asked me if I had any knowledge of the operation Greenspar had been running. He thought it linked with our man who was killed. No question, Duran didn't like Greenspar."

"That's an understatement. I saw the two of them go at it right after the raid. They were in Duran's car and Greenspar is lucky Duran didn't shoot him."

"Guns aren't the answer to all your problems," Contentus said. That rebuke was his way of telling me he was still pissed over my shooting Badman Tex. Given the circumstances, I'd do it again.

"I've known Greenspar since Vietnam days. He's a good guy."

"Everybody involved in this operation is a good guy," I quipped. "Regular Rat Pack. Obviously someone's not."

Before the phone went dead Contentus remarked, "Or you just haven't found the right person yet. Only been a week or so. It's early days."

"I have a room booked at the Isla Grand. You guys still there?" Tiny asked, when I shoved the phone back into my pocket. "Or did you move out?"

"No reason to move out. We found the microphones," I said.

"We searched before we left," Angella added. "Maybe do it again."

"I hate to break it to you, but you're no match for these guys. Shit, your bra could be bugged."

"It already has been." Angella replied, her face flushing ever so slightly. "I think I know what to look for."

"I wouldn't trust them under any condition. We're going back to the hotel and pack a few things. Stay checked in. Then we're going to move up island and find a place. No talking business in the car either. Can't trust anything. They play a dangerous game."

- - - - - -

A half hour later we were all checked into a neat set of condos going by the name *Beach House Vacation Rentals* located directly across from *Ted's* on the same side of Padre Boulevard as *Island Fitness*. A great place run by a guy named Mike, a former Marine, and his wife, Barb. We tucked Angella's car in the back corner of the parking lot where it wasn't visible from the street. The rentals looked freshly painted and well cared for.

A few minutes later we gathered in Tiny's room and I briefed him and Angella on my visit to the White House. When they were finished asking questions, I stood to leave.

"Before you leave," Tiny said, tell me where to get a paper on this island. Preferably something from the east coast."

"A block or so south," Angella said. "*Island Market*. Little place has everything. *New York Times* included."

"Speaking of papers," I commented. "Tell me what you know about Abigail Johnson from the Washington Post."

Tiny's head jerked in my direction. "What about her? She handles their homeland security desk. A real pro. She gets on a story, she's worse than a pit bull. Make your life hell, you cross her. She on to you?"

"Had a brief conversation with her at the reception. Caught me as I was leaving. She asked about Angella. Wanted to know why she hadn't joined me. I gave her some excuse and she rolled her eyes. Then she asked me about the bomb. She wanted background information about what went down."

"Did you give it to her?"

"Hell, no!"

"If she already knew about the bomb then giving her background is not a bad idea. But be sure she agrees it's background."

"How the hell you suppose she knows?"

"Abby Johnson knows everything. She's Cindy McNaughton's sister-in-law."

FORTY-FOUR

At nine the next morning I walked across the street to the gym.

"Good to see you," Teran called when I walked through the door. "Heard about the dead guy in the boat. Ruined someone's fishing day. Police have impounded the boat. Owner's really pissed."

"You know who the boat belongs to?"

"Guy down for a week. Him and a few buddies. Never seen them before. Not a good welcome to the island."

I turned to hang up my sweatshirt, and Teran commented, "Thought you couldn't start back yet."

"New plan. Let's get at it." That's the wrong thing to say to a trainer, but Teran is good at what he does. He had me do a series of exercises designed to warm up my muscles. Then he proceeded to test the limits of each muscle group individually.

An hour later he said, "Great job. You're still in pretty good shape. A little tune up here and there and you'll be a new man."

I didn't care to be anything new. I just wanted my old self back. I didn't tell Teran that.

I walked out onto the second floor deck and literally bumped into Joy Malcolm. I apologized, saying, "Sorry, my back was to the door, saying goodbye to Teran."

"Don't apologize! That was as close as I've been to a man in months. Rather liked it."

I had forgotten how much of a flirt Joy was. If I hadn't known better, I'd have thought she was serious.

"Hey, Big Guy, you're just who I was hoping to see. Come over here and talk to me." She led the way to a wooden picnic table and sat down. "Take a load off your feet," she called to me.

I reluctantly sat, and she leaned across the table, "What's with you?" she asked, "Every time you show up somebody drops dead. Well, not exactly drops dead. Is murdered. Serial killer, I'm certain of it."

"You get me over here to tell me that? Don't go spreading that around. It's not true."

"I looked it up on the computer. My friends say serial killers all kill the same way. But that isn't so all the time. Here we have the guy on the beach, his throat is cut. My friend, Hart, died of an overdose. This new guy, the one in the boat, bullet to the head. So it proves that serial killers can change their mod operandi. That's how you cops say it, right?"

"You're thinking of modus operandi. It's usually the same, but not always. Stop spreading—"

"I follow these things. Who's that big guy you were with last night? He's some hunk. Available?"

"What big guy?'

"Down on the pier."

"What were you doing down there?

"Trying to get a look at the dead guy."

"Why?"

"Tell me who the big guy is?"

"Friend."

"You're not telling me the truth. He's a cop. I can smell cops. Never seen him down here before."

"From Washington. Visiting."

"He making it with Angella?"

"No! And it's not your business if he was."

"I just wanted to know if he's available for me. I really don't care what he's doing with Angella. I figure that's your concern, not mine."

I stood to leave.

"Not so fast. I have evidence for you. May have seen the killer. May have seen the dead guy. That's why I was down there last night."

I sat back down.

"That's better. Now ask me nicely."

"Knock off the games!" I said, agitation getting the better of me. "What do you have?"

"Now, now, Big Guy. That's no way to treat an eye witness."

"Eye witness to what?"

"People walking on the beach."

"Who the hell cares about people walking on the beach?"

"You should."

"Why?" This was getting tiring. Good thing I didn't have the Beretta or I might have discharged it in her direction. Imagine how many anger management classes I'd have to take then. I slapped my palm on the wooden table. "Get on with it!" I said. "I have things to do."

"You're cute when you're angry. Now I know what Angella sees in you. Okay. I was standing on my porch. You were in my condo. You know what a good view we have of the beach."

I nodded, trying my best not to strangle her.

"I was having trouble sleeping. Comes from not having anyone to snuggle against. Went out on the porch for some air. Full moon. It was about midnight, maybe a bit later. Yea, more like one. Two men were walking along the water." She winked at me. "Who am I not to be interested when two men are walking on the beach at night? Got my attention."

"Anything special about these men?"

"Nothing really special about them at that time," she replied, pausing for effect. "But all men are special, know what I mean?" When I didn't reply, she continued, "After seeing the new dead guy's picture in the paper this morning, there sure was something special about the men I saw." Another pause. "One of them was the dead guy."

"How can you be sure of the identity? It was night. You were, what is it, five floors up? A long way from the beach."

"The build, the size, but most of all, the uniform. I noted at the time that he was wearing khakis and a blue shirt. Just like in the picture this morning in the *Press*."

"The man with him," I said, "can you describe him?"

"Tall. Almost as tall as your friend. But trimmer."

"Anything else you recall?"

"Isn't that enough? Is there a reward? I should have waited until they announced a reward. Cheated myself."

"That all you have?"

"Isn't that enough?"

Again, I stood to leave. "What's your hurry?" Joy said, with what passed as a seductive smile. "Day's young. We can take in the pleasures of the island."

"Got work to do. Thanks for the information."

Joy called out across the deck. "One thing I did forget. The tall man had a full head of hair. At first, it seemed to be too long. But it wasn't long, just full."

Joy followed me across the deck and now stood beside me. "You might want to come back to my place, Big Guy. It'll be worth your while." Her smile broadened, captured now in her inviting eyes.

Where's Angella when I need her? Or even Tiny? It was time to call her bluff—if indeed it was a bluff. "And, pray tell, Joy Malcolm, just exactly what do you have in mind?"

"What any healthy woman has in mind," she replied, toying with me.

"And that would be?"

"Show you my picture album, what else?"

That caught me by surprise. "Your picture album? That's a new one."

"You'll like it. I'm certain of that."

"And just why is that?"

"I took pictures of them walking on the beach. The moonlight gave pretty good silhouettes. You can do wonders these days with digital cameras. Even if I do say so myself."

- - - - - -

Joy drove me the few blocks to her condo. As good as I think I am at reading people, Joy has been and continues to be a challenge. She'd go from gregariously loud to recluse silent in an instant. It wasn't that she just stopped talking, she actually seemed to withdraw within herself. Then suddenly, she'd expand and the incessant talking would return. She was cycling from manic to depressive and back to manic faster than a traffic light cycles through its program.

During the drive, she was stone quiet—on red as it were. Once out of the car, she switched to green and began talking non-stop. She again told me how lonely she was since her husband disappeared. This was followed closely by how terrible it had been living with him. She ticked off a litany of how he had ripped her off by gambling away her money, taking men-only trips, having late-night meetings on the beach with Nationals, and on and on. She then proceeded to once again tell me how she had been ready to divorce John. That brought her full-circle back to missing him terribly. By the time we arrived at her fifth-floor condo, she was talking about her afternoon lover. In her mind he had been one of the victims in her serial killer theory. "Jimmy," she said, "you know full well the murders are all connected. And I have the killer's picture in my computer. Doesn't that rate a big reward?"

It wasn't so much what she was saying, but the fact that her hands were all over my shoulders and back that made me believe she and I did not share the same meaning of the word *reward*. I was reluctant to enter her apartment. This had all the markings of becoming uncomfortable quickly.

She put the key in the lock, patted my arm one more time, and twisted the key. By the time the door was fully opened she was again deadly quiet, her arms hanging limp at her sides.

Once in her apartment she went straight to her bedroom.

I waited in the entryway for her to return.

Realizing I hadn't followed her into the bedroom, Joy called, "The computer's in here. Come on in."

I reluctantly entered the bedroom. The curtains and door to the balcony were open and sunlight flooded in. The view of the beach and water was magnificent. I heard the surf even from this far up.

Joy had her computer positioned to allow her to use it and still see out to the beach. A nice life if you could get it.

"Here they are," she announced. "Look here."

On the screen, indeed in deep silhouette, I could see two men walking on a dark smooth surface. White streaks that I assumed to be surf frozen in time were visible on the far side of the men. The full moon was high in the sky behind the subjects. Moonlight reflected from the water onto the walkers. Based on the known location of the camera, the FBI lab would be able to determine the exact time the picture was taken from the angle of the moon. I wasn't sure if they would be able to reconstruct the walker's faces. But science sometimes performs forensic miracles.

Joy brought up a series of six shots. She had been accurate when she had said one of the men was tall and slender with a full head of hair. I would call it bushy. I was pretty certain the other guy was the dead medic, Seaman First Class Thomas Delaney.

"Please e-mail those to me?" I said, handing her one of my new cards. "Don't fail. Every one of them."

She held the card gingerly by the edge. She read the words and then commented, "Homeland Security? I thought you were a Texas Ranger. What gives?"

"Changed jobs. New assignment."

"What about Angella? I remember reading something about her in the paper a few weeks back. But I didn't know...is she with you also?"

"She is."

"That explains why you're here! You never did solve the last two murders, did you? And the Police Chief was shot. Oh, my God! There *is* more going on than I thought." When I didn't comment, she continued. "This new dead guy is connected to the others! I was right. There really is a serial killer on the loose down here. Oh, my God!"

"Joy," I said, trying to put Jack back in the box, "don't go making wild assumptions. This is not a serial killing. I need your help on this, so please do as I say. I want those pictures e-mailed right now."

"What about my reward?"

"Send the pictures! I don't have all day!"

That got her attention. Joy went silent. But she turned back to her computer, brought up the e-mail screen and dutifully attached the six files to the e-mail. She then carefully copied my e-mail address into the TO location, typed Joy's Pictures in the SUBJECT line and hit send. A little message popped up saying: **e-mail sent**.

"They're on the way. Promise me if this leads to the arrest of the murderer I'll get my reward."

"I'll see what I can do," I replied, knowing I was helpless on that score. I thanked her and walked to the door. Before leaving, I said, "Joy, I'd appreciate it if you didn't share the pictures, or even that you have them, with anyone. I'll be in touch."

Joy sat there unmoving. She was in full red recluse mode.

FORTY-FIVE

An hour later we were racing across the bridge on our way to Corpus Christi, a three-hour drive north. Tae-hyun had been located in a motel. All three of us were in Angella's car. Tiny was driving. Concern about bugs kept our conversation limited. At Tiny's suggestion, we detoured to Harlingen Airport to pick up a rental. That would free us to talk and would give us more freedom of movement.

At the airport, Tiny said, "It doesn't take three of us chasing Tae-hyun. I'll take the car back to the island and coordinate from there. You okay with that?"

Both Angella and I nodded in agreement and Tiny drove off.

I drove the rental while Angella was busy getting updates from the FBI on the situation in Corpus. "What did Tiny tell you?" Angella asked, when she hung up with the FBI. "Give me all you know."

Tiny had taken me aside and whispered the news in my ear. Angella had appeared miffed that she hadn't been included, but there hadn't been time. And until now, we had to assume we were being listened to. "Excellent work on the part of the FBI," I said. "The guy captured in Dallas, the cut-out with the transponder, had a scrap of paper with some scratch marks on it. Some alert agent guessed it was Korean. Jackpot. The translation was interpreted as *Plaza*. Another guess, or maybe it was the scratching itself, led them to think it was a motel where he was to meet. Agents were sent to every *Plaza* hotel, motel and flop joint within a thousand mile radius of Dallas. A motel of that name showed up in Corpus and the Bureau, smelling pay dirt, sent a team. They found Tae-hyun, alone in a room at the motel. That's all I know."

"Don't play Tiny's games. Okay? I mean, you could have taken me aside and told me what was going down. What would it have taken? Thirty seconds? Not even that long."

"Don't be so sensitive. You weren't being cut out."

"If the shoe was on the—"

"Probably shoot you. Just saying."

"I take that as message understood."

"Loud and clear."

"And another thing since we're clearing the air."

I didn't much like this clearing the air thing. When my former wife said that, I got an earful of shit. All the things I had done that she didn't like. She usually picked a time, such as when I was driving or otherwise not capable of leaving, to unload.

"You should review your anger management skills. Folks are getting to you—or should I say, you are allowing folks to get to you—much too easily.

"You're, of course, talking about sailor-boy Boyle. Man's an ass!"

"Ass or not, aren't you the one who told me to stay above it?"

"Do as I—"

"Message delivered?"

"Delivered."

For the next hour, we exchanged a few thoughts, but mostly we each contemplated what we had going for us so far. And that wasn't much. At the Sarita Border Patrol checkpoint, I flashed my credentials and asked to see the inside of the hut where the bomb had changed trucks unknown to the guards.

I don't know what I expected, but what I saw was disappointing. An empty green metal drive-in storage shed is all that I found. In a few minutes we were back on the road. Angella took over driving.

I took a call from Mark Cruses, who said, "I've asked around and the name of a Border Patrol guy keeps coming up. To be exact, he was mentioned twice."

"Name?" I asked.

"Te Burner."

"Any thing else?"

"Nothing much."

"What context was Burner mentioned?"

"Asking the guys about shift assignments, times, that sort of thing."

"Where did this occur? On the base—I mean station?"

"In town. At a watering hole called *Padre Island Brewing Company*. It's on Padre Boulevard in the middle of town."

"Great place. Has an upstairs patio."

"You got it. I'm grounding everyone until we get this settled. Time-off's been cancelled. Increasing our patrols. On another subject, Mother says she understands you're busy and wants to cook you a dinner."

"Don't know when that will be."

I promptly repeated the conversation for Angella, adding, "See, I can learn."

"Never thought otherwise. Now, who's being sensitive?" She reached across the seat and placed her hand on my knee. This time it felt comforting.

About twenty miles north, Angella said, "Hope you enjoyed your little nap. We've company. A blue Buick has been on our tail since the checkpoint."

I glanced in the side mirror and the car Angella was commenting on was pretty far back. Perhaps as far as two-hundred yards. "He's far back for following us."

"Thought that myself, but when I slow, he slows. Keeps a steady distance."

"Pull off at the next opportunity and I'll drive from there. We'll get a chance to check him out when he passes. See what he does."

In Kingsville, Angella pulled into a Dairy Queen parking lot. Our tail kept going. There was something vaguely familiar with his profile, but his head was turned away from us so I couldn't get a decent view.

I slipped behind the wheel. "He expects us to be a while. If you're right, he'll pick us back up when we leave. Unless you need to use the potty, I'm for getting back on the road."

"If you promise to stop down the road, I'm fine."

We hadn't driven ten miles before the Buick, which had apparently gone off onto a side farm road, pulled into the road behind us. "You'll get your wish for a stop sooner than you thought," I said. "He's back. Good catch."

I pulled into a Shell station about six miles up the road. Angella casually climbed out and proceeded to the rest room. The man in the Buick pulled up to a pump and put the nozzle in the tank. I couldn't determine if he was actually pumping gas or making a pretext of doing so. He then walked into the convenience store. I was waiting for him inside. He was tall and wiry and carried himself as if he was powerfully built. Except for the hair, he was a spitting image of the silhouette I had seen in Joy's pictures.

"I assume you wanted to speak with me," I said, coming up behind him.

"Who're you?" His eyes had the cool flatness of a professional. I'd seen this look plenty of times from hoodlums who took delight in bullying people. He was most likely carrying a weapon. Guys like this are always armed. If not a gun, then a knife.

"Let's put our cards on the table before someone gets seriously hurt," I said, giving him a chance to explain himself. "You're following us. That always makes me nervous. I'm with the Department of Homeland Security." I produced my badge. "Who are you?"

"Don't know what the hell you're talking about," he shot back. His eyes maintained their flatness.

"You're following us for a reason? Who you working for?"

"I don't take shit from anybody," he answered, his stance widening. "And I sure as hell ain't taking it from you!" His thin lips pulled back revealing prominent canines. His muscles tensed. He was ready to pounce. Someone else who needed anger management lessons.

We were face to face and one of us had to yield. From his standpoint, if he pulled his gun, he'd blow his cover—whatever that was. If he walked away, he'd at least be able to maintain his innocence. It was his move and we both knew it.

He turned away. As he did so Angella snapped his picture.

"Who the hell you think you are taking my picture?" His arm shot out for the camera.

But mine was faster. I caught him in the forearm and his hand shot upward. His other hand started toward his midsection. I had already noted the bulge of a rather large firearm tucked into his waistband.

"Don't pull that," I said, "if you want to keep all your parts." My hand was on my gun, my thumb having kicked loose the holster guard and the safety. Drawing wise, it was another standoff. One thing I knew. If I drew, I'd shoot.

He must have seen it in my eyes because his arm relaxed and he slowly brought his hand down.

"I ask you again. What's your name? Who you with?"

"Screw you both!" he hissed. "Next time we'll see who wins." He turned and left the store. Either he hadn't pumped gas or he decided it was a free gas day.

Watching him disappear though the door, I said, "Bet we get a match."

"If he's angry now," Angella said, "just wait until he finds the four flat tires. That'll make his day."

A mile down the road I said to Angella, "Send that picture you just took to Woody. See what she gets." The talk about pictures reminded me. "Have Woody forward you the pictures Joy sent. Also have her send them to the FBI for processing. They can call me for details of what I want."

A moment later Angella held up the screen of her phone. I read the message. RECEIVED NO PICTURES.

"I saw her send them! Shit! She played me for the fool! Should have taken her friggin' computer!" I exclaimed. "Get Tiny on the line!"

She speed dialed and handed me the phone. "I know you can't talk," I said when the big guy answered, "but listen. Joy Malcolm took pictures, there are six of them. Two guys on the beach the night the medic was killed. I'm pretty sure one of them was the victim. I believe the other is the perp. Pics are in her computer. Angella will give you Joy's condo address. Maybe take a jump drive or something with you. Get those pics, even if you have to take the whole damn computer!"

"On it," he snapped. "Put Angella on."

Angella didn't know the exact address but she did know the name of the condo.

"Unit 502," I called across to her. "Tell him ASAP!"

FORTY-SIX

We were getting close to Corpus Christi, located on North Padre Island about 200 miles due north of the Town of South Padre Island. But unlike SPI, Corpus is located on the mainland inside a sand barrier, while the town of SPI is on the barrier spit. I hadn't been here in over ten years, and the first thing I noticed was that several landmarks were gone. I suspected the demolition was the result of a hurricane, but could be just remodeling.

The phone rang. Tiny's name splashed onto the screen.

"She's not home," he announced, not bothering with a preamble. "Agents are posted."

"Screw the posting! Go in and get the computer! I'll deal with Joy."

"Need a warrant. We go in, those pictures will never get into a court room."

"Screw the court room. I just need to know who we got."

"Can't. Judge won't let you use anything you get. Poison fruit theory. You catch the perp based on those pictures, he could walk."

"Get the friggin warrant then. I saw the images. One guy was the dead medic. The other is either the murderer or a material witness. That should be grounds enough for the warrant."

"Take a few hours, but we'll get it."

Angella said, "Have him canvass everyone at the condo. Bunch of busybodies. Everyone pretends to mind their own business, but they pay more attention to the other guy than they do to their own spouse."

I started to relay her request, but Tiny cut me off. "Heard her. I'll have the locals do it. Ballistics came in on the medic. Powder burns suggest he was shot at close range. No shell recovery, but the bullet was found in the bulkhead. I understand there was very little distortion. Should be able to trace its origin."

"What do you make of this?" Angella asked me, when I handed the phone back to her. "Shooter collects the shell but leaves the bullet. A bit sloppy."

"Maybe. But maybe he had to get out of the boat."

"That means someone was coming? Or he thought someone was coming? In either event, we need to talk to everyone around."

"I'm sure they canvassed the area. When we get back we'll work the list."

"That's not consistent."

"What are you talking about?" Angella asked.

"From all indications, the medic was shot somewhere else—I'm thinking the beach—but the slug is found in the boat's bulkhead. Something's out of whack!"

A few minutes later, Angella announced. "Corpus is just a mile ahead. The motel is on the far end of town, set off by itself."

"You seem to know the place."

"Long story."

"Give me the short version."

"My husband…former husband…spent more than one night here. Not with me, I might add. Have the pictures to prove it. Enough said."

"Got it."

"Park here. Let's walk the rest of the way. No sense telegraphing our plays." Angella sure was a quick study. She was fully into detective mode, and this was only her second case that I knew about.

I followed her advice and we were walking up the sand-dusted road when my text message alarm sounded. The answer was back. Blue Buick was a Border Patrol Agent, name of Te Burner.

Bingo. A match with what Mark had found. So Mr. Burner was following us.

"Was he trying to find Tae-hyun through us?" Angella asked. "Or was he following us because he works for some agency—or someone—who wants to know where we are?"

"We'll just have to get our hands on Mr. Burner and find out."

FORTY-SEVEN

The only redeeming feature of the Plaza Inn was its room rate. Fifteen dollars, actually fifteen ninety-nine, a night. There were only two cars in the lot. The remainder were trucks, ten in all. All but one of them looked as though they belonged in front of a fifteen-dollar-a-night hot-sheet motel.

I walked over to the only vehicle with an intact paint job and knocked on the window. A sleepy-looking man rolled the window partially down.

I flashed my badge and said, "Mind telling me what you're doing here?"

The window went all the way down. The man, his eyes fully awake now, slowly reached his left hand under his jacket.

I tensed, ready to step to the side if he made a sudden movement. Angella, seeing me tense, flipped her jacket out of the way and put her hand on her holster.

In truth, if this man had bad intent, and if he was only partially good, one or both of us would be dead before we could get even one shot off. No amount of juking or jiving on my part would save me.

But instinct, borne of more than twenty-five years of doing this, told me that the man sitting in the late-model car was not bent on mischief. However, one of my partners, I think it had been Mark's father, had reminded me on more than one occasion that more cops than I care to count have died after making just such an assessment. But this guy had FBI written all over him.

My eyes never left his hand as it grasped something and brought it out. When the object broke free of the shadows it was too small to be a gun and too dull to be a knife.

I was still in danger, but my body involuntarily relaxed. He thrust his hand through the open window and held it so that I could read what he held. But that wasn't necessary. I already knew what it would say.

The only difference between what I held in my hand and what he held in his was the wording on the shield. His said, Department Of Justice Federal Bureau Of Investigation.

The door opened. I stepped back to allow him to join Angella and I on the weedy, cracked asphalt parking lot.

"I'm Jimmy Redstone. This is my partner Angella Martinez," I said, my hand extended in greeting. "And you're..."

"Special Agent Bromlee. I was told you two were on your way. Far as I know, he's still in there."

"What's that mean?" I demanded. "Is he, or isn't he?"

"I was told he was in there by the agent I replaced five hours ago. I left once, about an hour ago, to take a leak. Gone less than five minutes."

I wanted to ask him what the hell he was thinking, but thought better of it. Instead I said, "We'd better find out for ourselves."

"Where the hell can a Korean go?"

"You'd be surprised," Angella told him.

"How you propose we go about it?" Bromlee asked. A go-by-the-rules type of question.

"Knock on his door, that's how."

"What if he doesn't answer?"

"Break the door down," I replied, only half-kidding.

"Can't do..."

I was tired of these guys and their rulebook. "What room's he in?"

"Twenty-three."

I proceeded across the asphalt, paused briefly to listen for sounds coming from his room. We heard nothing. Angella ran around to the far side.

I knocked on the door.

Nothing.

I knocked harder.

Still nothing.

"Police," I called, "Open the door."

A moment later, when the door remained closed, I took a step back, lowered my shoulder, and slammed into the door.

The latched snapped loose and the door flew inward. I landed on the floor inside the room. Even before I hit the filthy carpet I knew the room was empty.

A moment later, Angella joined us, having found no window in the back. I said, "Gone. And judging from the time Agent Bromlee was off-site, I'd say he's been gone for about an hour."

"This guy is one slippery creature," Angella commented.

"He knew we were coming," I said. "He always seems to know where we are."

"Someone's feeding him information," Angella concluded.

"What do I say in my report about the broken door?" Bromlee asked. His pad out, ready to take down my statement. "Or about the illegal entry?"

"Hot pursuit works for me," I answered, not at all certain about the FBI's definition. But it sure fit mine.

"Hot pursuit!" the agent exclaimed. "It takes an active imagination to get there with these facts."

"Speaking of imagination, bet it takes a bit more creativity to explain your pee break and the loss of the target than it does about the B&E. I'll be interested to read what you come up with. I'll not comment when they ask me to review your report." Special Agent Bromlee stopped taking notes at that point.

Thirty minutes later I called Tiny after having interviewed the office clerk, as well as the motel patrons, all of whom professed to having seen nothing.

"Get back down here," he barked. "We can work on the murder while the FBI's looking for Tae-hyun. I'll have a copter ready for you. Get your asses over to the Coast Guard station. They patrol the shoreline regularly; should be a copter or a spotter plane available."

On the way to the station, Angella reminded me of our hijacking to Mexico. "Wasn't that ride initiated at Tiny's direction? Just asking."

"That time it was text traffic we followed. This time I heard his voice."

"Mexico is still Mexico," Angella replied, "regardless of how the message is received. Just saying."

\- - - - - -

Driving time to South Padre Island from Corpus is about three hours, give or take. It was exactly one hour and five minutes before we were aboard the copter. Because of heavy head winds and low-level turbulence, it took an hour and a half to cover the 180 or so air miles. By my calculation, the copter ride saved a total of between fifteen and thirty minutes. I don't know what the cost of the ride was, but I could visualize some clerk somewhere in the bowels of the government scratching his or her head wondering what the hell was going on. However, I wasn't so foolish as to think that anyone would approach General Jamison with the question.

I'll never get accustomed to spending money at that rate. In Texas the motto, at least of Contentus is: One riot, one Ranger. With the Feds it seems to be: Create a riot and then call the Rangers.

We stepped off the copter at the Coast Guard station, and Tiny was waiting with the news that a car had been stolen in Corpus a half-block from the *Plaza Inn* motel. "The owner had gone in for a six-pack and the car was moving down the street when he came out. Police have an APB out on it. You'd think they'd be able to find him in a few minutes. But they haven't. Probably went to ground immediately and ditched the car."

"Man's resourceful, no doubt about it. But he's heading somewhere and eventually he'll surface." Angella commented.

It was good to hear that Angella's optimism had returned. She asked Tiny, "Any luck with the canvassing of Joy's condo?"

"Nobody saw Joy leave. In fact, the only person who left the place was a delivery kid, some teen, works for *K's Jewelry & Beads*. Girl was delivering some home-made jewelry."

Angella said to me, "Mary, that's who owns *K's Jewelry*, runs the bead shop. People come in and pick out their own beads, stones, shells, that sort of stuff. They lay it out in the design they want and Mary puts it together. Great little place. I used to wear a bracelet I made there."

"Dead end,"Tiny replied.

"Maybe not," Angella replied. "Try the kid. Maybe she saw something."

Tiny nodded and placed the call.

- - - - - -

Once back to our rooms, Angella changed into a loose fitting tee, and it was clear Tiny was having difficulty keeping his eyes from her. Perhaps it was the stress lines that had formed on her face, making her look particularly vulnerable, but I felt the unmistakable yearnings of a male in heat. She was not wearing makeup and her skin, other than for the temporary stress marks, was perfection. I again renewed what I had known for a while. This was a woman I could become serious with. The feeling seemed mutual, but her behavior when the opportunity to do anything about it arose belied that conclusion.

We were all together in my room going over the files Tiny had brought with him. These appeared to be duplicates of the files I had received from Woody. I was still following my plan to check Woody's files against those produced by Tiny. We were going over them line by line and finding no discrepancies and nothing pertinent.

Two hours later, three things happened almost simultaneously. First, the kid working at Kay's, the only person seen leaving Joy's condo, turned out to be a sensational artist. The FBI report indicated she lived in Dallas and attended Booker T Washington High School for the Performing and Visual Arts. I knew the school to be one of the country's premier by-invitation-only public magnet high schools. The report, taken by an agent with the weird-looking name of McSlednehona, chronicled the fact that she had come down in the elevator with a tall, slender man carrying a computer. A sketch was attached to the report.

"Perfect likeness," I exclaimed, when the sketch finally appeared on my cell phone screen. It was a perfect match for Te Burner, the blue Buick Border Patrol agent who had followed us to Corpus.

"I agree," Angella said, excitement in her eyes. "That young lady nailed him!"

Tiny was already on his cell ordering Burner picked up. He also asked for a warrant to search Burner's house. Then he added, "Get agents over to his house. I don't want anything removed until we get the warrant. Find out where he hangs out and cover all possibilities. We want him and we want him now!"

No sooner had Tiny hung up than his cell buzzed again. He listened for a few minutes, then flipped the phone closed. "Stolen Corpus car's been found. In a shopping mall not more than five miles from where it was stolen. Police have canvassed every motel within walking distance and no Tae-hyun."

"Stole another car," Angella tossed out. "He's long gone from the area."

That was the second thing.

"Break time," Tiny announced. "I'm starved."

Angella suggested we call *D'Pizza Joint* and she volunteered to go pick them up. When she was gone, Tiny said, "A text came in while I was talking. Giving you a heads-up. Ballistics says the slug they dug out of the boat was a .45 caliber, fired from a PX4 Storm SD."

That was the weapon I was carrying, and I said as much to Tiny.

"And so is Angella," he added.

"You telling me something?"

"If the shoe fits...You're the detective. I'm a bodyguard. But she also was in the vicinity when Duran got hit. That's two for two."

"So were a lot of people. Including myself."

"What would you say if I told you a piece of jewelry belonging to Angella was found in Duran's garage?"

"I'd say you were full of shit! She doesn't wear jewelry."

"Didn't she tell us otherwise? Jewelry she made at *Kay's*," Tiny said, his jaw set hard. "Keep your wits about you, all's I'm saying."

The third shoe had dropped.

- - - - - -

The atmosphere in the room was somber when Angella returned with two large pizzas, one with sausage and one with double cheese, sausage and peppers. We sat in silence while we devoured the pizza. The disappointment had little to do with the pizza, which was excellent. It had to do with the fact that we were at a dead end, having found no discrepancies in the files. The good news, we had identified a possible suspect. The counterbalancing bad news—at least for me—was that Angella was in the mix.

I said to no one in particular, "We'll have a go at it in the morning. Maybe with fresh minds we'll see something we overlooked. Don't know about you two, but I'm calling it a day." It was now exactly twelve hours after we learned that Tae-hyun had vanished. The last time I had been in a bed, Angella had climbed in next to me.

I doubted if she was planning to do that again any time soon.

FORTY-EIGHT

In the morning, we reviewed the files once again and still found nothing. It is true that investigative work can be mind numbing, and it is particularly tedious when avenue after avenue ends in blind rat holes. But that's my job and that's the way it's done. When it pays off, the internal reward makes it more than worthwhile.

I asked Tiny to pull more files. He suggested we could trust Woody to do it for us, since she had not altered the files that she had already sent us. "That way, there will be less of a commotion; she knows how to finesse. My sources are not so subtle."

"Just get it done," I said. "Have her step down a notch in grade. We've looked at all the top ones. Also, what about *Her Highness*, Lucinda? She seems to have an inside track. And, you need to do Woody's yourself."

Angella had gone off to her room. When she returned, she asked, "Where to now, boss? I'm packed, what few things I have. Ready to move on."

I suggested we stay where we were until Tae-hyun came back on our radar.

Tiny, who was looking out of the window, announced, "We got company!"

I joined him and looked down. Sure enough, our friend in the blue Buick, Te Burner, was just climbing out of his car. He looked up, smiled, and started toward our building.

"Let him come," I said. "It's time we get to the bottom of who this guy is and what his angle is. Besides, we want him for questioning anyway." I positioned myself beside the door, gun drawn. I felt wobbly in the boot so I removed it and stood barefooted. Angella frowned when she saw what I had done, but took up a position in the bathroom without comment. She expertly positioned the door so that she could see through the hinge opening when the door opened. Tiny remained where he was.

We were ready for Mr. Buick.

Tiny's cell beeped, signifying a text message. He quickly read it and exclaimed, "Pay dirt! They got a hit on Igniter twenty minutes ago."

"Let's go," I said, reaching for my boot.

"Don't forget our visitor!" Tiny said.

Tiny was right. I had momentarily lost focus. In this line of work, that can be fatal.

A moment later, Tiny said, "Stand down!" Then he added, "Buickman just ran back out to his car. He must have access to my reports! Or the unit is bugged again. He's gone."

"Not so easy for him to get away. Angella, call the locals. Stop him at the bridge."

"No," Tiny said. "Let him run. We need to see where he's going. I'll get a car on him."

"Where's Tae-hyun?" I asked.

"The report came from Port Aransas."

"Port Aransas!" Angella exclaimed. "He's sticking close to the Gulf. Must be trying to meet up with someone."

"Or something," I added. "The fact that Mr. Buick bolted indicates that he lost Tae-hyun as well. He was following us, hoping we'd lead him to the target."

"So what's that about?" Tiny asked.

"Beats me. Why would Border Patrol be chasing him?" I responded.

"If it was official, I'd know about it," Tiny said.

"Rogue?" Angella injected. "Do we have his file yet?"

"Came in a few minutes ago. Can't see anything in it, other than the man seems to be a hothead. Here, see what you can make of it." He handed me the file.

I studied the file for fifteen minutes and had to agree with Tiny. Te Burner indeed had been disciplined and several letters were in his file detailing brutal treatment of immigrants. Apparently in his world that was not an overly bad thing to have done, so nothing of consequence happened to him. He hadn't even been passed over for promotion.

Then the fourth shoe dropped!

Contentus called. "Get yourself to a place where you can talk in private. And do it immediately!"

I stepped into the bathroom and closed the door. "Go," I said.

"Don't say anything, just listen," he snapped. "We got a problem. Ballistics matched the bullet from the boat to Angella's gun. We know she was on the dock about the right time. She says she was following Tae-hyun. SPI wants her held for questioning. Jewelry of hers was found in Duran's garage."

"She's being framed," I replied. "Evidence points to the murder being off the boat. No reason for the slug to be there."

"Maybe, maybe not," Contentus yielded. "I'll ask SPI to step down for a while. I'll tell them you'll keep her under surveillance. She can't leave the country. Can you manage that? Or should I allow them to step in?"

- - - - - -

A few minutes later we were in the car, destination Port Aransas. I had expected to be heading back to the Coast Guard station to catch the copter north. But when Tiny turned onto the bridge, I said, "What's with driving? Won't your friends fly us up the coast?"

He gave a sheepish look, then confessed, "Tried that. They're running low on budget. That's the official word. The real reason is your friend Captain Boyle said a three-hour drive would do you good. It's his way of reminding you he's still in command."

"Angella," I said, twisting to face her in the back seat, "I'm having second thoughts about chasing Tae-hyun. I'm for putting agents on him and following him that way. Might even be better since he somehow knows when we're getting close. When you repeat the same thing and get the same results, it's time to change your approach."

This wasn't the entire truth, and I felt a twist inside me when I said it. The fact that Angella was a suspect in a murder case and that I had been assigned to babysit her cut into me. I was positive she was innocent, but until that was proven, I had to abide by the rules set by Contentus. Just why I was still taking orders from my former boss, I didn't exactly understand, but this wasn't the time to question it.

"That was our original plan when we had the transponder put in him. We set out to let him run," Angella replied. "No reason to change now."

"I'm out-voted I see,"Tiny said. "I could use some breakfast, if that's alright with you. Angella, you live here. Name a good place."

"Seeing as though you are hungry, *Marchan's Restaurant* is the place. Sits back off the road next to a channel where the locals keep their boats. Get the shrimp omelet and even you'll have a hard time finishing it."

"Try me,"Tiny said. "Sounds like my kind of place. Then we can go back to the room and do the files one more time."

As I thought about it, it seemed to me Tiny yielded easier than I had anticipated. My conclusion: he was secretly relieved we were not chasing up north. If I had been told about the forensic findings, so had he. But the more I tossed it around, the more sure I was that the evidence had been a plant.

After we ordered, I asked Angella, "When was your weapon last discharged?"

"I've never fired it," she shot back, puzzled at the question. "Oh, I take that back. Sure I did. At the firing range. Why do you ask?"

"Curious is all."

"You're never just curious for the sake of being curious. Tell me what's troubling you."

"He's jealous,"Tiny injected.

"Jealous?"

"You kicked his butt on the range. He thinks you secretly practice."

"That's nonsense and you both know it."

"Now tell me—"

The waitress selected that moment to bring our breakfast. Angella had been right about the portion size. It was huge. But she was wrong if she believed Tiny couldn't polish it all off. He even had the waitress bring additional biscuits.

Tiny took one look and said, "Better bring me a second plate. This size is for kids." He never did respond to Angella's question, and she let it slide—at least for now.

Truth was, we both had fired our guns down there. I still had a vivid vision of her target with its near perfect hits arranged in tight clusters, first in the heart area, then in the forehead and then in each extremity. When I yelled 'eye', she nailed first the right eye followed closely by the left. The lady never seemed to miss what she had aimed at.

If Burner had been the killer, than in order to have obtained one of her bullets he would have had access to the shooting range. Seemed impossible.

Or, and this sent a shiver down my spine, Burner had an accomplice in a high place in D.C., possibly even at Homeland Security.

\- - - - - -

Mid-afternoon we were informed that Burner visited Tae-hyun for ten minutes at the motel in Port Aransas. Tae-hyun checked out a half-hour after Burner left his room. Tae-hyun was driving a stolen white late-model Honda Civic and was being followed from above by a spotter plane. The FBI agent at the motel had put a tracking device on Burner's car.

My cell phone rang.

It was Contentus. "Glad I caught you. Got a tip for you. Don't repeat this, just listen."

"Understood."

"The Igniter has taken a motel in Victoria. FBI is on the way."

"Roger," I replied, before I realized the line was dead.

Angella was busy studying information she had received on her phone. I hung up from Contentus and she announced, "I reviewed the latest medical reports. There's been a new cluster of sickness reported in Bexar County."

"San Antone!" I replied. "Suppose the bomb's there?"

"Makes sense," Angella answered.

If that were so, then logic suggested that Tae-hyun would be heading west toward San Antonio or maybe Austin. Instead, he holed up in Victoria slightly north of Corpus, and still near the Gulf of Mexico.

Tiny had spread a paper map of south Texas across the bed and was listening to reports of each man's location using a headphone connected to his cell. According to the black dots on the map, Tae-hyun was heading south on route 77 and was, in fact, coming back toward us. But Contentus had told me Tae-hyun was in Victoria. Something didn't add up.

"Where are you getting the information for those dots?" I asked Tiny.

"FBI coordinator."

"You sure they're accurate?"

Tiny looked at me as if I was an alien. "What's that supposed to mean?" he demanded, straightening himself to his full height. "You think I can't read a map? Or are you back to thinking I'm sabotaging the operation?"

"Just asking," I replied, puzzled by his sudden sensitivity. Perhaps it was the fact he was now towering over me, or perhaps it was the critical nature of the mission at this point, but I decided to let it play out. "I'm just confused is all because if our theory is right, he should be going toward San Antonio." There were only a few roads that could be used to go west, and Tae-hyun showed no sign of turning onto any of them.

I noted that Mr. Buick was heading north toward Victoria.

Following Tae-hyun's progress on Tiny's map was like listening to baseball on the radio. A lot of waiting, a burst of activity, followed by a lot of waiting. I loved listening to baseball, but when I did so I usually multi-tasked. That's what Angella and I were now doing; reviewing another big load of files while keeping an eye on the map.

At six-twenty Tiny announced, "Our man's in Brownsville. Border's been notified and he'll not slip across the bridge."

"With Burner's connections I wouldn't bet on it," I replied.

"I wouldn't bet on anything with this guy," Tiny replied. "FYI, Burner's been cut off in the system. He can't authorize a toilet flush."

None of this was making sense. Contentus had been quick to tell me Tae-hyun had gone to ground in Victoria, but hadn't yet called to tell me he was on the run. I wondered what game was being played and by whom. I called him and when he answered I said, "Tae-hyun's not in Victoria, he's in Brownsville. And just why are you involved anyway?"

"Nothing happens in Texas I don't know about. You think because the Feds are running this, my network's closed? Think again." As usual, when Contentus is finished, he's finished. My phone was again dead.

I looked over toward Angella and caught her dozing in her chair, her mouth slightly open. Seeing her, I thought of a conversation we had had in the hut in Mexico, late at night with the sounds of jungle frogs and other creatures screeching around us. It was clear she was probing to see how much of myself I was willing to reveal. "Why did your marriage break up?" She had begun. "You were married for over twenty years. What happened?"

I surprised even myself when I answered honestly. “I was teamed up with a woman partner. Before her I was known as a straight shooter, goody two-shoes kind of thing. The job was everything to me. Still is, actually. Always will be I suppose.” While I was talking, Angella’s expression remained steady. “We were on the fourth day of a stakeout deep in a wooded area, listening to drug dealers, recording their phone calls. She lay down in the back seat and took a nap. When she woke it was my turn. I moved to the back seat, but she didn’t leave. It was the first time I had ever cheated on my wife. Truthfully, I felt horrible and my partner knew it. We got drunk when the shift was over.”

“Is that how your wife found out?”

“Not really.”

“You can’t leave me hanging,” Angella had said, “So…”

“So, and this is classic stupid. We had gotten into it with the tape recorder on. Didn’t even think about it when the relief team arrived. One of them must have sent a copy to my wife. It was on the bed a month later with a note.”

“What did the note say?”

“Just a phone number. A divorce lawyer. The lawyer broke the news to me that I’d be moving out. Gave me a week to vacate, or the tape would go to my boss.”

“I’m sorry, Jimmy,” Angella said, touching me lightly on the arm, as if to console me.

“Serves me right. Now tell me about your divorce.”

“Same story, different woman. No tape. Pictures. It still hurts.”

Tiny’s voice broke into my daydreaming. He was giving the latest play-by-play development. Angella was now awake.

“He’s taken a room. Another dive. Actually, if I’m right, we’ll get a two-for. Buickman got to Victoria, pulled into a motel, waited a while and a few minutes ago turned around and is now heading south. Bet he ends up in the same place as Tae-hyun. Any takers?”

No one would bet against Tiny.

FORTY-NINE

Thirty minutes later we pulled into the Brownsville motel where Tae-hyun had taken a room.

Tiny made contact with a Secret Service colleague and all four of us took separate rooms. It most likely was the biggest night of the year for the motel, judging from its run down condition. Not even a paint job could help the place. A good dose of bulldozer was the appropriate remedy. "Sleep in your clothes," I told Angella, "or something might carry you away."

"Thanks, I needed that. Have to fumigate my jeans after tonight. Can we put in for hazardous duty pay?"

Tiny, catching only the end of the conversation and not realizing Angella's sense of humor, replied, "It's automatic. Any night spent in the field yields extra pay."

"A field would be better than this dump!" Angella responded. "Roaches are already living in my shoes."

"It's not that bad," Tiny said, mistakenly believing she needed calming. The nights I spent with Angella in Mexico were in much worse conditions than this and she handled herself remarkably well. She was one tough woman when the chips were down.

The progress reports on Burner proved Tiny right. He was indeed headed toward Brownsville with an ETA of two hours. We all adjourned to our respective rooms, with Orsen, the FBI agent, taking the first shift. Tiny was scheduled to follow. Then I was to be followed by Angella. Except, under my agreement with Contentus, I couldn't allow Angella to have her own shift. But I still didn't have a plan as to what I was going to do.

Three hours later, at the start ofTiny's shift, he tapped on my door. When I opened it, he said, "Burner's on the move."

I went to the window in time to catch a fleeting profile of the slender man walking from his room to the manager's cage.

I called Angella to be sure she was ready if we had to move out. "Any desire to pull the stems on his tires?" I asked.

"I wonder if he knows we're here?" she replied.

"I bet that's why he went to see the manager. Check on all this traffic."

Tiny joined me in my room. A few minutes later, Angella slipped in. "One big party. At least we know where he is."

Tiny, watching from my window, said, "Burner's on his way back to his room. Let's pay him a visit. Get this party moving."

Before I could respond, Tiny was outside, with Angella and Orsen on his heels. I didn't like the odds of a favorable outcome when five people, all licensed to carry guns, came together in a small room.

But, as they say, that wagon was already rolling.

A moment later, Tiny knocked on Burner's door. It opened and we all pushed inside, holding our badges in one hand with our other hands on our weapons.

Tiny announced, “Secret Service. Don’t reach for your weapon. We want to speak with you.”

“What the hell’s going on?” Burner, not one to be bullied, came on strong. “I’ll have you busted for this! You have no right to barge in on me.”

“Stop the bluster,” Tiny said. “We know who you are and who you work for. We shoot you, we’ll be national heroes before the media’s done with the story. You’ve been following Tae-hyun. I want to know who put you up to it?”

“I have nothing to say to you! Get out of my room!”

“We’re on the same team, my friend. Need you to cooperate before someone gets hurt in this mess.”

“I could ask you the same question. What are you doing here?”

This was going nowhere. “You make a good point,” I said, trying to ease the tension. “Who do you need to speak with in order to talk with us?”

“How about the President of the United States for starters, asshole?”

“You were doing fine, until the last part. I’m trying to do this the easy way. Best for you if you cooperate.”

“You want easy? Turn around and get your sorry ass the hell out of my room! That’ll be the easy way.”

My self-control was fading fast. “How about if I get General Jamison on the line? Will that work for you?”

“Who the hell’s that? I don’t answer to any General! Now get the fuck out of here!”

“Who do you answer to?”

“None of your friggin’ business!”

“I’m a federal investigator. I’m investigating Tae-hyun. That makes it my business—actually, the Government’s business.”

“Screw you!”

Tiny had enough. He grabbed Burner by the shoulder and spun him around. I don't know what Tiny's intention was, but Burner was having none of it. He reached for his weapon, which was tucked in his belt. It was halfway drawn before Orsen grabbed Burner's arm and twisted it far enough to cause the weapon to fall to the floor.

"Should have shot you, pull a gun on me like that!" Tiny said.

"I ever get the chance, I'll put a hole through your head sure as you're sitting here!" Burner snapped, his lips pulled back in a vicious snarl.

"That's enough," Orsen said. "You're under arrest for threatening the life of a federal agent." With that, the agent proceeded to cuff Burner. A search of his wallet confirmed what we already knew. He name was Te Burner and he did carry a Border Patrol shield.

"Well, Te," I asked one last time, "you want to tell us what your mission is? Maybe get the charges dropped? Or you going to continue being an asshole?"

"You assholes ever hear of the Fifth Amendment?"

"Why don't you just tell us about it?" Tiny replied.

I had not seen Tiny so animated in all the time we'd been working together.

"Stop harassing me, assholes!"

Tiny nodded to his colleague, and the agent, who was a big man, but not nearly as big as Tiny, pulled Te up off the bed where Tiny had pushed him. Angella held the door. Tiny said, "As you are well aware, if you try to escape, or cause us harm in any way, we're authorized to shoot. And shoot we will."

"You guys are really serious, aren't you?" Burner said on his way to the car, "How about we talk this over?"

"Talking time is long past," the agent replied. "Going for your weapon, threatening the life of a federal officer, changed all that.

You'll be lucky to get out of jail in time to collect your pension. You can make any deal you want with the Federal Attorney here in Brownsville. I happen to know him well. One tough son of a bitch—even if he happens to be my brother."

Angella turned to me when they were gone and asked, "You think Orsen's really the brother of the Federal Attorney?"

"I wouldn't bet against it."

"With Burner locked up we won't get any information," Angella lamented.

"Not really so," Tiny said. "When he learns he's being held for treason, which carries with it a possible death sentence, he'll talk. I'll brief Jamison and he'll talk to the Attorney General. Te's life is going to become complicated very soon."

"And while we were otherwise engaged with that knucklehead, who here thought to keep an eye on Tae-hyun?" I asked, realizing all too late that this whole thing with Buick Boy could have been staged to distract us.

Tiny went to his door and knocked.

No answer.

He knocked again.

Still no answer.

A third time without response.

I turned to Angella. "Check if there are any back windows. If so, guard them. In one minute we're going in."

"Hot pursuit?" she commented.

"That and President's orders. I trust he'll recall his conversation with me."

"He'll recall them all right," Tiny said, "but will he step up and acknowledge you? That's the money question."

The room proved to be empty. I should not have been surprised.

Tiny called the federal Marshal Service to watch the room in case he came back. Tae-hyun had ditched the stolen car and no car seemed to be missing. So he either took a cab or he walked. The manager had not seen a cab arrive.

A neighborhood search for him turned up nothing. Tiny was on the line to the local Secret Service detachment and FBI office. They canvassed cab companies, all to no avail.

"He stole another car," Angella said. "I'll bet on it. He did that on the island when we were chasing him. Grabbed a garbage truck."

"You think he's driving a garbage truck? I can have an APB put out for garbage trucks going north." Tiny's big grin told us he was putting Angella on. But he did get back on the phone, this time checking for cars reported stolen within a two-mile radius of the motel.

Within thirty minutes the report came back. A late model grey Honda Civic, license plate, Minnesota T23H3, was missing from a shopping center one block from the motel.

Tae-hyun liked Hondas.

FIFTY

When you are in Brownsville, Texas, unless you go south across the bridge to Mexico, which we were certain Tae-hyun had not done, there are only two directions you can go. North, or northwest. It would only be a matter of time until we found him. This time I was determined to take him into custody. I felt like a college kid on a scavenger hunt. Only, I wasn't certain I knew who was chasing whom—or even what the next clue was that we were supposed to find.

On the assumption that Tae-hyun would eventually head toward San Antonio, we started in that direction. Our destination, unless Tae-hyun was spotted, was to take a motel in Alice, halfway to San Antonio.

Angella once again checked the medical reports, and no new radiation symptoms had been reported.

That meant one of two things. Either the bomb was in or around the San Antonio/Austin area or it had been resealed and was no longer giving off radiation, so its movement could no longer be traced using the radiation reports.

I convinced myself that Tae-hyun now had the key and was on a mission to detonate the bomb.

Tiny believed he had yet to get the key, but that a new plan had been worked out as to how he was going to get it. "I'm basing my theory on the fact that he's not in much of a hurry to get to where he's going," Tiny remarked. "He's doesn't seem to be on a direct path. In fact, he's going in circles."

"Maybe he's meeting someone else. Or waiting for orders," Angella volunteered.

No one offered a theory as to how he was going to accomplish his mission, if and when he came into possession of the key. In fact, if the bomb was being held at an air base, how Tae-hyun planned to gain access to the base was beyond me.

We circulated his picture and description to every motel operator and gas station between Brownsville and San Antonio. We didn't expect it to take long before he was under surveillance again.

"If it was that easy," I commented, "there would be no pictures hanging in the post office."

- - - - -

It was the next morning when Tiny announced, "He's gone to ground, holed up at a motel about seventy miles from where we are now. We'll have a full team on him within twenty minutes. He's not going anywhere this time."

Our guess had been right. Tae-hyun was just south of San Antonio.

Angella, from the back seat, said, "This guy must be on juice; he never seems to sleep. He can't keep this up."

Angella was right, as it turns out. Tae-hyun didn't leave his motel room for two days, during which time we continued to have files of senior people brought in for us to review. A Secret Service team supplemented the FBI agents that had been assigned to guard the Korean around the clock.

Angella, after going through over two hundred files, commented, "These are mostly men. Who says a traitor needs to be male? Let's review the females as well. Tiny, can you get us files of top females? There's got to be something somewhere. This guy is being directed and his every move is being greased. Burner cannot possibly be doing this alone."

Tiny studied a text on his cell for a long while. Then looked up, "Speaking of that, our friend Burner has finally decided to save his ass. He began talking. His instructions were to distract us. He was assigned to prevent us from interfering with the free movement of the Korean."

"Where did the orders come from? Who issued them?"

"Down the chain of command, one to another. He's in Border Patrol, so it came down that chain. We've looked at all the files in that department and nothing jumps out."

"Let's review the files one more time," I said. "We're missing something."

"FBI and Secret Service experts have combed through those files,"Tiny reminded us. "They found nothing. Those folks don't usually miss anything."

"But we've narrowed the search. Burner is involved. We need to find connections to him. At least now we know what haystack we're looking in."

"What makes a traitor become a traitor?"

The question was asked by Angella. It stumped me. The more I thought about it the more I knew Angella was on the right track. I recalled reading years ago about Ted Hall, who had passed atomic secrets to the Soviets while working at Los Alamos. He defined his loyalty as being to the people and not to the government. He naively believed he was saving the people from stupid decisions his government was making and that's why he gave our secrets to the Russians.

Other people help the enemy because they don't see them as an enemy so much as having a different point of view. Some people do it for money, pure and simple. Still others because of fear of something.

I wanted to explore the fear angle, because I couldn't imagine a situation where I'd be so afraid of something I'd compromise my country. I said this to Angella. A few minutes later she asked, "But what if a loved one were under attack? Would you help them to the detriment of your country?"

"Would I let atomic bombs into this country if someone was threatening my son? The answer is no."

"Hate to say this, from what you've told me about your relationship, your son might be a bad example. What if you and your son were close?"

"I really doubt if I'd do it under any condition. Would you?"

Without hesitation, Angela replied, "I can't believe anything would make me do it." She returned the question. "If your wife was being held under a death threat, would you perform an illegal act?"

I thought about my conversation with Angella back in Mexico concerning Badman Tex. I could have brought him down without firing a bullet through his head. But he had killed a child, and he was scum. He was determined to kill others. I executed him, contrary to the oath I'd taken as a lawman. That certainly was illegal. "Don't know," I responded, thinking through various scenarios.

"For you to say you don't know is akin to others saying *yes*," Angella commented.

Something clicked. A piece of a thread was teetering on the edge of unraveling, but I wasn't yet capable of latching onto it. I kept thinking our connection to the leader is Burner. Why was it so hard to trace the thread upstream? And what about Homer Greenspar? That was Chief Duran's choice. Where did that lead?

"Let's assume for a moment it's Homer Greenspar," I said, trying to yank the thread end. "He was on scene in South Padre Island when we uncovered Tae-hyun. He didn't like it when Chief Duran raided his safe house. He had easy access to move Angella and I and drug dealer Santiago out of the country. And who better situated to coordinate the smuggling of Tae-hyun?"

Tiny looked at me, gauging how serious I was. "He's a long-time friend of General Jamison. You can't really believe he's involved."

"Everyone's suspect. He could be in league with Burner."

Angella gave me a look. "You're getting desperate."

Panic was more like it. Finding the traitor was going nowhere and I was certain we were being manipulated, puppets being led around. "Okay," I announced, "enough of this chasing in circles. Time to seize the momentum."

Tiny looked at me. "Okay, what's the new game plan?"

"Roll up the Korean. We'll do it when he's sleeping. Say midnight, one at the latest."

Tiny placed several calls. Fifteen minutes later he announced, "They'll have a full team here at midnight. Full armor, all out. Arrangements have been made at the Federal Detention Center. I say we get some shut-eye. Promises to be another long night."

"I'll vote for that," Angella, replied. "It'll be good to get him behind bars. This cat-and-mouse is going nowhere. And frankly, it's wearing me down. Is it always like this?"

"Not like this," I replied, "Especially since we seem to be the mouse." I didn't add, *And the cat's about to pounce on us.*

"You think we're in play as well?" Angella commented.

"They kidnapped us to Mexico. They want something from us. I just don't know what it is."

Tiny went off to his room and Angella sat finishing off a Newport. I said to her, "You seem to be taking to the investigator life well. You over your doubts?"

"Off and on. Is it always this way?"

"What way?"

"I don't know. Messy? Confusing? Mostly out of control."

"Never before been part of a large team, wouldn't know. As a Ranger, when I got assigned to a case, a ton of documents came with it. I'd ask lots of questions of lots of people trying to find a thread. Public corruption is just that way. It takes dog work for months, sometimes years, to root it out. Then it might take twice as long to get the necessary proof for a conviction. Sometimes we even knew who did it and what they did, but rounding up sufficient proof to please the lawyers was another thing all together."

"There's some of that here," Angella commented.

"There're too many players. The canvas stretches from here to Foggy Bottom. Even with a scorecard I can't tell the good guys from the bad."

"Burner can't be alone. He's got a D.C. counterpart. More than one, you suppose?"

"He's the field guy. Possibly he's working with someone down here who does the dirty work. Could be Greenspar, but

I doubt it. With his track record of violence, he doesn't require help. He's got someone coordinating from someplace where records can be manipulated and orders transmitted, all of which look authentic. Has to be someone with access to the inner workings of the system. Again, might be more than one somebody."

"As you said before, we've disrupted the timetable and they seem to be confused."

"I think the problem is that they're having trouble communicating with Tae-hyun. We keep him moving and they lose track of him."

"You think he's waiting for orders?"

"He knows what to do. Something's missing."

"For one thing, he doesn't know where the bomb is."

"That's assuming there's only one bomb," I said. "But even if he knows where it is, he's missing the key. We know he didn't have it when he was being detained. Maybe Burner gave it to him, but that supposes Burner had it."

"I'm thinking all this running round is because they can't locate the key," Angella said.

"Or they can't get Tae-hyun in position to get it."

"Maybe that's Jamison's plan," Angella continued. "It's our job to keep the pressure on. Didn't Chief Duran say that once? Disrupt their timing and we have a shot."

"You're getting good at this investigation stuff. Make a Ranger out of you yet."

"For what it's worth, you're a good teacher."

"We work well together. Good chemistry."

She drained the bottle and came over to the bed where I had propped myself. "Here, give me your leg," she said, sitting down next to me.

She proceeded to pull off the walking boot and toss it on the floor. Then she leaned close and kissed my forehead.

I tried to pull her head lower, but she slid from the bed saying, "The easiest thing in the world would be to climb in next to you."

"There's plenty of room."

"There's plenty of desire as well. But…it doesn't seem right. Not while we're on the case, anyway."

I didn't respond.

Angella said, "Don't look at me that way. You know what happened when you climbed in the backseat with your last female partner."

"I'm not married now."

"You never know when tapes will show up. Hell, we could be on Candid Camera right now for all we know." She kissed my cheek and whispered, "When we get together we'll do it right. Until then, keep your powder dry."

Before I could respond, Angella was across the room and had the door open.

She was right. And we both knew it.

A thought hit that I couldn't shake. Angella, or perhaps Tiny, had voiced it earlier. But with the rush of everything else I had dismissed the observation. If Tae-hyun was heading for the bomb, then why the deviation to Brownsville?

Timing. This was being timed. Or stalling. But for what purpose? I kicked that around for a while but fell asleep before I came to a resolution.

FIFTY-ONE

The knock on the door came at ten minutes to two. It was Tiny and it was show time. He was holding a vest and I reluctantly slipped it on, checked my Beretta and said, "Let's go."

I walked outside and was expecting to see federal marshals. But instead there was a full Immigration and Customs Enforcement team, with enough firepower to blow us all to the moon. There was also a stout woman in an ill-fitting suit standing off to the side. She didn't appear happy.

"What the hell is ICE doing here?" I demanded of Tiny. "I thought we were going to use marshals! ICE is part of the Department of Homeland Security, precisely where we're having the problems."

"This is what we have,"Tiny responded, not sounding pleased, but playing the good employee role. "This is what we use."

I wasn't happy, but there wasn't much I could do about it now. "Who's the Gestapo?"

"Federal Attorney. Mandatory for what we're doing. Too many civilians around."

"You expect trouble?"

"This is more down your line of work than mine. You tell me."

"Never know what to expect," I confessed. "Just serving a summons can be dangerous."

Angella wasn't present. It turns out Tiny, possibly based on the evidence they had against her, had decided not to wake her. I immediately went to her door and knocked.

Before she opened the door, the Commander gave the all-go signal and everyone went into action. I quickly told Angella what was going on. She frowned, but said nothing. The door closed and a moment later she was beside me ready to go.

But it was already too late. The Korean was on the ground in front of his room, his arms pinned behind him. No shots had been fired, in fact, no words had been spoken. These folks knew what they were doing. Either good training or lots of practice.

A search of Tae-hyun and his room turned up no weapons, no written instruction and no extra clothes. Most important, no key. The man traveled light—but most unsanitary.

I leaned down so I could look him directly in the eyes. He wore the same expression as the last few times I had seen him; a mixture of resignation and fright. But this time I saw something I hadn't seen before. A mocking expression, as if to say, *if you think this is over, you're a fool.*

The nagging feeling was back. We were being played, but I didn't understand the game.

He was gone before any of the other motel occupants even realized anything was going on.

The grumpy woman walked directly to where Angella and I were standing. "We need to talk," she announced, not bothering to introduce herself. "We can use your room."

She marched directly into Angella's room and waited for us to enter. Tiny tried to follow and she told him to get lost.

"Polite lady," Angella whispered, when she thought Miss Lawyer was out of range.

The lawyer turned abruptly toward us and barked, "You'd be out of sorts yourself getting dragged out of bed in the middle of the night! This could have waited 'til morning. But not you guys! You want it your way, on your time. Middle of the night macho bull crap. Don't give a damn for nobody!"

I had had about all I was going to take. I moved a step toward her and promptly winced from the pain in my ankle.

"You okay?" she asked, a smidgen of genuine concern in her voice.

"Nothing a few weeks off my feet wouldn't cure. You came in here to talk, so talk."

"My name is Brea McFaren," she replied, her tone noticeably more civil. "As you may have been told, I'm an Assistant U.S. Attorney assigned to San Antonio."

When neither of us responded, she continued, "And you're Angella Martinez and you're Jimmy Redstone." McFaren pointed to each of us in turn.

She didn't offer us her hand in greeting, so neither of us offered ours. This certainly wasn't starting off on the right foot. I had to assume she had better things to do than stand around chatting in a two-bit motel room at two-thirty in the morning.

"As you may have surmised, this is not a social call. Brownsville FBI is investigating a murder on SPI. Coast Guard medic." She consulted her notes. "You were both in the vicinity at the time of the murder. So was Tae-hyun. Now he's here and so are you two."

"And what have they found so far?"

"I'm here to ask the questions, not answer them. Can you both account for yourselves at the time the medic was shot?"

"Exactly what time was that?"

She again consulted her notes. "Between midnight and two in the morning, three days ago. That would be Tuesday of this week."

"You don't seriously think we—"

"Just answer the question. Where were you each?"

I looked her directly in the eye. "I'm not in the habit of keeping a log of my time, so I frankly don't know where I was when he died."

"And you, Ms. Martinez, where exactly were you?"

"I can't really be certain."

"So neither of you have any idea where you were. How convenient."

"I didn't say I didn't have any idea," I replied. "I certainly have *an idea*. I just have no intention of telling you."

"And you Ms. Martinez, do you have *an idea* of where you where?"

"Yes."

"And where would that have been?"

"Same answer," she said, pointing at me.

"So this is the way you want to play it?"

We both nodded.

She flipped open her notebook. "Please give me your addresses. Starting with you, Mr. Redstone."

I gave her the Arlington address. It's where I live when working in the District.

"And you, Ms. Martinez?"

"In the apartment also."

"You two live together?"

"We have separate bedrooms in a rental apartment."

McFaren raised an eyebrow, looked hard at Angella and asked, "Mind giving me the address?" She noted Angella's response in her notebook. "So it's your official statement that the two of you share the same apartment in Arlington, Virginia."

"Yes," we each replied.

"And I have it here that each of you maintain you own bedrooms in a common apartment. Is that accurate?"

"Listen, lady," I barked, "It's late! I'm tired and we don't appreciate games! The bloody apartment is being paid for by the government. Our sleeping arrangements are none of your business! You think we're trying to hide something, you're nuts. Now ask us what you want to ask us and get the hell out of here!"

"I will ignore your manner, Mr. Redstone, but for the record I don't appreciate being spoken to this way. I must say, however, that you appear overly sensitive about your sleeping arrangements. Personally, I don't giving a flying hoot what you two do behind closed doors. I'm just trying to establish for the record if you have alibis for each other or not."

"For the flipping record," I replied, "get your ass out of here! And do it now!"

She looked from me to Angella and back. "I believe I'm right in thinking this is not your room Mr. Redstone. So your rather impolite instruction to leave is of no effect."

"It's my room," Angella quickly added, "and I say the same as he does. Get the hell out of here!"

"I'm sorry this has deteriorated. You're both being uncooperative. I was hoping to avoid this, but I'll just have to serve this paper on both of you." She reached into her bag and produced a folded sheet of paper. She unfolded it and held it up so that we could both clearly see the seal of the Justice Department imprinted across the top. She handed it to me, "You will each note that this is directed to both of you. You are both ordered to appear at ten tomorrow morning at the Federal Building in San Antonio to answer questions under oath pertaining to your actions and activities with respect to the shooting that took place on South Padre Island at about three in the morning of November twenty-eighth. I must also caution you that you are both suspects in that murder and that if you don't appear a warrant will be issued for your arrest. Do I make myself clear?"

"Get the hell out of here!" I barked. "I don't know what game is being played, but we have nothing more to say."

"That remains to be seen, Mr. Redstone. But a word to the wise. There is evidence enough to hold you. We have a witness who places you, both of you, on the boat where the medic was found."

"What witness can you possibly have?" Angella asked, her face flushed with anger, her eyes darting back and forth between myself and McFaren.

McFaren thought for a long moment before she answered. Federal investigators are trained to ask questions and never volunteer information. In fact, federal law limits bidirectional discussions. But federal lawyers have wide discretion, and McFaren was obviously considering just how much discretion she would allow herself.

Finally, she looked at each of us, and in a much softer voice than she had been using said, "We have sworn testimony from Border Patrol Agent Te Burner stating that he personally witnessed your presence on the boat at the time of the murder."

"Payback time!" Angella responded.

From long experience on the other side of these interrogations I knew that the more we said the worse it would become. Burner had been arrested. McFaren knew that. She also knew that his statement was most likely false. So why the hostility?

"And just what do you mean by that statement, Ms. Martinez. Payback time?"

"Angella," I said, holding my hand up to stop her from saying any more than she already had, "I believe it would be better for us to visit with Ms. McFaren in the morning. This is not the place, nor the time, to be answering any more questions."

Angella remained quiet, prompting McFaren to ask, "Is that your position as well, Ms. Martinez?"

"That is my position as well," Angella wisely responded. "The morning will be soon enough."

"Okay, let the record show that you both refused to answer questions, even after being informed of the seriousness of the situation. In my book, that's interference with a criminal investigation."

I opened the door for her. "In my book that's bullshit! So just please leave, before this deteriorates even further."

"Is that a threat?"

"When I threaten someone, they know they're being threatened! I was just stating a fact."

"As you wish." She took a long moment to write some dissertation in her notebook. Then she marched out of the room without a further word.

"What day is that? The twenty-eighth I mean?"

Angella, after consulting her calendar, replied, "Sunday. I should remember that. That's the night you flew in late after your White House visit. You were with Lt. Garcia if I recall right, over at the hut where Tae-hyun had been holed up. I was following Tae-hyun. But I was on the dock. I heard nothing."

I dialed Tiny's cell. No answer. The call went to voice mail.

I tried again.

Same result.

I called his room. On the twenty-first ring I hung up.

On the way to my room I noticed our car was gone as well.

FIFTY-TWO

Brea McFaren had changed suits. At least this one didn't appear as though she had slept in it. This morning she wore a faint smile, a vast improvement from last night. She even offered to shake our hands in greeting.

But that was as far as the pleasantry went. Once we were in her office with the door closed, the badgering began anew. She had typed up our statements from the night before, meager as they were, and slipped them in front of us.

"If this is an accurate account of what was said, minus your nasty comments, I would ask you both to sign. Please remember that making a false statement in an investigation is a criminal offense."

I don't know if she was doing it on purpose, but I found her tone, as well as her content, demeaning. Even Angella was bristling. This was not going to go well, and I gathered myself for a siege.

There was nothing false in the statement. It contained our names, the time of the discussion, the address of our Arlington apartment and a brief summary of what had been said. The part about me asking her to leave or refusing to answer any questions had been omitted.

I signed my paper and Angella signed hers. This was all extremely foolish and more of a charade than I cared to be involved with. Time was of the essence. We needed to be done with this and get on to the business of interrogating Tae-hyun.

"Thank you both," McFaren said, still smiling pleasantly. "You do understand that if you don't actually reside in the Arlington apartment you are guilty of giving a false statement?"

Something was wrong. Her inflection was wrong. She already knew something we didn't. "What are you getting at?" I demanded. "There's a bee in your bonnet, and I want to know what's troubling you. We're law enforcement officers doing a job for..." I almost said the President, but thought better of it. "...for Homeland Security."

"I know who you are and who you work for. But you're not the only people investigating that Korean. And right now you two are in the eye of the storm. The medic who removed his transponder was murdered and there is evidence ...never mind that for now. Truth is, we've checked the lease records. The Arlington apartment is not leased to either of you. Does that surprise you?"

"Of course not," Angella responded, "We've subleased it from the owners for six months. Signed the papers last week."

"Not according to the owners. They were surprised to hear that anyone was living in their apartment. And to say the least, they were most upset."

"That's crazy!" Angella responded, red streaks working their way up her neck. "We signed a sub-lease. I have a copy."

"Can you please show it to me?"

"You think I carry a lease around with me? It's in the apartment."

"Afraid that's not accurate," McFaren said, her lips curling upward in satisfaction. "We've taken the liberty, with the permission of the owner I might add, to take a peek into the apartment. Didn't find a trace of anything belonging to either of you. No clothes, shoes, underwear, nothing."

"That's because we threw it all out!" Angella was angry now and even I was struggling for control.

"And just why would you do that?" McFaren pressed. "You threw out the lease as well?"

"I don't know what happened to the lease. But everything else was bugged!"

"Bugged? As in bedbugs and things?"

"No, you fool, like in microphones!" Angella exclaimed.

"I don't follow. Please elaborate. And for the record, this is all being recorded, so you might want to watch your language."

Angella proceeded to tell McFaren about the microphone strips stuck to our clothes. The more she talked, the deeper we were going. I tried to interrupt, but McFaren took charge. She warned me that if I wanted to remain in the room I'd have to allow Angella to tell her story her way.

McFaren again turned her attention to Angella. "And it's your position that a man named Tiny, real name, Kelvin Jurald, a man who works for the Secret Service, can vouch for all this."

Angella nodded her agreement.

"I want it on the record, Ms. Martinez. Nodding won't cut it."

Angella glanced at me. Seeing my approval, she said, "Tiny can vouch for everything we said. Is that clear enough for your record?"

I tossed Angella a glance, trying to warn her to be careful with her gratuitous comments.

"You know what you can do with your record, don't you?" Angella continued, not heeding my warning.

"Why don't you tell me?" McFaren said, baiting her. "I'm sure you're about to anyway."

"You can take that record of yours and—"

"Enough!" I interrupted. "Angella, think before you speak!" I had seen this all too often. At this point, we had no idea where all this would lead. But one thing I could bet on was that anything said would be used at a later time, perhaps in a different context. And it would never be used in our favor.

My partner glared at me. For a moment I thought she'd tear my face off. I had never seen Angella this angry. This was a side of her I didn't know existed.

I tossed around several options to end this, now worried that Angella would say something that we would later regret. But before I worked through the scenarios, Angella's remarkable ability to control herself came to the rescue. Under fire, the woman was as cool as anyone I had ever worked with. When I had lain near death in the South Padre Island marsh, she had held my neck closed with one hand and calmly directed the SEAL rescue operation with the cell phone in the other hand. For my part, I had mostly passed out. I would like to think it was from loss of blood. But a part of me knows I had given up.

Angella was saying, "…and…and take the record and do what you'd like with it. There's nothing in there that's not one hundred percent accurate."

McFaren waited to see if Angella would say more, giving her a chance to hang herself. But when Angella's cold-steel eyes bore into her, I knew she was back under control.

And so did McFaren. The attorney consulted a file on her desk making an exaggerated pretext of studying several pages. “Seems a lot of things have been traced back to this *Tiny* fellow. It also seems nothing ever checks out exactly right. I mean, Tiny always seems to be a dead end.” She flipped a few more pages and then studied us, her eyes going from Angella to me and back to Angella. “You know what else is strange here? Let me tell you. And I'm saying this as a friend.” She paused for effect and looked each of us in the eyes. “Your friend Tiny, real name Kevin Jurald, has been on medical leave from the Service for over a year. Man was badly injured in a training accident. Isn't expected back anytime soon.” McFaren made no attempt to hide her triumph. The bomb having been lobbed into the room, she now sat waiting to see the damage it had caused.

She got absolutely nothing from my partner. Angella remained stone cold. Not so much as an eye flutter. I made a note never to play poker with her.

Sensing she had met her match, McFaren asked, “So do you still want to use him as your alibi?”

“Something's wrong,” I said, stating the obvious. We were being recorded and anything we said would be damaging. The more we tried to explain, the worse it would get. “We've been assigned to work with Mr. Jurald. I have every reason to believe he is who is says he is.” In a feeble attempt to redirect to conversation, I said, “Have you checked us out? I mean with Homeland Security.”

“We're working that right now. When was the last time you were in your office?”

Actually, the last time for me was following the President's reception. I gave her that information, but withheld the part about my private conversation with the President. Then, reading

McFaren's face, I said, "You're about to tell me there's no record of me going into the building about nine, nine-thirty that night and meeting my secretary, Woody."

"Woody. That's a new name. What's his full name?"

"He's a her! Full name; Lisa Wood. Longtime employee of Homeland Security or whatever it was called before that."

McFaren dutifully punched her name into the computer. She studied the screen for a long while. Then she pressed some keys and her printer came alive. "There is an Alisa Woods. I suppose that could be Lisa. She's been with INS, seems forever. There's no record of her being assigned to you at Homeland Security. And there's no record of her being in *any* government building on the night in question." She paused for effect. "As you rightly guessed, there's no record of you being in any government building either."

"Who do you report to?" I asked, knowing this would now degenerate even further. We were clearly being set up by people with access to records at the highest level.

"I don't see the relevance of—"

"Listen to me, lady. As you most likely know, we are working on a national security matter. I must speak to the top person at Justice. How about the Attorney General for starters."

"You're delusional! I couldn't get to him if I tried. Need to go through command."

"Then do it. And do it now!"

"Mr. Redstone, I don't believe you understand the seriousness of the situation. You both are suspects in a murder investigation. Ms. Martinez is on record with a far-fetched conspiracy that people, unnamed people, are monitoring you by pasting microphones in your clothes. Also, a piece of her jewelry was found at another crime scene. A bullet fired from her gun was found at the murder scene of the Coast Guard medic. We have a sworn statement of an eyewitness who saw her on the dock at the time of the murder. Until this starts making sense, I'm not going upstairs with anything."

"Are we under arrest?" I asked.

"Not yet."

I stood to leave. "Then you have a choice. Arrest us or let us go."

"Don't force my hand, Mr. Redstone. I have enough to hold Ms. Martinez, and I'll play that card if I must. She's not leaving here until I say so. Sit down and behave."

I looked to Angella and while I knew she would follow me out the door, I also saw her expression saying, *sit down, play this hand*.

I studied McFaren a long moment. "I won't call your bluff," I said as I settled back into my chair, "but let's understand something. You're in the middle of a national security problem the likes of which you can't imagine. You can help us—actually help your country—or you can be a national goat. I suggest you work with us."

"You keep talking about national security, Mr. Redstone. How about letting me in on your little secrets."

"Turn the recorders off. Anything we say must be off the bloody record."

"Just a minute and I'll confer with my boss. Be right back."

This was not what I had expected. When you don't know the good guys from the bad it is impossible to navigate through the shoals. We were heading for the rocks and I felt helpless to correct course. Right now, disaster was on the close horizon. What I didn't yet know was the extent of the disaster.

FIFTY-THREE

We were alone in McFaren's office. Everything we said was being recorded. We were also most likely being video taped. I nodded to Angella to remain silent.

We waited.

And waited.

It was the better part of an hour before McFaren returned. With her came a well-dressed man in his early sixties. McFaren introduced him as J. B. Hastings, Jr., United States Attorney for the Western District of Texas, San Antonio division.

"Just call me JB," he said. His smile was spread across his face and his hand was out in greeting. A true country gentleman, or so he wanted us to believe. In Texas we had more than our fair share of 'ole country boys who could smile broadly while chopping off your hands and feet the instant your guard was down.

"I want to thank you both for dropping by," JB began, the smile spreading even fuller. "I hope you've been treated pleasantly enough. Brea has filled me in on your discussions of last night and this morning."

"I wouldn't exactly characterize our appearance here this morning as being on our favorites list," I answered, "but since we've been here, our needs have been met."

"I appreciate the kind words. Let me just say this. I've run some additional checks on your stories and it unfortunately appears that what you have told us simply doesn't match what we have verified. Mr. Redstone, you being a seasoned veteran and all, I don't have to draw a detailed picture for you. Suffice it to say, the two of you are standing in some mighty tall cotton. I've placed a call to Miss Woods. She's not called back as of yet. We have, however, confirmed from the official records that she's not assigned to either of you two."

"That's the problem," I responded. "Everything about our involvement in this case has been erased. Tell me this, do I hold the level of GS14 in Homeland Security or not?"

"Good question. Brea couldn't find it on the official chart. But I called a friend who confirmed it. That's why I'm here and you're not locked in the basement."

"Does Operation Domestic mean anything to you?" I asked, carefully watching his eyes for any brief recognition.

"Not a thing. Should it?"

He was lying. I had caught the faint eye movement. "If you don't already know," I said, "then I'm afraid you're not cleared to know. Let's get the Attorney General on the line. Or if you wish, General Maxwell Jamison, so we can get to the bottom of what's going on. Time's wasting."

"I'm afraid it doesn't work that way. We don't take orders from the military. You'll have to give me something tangible, something to persuade me to go up the line. Otherwise, we'll proceed the way we're going."

"We can't. But the President of the United States can. Get him on the line!"

That got his attention. "Care to tell us what might the President have to do with you and with this Operation Domestic?"

"Call him and ask."

"What the devil you talking about? I'll not be calling the White House. They'd have me put on crazy leave. Early retirement's all I'd get for my efforts."

I debated as to what to tell him and decided that I could at least tell him I was working for the President.

"And I suppose you're now going to tell me you met the President personally and he issued you orders." JB said, his tone one of dismissal. "Brea is right, you're delusional."

"Matter of fact," I said, "we did meet the President." I was sounding more foolish by the moment.

"I can easily check the logs. As you know, every visitor the President sees is logged in by the Secret Service. Our office has access to the log." He went to McFaren's computer, typed in long strings of data and waited for a response. In about a minute he came back around the desk. "Not surprising, Mr. Redstone, but there are no records of either of you meeting with the President in the past month. Care to elaborate further?"

I was not surprised they had no record, given the manner in which both visits occurred. "I was on the guest list this past Monday. Check that."

Again JB consulted the computer. In less than a minute he asked McFaren to show him a file. Finally, he said, "Now we may be getting somewhere. Indeed you were in the White House for a reception. Shows you came through the gate at seven-oh-five. You left at nine-twenty."

I looked to McFaren, who averted her eyes. "This is all bullshit and you both know it! Let's call the President and he'll verify us!"

"The President was in the apartment with you two?" McFaren asked, a smile again spreading across her face.

"Don't be obtuse! The only evidence you have of Angella being involved in the murder is a rogue Border Patrol Agent trying to save his butt! The man was arrested for threatening our lives. This is a set-up, and you know it as well as we do."

"We'll have none of that!" JB immediately shot back. All pretext of a smile gone. "There are major discrepancies in your story, and we plan to get to the bottom of this."

"Please arrange a private phone line. I need to make a few calls."

"We are not finished with our investigation, so if you are planning on leaving I'd suggest otherwise." JB said, his eyes now devoid of any pleasantry.

"I'm sure you're aware I'm a former Texas Ranger, so you know I understand the system. Lawyers try cases and investigators investigate. So I suppose what you need now is the FBI to investigate. You lawyers are not the right persons to, as you say, get to the bottom of this."

Now it was McFaren's turn to flush.

"In the normal situation you would be right," McFaren responded. "But in this situation we've been requested to detain you for further questioning."

"How about my one phone call? Courtesy to a fellow government employee, if you will," I replied.

"Listen, Redstone, you're not exactly an unknown to this office," JB said, his smile returning. "I know a bit about you. San Antone FBI office investigated the Badman Tex situation. I reviewed the report. If it were up to me I would have hung you out to dry. But now your cover is gone and I've got you in my sights."

I was on my feet moving toward him. Angella put her hand on my arm and pulled gently, but said nothing. The reminder that we were in this together did wonders. I stopped well short of his personal space. "Now that you got that off your chest, I hope you feel better. At least I know where I stand. Now I'd like to repeat my request for a phone call."

"Okay, Brea, let him use your phone. Be sure it's not being recorded." He looked to me. "You get one call." His grin returned. "Don't waste it on the White House switchboard."

McFaren reluctantly turned her computer off and followed JB out of her office. I called General Jamison, who was out and not available.

"What now, boss?" Angella asked. "Seems our cover's gone south."

My cell phone rang. It was Cindy McNaughton. "Where the hell are you?" she demanded. "I've not had any report from you in days! Gone silent. I don't like it."

"Hold on a moment," I said, "this is not a good time. We're being detained in San Antone by some Federal Attorney name of Hastings. Goes by JB. You know him?"

"I know *of* him. Straight shooter from what I hear."

"They believe Angella and I had some part in the death of the medic on SPI. As you must know, the medic removed the transponder from Tae-hyun."

"I understand Tae-hyun's back in custody. Being held in San Antonio. Is that what you're doing down there?"

"We're being detained at the orders of someone, don't know who. I need someone to tell JB to free us immediately."

"Put him on the line."

"He's not here. Hold a moment." I asked Angella to see if she could find Brea and JB.

"There're out here," she announced when she opened the office door. "Didn't go far."

I handed the phone to JB, who made a questioning face, but put his ear to the receiver. After a while he hung up.

"Well," I said.

"Well," he answered. "I don't take orders from a retired General's paramour. You'll remain with us until we sort this mess out." He turned to leave.

"I need to interrogate Tae-hyun, the Korean, you brought in last night," I called after him. "It's critical that I speak with him. If you won't let me leave I must call the President immediately!"

"You are indeed deranged! I'd be insane to allow you to harass the President. Even if I let you go, which I'm not prepared to do, you couldn't speak with that Korean."

"And just why not?"

"ICE brought him in under Border Patrol custody. Was transferred to Lackland Air Force Base for safekeeping."

FIFTY-FOUR

JB took his leave and his underling McFaren now seemed to be going through the motions, primarily, it seemed, as a way to detain us. Since Tae-hyun was secured, the immediate pressure was off the bomb hunt. Now the treason investigation took center stage.

I played along for a while, harboring the hope she'd allow something to slip that we could use to jump start what seemed to be a dead end. The behavior here in San Antonio was bizarre, and I wanted to know just who the maestro was.

On the theory that no one was exempt, I wondered if McNaughton had really told JB to free us. Perhaps she herself had issued the order for further detention. That would certainly be a game changer.

The cast of suspects was going in the wrong direction, expanding and not contracting. No wonder the President was concerned. It was more than just the prospect of an atomic bomb going off in his backyard. That was catastrophic. But political animals being what they are, to compound the nation's worst disaster with the fact that it was orchestrated by a person he personally selected would be politically devastating.

And where was Tiny in all this? In fact, who was Tiny? Had he actually given us the right file information to review? If Tiny was in league with the traitor, we had no chance.

McFaren was doing a masterful job of not imparting any useful information, and I was at the end of my patience. In response to a question pertaining to the circumstances under which I first met Angella, I'd had enough. I barked, "You're fishing! This has all been well documented by General Jamison, and I must assume it's all in that blasted computer of yours."

"I appreciate your frustration, Mr. Redstone," McFaren repeated for perhaps the fifth time. Her smile was also practiced, appearing this time exactly as it had the last time I protested. "I am investigating a crime after all. Your continued cooperation is very much appreciated."

"Cooperation is hereby over!" I announced. "I don't know if Angella concurs or not, but for me, I'm finished." I stood and walked toward the closed office door. "I'm not answering another question and I'm not remaining in this building another minute. We have work to do."

I opened the door and held it for Angella. She passed in front of me and was in the outer office when McFaren called, "Not so fast, Ms. Martinez. I must insist you remain here. Mr. Redstone is free, for the moment, to leave if he wishes. But I must ask you to remain."

Angella's anger flared and her face flushed. She spun around and loud enough for people in the hallway to hear, exclaimed, "You're harassing me! You have no reason to detain me!" Her voice cracked with emotion. "This is pure bull shit!"

McFaren was ready for Angella's barrage. "I'm afraid you can't leave. I am placing you under arrest."

At that instant, apparently responding to a signal McFaren had sent, two marshals appeared. One of them snapped a handcuff around Angella's right wrist. The other took up a position several feet away, his hand on his holster. The first one said, "Please slowly remove your weapon, and hand it to me."

Angella glanced in my direction. I nodded and she did as she had been told. For Angella's sake, that outcome was infinitely better than if she had tried to draw on him.

After she handed him the Beretta, he twisted her arm behind her and snapped the cuffs on her left wrist.

"Get your hands off me!" Angella demanded. "Don't touch me!"

The marshal replied, "Please calm down, Ma'm. You're under arrest. Resistance on your part will be dealt with severely."

"What the hell's this about?" Angella demanded, directing her attention to McFaren, who had remained behind her desk.

I said, "Let's all go back into Brea's office and get to the bottom of this." I couldn't imagine this scene transpiring without Cindy McNaughton's blessing. Certainly JB knew what was going down. But nothing made sense.

"Jimmy, for God sakes do something!" Angella pleaded. "Why am I under arrest?"

I turned to face McFaren, who had come out from behind her desk to meet us at the door. "Ms. Martinez, you have been placed under arrest at the request of the South Padre Island police for the murder of Chief William Duran." She held a paper in her hand. "I have the Warrant right here."

It is fundamental that a murder charge implies that the victim is dead. Angella gasped and tried to free her hands when the import of what McFaren had just said hit her. The marshals on either side of her misinterpreted her movements and leaped to restrain her.

The air had been sucked from the room. A wave of dizziness swept over me as well. I felt as if I was helpless as in a dream. I wanted to hit the reset button, to start the program over.

But it was not a dream. Nor was it a computer game.

Angella was sobbing. "Oh, my God, he's dead! His poor family! I can't believe it! The Chief's dead!"

McFaren impassively said, "You have the right to remain silent and anything you say or do can and will be used against you. At this point I will ask no further questions of you. I will address myself to Mr. Redstone. Ms. Martinez, if you wish to remain in the room, that is your choice freely made. Otherwise, I'll have the marshals take you down to the processing center. What is your wish?"

"Remain here," Angella murmured, unable to form the words properly.

"Duly noted," McFaren commented. "You can sit in that chair and I'll ask the marshals to step back. Please keep in mind you are under arrest. Do not make sudden moves."

I struggled to regain control of myself, fighting a losing battle. But this battle was not only for myself, it was for my partner. I had to get control of myself. Turning to McFaren, I asked, "When did Chief Duran pass?"

"About two hours ago."

"I thought he was recovering," I stupidly said, working to gain equilibrium.

"He had a set-back this morning. Before he died he called Angella's name and repeated the word *home* several times."

My mind began to focus. "So what is the evidence against Angella? Surely not because he called her name."

"That and the fact that Angella was in his garage at the time of the shooting. Evidence points to the fact he knew the killer, expected the killer to be there. His deathbed comments link her further. As I said earlier, jewelry of hers was found at the scene."

Angella started to respond but I cut her off. "That's bullshit evidence!" I exploded. "You know it'll never hold up! You won't get an indictment with the shit you got."

"Hey, take it easy. I'm only the messenger in this arrest. We're acting as a courtesy to the SPI police. This is not our jurisdiction. Unfortunately for Angella, you're neither the judge nor the jury, Mr. Redstone." She glanced at papers on her desk. "And, for the record, they have more than what I've given you."

"And what is that?"

"As I told you before, she is linked to the scene of the boat killing. Enough said on that topic. In fact, Mr. Redstone, there's evidence you're a co-conspirator, so I'll say nothing more to you about the facts. You're free to leave. Angella will be taken to processing and is scheduled to go before the magistrate in the morning. She'll be spending the night with us."

If ever I wanted to cold-cock someone it was now. But that would serve no useful purpose other than to send me to the processing center along with Angella. But the idea was tempting. One thing I knew from my years as a Ranger is that it took a special kind of psychopath to premeditatedly kill a police officer. Nothing, and I mean nothing, catches the attention of every law enforcement officer in the world quicker than a shooting under these circumstances. Another thing I was absolutely certain of: Angella was not a psychopath. The more I worked this over, the more heated I became.

McFaren, apparently reading my mind—or my eyes—retreated behind her desk.

I stood helpless as Angella was escorted out of the office. The depth of pain radiating from her seared into me so deeply that I couldn't even manage a decent goodbye. Nothing I could have said would have lessened her agony—or mine.

FIFTY-FIVE

"There's nothing I can do at this moment, Jimmy," Contentus said, trying to console me the best he could. The Texas Rangers had automatically been called to investigate when Chief Duran was shot. "Look, I can't go into details with you because of your involvement with Angella. But the time-line we developed did put her in the vicinity of Duran at the approximate time he was shot. There is also some evidence that her initial meeting with you when Nelson was found on the beach with his neck cut was not a pure accident."

"What are you talking about? You know damn well Angella didn't shoot Duran! She could no more pull that trigger than I..."

"Don't go there! My point is simply that from the very beginning she might have, and I emphasize *might have*, been told to get close to you."

"But you and I both know it wasn't her," I protested.

I was unnerved by the hesitation before he replied. "It's not important what you and I know—or think we know. This is a murder investigation, I grant you that. But because of the national security implications the Feds have taken over jurisdiction. My hands are officially tied."

"The Feds? McFaren told me the SPI Police made the arrest!"

"Not exactly right. SPI wants to question her, certainly. But the Feds took control. This is being run from Brownsville."

The Brownsville office had federal jurisdiction over the SPI murders, but only if they were related to federal crimes. I said to Contentus, "The Feds tried to take over when Nelson was found dead back when this whole thing started," I said, pleading for understanding. "You ignored them then; that's how I got involved. Ignore them now."

"I can't get into it with you what we're doing and not doing. But keep in mind you met Angella through Duran. You don't know anything about his involvement—or lack of involvement—in the smuggling operation and you don't know anything about Angella's either for that matter. This thing's a wild fig!"

His reference to wild fig implied a deep root, such as the 400-foot root of a Wild Fig tree someplace in Africa. "That's bullshit! If it wasn't for her we wouldn't have captured the Korean in the first place!"

"Look, Jimmy, you did a magnificent job of investigating to track down how they were planning to bring the bomb ashore and how it was going to be transported. We allowed you to intercept it, with Angella's help. She may have saved your life, but you did the detective work, not her. You put the pieces together. She saved your life—but we don't really know her motive."

What Contentus was saying, from an investigative standpoint, was accurate. But there is more than hard facts involved in solving crimes. One thing I know is that Angella is neither a traitor to her country nor a murderer. But, and this hurt to even think about, for all we really knew Duran was into this up to his badge.

I changed the subject away from Angella because this line was going nowhere. "What if Duran was killed because he knew too much? Maybe he figured out who was behind all this? Then what?"

"Then we have another ball game. That's what I'm concentrating on now."

"Pardon me for asking, but I thought you were out of this investigation. What gives?"

"Let's just say, where there's a Ranger involved, I'm involved. Leave it at that."

I'm the only Ranger involved. Angella never was. Was I the next one to fall? A thought struck. "And what if, just what if, the whole idea is to isolate me? One way to do it is to remove Angella. Another is to remove any evidence I ever spoke with the President. Without that, I have no credibility. There is no record of me going to the oval office. The only proof I can think of is the fact that Duran and you were present. Duran is gone."

"Are you suggesting my life's in danger?"

"Just keep open the possibility."

"Jamison was there as well."

I then told him about my conversation with General Jamison's unofficial second in command, Cindy. "On the surface, she was supportive, but she could have been the one to instruct JB to hold us. Clearly, someone high up wants us out of the way."

"JB's got a stinger under his saddle for you as it is. Ever since the Badman…"

"He told me as much."

"I'll bet my life on Jamison," Contentus shot back, "but you could be right about his lady friend. But why?"

"Why is what *we're* about," I needlessly reminded Contentus. "I need a good lawyer for Angella. Any suggestions?"

"I'll ask around. Should have that for you in a few hours." After a brief silence, he added, "I would be remiss if I didn't at least caution you to approach Angella with your training, not your heart."

"Duly noted," I replied, without adding that I had no intention of following his advice.

I have spent most of my adult life investigating situations, maybe not as critical as this, but every bit as complicated, and doing it essentially alone, or at most with a single partner. I've never been a real team guy. I've put in tedious months running down dead-ends without ever once thinking how lonely a life it was. But the thought of not having Angella was debilitating. Actually, it was more than that. I trusted her with my life, and that was more than I could say for anyone else I was working with on this assignment.

I called Woody. It was time I started rounding up the pieces. I was surprised to find her answering the phone. She assured me she was listed in the database as my secretary and offered to send me the link so I could see for myself. I declined, knowing I was no match for her technical abilities with the system.

I called Tiny and he answered on the first ring. Before I could say anything, he said, "What the hell's going down with Angella? I tried to work some magic to spring her, but got it rammed up my butt! Haven't taken heat like that for years. Cheeks are still smoldering! What gives?"

"You tell me!" I shot back, frustration taking command. I had to vent on someone and Tiny was certainly the right person. "You're the guy left us high and dry. You tell me what's going down?"

"What's that supposed to mean?" Not a trace of joviality remained in his voice.

"Just like what it sounds! She's under arrest for murdering her old boss. It's pure bullshit! When we told them to check with you at Secret Service we were told you were on medical leave and had been for months. What gives?"

"How the hell should I know? I'm here. Never been on medical leave. Someone got their wires crossed."

"Someone got their wires crossed all right! Just who that someone is remains a mystery—for now! How the hell am I to do my job when I can't trust anyone?"

"Either trust me or quit! Simple as that. You call it either way."

I had no intention of quitting. That's what this was about. Forcing me to go away. Angella was the pawn in that game. "Where are you?"

"Not far from you. I got out of there when that McFaren character came after you guys. She's trouble and I had the files. They get onto the fact that we have the files in our possession outside of a secure building then we have more trouble on our hands."

I had an idea. "I'll call you back in a few minutes."

I called Contentus. Before I could say a word, he said, "Call from a pay phone."

It's surprising how few pay phones there are any more. But thankfully there still are some at the Federal building. "What's this all about?" I asked Contentus five minutes later.

"Turn off your cell and remove the battery."

Contentus doesn't play games and to my knowledge hadn't lost his mind. I did as instructed. "Done," I announced. "What gives?"

"All that running up and down highway 77 to Corpus, to Port Aransas, to Brownsville got me thinking."

"Timing," I interrupted. "They're timing something."

"Partially. But remember I called you and told you Tae-hyun was in Victoria?"

"You were wrong about that as I recall."

"It was a plant. I was testing out a theory. Your cell is compromised."

"Shit!"

"Worse than that. That's what the *timing* is about. They've lost something. Actually, I think they lost both the bomb and the key."

"Jamison took possession of the bomb smuggled in by Tae-hyun," I said. "I don't know about the key."

"Jamison can't have the bomb. He's considered military. Under some 1950s law, all atomic material must be civilian owned and controlled."

"I'm not following."

"I won't get into the specifics, but suffice it to say, the bomb must be delivered to a civilian facility and the military cannot keep possession of it."

"Is that why they didn't fly it directly to Guantanamo?"

"I'm guessing that's the reason. But Gitmo is a political mess, so there may be other reasons."

"So where is it?" I asked, knowing full well that if Contentus knew he would have already told me. I was also concerned that political considerations could be jeopardizing the lives of millions of people.

"Somewhere in Texas. I can't get the exact information, but I'm working on it. Because the military is not allowed to have the WMD, it follows they are not keeping open records."

"Why Texas?"

"Because the civilian facility where these things are maintained is in Texas, that's why."

"Do you know who's at the other end of my tapped phone?" At first I was going to throw it away. But perhaps a better plan was to use it for bait.

"Not exactly."

"Am I right in thinking I'm to keep the phone to feed them false information?"

"You got it! I don't know if it transmits all the time or just when you're live on the line. So assume the worse. If you keep the battery out I think you'll be safe. But if you do that, they will catch on."

"So you want me to walk around as if I'm bugged."

"Take the battery out when you need to, but otherwise yes. Assume you're wearing a wire."

"Just what agency am I working for? State or Federal?"

"Let's just think lend-lease."

"Angella?"

"SPI terminated her."

"What's going on with her?"

"She's now bait."

"Elaborate, please."

"The jewelry, as far as I can tell, was a plant. So was the slug from the boat."

"You certain about the slug?" I was pleased to hear the news, but I wanted to hear for myself what the supporting evidence was.

"Fragments of a target were imbedded in the tip. The fragments, I should add, matched the material used in the Homeland Security target range. Conclusive, I'd say."

"Shit! She's being framed by someone with access to our offices, everything."

"You need to work on your vocabulary," Contentus responded, "especially when you turn the phone back on."

"That is the toned-down version. Want the rest?"

Ignoring me, Contentus said, "We'll get her out of jail, but not before we allow it to play a bit longer. You, Redstone, have to play this as though you don't know about the bullet forensics."

"So why'd you tell me?"

"Because you're acting abilities exceed your anger management abilities. I don't want you shooting anybody."

"Thanks for the vote of confidence. How about setting up an appointment with the top FBI person in San Antone?"

"I'll do better than that," he responded, "I'll get it set up from the Director himself so there'll be no misunderstanding. What is that operation code again?"

"Operation Domestic."

Contentus called back in twenty minutes on my again active cell and gave me the name and address. "He's waiting for you. Name's Sylvan Jacobs. Special FBI Agent. One of the best there is. Man's on the fast track. Knows everyone. I've had the pleasure of working with him on several matters over the years and he's a straight-shooter. Books no bull from anyone. But I warn you, he's a no-nonsense guy. The Director gave him the green light and briefed him. Good luck."

I called Tiny back and told him about Jacobs.

"Good move. I've heard of the guy. At least we'll get it straight."

FIFTY-SIX

An hour later, Tiny and I were in Jacobs' sparse office in the Federal building two floors below where we had been earlier in the day with Brea and JB. His office was neat, as if he had just moved in. A picture of his wife and two children sat on his otherwise clean desk. Not a file was in sight.

"I know why you're here, Mr. Redstone," Jacobs began when the door closed. He was an imposing man, over six-five, but appeared small next to Tiny. "But tell me why Mr. Jurald's with you?"

"He's Secret Service and was assigned to me by General Jamison. I believe you know the good General."

"I do. Go on."

"Tiny, that's what Jurald goes by, is Secret Service working with me. But when I told JB and Brea about Tiny and explained he could verify my status and whereabouts, they checked and found he was on medical leave."

"So, you brought him here so I could verify who he really is. Am I understanding you correctly?"

"That's right." I had to admit, Jacobs was quick witted. Note to self: Don't underestimate the man.

Jacobs turned to Tiny. "I reviewed the files they compiled on Martinez and Redstone, and I must say the situation is confusing, at best. Mind if we do a fingerprint test? Clear this up in an instant."

It's funny how I hadn't even thought to ask Tiny for his prints. The basics sometimes get overlooked. I studied Tiny to see what his response would be. But without hesitation, he said, "Go for it. We need to get this under control and the sooner the better." The guy was cool under fire. I suppose that is why he works for the agency tasked with keeping the President alive.

Jacobs stepped out of the office for a moment and then returned. "It'll be a few minutes before the technician gets here, so let's continue and see where this all leads. While we're waiting, I must tell you, Mr. Redstone, the file on Angella doesn't look good for her. But there are some major discrepancies, all in her favor. I know you hired the best lawyer in the city, but frankly, that's a waste of time in this situation. There's a National Security Alert on her. She's not eligible for bail. In fact, she's being held as an enemy combatant, a terrorist, if you will. There won't even be a hearing for several days—if then."

"You can't do that!" I exploded. "She's an American, not some Foreign National! She has rights!"

"You're yelling at the wrong person. I investigate; the U.S. Attorney brings the charges. Go up two floors and yell at them. Now calm down or get out of here. Do I make myself clear?"

"Regardless, she has rights!" I said, defiant, but in a softer voice.

"Not when an NSA is issued. Her civil liberties have been suspended for the time being."

The lab tech knocked and came into the room. He opened a small bag and pulled out a device the size of a cell phone. He flipped a switch and a small glass screen took on a green tint. "Place your fingers on the finger outlines," he said to Tiny, pointing to images that had formed on the screen.

Tiny looked from me to Jacobs. For an instant I thought he was going to bolt from the room. He kept his hands in his lap and Jacobs finally said, "Well, Mr. Jurald, don't keep us waiting."

"There's something you should know," he began, his hands still in his lap. Then he stopped talking.

"We're waiting, Mr. Jurald," Jacobs repeated, this time a flash of anger creeping into his tone. "This is a simple matter. Let's get on with it."

Tiny slowly raised his right hand, studied the green glass and carefully placed his fingers on the outlines. As soon as the tips touched the glass he yanked them back.

The technician said, "Good. That registered." He waited about fifteen seconds and then held the device up so that he could read the display. Satisfied, he laid the small machine on the desk in front of Jacobs.

"I can see what's troubling you, Sir," Jacobs said, his face revealing nothing. "You are not with the Secret Service at all. Am I correct?"

My stomach muscles tightened as if to say, "Here we go again."

Jacobs waived the tech from the room. When the door closed behind him, Jacobs continued, "In fact, your name is not Jurald is it?"

"No it's not," Tiny confessed.

"Your name is Emerson Sommers."

"That's correct."

"Mr. Sommers, please inform Mr. Redstone as to your proper employer. I'm sure he's anxious to know."

"Central Intelligence Agency. Sorry, Jimmy, but CIA is not permitted to investigate internally. It was thought wise to not tell you my real identity. This of course is a terrorist operation and, as you know full well, the President is very much concerned that someone at the top, perhaps even in the Secret Service, is working for a foreign power. So I was asked to head up the investigation. I requested you so that we could watch internal as well as external."

Jacobs looked from Tiny to me and back again. "Gentlemen, I think this is best resolved with me out of the room. Please excuse me. Be back in ten."

While he was gone, I said to Tiny, "I feel duped and a fool. A puppet dancing on a string! You could have leveled with us."

"It's illegal. CIA is forbidden to work internal investigations. Now that you know you could have the honor of joining me in prison. We need to finish the operation. We need to find out who's manipulating this and end it once and for all."

"I take it then that this has happened before."

"Not so serious, but yes."

"Then why not just take the bomb out to sea and set it off? Or deactivate it? Or bury it on the sea floor?"

"Two reasons. It's illegal for the military to have possession of atomic weapons without strict controls and civilian oversight. For now, I believe, they're claiming Jamison is civilian, since he's retired. Attorney General is having a bird. Second, there are more rogue bombs out there. Maybe not in this country right now, but around. We need to find the top guy and stop this. Or it will happen again. Next time we may not be so lucky. These people learn from their mistakes."

"We have Burner. That puts a crimp in their plans."

"Only temporary. FBI got a warrant and searched his apartment. Not much, but they did find a cell phone registered in Angella's name. One message was on it. Outgoing. **Key in my bag.** May be other messages, but if there were any, they've been erased. Lab is checking."

"Who was the message sent to?"

"That's the crazy part. To Burner."

"Burner? He sent it to himself?"

"It's more planted evidence. Only he didn't get a chance to plant the phone. It all ties in with what they have on Angella."

What Tiny didn't say was that it could have actually been Angella's.

Before I could inquire further, Jacobs returned. Tiny immediately asked, "Am I properly verified?"

It hadn't crossed my mind that Jacobs had left us to check on Tiny. I might be losing it.

"The CIA Director personally vouched for you. Says you're the best there is. Tells me you're on assignment and doing exactly what you are supposed to be doing. That's good enough for me. Now where do we go?"

"Two things we need to do," Tiny replied. "One, find the traitor. Two, be damned certain Tae-hyun does not get anywhere near the bomb."

"Doesn't he need the detonator key?" I asked. "He seemed to be hanging onto it for dear life when we caught him the first time."

"Don't know for certain," Tiny answered, resigned to play the hand we had been dealt. "We studied the original specifications, and there was a way to rewire it to bypass the key. Don't have any way of knowing if the Koreans changed that, or if Tae-hyun had been taught how. We are suspecting not, but you never know. Also, more than one detonator may have been smuggled in. Maybe the bomb has a code? But truth is, the detonator key, the one he originally had with him, is missing. I think that's why they hijacked him to Mexico. To find out where the key was hidden. They thought he was to meet someone to get it—or to get a new one. What we know is that he had it, then lost it."

I was slow! I suppose that's what happened when you get distracted. I turned to Tiny. "Do you know where the bomb is? Our original thought from the radiation sickness patterns was that it was in this vicinity, somewhere around San Antone."

"You're not going to like this."

"Try me," I said with more bravado than I felt.

"It's at Lackland."

At first I thought Tiny had said Lackland to get a rise out of me. But he was serious. I could see it in his face.

"That's where the Border Patrol, under INS instructions, took Tae-hyun!" I was putting two and two together and for once in my life I hoped it didn't make four.

"How do you know that's where it is?" I asked. "The bomb I mean. Contentus…I thought that information is top secret."

"Intercepted a message to our friend Burner."

"So, exactly when were you going to tell me?"

"Wasn't important until Tae-hyun was taken there."

"Everything's important!" I barked.

Jacobs leaned forward, his large hands flat on his desk. "Now that you have my full attention, what can the FBI do to help? Tiny, please bear in mind I do not have a Top Secret clearance."

I responded. "For starters, we need to find out who Burner is and where he's been. Who hired him? That sort of thing. He didn't just make up that eye-witness report. He was instructed to do it."

"FBI's already working that. Anything else?"

"Check out the background of our secretary, Lisa Woods. The woman's been around the block. I don't trust her." I didn't add the fact that she had given me my cell phone and had access to Angella's accounts as well.

"I got a list going. That it?"

"JB. Too many of the things he looked up didn't come out right. He's up to something."

"I can't investigate a U.S. Attorney without high up approval. You willing to go upstairs? I mean to the Attorney General."

Something Angella—or Tiny—had noted earlier triggered a thought. We were here because Tae-hyun detoured. That detour may not have been random. Someone with high level connections wanted us here. "Talking to the Attorney General could tip them off," I said. "Can you just check to see if he has any connections to Jamison? Or to Homer Greenspar at INS, or to Burner?"

"Who is Homer Greenspar?" Jacobs asked.

"INS, Assistant Deputy. He was on SPI and got into it with Chief Duran on several occasions. He was in Duran's face when we raided a safe house. That's where we first found Tae-hyun."

"I can do simple background checks. Routine stuff. The list is still open."

"Get Angella out of jail!"

"After I got off the phone with you," Tiny injected, "my magic started coming back. Release can be arranged. But it comes with a caution—and a promise. The caution is she could be working for the enemy. The promise is that you'll prevent her from sabotaging the operation. And you will not tell her I'm CIA."

"And you'd get her released? Why?"

"The same reason you released Tae-hyun. Let her run. She won't get out of the country."

I pretended to think it over just so I wouldn't appear desperate.

I didn't fool either of them when I said, "I promise."

FIFTY-SEVEN

It took the remainder of the day and most of the next before Tiny's *magic* could work through the system. Apparently, the signatures of the Director of National Intelligence, Tiny's ultimate boss, as well as the Attorney General, were required before JB Hastings reluctantly signed. During the process, Hastings had made himself scarce, requiring Sylvan Jacobs to track him to his farm in northeast Texas, over two hundred miles from his office in San Antonio.

Angella was tense, drained of color, her mouth a tight line, when the marshals brought her upstairs to Jacobs' office. I threw my arms around her and pulled her close. She didn't resist, but she remained rigid, her lips seemingly frozen together. Her hair smelled of urine and her clothes were a mess.

Tiny, returning from the men's room, took one look. "Prison life doesn't suit you, young lady."

"So look who's here," she snapped, exhaustion yielding to anger. "Nice to see you looking so well! Glad you could make the reunion."

"He's on our side," I commented. "They had it wrong. There's more here—"

"That's not all they have wrong! They refused to allow me a single call! Have you lined up a lawyer? I'm being framed!"

"Got it under control," I said, not very convincingly. "We'll fill you in later. Let's get out of here. Too many snoops around. And besides, you need something fresh to wear—and a long hot shower."

- - - - - -

In the car, I said, "Tiny worked his magic to get you released. SPI withdrew their request, and for now the Feds have stepped down. Let's just say they're willing to wait for more evidence before they make their next move."

"That's all nonsense!" she said, her face again animated. "I did nothing! I'll fight them!"

"And lose. At least for now. It's stacked against you. You've been labeled a terrorist and God help you if they move forward. You essentially have no rights."

"They can't—"

"Not only can they, but they did," I replied. "Only the fact that we were assigned to this by the President is allowing you to walk free this moment."

We drove in silence for a few miles. Then I said, "We have work to do. Any preference where we stop to get you something to wear?"

"Nordstrom. Macy's. Hell, even Wal-Mart. I don't care. I stink!"

It was well after dark when we found a decent motel and got checked in.

"Give me an hour, gentlemen, and I'll be good as new," Angella said, struggling to be upbeat. "I'm starving, so let's go treat ourselves."

There was an upscale steak house across the street. We agreed to meet there in one hour.

As it turns out, I was the last to arrive at the table. Tiny and Angella were in an animated conversation. Angella's eyes were sparkling and her mouth was turned upward in a wide-open smile. After the ordeal she had gone through, she was surprisingly chipper. I felt awkward. To be honest—jealous.

I had no reason to be jealous of Tiny; he was, after all, a married man. But was he? The only thing I could verify about him was that he was CIA, going under an assumed identity. The way he looked at Angella I doubted if he was married. And if he was married he didn't seem to care. From my limited experience with the CIA, nothing was what it seemed. Your best friend could be CIA and you'd never even know.

Their conversation wound down when I approached. "Hey, I didn't mean to disturb you two. I'll take another table if you prefer."

"Don't be silly," Angella said, a bit too quickly. "We were waiting for you before we ordered. But we did get started on the Merlot. On an empty stomach no less."

"I'm sorry to be late. Contentus called to fill me in. Actually, he called to give us a heads-up. JB is furious we went over his head to spring Angella. Apparently, that stirred up an internal fuss at the highest levels. He's gunning for me."

"Turf wars go on all the time," Tiny commented, draining his glass. "Let it roll."

I had the waiter get me a Bones. He refilled Tiny's glass and Angella held her hand over the top of hers. I ordered my steak rare and Angella followed suit. Tiny asked for the Texas cut, twenty-four ounces of meat medium-well.

"You'll need a table by yourself just to hold the cow," I quipped.

"Can't help it if I worked up an appetite. A pitcher of beer will help to wash it down."

Tiny, aided by the beer, then proceeded to tell stories about his life in Paris and India and I overlaid what he was saying onto a CIA persona. In that context, his adventures took on a different meaning, one that I could not share with Angella.

After dinner we went back to Tiny's room and began laying out a plan of attack. Tiny took the assignment of tracking down all he could find on the Korean, all in keeping to the spirit of the law that prevents CIA from investigating American citizens within the country.

I was assigned to concentrate on the files and ferreting out the traitor. And Angella, because of her special personal interest in the outcome, was asked to gather everything she could on the death of Chief Duran.

Our FBI contact, Sylvan Jacobs, left word on my cell that Te Burner, our blue Buick Border Patrol nemesis, is no longer in custody and is thought to be in or near San Antonio. Jacobs guessed Burner was continuing with his assignment to disrupt us and warned me to be on the alert. The message ended with the ominous warning, "He's known to have a mean streak. Been disciplined twice for abuse of illegal aliens."

"Can we take him into custody again?" Angella asked. "Catch him jay walking or something?"

"Not a chance," I answered. "See how fast he got out. Someone is working the system. He's free to come after us—or whatever his mission is. Until we catch him doing something illegal, I'm afraid that horse will have free rein. Speeding tickets won't cut it."

"If he's true to form, he'll find us before we find him," Tiny added. "Most likely when we least expect it. Sleep with your weapons handy."

Just what we needed.

FIFTY-EIGHT

I awoke to what I thought was my cell phone alarm, but it was Jacobs calling. He had beaten my alarm by an hour. "Early riser," he explained. "You got my message I assume about Burner. Watch out for that guy. I'd put a tail on him, but he's too good and it would tip him off that you've got cover. We'll watch from afar, but you'll have to take care of yourself."

"Warned should be enough," I replied. "Thanks."

"Another piece of information. The background check on JB is sterile as I expected it to be. I've worked with him for years. He's good. But here's the interesting part. His father served in the same Air Force unit as did a very young Homer Greenspar. They were based at Tan Son Nhut in the late sixties."

"How did you track that so fast?"

"Sometimes you get lucky. JB holds a Top Secret security clearance, allows him to work on national security cases. That means the FBI checked him out from birth. We personally interviewed his mother and father, as well as a hell of a lot of other folks. Father was justifiably proud of his service to the country. Showed our investigator a picture of himself with Homer. Father was serving his third tour in the capacity of a trainer. Homer, a new guy, was a star. They were each holding up three fingers. Homer had shot down three MIGs."

"So Homer Greenspar is a war veteran?"

"Ace. The guy is fearless. You take care, and I'll check back later."

It was six-thirty in the morning, but I felt like I had only slept an hour. I tried to get back to sleep, but instead tossed and turned trying to get comfortable. A million thoughts raced around, nothing holding long enough to make sense. I tend to work in patterns, but this time I simply had a bunch of loose ends. The only pattern I could force was one of a spiral. On reflection, it was a death spiral.

At seven, I climbed into the shower and came out a while later to answer the phone. How long it had been ringing I don't know. An extremely agitated Angella greeted me and asked me to come to her room as soon as possible. She had been trying to reach both Tiny and myself. So far, Tiny had not responded. She refused to tell me what the problem was, perhaps because of our negative experience with tapped communications.

I pulled on a pair of jeans and the new Texas sweatshirt I picked up when we went shopping yesterday. She greeted me wearing jogging shorts and a tight-fitting top with long sleeves. She was visibly shaking.

"What happened?" I asked, eyeing the bed behind her where her purse sat open, surrounded with what appeared to be its contents. To call it a purse is a misnomer. It's actually very small, and she keeps it strapped to her belt.

"I did a dumb thing," she replied. "Went for a jog and when I came back my room had been tossed."

"Anything missing?" We had been traveling light, so I couldn't imagine what anybody would want.

"I think it was done by someone who wanted me to know they had been here. Could be Burner. Everything in the room was thrown around. A few tops, a couple pairs of jeans, sneakers, underwear. A few things in the bathroom knocked over."

"And your purse," I added. "Anything missing?"

"I think nothing. But when I was released from custody yesterday they handed me a printed inventory. It's in the car, in the back seat."

"Let's check the list against what's here," I suggested. I started for the door.

"Don't bother. Tiny's not here and neither is the car. Guy disappears at the most inopportune moments. He's spooky."

I wanted to tell Angella how close to the truth she had hit, but wisely held my tongue. I dialed his cell and while I was waiting for him to answer, Angella said, "I've called several times. No answer."

I hung up and a moment later my cell rang. It was Tiny. "What's up? I see you and Angella have been calling."

"Someone broke in and tossed her room. Where the hell are you? And when will you be back?"

"I can be there in twenty, just finishing up here."

"Make it ten." Taking a page from Jamison and Contentus, I hung up. I turned to Angella, "While we're waiting, let's check with the office. Maybe someone saw something."

"Not likely, but we've nothing better to do."

Angella was right, no one saw anything. But luck was working for us. The surveillance camera had caught a blue Buick pull in at six-twelve. No one got out of the car until Angella was seen walking out to the street at six-thirty-five. The man in the car then waited five minutes until six-forty. He then went into her room and was back in his car and gone by six-forty-three.

"Three minutes and I feel totally violated," Angella said. "At least we have a positive ID on him."

"That's the least of our problems. You're right, that mess he made was deliberate. Burner's calling card. He'll be back."

"I'll shoot his nuts off he comes near me."

"Speaking of guns, is yours safe?"

"I had it with me. Jogging with a Beretta is not my idea of proper dress code, but I'm taking no chances 'til this thing is settled."

"Good plan."

"What's a good plan?" Tiny asked, coming through the door.

"Forgot how to knock?"

Ignoring my remark, he said, "What's going on?"

He remained silent while I filled him in. One thing about Tiny, he listens well and absorbs facts faster than anyone I'd ever worked with.

When I finished, he said, "I'll get the surveillance tape. That'll come in handy when we get our hands on Burner."

While Tiny was gone I retrieved the inventory list from the car. It was exactly where Angella said it would be.

We checked off each item as we put it back into her purse. When we were finished, one item remained unchecked. A locker key.

"A locker key?" I asked, puzzled. "A locker key?"

"I have no locker. What the hell's a locker key doing in my purse?"

"Maybe it's not a locker key. Maybe it's a house key? A car key? Some other key?"

"Those keys are all on my car key chain, which is right here." Angella retrieved a key chain from the bed and counted out the keys to show me they were all in place. No extras, none missing.

"So he took a locker key you didn't know you had. That makes no sense."

"What makes no sense?" Tiny said, coming back into the room.

"If you'd stay in one place long enough, we wouldn't have to repeat things twice," Angella answered, only half kidding.

Angella told him about the missing locker key. He immediately grabbed his cell and placed a call.

"Who are you calling now?" I asked, trying to keep up with the man.

"Sylvan Jacobs."

Angella's face took on a puzzled expression. "Who's Sylvan Jacobs?"

"If you'd stay out of jail, you wouldn't have to ask," Tiny replied, smiling broadly. "Anyway, procedure calls for them to photograph everything that was inventoried. Jacobs has access to the pictures and can text them over here."

I was impressed with Tiny even if he always seemed to be going the wrong way. Perhaps, that's just how spooks operated. While we waited, I filled Angella in on Jacobs.

In ten minutes Tiny had the inventory pictures on his phone.

Angella's eyes went wide. "Oh, shit!" she exclaimed. "You'll never believe this! Remember when I disabled the boat in the marsh when we caught Tae-hyun?"

"You took the spark plug, if I recall."

"Before I thought of the plug, this key was in Tae-hyun's hand. I figured it was the ignition key to the boat. I grabbed it from him and threw it in my bag."

"Tae-hyun had been holding it?" I exclaimed. "It wasn't around his neck?"

"He had it clutched in his hand."

"And you took it from him?"

"Yes."

The air came out of me. It was as if I had taken a blow to the stomach. Tiny looked sharply at both of us, his eyes boring in on Angella. He said nothing.

I suffered a second blow, but this one felt like it landed on my chin. I had just recalled the cell phone that had been found in Te Burner's crib. The outgoing message had said something to the effect that the key was in her bag. Coincidence? I don't believe in coincidences any more than I believe in Santa Claus. However, as between the two, I'd put my money on the jovial fat man.

Angella had not yet realized how bad this all was for her. Possession of that key in and of itself was grounds for her arrest. Coupled with whatever evidence there was pertaining to the murders of Chief Duran and the medic, if the key proved to be the missing igniter key, Angella would be lucky to get off with a life sentence.

Treason—as well as murder—are both punishable by the death penalty.

FIFTY-NINE

"I simply didn't remember it was there," Angella pleaded. "When I took it from him I thought it was the boat ignition key, nothing more."

"Even so, it was evidence from a crime scene. You had to log it," I said, struggling, but failing, to find a decent rationalization.

"You were bleeding to death, for God's sake! When they evacuated you out of the marsh I thought you'd not live to make it to the hospital." Tears filled her eyes. "You think I was focused on a boat ignition key? I was trying to hold it together, suck it up as they say. You can't imagine. Everything was happening so fast! SEALS were coming out of the sky. Coast Guard emptied three landing craft right next to where I was standing. Men with assault weapons poured in from every direction while a massive medevac helicopter hovered directly over my head. It was chaos! My God, it seemed like half the United States military had invaded! I was worried sick, thinking you had died. They air-lifted you out of there, and that gave me hope you'd live. The last thing I was worrying about was a stupid boat key!"

I remained silent, digesting it all. Picturing what she had been through. I had read the reports and I did have to admit that Jamison had spared nothing. They indeed had come from land, sea and air.

"Can't you believe me?" Her eyes begged for acceptance.

I knew what she was going gone through. I had once lost a partner in the line of duty. He died in my arms and all I could think of at the time was putting a bullet through the perp's brain. I know it's wrong, but it's what sometimes happens. Wearing a badge doesn't make you less human-—it just gives you more responsibilities. Sometimes you fall short.

"I understand," I replied, "what you went through. But you need to log in everything. It's always chaotic, but you need to focus on the job."

Tiny sat passive, listening. From my meager knowledge of CIA operatives, I supposed he had seen this play out many times in the past. And I certainly wasn't naive enough to think the CIA always played by the rules. Yet, his duty was to find the traitor, and he would remain focused on the end game at all costs. Following his heart was not the proven method. He followed the facts.

"I was focused on you! My job was to save your life! I did nothing wrong. A boat key. That's what it was. A damn boat key! And you're not supporting me! I can't believe this!"

Angella fell silent and I waited for Tiny to take the lead. He looked to me. "You're in charge of the internal-traitor portion of this operation," he said, backing away from confrontation with Angella. "It's your call."

Angella, not catching the subtlety of what Tiny had said about the division of responsibility, continued to plead her case. "I understand how this looks. But if it means anything, I could no more turn against the United States than I could shoot my own mother. You, of all people, must understand that. We're partners after all."

"I know that Angella," I consoled, "but truth is, there's too much going against you at the moment. I'm willing to meet you half way. I want your ammunition. You keep the weapon. If we get into a jam, I'll feed you what you need. Promise me not to load with live ammo without my permission."

"That can get me killed. That what you want?"

"Of course not. I'm sorry about this, but you can drop out of this investigation if you wish. Go on admin leave. Nobody would fault you if you did. Might not be a bad idea."

"I'm in this all the way!" she snapped, not backing away. Her eyes burned into me with a mixture of hatred and contempt. "I'm not a quitter! I'm being framed and you know it! If you won't help me clear my name then I'll do it alone!"

I wanted to take her in my arms and tell her everything would be all right. Instead I said, "I'm sorry, Angella, but I don't see any other way from here."

She abruptly turned, walked across the room and retrieved her gun. Coming back toward the bed, she held the gun at her side. From what I had observed, and from Tiny had said about her abilities, we were both now vulnerable.

I trusted her, maybe foolishly, to do the right thing. I couldn't see what Tiny was doing, but I didn't sense any tension in him.

Angella continued toward us. She slowly raised the Beretta over the bed and with a flick of her finger released the magazine, allowing it to fall onto the bed.

My heart sunk, but I knew this had to be the way. Contentus had told me about the traces of target on the bullet, but truth is,

I hadn't seen the report myself. I would turn my attention to the medic investigation in due course. Particularly, if he had been killed somewhere else, the slug in the boat would mean nothing.

Tiny, watching from across the small room, said, "Okay, let's move on. I've determined Tae-hyun was born in Vietnam in 1970 of a Korean mother."

"Korean mother in Vietnam. What about the father?"

"No father listed. That doesn't mean anything. The records in those days in that part of the world were miserable. I've checked with a few folks who were there at that time, and their best guess is that the mother was, let us say, working the troops. In the late sixties and early seventies it was wild over there. And that's an understatement. Kapish?"

Angella slumped into a chair, her head in her hands. After a while she looked over to us and said, "Would it be okay if I went back to the island? I could work on my piece of the puzzle from there. That's what I'm investigating anyway, bring me closer to the evidence."

I thought about the pros and cons. I could get Contentus to assign someone to watch her for me. But I rejected that idea. Making up my mind, I said, "If Tiny has no objections, neither do I."

Tiny nodded his agreement.

Angella immediately retrieved her cell and booked a flight. "Mind dropping me at the airport, plane leaves at noon?" Her voice was flat. The fight had gone out of her. I hoped that was only temporary.

The short ride to the airport was made in silence. I hated to have her go. She had been rock solid as a partner—and as a friend. She refused our offer to go inside with her, so I stood beside the car waiting for her to slip out of the back seat.

At first she refused to look at me. I put my hand on her shoulder. "Angella, I want you to know this is as hard on me as it is on you."

She pushed my hand away. "How the hell can you know what I'm feeing? No one's accusing you of being a murderer. A murderer and a traitor to the country I love! You think you know what I'm feeling! I'm leaving because you have no trust in me. I've as much invested in this investigation as you have, and this is the thanks I get! You're as bad as they are! You're all shits!"

She stormed into the airport and I wondered if I would ever see her again as a free woman. I hated myself for thinking such a thought. But there it was, front and center. Trouble was, I knew she was being framed, and yet...

Back in the car, Tiny said, "I'm surprised you didn't lift her passport."

"She's not going anywhere. Angella is solid. That's not our main concern at this point. I think this is payback from Lt. Malone down on the island. Never did get her first name."

"Carrie. Carrie Malone. Not a bad person if you get to know her."

"And just how..."

"Snooping around while you guys were off chasing up to Corpus. She knows Angella and knows she didn't do it. But you got in her face and she's got a burr under her saddle. Anyway, I put a watch on Angella's travel. We'll be notified of her movements."

"Do you really believe she's a threat?"

"Someone is. In my experience, anyone can do anything at any time. In the field, life expectancy goes down dramatically when you relax that rule. Countless agents have died following their hearts instead of their minds. Kapish?"

"Sometimes in my line of work the most difficult crimes are solved with instinct."

"Maybe that works for traditional criminal activity. But terrorism is a political act, practiced by fanatics. Politics is not often rational. They don't adhere to human nature. There's nothing to justify them taking their own lives. Yet they do it all the time. Instincts are useless against them."

"But some things you know to be right, and I tell you, Angella is a good kid."

"Do good kids shoot like she does? That woman is highly trained. Question is; by whom? What you saw on the firing range is the tip. She's even more deadly than that."

"How do you know about her scores?"

"It's my job to know everything there is to know about both of you. How the hell you think I stay alive doing what I do? Your friend was trained by the best. FBI is covering that angle."

"So why did you spring her?"

"See where it takes us. Shit, she already let them have the detonator key. My guess, her part is finished. She's delivered! Unless…"

"Unless what?" I demanded.

"You can fill in the *unless* as well as I can."

"So you don't believe her story?"

"It's not important what I believe. She was separated from you in Mexico, wasn't she? Could have picked up the key then. That could explain the little excursion you two took. They know our every move. She was in the vicinity of two key deaths. You're the one who keeps getting hurt. Her wound was superficial. Need I go on?"

"I don't…"

"Neither of us knows anything for sure. Don't even know for certain if that was the detonator key. Could all be coincidence."

"Declaring her a terrorist and keeping her from a lawyer was certainly not right. They go that route, they'll hang her."

"Fairness!" Tiny said, sucking in a deep breath. "Our Constitution is designed to protect its citizens from Government's normal tendency to act heavy handed. It was never conceived to protect people who don't want civil liberties, who don't believe in them, who hate the very notion of freedom. Fairness, whatever that means, is not a concept even remotely applicable to terrorists who want to destroy our very fabric." He took a deep breath. "Sorry, pardon the rant. Let's get on with our work."

The passion Tiny displayed was actually refreshing. I gained a new respect for the man. "I'm convinced this is being orchestrated from the INS. Too many roads lead in that direction. We know about Burner. But Homer Greenspar's name also keeps popping up. I've studied his file carefully. Nothing!"

Tiny remained quiet for a while. When he next spoke, it was with a quiet resolution. "When we're back at the motel, let's do it again. Something's bothering me and I can't place it. This all takes a top operator. Someone highly trained. You can't be inside this deep and hold amateur status."

"I'm hungry. You mind if we stop for lunch? We can review the files then."

Tiny pulled into the next shopping plaza. He spotted a place called *Original Taj*. "I'm up for Indian if you are."

And that's where we were when a major breakthrough came. As it turns out, it played to our advantage not to have been at the motel. We found out later, our rooms had again been compromised.

We were doing a chronological review of Greenspar's life year by year. Tiny was cross-checking the data for each year to be sure it passed the sniff test. Everything was perfect through nineteen sixty-eight where his college transcript showed he graduated with a BS in Accounting from Washington State. Graduate school for finance followed. According to his grades, he did exceptionally well for the next two years, eventually being awarded a master's degree from Indiana State College in nineteen seventy-one. That put him in Indiana in the nineteen seventy/ seventy-one time period.

"Bingo!" Tiny exclaimed, knocking over his empty mango lassi glass. "Angella getting busted is turning out to be a blessing!"

"You lost me!"

"Remember what Jacobs told us about JB's connection to Greenspar? JB's father and Greenspar flew together in Nam in the late sixties, is what Jacobs said. Unless I'm missing something here, I don't see where our friend Homer had flight training. In fact, I don't see any military at all in this record. And it's hard to be in Indiana and Nam at the same time!"

"No one leaves military off their record unless something's wrong. How do we check?"

"Jacobs can run this down in a few minutes."

We had our answer in less than thirty minutes. Jacobs called and said, "The hardest part of this was to obtain his social. That required calling in a few favors. It took five minutes after that. Major Homer Greenspar flew for the Air Force and was stationed at Tan Son Nhat in nineteen sixty-nine just as the picture showed. By the way, the FBI background security check on Greenspar has all of this information. The Homeland Security file does not."

I had barely digested that news when Tiny exclaimed, "Jackpot! Jacobs says there's a note in his file indicating he was disciplined for having a prostitute on base several nights."

"We got him!" I exclaimed, getting caught up in the moment and barely able to conceal my excitement.

"One further note," Tiny relayed, "and you'll love this. He was denied permission to marry the woman. She was denied permission to enter this country."

"Can we tie Tae-hyun to the woman?"

"Not by name. The best way would be by DNA. We have Tae-hyun's. That's routine when a terrorist is arrested. I have the printout in my file. Now we need Greenspar's."

I took Tiny's cell and told Jacobs about the retrieved key. He responded by saying, "We'll put a watch on Angella and a closer watch on Burner. He's the one most likely took the key."

"What about Tae-hyun? Is he secure?"

"When he leaves his cell he's under heavy guard, cuffed hand-and-foot, and his head is covered. There's no possible way that key can get to him. Or him to the bomb."

The terrorist and the bomb were now residing at the same location. That couldn't be a coincidence. If it was, Santa was alive and well. Burner, or Greenspar, or a player yet to be named, had the igniter key. I didn't know how those three moving parts would come together, but I was willing to bet that some group of somebodys certainly had a plan for it to happen.

My guess: we wouldn't have long to wait.

SIXTY

I suggested briefing the President.

"To do so," Tiny thoughtfully responded, "we first need to brief Jamison."

We discussed the briefing with Sylvan Jacobs to get his take on what we should and should not say. His response was to rethink our plan. "Speaking from the FBI perspective," Jacobs said, "all you have is circumstantial evidence. You have no actual fact tying Greenspar to anything tangible. Perhaps he even had a child in Nam. So what? So did any number of guys."

"But, as INS Assistant Deputy, he's in a perfect position to move people in and out of the country. That's been central to this operation from the start. And there is the matter that his file's been altered. And if Tae-hyun is his child we have him," I insisted, pumping up my enthusiasm. I wanted to believe we were on the right trail.

"Hate to break it to you, but even if we get a positive DNA match, that won't be enough." Jacobs was holding my toes to the fire. "I don't have to tell you, Redstone, to be careful not to close your net too soon. He's the only lead you have, so he looks good. Get someone else in the crosshairs and then see how Homer holds up."

I wasn't sure if Jacobs was convinced of his position or just testing the evidence. But one thing for sure, he wasn't enthusiastic about lending his name to a briefing of the President.

Stepping back from it, he made good sense. We were still a long way from reeling in the fish, even assuming we had a fish on the line.

A priority call came in while we were talking. Jacobs asked a few rapid-fire questions and hung up. Turning back to us, he said, "Just got a positive match between the slug they recovered from Duran's skull and the weapon assigned to Angella."

I thought about what Contentus had told me about the slug they had found in the boat being contaminated with the target fibers from D.C. This, however, was a different gun. "I know that to be impossible!" I exclaimed. "I was with her during the critical period."

"And what time frame would that be?" Jacobs asked, leaning forward in his chair.

I thought about what Angella and I were doing during that period and then added. "Truth is, we weren't together the whole period. She had left to go meet Duran. But I can't believe..."

"Don't fight the evidence," Jacobs cautioned me. "It'll take us where we need to be."

Over the years I admonished many a young detective the same way. Yet, here I was falling into the classic trap. On a positive note, I remarked, "I believe there are pictures of the killer. Tall thin guy with bushy hair."

"Lots of tall thin guys with bushy hair. Burner is tall and thin. But his hair is sparse. Need something better than that, I'm afraid."

"What we need is to find those pictures." I addressed Tiny. "Any luck?"

"Nothing from the locals. Want to put Angella on it?"

"Good thought. Why don't you ask her? I'm not sure she's listening to anything I suggest. Pissed at me."

Jacobs leaned back in his chair. "I'm troubled about a few things. Angella is wanted for the murder of the medic. Now she's implicated in the murder of Duran. Tell me why she'd be involved in both. Is it your thought Duran was part of the bomb smuggling?"

"I was afraid you'd go there," Tiny said. "We don't yet know that the Chief was involved in the smuggling in any way. But it remains possible."

"If it was unconnected, then it seems a stretch to think she was involved with both murders."

"There's some talk of a love triangle," Tiny injected. "Could be all domestic stuff. Happens all too often. Duran moved Angella along faster than normal. Put tension on the marriage."

"Angella is good at what she does," I responded, again coming to Angella's defense. "She was promoted based on her abilities. Tiny, you said so yourself. She's good."

"She saved your life. That's why she's been allowed to run free. Payback for a job well done. But that doesn't prove anything."

My cell went off and Woody's name popped up. She wanted to know if we were coming back to D.C. anytime soon.

"Why," I asked, puzzled at the seemingly innocent question. "Is there something that we need to attend to?"

"Nothing urgent. I just hadn't heard from either of you and I was getting concerned. Anything more you need from me? Were those files of help?"

"Nothing now, Woody," I responded. "We'll keep you posted."

"Let me know what your plans are so I can get what you require."

"You can get us everything you have on a Border Patrol Agent name of Te Burner."

"Should I deliver what I find to the Woodside Motel? That's where you're staying isn't it? Or do you want them somewhere else?"

Something in her tone was off. No, not tone. Timing. Timing was off. She had delayed a fraction too long before responding.

"That'll work," I said, waiting for her to say something more. But she remained quiet.

"I'll have them printed in San Antonio and hand delivered."

"Tell you what. E-mail them to Special Agent Sylvan Jacobs, SA FBI."

"What was that look on your face?" Jacobs asked, when I flipped the phone closed. "Something was said you didn't like."

"Woody. My secretary. Something about her troubles me. Can't place it. My immediate question: How the hell did she know where I was staying?"

"Did you use your credit card to pay for the room?" Jacobs asked.

When I said no, Tiny confessed that he had used his, but he doubted Woody could trace it.

"Let's get a coffee," I suggested, "while we wait for the files to arrive." I addressed Jacobs. "You joining us?"

"Go without me. Have work to do."

- - - - - -

Tiny suggested we stop by the motel to search for microphones. Sure enough, he found small transmitters in each of our rooms. Someone was listening to our conversations from not very far away. He motioned for me to join him outside. "Let's take a spin around and see what we can see."

Our surveillance turned up nothing, but we knew someone was there. That someone was highly professional and had access to state-of-the-art equipment. "Take it from me," Tiny commented, "you can't buy these toys on the open market. The size of this microphone is smaller than a hair. I'm willing to bet the transmission is coded and the power is obtained by a combination of sound and light."

"How did you find such a small thing? I can barely see it."

"Know what to look for. Been trained in their placement. This is professional grade. And planted by someone with the same training I had."

"More confirmation that this is an inside operation," I commented to Tiny.

"Inside operation is no longer in question. What we need to know is who is running the show. We have our eyes on Greenspar and that horse's ass, Burner. But they can't be doing this alone. There must be someone in D.C. that we're missing."

"I think it's time we talk to the General. I also think we need to do that in person. I'm still not comfortable with long distance commutation. Too much is lost—or not said."

Tiny thought a moment and then said, "I agree about the face-to-face. But that's a bit hard to do since Jamison isn't taking my calls." Tiny had a quizzical look on his face. The first I had seen that expression.

"I was thinking more in terms of Ms. Lucinda Westminster McNaughton. Cindy may have some thoughts. Besides, I want to talk personally with the Korean, and she can make that happen, security or not.

"Can you get us—or at least me—to D.C. tonight?"

"Does a duck swim? We're only a few miles from either Lackland or Randolph. Bet there's a flight leaving soon. Always is. Let's go pick up the files. By then I'll have it arranged."

"We can pick them up ourselves from Woody."

"No sense letting her know we're coming. She was concerned about my movements last I spoke to her. Too concerned. Let this be a surprise. Less she knows the better."

SIXTY-ONE

As it turned out, Lucinda McNaughton was busy for dinner, but agreed to meet us at nine-thirty in the lobby of the old Willard Hotel, which, she reminded me, was now called the Intercontinental. I wouldn't have known the difference. The name Willard meant nothing to a Texas boy.

Tiny booked two rooms. He had been right, we were booked on an Air Force jet that was leaving for Andrews and scheduled to land at seven-thirty. The timing allowed for showers and room service.

More good news came by way of Angella. She called to tell me about a long talk she had had with Chief Duran's widow.

"How'd you manage to get her to talk to you? You being the *other* woman and all." My humor was either lost on Angella or she ignored me. But truth is, my stomach was knotted when she was on the line. I had to agree with Tiny, it didn't look good for her.

"Perhaps I was really convincing," Angella was saying. "Maybe Contentus said something to her? More likely, she just needed to believe my story. I don't know. But she did tell me her husband had been investigating the smuggling. He had mentioned to her he was convinced someone on the inside was behind it all, and that he trusted no one."

"Did she narrow it down at all?"

"At first she refused to discuss it. But when I was leaving I gave her a big hug. She whispered that Homer Greenspar and her husband had gotten into it several times over illegal immigrants."

"Any specifics?"

"Nothing specific. But get this," she exclaimed, her voice taking on a much lighter mood. "You know I was tied to Duran's death because he said my name several times before he died."

I recalled what McFaren had told us. Something to do with Angella and home. I repeated to Angella what I remembered.

"That's not exactly what was said. What he said to his wife was...better get my notes so I get this right." The line went quiet for a moment. Then Angella was back. "And I quote, 'Angella's case. Tell Angella, Home.' He died saying *Home.*"

"Are you implying he was trying to say *Homer*?"

"That's exactly what I think! Hildy, that's Duran's wife, she asked me to call her Hildy, believes he was to meet a Fed at the house the night he was shot. Something to do with the border. But she has nothing to back that up."

"Anything more for us?"

"Nothing now."

I told Angella about our motel being bugged and warned her to watch what she was doing—and what she said. I also suggested she check to see if Joy was back. "I assume she hasn't resurfaced. But we need to find her and get copies of those pictures."

"She hasn't surfaced. Been keeping my ear to the ground. No one's heard from her. I'm working with the locals. Listen to me.

Even I'm calling them *locals*. I have a list of everyone they spoke with at Joy's place. I'll follow up."

I called Sylvan Jacobs and repeated what Angella had said. I finished to silence on the line. Thinking I lost him, I said, "You still there?"

"Just thinking this thing through. Got a few holes here and there. First, I know it can happen, but it's difficult to think Greenspar would sacrifice his own son. So that doesn't add up. Second, Duran's last word, 'Home,' could mean Homeland Security and not Homer. Let's take this slow."

\- - - - - -

We landed at Andrews a half-hour early. Tiny had arranged for a car to meet us. Jacobs called a few minutes after the car passed through the front gate. "Got the info on your secretary, or whatever she's calling herself. I'm not comfortable on the cell with this."

I told him we were almost in the city and staying at the Old Willard. He said he'd have a District agent hand carry it to us.

"Any luck picking up Burner?"

"Guy went missing. Fell right off the screen. One minute we have him, the next he's disappeared. Seems to know exactly where you are."

"Where was he last seen?" I asked, thinking back to what Contentus had told me about my cell being bugged.

"Right here in San Antonio. About three blocks from your motel. Now he can be anywhere. He has priority access to planes, you name it."

"Tiny cut him off!"

Jacobs said, "Give me a minute. I'll check the system." A few minutes later, Jacobs was back on the line. "No record of him being cut off."

"Can't you trace his usage?"

"Tried. Dead end. Seems he may have another identity for such things. We're working it."

"I know he killed the medic. He stole the pictures. Probably also has Joy stashed somewhere, hopefully still alive. Only problem is, he doesn't have fuzzy hair. I definitely saw fuzzy hair in the picture."

"Halloween hair," Jacobs replied. "We need the photos."

"Angella's on it. Talk later."

When the phone went dead I said to Tiny, "Thought you cut Burner off."

"Did it myself."

"He's not now! Jacobs checked the system and he's free as a bird."

"Can't be!" Tiny immediately pulled out his iPhone. He busied himself until we were almost at the hotel. Finally looking up, he sighed, "That's strange. No record of me cutting him off. I tried again. This time the system wouldn't allow me to take action. Seems I don't have the required permission. That's bullshit! I'm cleared for the highest level."

"Obviously you're not. At least not any longer. Somebody telling you something? Better check to see if there's a For Sale sign on your front lawn."

Tiny threw me a look that clearly said *back off.*

"If the shoe fits..." I replied, moving against the side of the car out of his immediate reach.

The car dropped us in the hotel driveway and we walked inside, only to find a long line at the front counter. A tour bus of geezers took up a good portion of the lobby. Their loud shirts and even louder voices made them obnoxious. By the time we actually got checked in and to our rooms there was barely enough time for the long-awaited shower. Eating would have to wait.

A while later I opened my room door on my way to meet Cindy and found a young woman standing in the hallway. She was tall, slender and dressed casually as if waiting for a friend to join her. She approached. “Mr. Redstone?”

“Yes,” I answered, taking note of her effortless grace.

“I have a package for you.” She reached into the leather bag hanging from her shoulder and retrieved a manila envelope. Holding it out for me, she said, “I believe you are expecting this.” I must have appeared blank because she continued, “From Mr. Jacobs.”

“Oh, yes. Yes, indeed. Thank you. Only I hadn’t expected it to be delivered by such a…a well, attractive delivery person.”

She looked me hard in the eye. “Don’t let the clothes fool you. FBI is keeping up with the times.”

“I must say it is,” I replied, my mind flashing to Angella and missing her more than I cared to admit.

“Need to sign for it. It’s on the other side.”

I flipped the envelope over and found the paper. I signed on the proverbial dotted line.

“Prints as well,” she said, pointing to a blank area next to my signature.

I pressed my thumb onto the paper but saw nothing when I pulled my hand back.

Without a word, she then ripped the signature page from the envelope, folded it and slipped it into her bag. She turned and walked toward the elevator. I retraced my steps back into the room and opened the envelope. I checked my watch and realized there wasn't enough time to study the file. I slipped the envelope under the cushion on the reading chair in the corner of the room and went to fetch Tiny.

- - - - - -

"Thank goodness the tourists have cleared out," Tiny said when we arrived back in the lobby. "They're probably all sleeping by now."

Our timing was perfect. Cindy was walking toward us. I had to admit, for a woman in her mid-sixties, she still carried herself as though she was being presented at her cotillion.

"Hello, gentlemen, nice to see you both again," Cindy said, her lips upturned, her face fully involved in the smile, her perfect teeth a definite asset.

"Likewise," I replied, extending my hand to her.

"Forget the handshake, give me a hug, Cowboy."

I was puzzled, but followed her lead. When Tiny wrapped his arms around her she all but disappeared.

"Careful," she teased, "you'll crush me."

The ceremony over, I said, "I noticed lounge areas on the landings." I nodded in the direction of a series of indoor stepped terraces where a few people were having drinks. "We can talk in private over there," I said, pointing to an area in a corner devoid of people.

"Nothing's private here. I can see three investigative reporters from where I'm standing."

I followed her glance and sure enough, sitting talking to a man who I guessed to be in his late seventies was the reporter, Abby Johnson, I had briefly met at the White House. She was the

Washington Post Homeland Security guru. She was also Cindy's sister-in-law. D.C. was indeed a tight little world.

I wasn't sure if she saw me or not, but Cindy was right. This was not the place to talk.

"This is Cold War Berlin," Cindy was saying, "only transported to the District. I have a residence upstairs. Come."

She swept across the lobby with the two of us trailing behind. She waved gaily to several people, none of whom I recognized.

We approached a group of private elevators set off in the corner and she held her purse against a discreetly placed pad. A small elevator door slid open.

Once inside, she placed her purse against the keypad and pushed the button labeled PH. In a few minutes the doors opened and we stepped directly into the foyer of a very lavishly furnished apartment. The skyline of the nation's capitol was visible through the massive windows framing the living room.

"Make yourselves at home, gentlemen. The bar is stocked. Please help yourselves. As the cliché goes, I'm going to slip out of these tiresome clothes into something more practical for a discussion." She marched toward what I guessed to be the bedroom wing of the suite. Before disappearing, she said, "The kitchen's over there and there's cold cuts and cheese in the refrigerator and fresh bread in the pantry. Feel free to make whatever it is you want. I've just eaten, so don't worry about me. But you can pour me a scotch if you don't mind. It's been one of those days."

I immediately headed for the kitchen and set about making sandwiches for Tiny and myself. I had seen his appetite and knew he had to be starving. "Turkey or ham?" I called to him.

"One of each. I'll get the drinks. This is some pad. Wonder what it costs?"

"As they say, you have to ask, you can't afford it."

SIXTY-TWO

Cindy was back before I finished with the sandwiches. She gathered her drink and switched on a satellite music channel. Then she pulled a hand-held gadget from her purse and slowly walked the room. By the time she completed her tour I had finished my supper preparations. The sandwiches were on the bar counter.

"From what I've been told, you gentlemen should obtain one of these." She held up the gadget for us to inspect. It looked like a small portable radio, being slightly larger than a cell phone.

Tiny said, "That would come in handy. I do it the old fashioned way."

"Wear the sucker out as many bugs as we've found," I commented.

Cindy said, "I'll have one delivered to you tomorrow. Go ahead and eat." She had changed into jeans and a loose fitting pullover. Her hair was now down, but she still retained her regal appearance. She sat in the corner of a large wrap-around white sofa sipping her drink. As dainty as I tried to be, I still managed to feel out of place as I ate the over-stuffed sandwich. Tiny, who had settled on the far end of the sofa, must feel like a misplaced elephant among all the glass and porcelain objects.

"Gentlemen, your timing here tonight is perfect. First, before I get on to what I have to say, I need to be brought current on everything that you've done so far. And don't leave a bloody thing out. Nothing. I want it all. The good, the bad and the stupid."

I glanced at Tiny and he nodded. So I told her everything I knew, including our suspicions of Homer Greenspar and Te Burner.

She was a patient listener, slowing working on her Scotch while I spoke. When I finished, it was past midnight and I expected her to be impatient. Instead, her eyes were alive, but there was a definite tenseness in her body movements that I hadn't sensed earlier.

I pointed to my boot as an example of something stupid.

"You don't consider Angella's behavior stupid?"

Assuming Cindy was speaking about Angella going for a morning jog without an escort, I relied, "She's a police officer. And she carried her weapon when she went jogging."

"Actually, I was thinking about the key she had in her purse more than the run. Evidence being withheld. But even more than that. That key being in their hands can be devastating. That's what I consider stupid—or worse."

"Not her finest day, I'll concede that much," I responded. I didn't like where this was leading. Clearly, General Cindy had no thoughts of coming to Angella's rescue. That didn't bode well for either of us.

"Speaking of fine days, you let her run free to investigate the very murder she's suspected of committing. That the way you Cowboys do things in Texas?"

We were being set up. Already had been from the look Cindy flashed across the sofa. There was not much I could do about it at this point. “She’s being framed. Evidence was planted.” I sounded lame, even to myself. My assessment was confirmed when Tiny winced. He wisely, for him, remained silent.

Cindy leaned forward, looked from me to Tiny and back again. “What I am about to say is between the three of us and is to go no further. I’m not one to be crossed so I trust you both understand.”

She paused to be sure we were both with her. Her eyes narrowed. “Cowboy, I have information that leads me to believe your old boss Contentus has been feeding you information. Is that accurate?”

“It is,” I confessed.

“And is it accurate to assume information is flowing in both directions?”

Now I was in the cross hairs. I didn’t think there was any way she could know what I had said to Contentus, but I couldn’t be certain. “It is,” I replied, deciding in favor of honesty. I didn’t have any chits in the Foggy Bottom Bank, so no one would come to my rescue if Cindy, or Jamison, came gunning for me.

“Thank you for being honest. Our understanding was that you were to feed me what you had first. Was it not?”

“It was.”

“I’m disappointed, to say the least. I thought it was clear not to cross me. Martinez is in difficulty and I suppose you’d like it if I were to call off the dogs.”

“It’s trumped up. The bullet—”

“Loyalty, Cowboy, begets loyalty. And I’m sure you know the corollary.”

“But, I—”

"Off the reservation is off the reservation! We'll just let her situation play out. The problem is, information is fragmented, some here, some there. Our enemies are counting on us not getting the pieces together. And so far they are right. Time works in their favor. My assessment is they expect to be caught. Just as long as their mission works, they've done their good deed. Spend eternity with virgins—or whatever their dreams entail." She paused to let that sink in. "By not sharing what you have, you're helping them."

"I was—"

"Not now. You'll have plenty of time later—if there is a later—to explain your actions. And the actions of your lovely partner."

Her smile was gone. Hard lines now radiated from the corners of her hard-set mouth. Her eyes bore into me. I saw her, not in casual clothes, but in the uniform of a Marine General facing down an errant officer.

After several seconds, Cindy rose and walked to the window, keeping her back to us as she stood looking out over the nation's capital. Her head was perfectly still, her arms hung at her sides with thumbs facing forward. Nothing moved. It was as if she was standing at attention.

Cindy remained in that posture for several minutes before returning to her seat on the sofa. She again focused her full attention on me. It was as though Tiny was not in the room. The intensity in her eyes had softened, but her face was still set hard. "Cowboy," she began, "we have here the classic moving target. Whatever is going on is designed to inflict great physical and emotional damage to the country, much as 9-1-1 did. But this time it is also designed to weaken and possibly bring down the President. As I'm certain you're aware, his approval rating is falling. Some of it, frankly, he brings on himself. Some of it comes with the office. But a great deal is being orchestrated by his enemies, both domestic and foreign. Bear in mind the weaker he is at home, the weaker he is around the world. Vulnerability, even if only perceived, is always exploited."

"What—"

She held up her hand, signaling me to remain quiet and listen. "China lent us a ton of money over the past few years. Now they're making demands. Demands that, quite frankly, we may not be able to meet. Couple that with terrorist groups everywhere making demands, hijacking ships, blowing up train and bus stations, putting bombs in underwear and flying into our country. The U.S. is on the defensive. If this bomb goes off, beside all the other damage that will occur, it will politically devastate this government. I wouldn't be surprised if impeachment proceedings were held."

"Then why not remove the bomb from the country?" I asked, when she fell silent.

"And put it where? Even acknowledging we have it is devastating. We can't just dump it in the trash, or bury it at sea. We certainly can't detonate it."

I wondered if a weapon as dangerous as this could be dismantled. You can't get halfway through the process and then say, "Whoops, guess that won't work." I dismissed that thought. Instead, I said, "Then store it underground in some nuclear arsenal."

"That's where the rub comes. I can't get into it and even if I could, I don't profess to be an expert. But from what I know, the Atomic Regulatory Act of 1954 set very close controls on the possession of atomic material. The short version is that the Department of Energy takes the position that they must, under the law, take control of the atomic material in the bomb. They believe the law forbids military control in this situation. The Attorney General is working on this very issue. But the real problem is that your friend JB out there in San Antonio is demanding the bomb be turned over to the Energy Department immediately. They have facilities for handling atomic material. He's preparing to take the issue to Federal Court. JB's politically savvy and wouldn't be doing this if he didn't think the court would go along with him."

"So, even though the bomb is on Lackland Air Force base, JB has authority to have it moved?" I managed to ask, even while I sorted through the tangled factual threads swirling in my mind.

"It's federal property. He's a federal attorney. Military is not exempt from civilian control. His position is that the atomic material is wrongfully on a military base because the law requires it to be under civilian control. He's furious the military won't turn it over."

"Furious or not, the Air Force has the bomb secured. Its location is top secret. He can't very easily go to court and make it public."

"The court can hold private hearings if the judge wishes. But here's the kicker. My sister-in-law Abby Johnson, I believe you met her, somehow got the story. Before you jump the dog here, Cowboy, it wasn't from me. Some snitch from Homeland Security told her about the bomb and where it's being held. That's how JB found out. Abby called him to confirm."

"Can't you declare national security or some such thing?"

"That's exactly what Max did. President's going along for now. Post put a lid on the story. But the information will get out. It's only a matter of time. If the Post doesn't publish, it'll go to Wikileaks or some other blog. It's a ticking bomb. No pun intended."

"So what's the plan?" I asked Cindy, knowing this was not an idle conversation. Marine Generals, retired or not, always have a plan.

"The obvious. Find out who's orchestrating this and cut their communication paths. I believe we have less than twenty-four hours, and that's stretching it."

"My best guess if you push me right now is Greenspar, with help from Burner. From the outside it appears to be North Korea."

"Don't be so quick on either. Take North Korea. It is not a certainty they're even aware of the bomb. We've made several back-channel overtures and nothing leads State to conclude they're aware. We're working that angle, but all indications are it is not them."

"Greenspar?"

"Greenspar presents a touchier situation. Suppose, just suppose, he's the person. That means the President appointed him and the FBI cleared him. Jamison vouches for him. Says the man bleeds red white and blue. If it's Greenspar, all hell will break loose. Again this will undermine the President—and Max as well."

I sat upright. "Are you saying we should forget about Greenspar? If you are, then we shouldn't be having this conversation. He is a prime suspect and I won't be—"

"Keep your powder dry, Cowboy. It's delicate. So delicate, in fact, that the President couldn't allow the Secret Service to handle the investigation. That's why you're here. That's why Tiny was brought in. You work for us and you do what we say. This isn't Texas."

"So I can be the fall guy! A Texas outsider nobody has anything invested in. Someone you can hang out to dry. That's where you positioned me. You spoke of loyalty before. Lip service."

Tiny spoke up for the first time. "And a CIA guy who has no right to meddle in internal affairs. You can hang both of us out. Great cover."

"Being blunt, in a word, yes. But even so, your roles are critical to the future of this government. If, indeed Homer is behind this, we had better have ironclad proof, because we get only one shot at him. Imagine what will happen if we name him and we're wrong!"

Tiny responded. "You're saying that if we name Greenspar and can't convict him, the public won't trust the President?"

"More or less you got it right," Cindy said, her body going tense again. "I'm not a doomsayer, but can you imagine the chaos that'll occur if this is screwed up?"

It was my turn to glare. "So unless we're lock tight on Greenspar—or on anyone else appointed by the President—we better keep it to ourselves."

"You got me, Cowboy. No leaks to the press about Homer. No hints. No visibility at all."

"You've heard all that we have," Tiny pressed, "what's your take then?"

"Candidly, I agree it looks to be Homer. Except, I know him too well. Just like you're certain Angella didn't shoot her former boss, I know Homer didn't plan or execute this. You said yourself, heart trumps logic. This is one of those times."

"Speaking of heart, let's get all the cards on the table so I understand all the forces at work here. Rumor has it that you and Jamison are more than employer and employee. Is that accurate?"

"I'll answer your questions as part of your investigation, but only off the record."

"Agreed. How long a relationship have you had?"

"I suppose you mean romantic relationship. I've known him as a fellow officer and friend since Officer School. The romance began in Vietnam before he was captured. Look, it's an open secret. We're not hiding it, but we're not flaunting it in his wife's face. She has her own life, shall we say. While Max, General Jamison, was on active duty, he didn't believe divorce was the right option. I don't necessarily share his view, but that's just the way things play out in life. You'd be absolutely amazed at how many politicians are, shall we say, less than monogamous."

There was so much more I wanted to know, but I sensed I had worn out my welcome with that line of questioning. So I asked her why they had not moved the bomb to Gitmo, or some other secure place before JB got into the mix. "No one in his right mind would allow both the Korean and the bomb to be in the same location. Yet they are both at Lackland, from what I know. Someone high up had to orchestrate that."

"Good question. Good observation. Tae-hyun was taken to the base under orders from Homeland Security. Max was furious when he heard where Tae-hyun had been moved. He'd move the bomb out of there, but as I said earlier, his hands are tied on that. Department of Energy, supported by JB, is demanding custody. Under law they seem to have every right. If the President allows the bomb to remain with the military, there most definitely will be impeachment proceedings."

"I'll feel better when it's physically impossible for Tae-hyun and the bomb to come together," I said. "We've been manipulated, worked like puppets, so that Tae-hyun could get the key and then get put into place near the bomb. He could never have broken into the base, so it was genius to have him arrested and locked up at the base." All that was now missing was putting Tae-hyun together with the weapon. The timing was now making sense. They had been delaying in order to move everybody into place.

They were also being held up because the igniter key, thanks to Angella, had gone missing after Tae-hyun's first arrest.

"Speaking of arrest," McNaughton said, "I recall that you ordered Tae-hyun arrested."

"I did, but only because we were being run around. I didn't want to lose him again."

"Someone manipulated that as well. They got your measure, knew you'd roll him up."

I wanted to explore that further, but time was indeed critical, and it wasn't on our side. We had to move on. We could sort out who did what to whom afterward—if there is an afterward.

"What do you require at this point?" Cindy asked, apparently assuming we would continue the investigation even after she had admitted we were being set up to take the heat.

"For starters, I want my partner back. You're right, I want your help getting her freed from the bogus charges."

"Go on," Cindy replied, not committing one way or the other.

Now it was my turn to study the city from the penthouse window. Unlike most large cities I've been in, Washington seemed frozen in time. I doubted if I could ever understand the mentality of this place. Our nation's capitol is supposedly made from little bits of all of us. But it is foreign to most. Here, it's not about what reality is; it's about what people think reality to be. Perception replacing reality. Maybe that's why nothing seems to be moving. Nothing's real.

Cindy's voice broke though my thoughts. "When you have reason to think detonation is imminent, then you must, at all costs, get word to Max or myself. The code Domestic Disturbance will trigger an Executive Evacuation to the underground shelters for everyone in government who needs to survive. Let's hope it never gets to that point, but we need to do what we need to do. The evacuation plan is extensive and will effectively shut the country down within minutes. Senators and Cabinet Officers will be relocated. The President and Vice-President will be secured."

"Has it ever been employed? The evacuation code, I mean."

"September eleventh. I can't say more. For your information, I'm not on that list. Max is."

"The bomb's in Texas," I reminded her. "At least it's not at Andrews. Not the one we were trailing anyway. No need to close down the government here. Maybe in Austin."

"They won't take a chance. No telling what other surprises are in store."

Then I remembered the radiation patterns and how they had extended up the east coast. Maybe we were the decoy—the clown distracting the bull. But I kept that to myself. I changed the subject. "Please arrange for us to talk in person with Tae-hyun? As soon as possible. By *us* I'm including Angella."

"Got it." She reached for her purse. "Here," she said, handing me a small envelope. "When you go on base each of you must wear one of these. There are three of them."

I looked inside and saw what appeared to be three ribbons.

"You look puzzled," she said, "they're the latest radiation detectors. Got sensor chips inside. Not only do they warn you about radiation, but when the level gets dangerous, they sound an alert. A beeping at first, and as the level reaches toxic levels it becomes solid."

"Three?" Apparently she had planned all along to have Angella rejoin us.

"I must warn you, however, if you're thinking of having Angella rejoin you that could present a problem. For a woman of childbearing years, by the time the strip goes solid, reproduction is severely compromised. Unfortunately, it's permanent—and life threatening. Men have a bit more tolerance, but having children is out. Now, if you gentlemen will allow me, it's late and I must get my beauty sleep."

SIXTY-THREE

In the morning, I found Woody's file lying open on the chair in my hotel room. I had read through it before getting in bed, but I didn't recall leaving it open. I saw no evidence that anyone had been in the room. The chain on the door was still in place. I reminded myself that a bit of paranoia is what keeps detectives alive. Too much was paralyzing.

I called Tiny and we agreed to meet in the lobby. I took Woody's file with me, as well as the file Woody had prepared on Te Burner. We sat near the back of the restaurant. While waiting for our eggs to arrive, I opened Woody's file. As had now become our routine, I followed the years while Tiny concentrated on the substance for each year. In Woody's case, we found nothing more than her assignments at Immigration and later at Homeland Security. She started at age 34 as a classification clerk working in a pool with a group leader.

We traced her progress for two years until Tiny exclaimed, "This is interesting! She worked four years for our good friend Homer Greenspar!"

"Indeed! The net draws tighter."

"*Circumstantial*, as the lawyers say. Let's move on."

"Okay, 1989," I said, "assigned to a department called Research."

"You skipped two years. She left Homer in '86, I thought you said."

Checking back, Tiny was right. I searched the file and found nothing for the years '87 and '88. She remained in Research for ten years, becoming a manager in 2000.

"Where was she on 9-1-1?" Tiny asked, stress lines again forming along his jaw.

"Manager of Research, Iranian desk. After the merger into Homeland security she became something called Trouble Shooter."

Tiny continued to focus on the missing years, asking me several times to go back and make sure a page had not been overlooked. Something was clearly troubling him.

The remainder of our review revealed that she had a number of temporary assignments, lasting from a few months to a few years, up to the time when she was assigned to Angella and I. All the years were accounted for, with the exception of the two between '87 and '89.

We ate our breakfast in silence and then opened Te Burner's file. Undistinguished career in his early years. Came to Immigration in '87 after serving in the military. No history of where he served, but he was with Army Special Forces. So that was where he had been trained. Those guys are on par with the SEALS. Not to be messed with.

I studied the file further and then said, "In 1990 Mr. Te Burner went over to Border Patrol. Says here, and I quote, 'Suggest counseling. Detainees are complaining of abuse.' Seems they all managed to get themselves slashed in the neck while under his care." I read further and then elaborated, "Burner was placed on administrative leave in 2004. Reinstated in 2005. Nothing further in his record."

"Do you have a year-by-year listing?" Tiny asked.

"Not here."

"Is this the file Woody prepared?"

"Yes," I responded nodding at what Tiny had already digested. "Someone, possibly Woody, is hiding something."

"They could have both been at Immigration during the two missing years in Woody's file." He absently ran a napkin across his lips. "Time to call Jacobs and get the FBI's side of both of them. We also need to review the military records of both Greenspar and Burner."

"What's troubling you?" I asked Tiny. His eyes had narrowed to slits and he was concentrating harder than I had ever seen him.

"The timing. You mentioned the Iran desk. Woody was working it for Immigration on 9-1-1. She came to Immigration in 1980 just after the Revolution when Shah Mohammad Reza Pahlavi was ushered out."

"If there's a connection, that's a stretch."

"The U.S. was not exactly passive in the Revolution. A lot of our military and others were over there. She's the right age. Mid-sixties now, would have been mid-thirties then. Idealistic. Ayatollah Rujollah Khomeini turned the heads of a lot of our young folks. The Islamic revolution was very popular among a certain group of young people."

"How do you know so much about Iran? I certainly don't," I confessed. I suspected that when he had said *others* he was referring to CIA operatives.

"My training and background is much different than yours. Let's leave it at that."

I called Jacobs, who dutifully noted our request to follow up on Woody. Then he added, "Think you better get back to Lackland. The merchandise was turned over to Department of Energy and they have taken charge. It will be moved late today. I'll explain later. My hands are tied. Can't stop it."

"That's a good thing. They'll get it off the base and away from our problem child."

"But until they do, security is low. They've ordered the military to stand down. Your pal Jamison is furious. He's ordered perimeter guards, but they have to remain hundred yards back."

"Makes no sense."

"Governments don't exist to make sense," Jacobs answered matter of factly. "They exist to make the rules."

Walking back through the lobby, a familiar face appeared out of nowhere. Or so it seemed.

"I see you met with Cindy McNaughton last night. Want to tell me what's going down?" It was Abigail Johnson.

"No comment." Cindy had told us that Johnson knew about the bomb. No sense in confirming it.

"I know more than you think, Redstone. For example, I know that a medic who removed a tracking device from a Korean was killed. I know your partner is, shall we say, a *person of interest*. Might even be the prime suspect. A source even says a bullet found in the boat where the medic was killed came from her gun. I also have reason to believe that the Korean has been captured. He's being held at Lackland. How much of this will you confirm?"

"No comment."

"I also understand there's a rogue A-bomb being held at Lackland contrary to the Atomic Energy Act."

"No comment."

"I'm running the story as I have it. You want the country to believe some Korean spy is about to detonate a WMD that's your business. Don't think the President will approve. He's into this up to his hairline."

I caught Tiny's eye. "I'll meet you at checkout in say ten minutes."

He studied Johnson a long moment. Then nodded and walked off.

I couldn't determine if he knew who she was or not. From our previous discussion, he seemed to have known her, and I couldn't imagine Tiny working in this town for any length of time and not knowing the Washington Post reporter who covered domestic terrorist activities. But yet, here he was, with no recognition in his eyes. In the world of spooks, nothing's ever as it seems to be.

"I'll confirm a North Korean's been recaptured, but no attribution," I told her. From what Cindy had said, the Post was not going to run the story for a day or two anyway. By then, this would be old news, one way or the other.

"Deal." She said, her eyes going softer. "Can you confirm the atomic weapon?"

"Can we go off record?"

"Depends on what you give me."

"I'll give you the full story, but with a few caveats."

"Depends. Let's hear the conditions?"

"Tell me who the snitch is?"

"No way," Abby immediately snapped.

"Hear me out. I want the snitch because I think that person orchestrated this operation and is a traitor to our country."

"What draws you to that conclusion?"

"I'm making a leap here. Stop me if I'm wrong. Someone at Homeland Security tipped you to the bomb. I'm assuming that same someone told you a bullet from Angella's gun killed the medic. That true?"

"Assume so."

"The bullet information has not been released. In fact, it was a plant. My conclusion is that the person who tipped you is the mole who's running this operation—or very close to the mole."

"Go on."

"Delay the story for two days."

"And?"

"And leave out the fact of the atomic weapon."

"How about two out of three?"

"Which two?" I asked.

"I'll delay the story two days if you promise me I can release it before others get it."

"Good."

"I'll not tell you the snitch, but I will let you guess a few names. You guess right, I'll confirm. I wouldn't normally ever do that but I do have my concerns about the person who gave me the story."

"That'll work."

Before I got a chance to give Abby my list of names, my cell rang. It was Angella. She had found Joy. "At a rehab center. Place called *Origins*. They do a great job down here on the Island. She's detoxing."

Angella went on to tell me she had found Joy by tracking down Joy's friends. They had decamped from *Louie's Backyard* and she had found them at a beach place called *Boomerang Billy's.*

"Long story short," Angella said, more upbeat than I had heard her in a while, "Joy sent the pictures to a few of her friends before she left her apartment. I have copies and they're on the way to the lab. I blew one up and it does look to be Burner wearing what looks to be a wig."

I thanked her and hung up.

"What was that about?" Abby asked.

"May have solved the medic's murder."

"Give me the story?"

"Depends. Now how about the snitch? My first name is Te Burner."

"Guess again."

"Homer Greenspar?"

"God no! You got to be kidding you think he'd get involved in something like this. Homer's a good guy. Known him forever. You're off in the weeds." Johnson studied me with a practiced eye. After a moment of silence, she said, "With your reputation, I would have thought—"

"Lisa Woods?"

"Bingo. What took you so long?"

"Just what do you mean by that?"

"Woody's not what she seems."

"Keep going."

"Ran into her years ago. Many years ago. In Iran. Hot spot for my kind of work back then."

"Who did she work for over there?"

"You have to be kidding! She's CIA. Maybe not now, but she was back in the day. She was one of the best operatives they had over there. She's a trained agent."

"CIA?" I was stunned. "You certain?"

"Would I get something as important as that wrong? She was trained CIA. Don't know what she is now. Something happened, I have my guess on what, but something happened and she was busted out."

"What's your guess as to why?"

"One of two reasons. Maybe actually both. She converted to Muslim. But I don't believe that was the reason. Although, back then one never knows."

"Keep going"

"Pregnant. I don't know for certain, but she left the country and disappeared. Mind you, CIA operatives are always disappearing. But I had my nose to the ground and when I tell you she was gone, she was gone. No other postings. Nothing. Came off the government rolls. No trace. It was as if she ceased to exist. Then she popped up years ago working admin jobs. Got me thinking."

- - - - - -

We had just taken off from Andrews on our way to Lackland when I called Angella. She told me she had reviewed Duran's private notes. The Chief had made mention of the incident with Greenspar at the raid on SPI island where Tae-hyun had been flushed from the safe house. "Jimmy, I don't know why it took me so long to think of it, but ever since that incident with Burner on the way to Corpus it's nagged at me. I knew him from somewhere, but just couldn't place it. Focus on the raid. Remember the resolution of the feud between Duran and Greenspar?"

"Greenspar drove off with his informants."

"Precisely! And one of the so-called informants was none other than Burner himself! Duran had pictures in his file and I compared them to the picture I took of Burner at the gas stop when you confronted him. Bingo! That man is in it up to his eyes. I think that's what Duran was onto when he was killed."

"Good work. Keep digging. I think Burner planted the bullet and probably planted your jewelry as well." I considered how much of what Johnson had told me I should pass along to Angella. I decided on full candor. I outlined my conversation with the reporter and concluded with, "Woody seems to be orchestrating all of this."

"Is she really high enough to get all the clearances?"

"Judging from how she works the system, I'd say she has passwords and code names for lots of people. She practically lives in the office."

"When do you plan to talk with Tae-hyun?" Angella asked, not reacting to my conclusion concerning Woody. "I assume Mommy Long Legs gave you the okay. Am I right about that, Cowboy?"

"Is that professional rivalry I'm hearing, or just good ole' fashion jealousy?"

"Did you do anything to make me jealous?"

Beside admiring Cindy's gorgeous figure, and perhaps studying her legs a bit longer than I should have, I had nothing to fess up to. "Of course not. Tiny chaperoned me the whole time."

"That's what I'm worried about. I'm not sure they even know right from wrong. And even if they did, spooks don't talk."

I was now at a crossroads. If Cindy hadn't given me the lecture about radiation poisoning taking away Angella's reproductive capacity and putting her in grave danger I would not hesitate to have her with us for the meeting with Tae-hyun. But the thought of her compromising her reproductive system gave me pause. The professional in me fought for giving her the facts and allowing her to make up her own mind. I knew what her answer would be. But the chauvinist shut me down. I simply could not do it.

“Hey, I asked a question and you deflected. What about Tae-hyun? Did you get permission to talk to him?”

“Tiny and I will interview him tomorrow.”

“I’d like to be there,” Angella replied, stopping short of demanding.

“Need you doing what you’re doing. Tiny’s going to conduct a debriefing. We’ll have it on tape. I’ll call if anything important comes up. Hey, better yet, we’ll send it to you live.”

The silent line told me all I needed to know. She was pissed.

I relented. “If it means that much to you, come on up to Lackland today. We land at three-thirty. Interview is set for four. Be at the front gate by four and join us. This is on a fast track.”

“Why did you lie about the interview time?”

“I know you’d want to be there and we need you to remain where you are.”

“You could have said as much straight out,” she barked. “If you want me here, I’ll remain on the island. Let me know how it goes.” Her voice had softened, but she remained pissed.

SIXTY-FOUR

Our flight was diverted to Randolph because, as the pilot informed us, "Lackland is closed to all traffic. Have you on the ground by fifteen hundred hours. It's only a short car ride from one to the other."

Tiny had tried to reach General Jamison to open the base to us, but we had only been told about the diversion ten minutes before landing. By then it was too late.

"Listen to this," Sylvan Jacobs said when we landed, an unusual note of anxiety in his voice. "Greenspar did a stint in Iran, flew some cover missions. Also, and this is what you are looking for, he had an affair with a young CIA agent. She became pregnant with his child." Jacobs, who was normally as calm as they came, allowed his voice to rise slightly.

Tiny and I were parked in the holding lot across from the front gate of Lackland Air Force base, waiting to see if Angella was coming. Jacobs was on Tiny's cell, the speaker turned on. I had tried several times to reach Angella, but she hadn't answered her phone.

"That seems to be Greenspar's history," I replied. "In Nam he got a prostitute pregnant. In Iran he got a CIA operative pregnant. A real winner. What happened to the agent? The baby?"

"Slow down, Redstone," Jacobs said, "God only gave me one mouth. A big one, admittedly, but still only one tongue."

"Sorry."

"Hope you're seated for this. The CIA operative was none other than your supposed assistant, Lisa Woods. She even went by Woody back then."

I feigned surprise, but in fact, the reporter Johnson had tipped me off. "Any possible mistake?" I asked, knowing the answer.

"One in the same. Getting pregnant for a female CIA operative back then meant dismissal. She was deeply infiltrated into the Khomeini coalition and according to her file was a devoted disciple of the Ayatollah. She's fluent in Farsi and a note in her CIA file indicates she converted to Islam prior to her assignment in Iran." Johnson had nailed that as well.

"What's it all add up to?"

"For one thing, we can have Greenspar suspended because he knows her background and didn't report it."

"If she was underground CIA, it is possible he never did know." I was turning the tables on Jacobs. "As you say, *circumstantial*."

"You're right. But follow me. If she's behind this, then it's not a North Korean operation at all, but a terrorist mission being run from the inside. That's what the President is afraid of, being attacked from inside. He's dead on."

"What about Burner? Angella has tied him to the murder of the medic and being at the safe house where we flushed Tae-hyun." Thinking of Angella, I hoped she was not still pissed.

"A couple of interesting points there also. First, that Dallas kid sketched Burner leaving the condo with Joy's computer. Dead on. Angella says the picture Joy snapped is Burner." Jacobs said, slowly building the case against Te Burner.

"Cut to the chase." I said, anxious to know where this was going.

"Those missing two years from Woody's file were years where she worked for Burner directly. That information was in the copy I delivered to you. Someone removed it, probably while you were up with McNaughton."

"Most likely Burner, or possibly Woody herself," I said, remembering my feeling that someone had been in my room. Only I had the time sequence wrong. A chill ran down my spine. These people seemed to move with impunity.

"My money's on Burner," Jacobs said. "He somehow got to D.C. without us knowing. Man's slippery. But we do know he caught a flight back to San Antonio from National. We finally managed to cut off his government access, as well as Woody's, so he had to fly back here commercial. Landed two hours ago. They both now know we are on to them. This is now all on a tight fuse. They need to detonate that bomb today, because by tomorrow it will be dismantled."

"There might be other bombs. This could all be a decoy operation to keep us from the main event," I cautioned.

"Could be, but I doubt it," Jacobs said. But there was much less confidence in his voice now. "For starters, there's not enough radiation sickness anywhere else. Second, ...well, there is no second." The line went silent for a while. I assumed Jacobs was thinking. Finally, he said, "That, of course, means Burner is heading for the base. The guy is good. So be careful."

"He seems to know our every move," Tiny added. "Are you sure Woody's cut off?"

"Positive," Jacobs responded. Again the line went silent. When Jacobs next spoke it was with an apologetic tone. "Redstone," he began, "throw away your cell phone. They planted a GPS chip as well as a voice chip in the phone. That's how they know where you are and what you're doing."

I immediately yanked my phone, pulled the battery out and tossed them both in the back seat. I had been tipped by Contentus, but I didn't want them to know. "How do you know about my phone?"

"Contentus called and told me," Jacobs confessed. "He told me he guessed what they were up to and to prove it to himself he called you and told you Tae-hyun was in a Victoria motel. That was concocted by Contentus. When Burner turned north he knew your phone was bugged."

"Bait!" I said. "Now I know how the worm feels! You guys have been feeding me information just to see what the other side would do. You'll stop at nothing."

"The Limburger shouldn't complain about the Munster," Jacobs replied.

"The Limb..." It had taken me a moment, but then I understood he was taking another jab at my handling of the Badman Tex situation. I had the distinct impression that would never go away.

"Can you arrest Woody for lying?" I asked, changing the subject before this conversation deteriorated.

"She didn't lie. No one asked her. She hired on as a clerk after she left the CIA. Back then no one thought to check the backgrounds of the support help. It's certainly not illegal to be Muslim, or to speak Farsi, or for that matter, to be former CIA. But, truth is, all arrows point to her as the leader."

It also fit with what I got from the reporter. "An atomic bomb is going to blow the country to hell and we sit on our hands and watch! That's bull shit!"

"Tell that to the folks in the World Trade Center!" Jacobs shot back in frustration. "Our way of life handcuffs us."

Tiny, who had sat quietly throughout my conversation with Jacobs, said, "Let's get on with this. Time's wasting. It's four-ten. We're late. We'll sort out who did what to whom afterwards."

"You're assuming there is an afterwards," I added.

"Have more faith," Tiny responded. "The white hats always win?"

What I wanted to say was, "Sorry, I seem to be color blind." Instead, I replied, "It seems to always be scripted that way. We can only hope."

I used Tiny's phone to check with Cindy to see if we were still a go for the visit. As usual, she had performed her work effectively. She said Tae-hyun had been moved from isolation to the interview room over an hour ago. "Followed up myself," she commented. "By the way, Energy won. Preparations are underway right this moment to transfer the device to a facility in Amarillo under the Department of Energy's oversight. From what I understand, it will be trucked up there tonight."

"Got to be nuts getting near that thing," I said. "I hope they shield it properly this time."

"They're working on it now. Building a housing for it. It'll be in a Demron shield. There's nothing to worry about."

I didn't think it appropriate to comment on the obvious. No one's safe around an atomic bomb—and particularly not one from the fifties.

The Commanding General was not waiting for us at the front gate as Cindy had promised. In fact, the reception we received was not what I had expected. We were ushered into a small building off to the side, the door was closed and locked behind us. Looking out I saw two massive German shepherd dogs glaring back at us, their teeth bared as if daring us to come out.

"What the hell's going on?" I asked Tiny. "We're not the enemy!"

"Someone certainly believes we are. It's never good when men with assault weapons are pointing inward toward you. To them, we're the enemy."

We remained locked in the building for what seemed an hour, but was closer to fifteen minutes. Tiny finally called Cindy to see what the hell was going on. Her line rang to voice mail and it took another ten minutes before she called back.

"What's going on down there?" she demanded. "System says Tiny cleared in about an hour ago!"

"He certainly did not! We were on the phone to you at that time. We're now locked in a guardhouse surrounded by angry dogs backed up by Marines with their weapons at the ready. What gives?"

"Beats hell out of me! I'll have Max work this directly."

A minute later General Jamison was on Tiny's cell. He held the phone out to me as though it was burning his fingers.

"Redstone!" Jamison shouted when I came on the line. "I understand you're in the guard house at Lackland. That right?"

"Right."

"Should leave you there if I had any brains. But got a job to do. Base commander is on the conference bridge. General, tell me again who entered the base about an hour ago to see the Korean?"

"A man named Kelvin Jurald," came the crisp response.

"Did you personally see Mr. Jurald's ID?"

"I personally did, Sir, as I had been instructed."

"Did you have a picture ID of him sent from Homeland Security?"

"I did Sir. It matched his ID perfectly."

"How tall is this Jurald?"

"About six-seven or six-eight. Weight about one-sixty."

"The real Kelvin Jurald is closer to seven feet. Goes about two seventy if he's a pound!" Jamison barked. "We got ourselves a problem."

"The man I allowed onto the base was certainly not that large. He's with the prisoner now, Sir. According to the protocol I was given, his badge gives him unescorted access to the base. We have no procedure for rescinding that access without removing the badge from his person."

"Please escort the two men you have in the guardhouse to the prisoner. And take the imposter into physical custody! By God, whatever you do, do not allow the Korean anywhere near the device transport. Is that clear?"

"Yes, Sir." The line went dead.

Less than thirty seconds later the dogs were on leashes being led away. The door to the guardhouse flew open and one of the Marines who a moment ago had his automatic weapon trained in our direction was now rushing us to a jeep parked a few feet away.

"I don't know who you two are," the guard called over his shoulder, "but I've never heard the Commander use such language. He's pissed."

I had to hold on for dear life as the jeep raced across the massive base heading toward a small brick building. Off to the right, about a mile further than where we were seemingly headed, a large transport vehicle was backing out of a hanger. Armed guards, facing away from the vehicle, formed a secure perimeter.

Workers, civilians judging from their outfits, or possibly military in work attire, moved in every direction. Golf carts seemed to be the primary mode of transport with an occasional Jeep weaving among them.

Our driver pointed in that general direction. "Some special device headed out. Be glad when it's off the base. Been nothing but lockdown since it arrived. All leave's been cancelled."

I reached for my cell phone, momentarily forgetting that I had left it in the car. I wanted to inform Sylvan Jacobs what was going on.

"If you're thinking of making a phone call, forget it," the driver yelled over the wind noise. "You're entering the black-out zone where cell phones are jammed for security purposes. Only military communicators work out here." He tapped a large walkie-talkie-looking object hanging from his belt. "You can use this if you need it."

The Jeep slammed to a stop in front of the interrogation building and the driver raced inside, his assault rifle again in position to be fired. Apparently he had been assigned to apprehend the imposter.

Tiny and I both climbed from the jeep and drew our guns as well. Neither of us had any intention of allowing Burner, or who ever was inside, to escape. I turned to Tiny, "How about you escorting the creep to the guardhouse? I'll speak to Tae-hyun and get what I can from him. We can do the debriefing later. Come back when the perp's secure. You okay with that?"

Tiny shook his head in agreement. "It's your show, *Cowboy*."

"Don't friggin start!"

A moment later we switched to plan B when the Marine raced out of the building and announced, "Got a real problem! Imposter's gone! Coburn, says he was only inside a few minutes when the prisoner collapsed. Coburn ran into the confinement room to see what happened. The imposter slipped out and headed toward that transport parked over there. He has base clearance so he was allowed to proceed. Imposter's name is Jurald."

"Get me over there as fast as you can drive this heap," Tiny yelled, forcing his large frame back through the narrow opening of the Jeep. "Tend to Tae-hyun and get your butt over to the transport as fast as you can," Tiny yelled in my direction as the jeep quickly gathered speed.

I shouted back, "Call Jamison. Tell him Domestic Disturbance!"

SIXTY-FIVE

I put my weapon away and pushed the outside door open. A young Marine, who I assumed was Colburn, not older than twenty, was sitting inside. He snapped to attention when I came through the door. He studied my ID and quipped, "Seems IDs aren't worth a damn these days. Everyone's got one! Commander said to let you in. I let you in. Prisoner's in that room. Call if you need me. I'm not permitted to listen. The room has no windows, so he's not going anywhere. Yell loud if you need me, otherwise I can't hear you through the brick."

Clearly, he was not happy with his assignment, especially since I was a civilian and the prisoner was a civilian. He hadn't gone through Marine training to play babysitter to civilians. I resisted the urge to tell him to suck it up.

Tae-hyun was huddled in the far corner with his back to the door. Using my well-practiced technique for easing into an interrogation I softened my voice and said, "Good afternoon,

Tae-hyun, we've met before. My name is Jimmy Redstone and I'd like very much to talk with you."

Tae-hyun didn't move.

"I assume you understand English. Do you speak English?"

Still no response.

I moved closer to the inert body and the thought crossed my mind that Tae-hyun was dead. It didn't make sense that Burner would kill him, but something was wrong. Maybe he was sick?

I bent to feel for a pulse. "Are you okay?" I asked. "Are you hurt?" I extended my hand toward his neck to feel for a pulse.

Without warning, his right elbow came up hard and caught me square in the groin. I gasped in pain. Both my hands instinctively dropped to protect myself. He flung his body against my legs and simultaneously grabbed both my ankles. I fell forward.

In an instant he was on top of me. I landed with my arms pinned to the floor underneath my body. The pain from the initial blow was devastating and I had trouble clearing my mind. He retrieved my gun and jumped off me.

In English worthy of an English major, he said, "Sorry to disappoint you, Redstone, but your Korean friend has taken leave."

At first all I could focus on was the debilitating pain radiating from my crouch. I did not understand the import of what he had said. Nor did I comprehend the simple fact that the man standing over me was nearly two feet taller than Tae-hyun. It also took several more seconds before my eyes cleared enough to focus on the face of Te Burner—minus the big hair. The blue Buick rogue Border Patrol agent was finally in a location where he couldn't escape and there was nothing I could do to apprehend him—at least not while he hovered over me.

"You can get off the floor," Burner said, his lips curling into a lopsided smirk. "But do it slowly and keep your hands where I can see them. If you make any loud noises I'll put a bullet in your brain."

The pain was so intense that a bullet would have been a relief. I was gasping for air and it was difficult to get up. I paused on one knee to catch my breath—and to gather strength.

Then it came to me. I finally understood what he had said about Tae-hyun. But the impact of realizing who was speaking was even greater. This was the man best known for slashing the throats of his captives and killing the medic. He is also the most likely person to have killed Chief Duran as well.

I ran my fingers lightly along the scar that had been inflicted on my jugular when we captured the Korean the first time. I was lucky. My left shoulder had taken a bullet in an earlier incident and my foot was still not healed from the episode in Mexico. I was no match for Burner, and he knew it.

"Don't worry, Redstone. I won't bother cutting your neck. I had to go through screening to get in and they took my knife. I'll make it quick and fast. A bullet to the brain."

"Like you did to Chief Duran. Only he lived several days."

"Pity. Chief got his nose where it didn't belong. He was a good man. Liked him actually. But business takes precedence, don't you agree?"

"It doesn't matter to you whether you like someone or not. You thrive on violence."

"Can't let people get in the way."

"In the way of what?"

"Suppose there's no problem telling you now. In a few minutes, if all goes according to plan, we'll both be dead. And if the plan doesn't work, I'll not get out of here alive anyway. Kind of a no-lose situation for me."

"Sounds more like a no-win plan. You can call it off. Stop the detonation."

"Too late for that. There's no way to communicate with Tae-hyun at this point. Took me a while to figure out where the key went. Piece of cake after that. Tae-hyun will do the rest."

"What's his involvement in this? I mean why him?"

"Disillusioned young man. Mother got pregnant from some military guy in Nam. Country wouldn't let the mother or the kid in. He's getting his revenge. If it wasn't him it would be some other idealistic kid, righting wrongs they don't even understand."

"Is he Greenspar's kid?"

"Shit no! Homer's kid is Anglo. With Woody."

"Greenspar had a child by a Korean woman as well."

"Imagine that!" Burner exclaimed. His face came alive at the news. "He was whacking them good everywhere. He wasn't alone. There's a whole legion of children left behind in Nam, and even in South Korea. They hate us for the way they were treated. It's easy to find one who'll dedicate his life to messing with good 'ole America. We have a positive knack for getting people angry with us."

"And you? What's your great bitch?"

"You might say I was recruited by Woody. She taught me the virtues of Islam."

"You can be Islamic and still not kill innocent people." I was getting angrier by the minute and I kept reminding myself he had the gun. "You're a coward, killing innocent people."

"They're not so innocent. You want to know how this government you love so much treats its people? You really want to know? I'll tell you." It was Burner's turn for agitation. He was waving the gun wildly as he spoke. Actually, he was beginning to rant. "Greenspar gets a woman pregnant—now you tell me two women—and what do they call him? I'll tell you what they call him. They call him Ace! Gave him a promotion. That's what they do. But let a woman get pregnant and you know what they call her. They call her a slut! A slut with low moral character! They throw her out! Woody was one of the best agents they ever had over there in Iran, and they discarded her like filthy bathwater!"

With all the noise Burner was making I expected the guard to come in at any moment. The problem was, if he opened the door Burner would most likely fire at him. I was determined to not let that happen. Or at least if it did, to take full advantage of the distraction.

I studied Burner's movements and realized that the safety was still on. I planned to jump him the instant he turned toward the door.

But the door remained closed.

"So where's Woody's child now?"

"That's none of your friggin' business!" he shouted. "Stay out of my personal life! That's the trouble with you bureaucrats! You can't keep your stupid noses out of other people's business! She's a good kid! You leave her the hell out of this! You hear me?" He was shouting and becoming more agitated as he ranted. "You leave her alone, you hear!" The gun was waving in an arc. One moment the muzzle was focused straight at my face, the next off to the side.

Suddenly the door flew opened.

Burner turned in that direction, leveling the Beretta at the young Marine Colburn. He pulled the trigger before I could move fast enough. But the safety pin was still engaged. He found the release button and pushed it with his thumb. At that instant I swung my arm upward and it connected with his hand.

The bullet lodged in the ceiling.

I jumped him from the side and we both tumbled to the ground. Out of the corner of my eye I saw the guard point his semi-automatic pistol at our rolling bodies. I had one hand on my gun, but could not dislodge it from Burner's grasp. If it fired again, the most likely to be hit would be the guard.

And he knew it. He retreated so that the door would shield him. A second round went off and hit the doorframe above the guard's head. A third bullet glanced off one of the two chairs in the room, hit a sidewall and ricocheted back toward me, hitting the wall just behind my head. Brick fragments stung my neck. One piece tore across my cheek.

The guard took aim at Burner, but in point of fact, he was protecting himself. If both of us were hit he probably wouldn't miss a night's sleep over it.

Burner pulled me to the floor and rolled on top. I struggled to prevent him from pulling the gun free even though he was pounding my hand against the concrete floor.

He dug his fingernails into my jugular scar and warm blood squirted out, snaking its way down the side of my neck. I managed to punch a finger into his left eye and he answered with a deeper rip of my throat.

Then the marine fired and my hand slammed against the wall. The grip Burner had on my throat eased, allowing me to twist away from him. My hand throbbed. Blood was running free, but the gun was no longer in his. Several fingers from his right hand were gone. He tried to sit up but instead his body fell over on his side.

I retrieved my gun and with my left hand picked it up. My right hand would not function.

The guard ran over, ripped the front of the shirt from Burner and wrapped it around my hand to stem the bleeding. He grabbed my arm, pulled me up and walked me out of the room. He slammed and locked the door behind us.

"He'll bleed to death," I said, when he pushed me out into the open air.

"That's his friggin' problem! Serves the cockroach right! You're the priority. Need to get your bleeding under control." He examined my neck. "Not too bad," he pronounced. "Got to concentrate on your hand."

"I'll be fine," I lied. "Just get me over to that transport, that's the real priority." I pointed toward the direction I thought it was.

"If that's your orders, then so be it. Let's go."

I followed the young Marine outside and noted a large group of people gathered around one end of the transport. I had no way of knowing if Tiny had captured Tae-hyun or even if Tae-hyun was even near the transport.

I had lost track of time and had no idea how long we had before Tae-hyun destroyed a good portion of Texas. I wondered where Tiny had gone. I hoped this was not of the times he chose to disappear. Had he warned the President?

The guard appeared from around the side of the interrogation building with a golf cart and a moment later we were heading across the tarmac toward the crowd. The closer we got to the transport, the larger the crowd appeared. They were mostly Marines with their weapons pointed toward the transport.

A few minutes later I made out Tiny's frame towering above everyone.

"What the hell happened to you?" he asked when he saw my blood soaked shirt and the towel wrapped around my hand. "Tae-hyun get the best of you. That little ..."

"They switched! The Korean is in there. He has the key! Burner and Woody are the ones behind this. Burner is locked up in the interrogation shed. From what I gather, Greenspar is being framed."

"Shit! We've been standing guard waiting for Burner to come out. Didn't think he could set that thing off. Didn't want to storm it, no telling what might happen. Now you're telling me Tae-hyun's inside. What about the detonator key?"

"Tae-hyun has it. At least that's what Burner said."

"I only hope this is the only bomb they have. This could be timed to coincide with others. Maybe one near Washington? Possibly on a train coming in from, say, New Orleans. Lot's of possibilities. Did you call the code in?"

"What code?"

"Domestic Disturbance! Do it now. Call Jamison—or the White House. Shit, any second this can blow! Need to go in and get him out. He's probably assembling some mechanism or something. Maybe there's a fuse? Don't know how long a timer that thing has!"

Tiny borrowed a military phone and placed the call to Jamison. He handed the phone to me. When the General came on the line, I said, "Domestic Disturbance."

Jamison, always in command, without any trace of emotion, replied, "We'll execute immediately. How long do we have?"

"Don't know. Tae-hyun's been alone with the bomb for about twenty minutes. Could be any second."

"Do nothing to speed him up. We need all the time we can get. You have any reason to believe there's more than one?"

"Nothing either way."

"Gut?"

“This is isolated.” That was a pure guess, but if Burner was at the top then there was only one.

It didn’t take much imagination to visualize the actions that were about to take place. The President being escorted out of whatever meeting he was in. The others left to wonder what caused the sudden departure. Congress interrupted while key members were rushed to safe and diverse locations. The men and women of the Supreme Court, their black robes trailing behind them, fleeing their chambers. The Government being protected by men and women who pledged to substitute their own lives to save the lives of those they were sworn to protect.

And what would the press be told? The ultimate reality is what the press knows and reports. Nothing else exists. But Abigail Johnson knew. Would she be allowed to live to write about it? Right now, that was her problem—not mine.

I used the military phone to call Jacobs. I reported what I had found out about Woody and Burner. He asked a number of questions and before I hung I was assured the FBI would take her into custody immediately.

A siren sounded in the distance. My guess is the base had just gone on full alert. All around us uniformed men and women flowed like streams of water out of buildings scattered as far as I could see. In less than five minutes, jet fighters were in queues moving toward the center of the massive base. Soon the planes, their engines blaring and spitting dark exhaust, were racing down the two parallel runways lifting into the air in pairs. The sky filled with wave after wave of them, their wing tips seemingly touching as they rose and banked off to the east in perfect formation.

Two large Sentry early warning and control planes lumbered down a runway, their circular antennas jutting upward from their massive fuselages. I suspected that essential communication control would soon be transferred to the air out of harm's way from an atomic blast and the terrible after-shock that would follow. A few minutes later one of the Sentries headed north toward Dallas. The other went southeast, and I guessed it would soon be out over the Gulf of Mexico.

A third Sentry was towed from a hanger and soon it also moved toward the runway. I suspected that one would head west.

I hadn't realized just how fast the planes could be launched and how many people it took to get them off the ground. Planes of every variety, from large intercontinental bombers to small single-person trainers, were now moving into launch position. Several helicopters went straight up and then flew northwest in formation. Other formations flew south.

My young Marine escort leaned toward me, his eyes wide in anticipation. "The government just went into full Red-Alert. That means every military plane in the country will launch and every naval vessel capable of moving will put out to sea. Don't want them getting caught on the ground or in harbor. We've practiced this, but not to this extent. Never seen three E-3 Sentries go up together. They're preparing for heavy stuff."

"That transport," I said to the kid, "is ground zero. Let's see what we can do to change the dynamic."

"What the hell's in there?"

"Classified. You'd have to shoot yourself if I told you."

The kid's eyes went even wider. Then he gathered himself, threw a smart salute and announced, "I've been given orders to follow your command. Most unusual, Sir, but I'm here to serve. Let me know what you need." He snapped the safety off his weapon and stood with it cradled in his arms, his feet planted for action. He was ready.

The real question: Was I?

Off in the distance, a commercial flight, low on the horizon in preparation for landing a few miles away at San Antonio International Airport, suddenly banked toward the west. A moment later its nose pointed upward as it regained height, white vapor trailing from its engines.

The trauma to the normal way of life of Americans across the country caused by the events of September 11th had faded, but I imagined that if the bomb sitting less than ten yards from me detonated, the consequences would be even greater. Even without detonation, the sheer magnitude of the actions now being taken by the government were putting countless lives in harm's way. Unfortunately, with all this movement of people and highly sophisticated machinery, bad things were bound to happen to good people.

Tiny walked over. "Just got word the President is on his way to the underground command center. We need to hold another five minutes. Ten would be better."

"Going into the van runs the risk that he'll set it off. But other than that, there's not much we can do to delay him."

Tiny replied, "Something's stymied him so far. I'm thinking maybe he's already activated it and it has a built-in timer to allow the operator to get clear."

"Not likely," I replied. "How far could he run? Not far enough to be out of the range of a monster like this. No, something's gone wrong." Then I remembered the envelope Cindy handed me last night. "Here," I said to Tiny, holding out a ribbon, "Put this on." I slipped Angella's back in my pocket. Silently thankful she was not here. That's what's wrong with partners becoming emotionally entangled. Call me soft, but the pictures and horror stories from Hiroshima and Nagasaki filled my mind, and I couldn't watch while that happened to her.

As we counted down the time until we could chance going in, the sky continued to fill with aircraft of every size and shape, from jet fighters and bombers to more Sentries and attack helicopters. On the ground, a literal army of armored trucks, transports and tanks, all filled with people and equipment, snaked across the ground away from where we were parked.

"How are they going to explain this to the press?" I asked Tiny.

"I think that's the least of their concerns at this point," he answered. "From what you told me about the leak, it's already out."

"Knowing how they think in Washington, I'm certain they even have that worked out."

"Look around. You think this won't cause panic?"

"They can cover for this. Pre-planned military maneuvers, some such thing. Trump up some small invasion of a hapless country, if need be." Tiny replied. He took a moment to study what was going on, and then commented, "Mexico. They'll cover by saying they were asked to help with some drug-related bust going on in Mexico. Maybe a border control issue. If what Jamison said is true, they've already launched against North Korea. They could cover it that way."

"Korea had nothing to do with this! There's no call—"

Tiny grabbed a military phone and called Jamison. His line was busy. He then tried Cindy. Her line was busy as well.

He redialed and handed the phone to me. "Here," he said, "you got a better relationship with her than I do." Her phone answered on the second try. "It's not Korea!" I exclaimed, "It's internal!"

"I know," she answered. "Jacobs informed me."

“Don’t launch the counter-offensive. It’s not—”

“Doesn’t matter. The planes are launched and on their way. The bomb goes off, North Korea ceases to exist.”

“We’re destroying the wrong country!” I exclaimed. Well, maybe the right country, but for the wrong reason, I told myself. Shades of the Iraq invasion. It was senseless arguing with the former Marine general.

“Sometimes these things happen,” McNaughton answered. “If you think for one minute this Government will allow the public to know this is internal, then you’re a fool. If nothing more, Korea makes a great cover.”

“But Woody will talk! She didn’t plan all this to have it fizzle in rumors and speculation. She’s already leaked it to your sister-in-law. One way or the other, the story will come out.”

“That remains to be seen,” McNaughton replied, her voice cold. We’ll deal with Woody.” The line went dead before I could remind her that there were others as well. Burner, for one.

“They launched against the Koreans,” I said to Tiny, “Won’t call it back.”

“Wasn’t Jamison a POW? I’d bomb them out of existence too, they did to me what they did to him. It’s payback time.”

“He was in Hanoi,” I reminded Tiny.

“Who do you think worked with the North Vietnamese?”

“It’s not right!”

“What was that Jacobs said about the smelly cheese?”

“Not you too!”

We waited another ten minutes. Then I said, “Shit! I just had a thought. Just came to me! He’s rewiring the sucker. The key may be wrong. That’s what’s taking so long. You don’t light these things with a fuse!” I checked my watch one final time. “Okay. Time’s up. It’s been too long as it is. If he’s having a problem, we still might have time to intercede and stop him. I'm going in."

"I'll inform Jamison."

This time Tiny got through. Jamison's reply was characteristically short. "President's secure. Good luck."

I told our Marine guard to get everybody out of Tae-hyun's line of sight and to be quiet. I had no idea of what was going on inside the trailer and I didn't want to spook him when the trailer doors opened. I said to Tiny, "I don't imagine he has a weapon, but with him you never know for sure. I'm going in. Stay out of sight. I won't be able to grab him with my hand as it is, so I plan to chase him out. You grab him when he comes through the door."

Tiny nodded and handed me the communicator he had been using. "I've turned the talk channel on. It'll pick up everything said in there. It's all secure. We'll monitor from out here."

I snapped it on my shirt. I imagined Jamison in some underground bunker somewhere watching everything we did. I didn't ask Tiny because I really didn't want to know. If I was successful, they wouldn't care how I accomplished the mission. If not, well, if not there'd be nothing left of me to care. Another one of those no-lose situations. But it felt more like a no-win to me. It's all in how you look at it.

I opened the door and waited.

Nothing happened.

I sat on the rear ledge and heaved my legs up, twisting as I did so, allowing my feet to land inside the trailer. I wasn't exactly silent, so he must have seen me by now. I tensed, not knowing what to expect.

Still nothing.

I started forward. My stomach locked tight and my pulse going off the chart. I reminded myself that dead is dead. It didn't matter if it was a bullet to the brain or an atomic bomb. Except the WMD took out a whole city.

Before I could move any further into the vehicle, something grabbed my ankle.

I glanced back and was relieved to find it was Tiny's large hand. He motioned me to move close to him. He pressed a military phone against my ear.

"The FBI just found Woody dead," Jacobs said. "Died of an apparent heart attack."

"So that's their solution. So why do you sound upset? It solves a million problems."

"Body was still warm when the FBI got there," Jacobs replied. "I'm convinced the CIA was tipped and got to her. You're buddy Tiny's orchestrated it."

"You don't know that for a fact," I said automatically defending Tiny. "He's right here with me." I pressed the receiver against my chest and said to Tiny, "Did you tip the CIA?"

"I reported the situation to my command. Why?"

"Woody's dead."

"Good riddance!" He paused then said, "Hey, don't lay this on me. How they handle things I won't vouch for."

I snapped the phone off and handed it back to Tiny. There was nothing I could do about a dead woman. My business was stopping the Korean from detonating the bomb. That took all my concentration.

I started crawling on the floor of the trailer slowly making my way to the front where I supposed Tae-hyun and the bomb were located. Four feet into the trailer and the blood-soaked shirt that had been wound around my hand slipped away revealing a deep slice where the bullet had cut a path across the knuckles.

I think I saw bone, but that was tomorrow's problem. Assuming there would be a tomorrow.

I concentrated my vision forward, trying to see into the deep shadows. It took a while, but up ahead the outline of a steamer-trunk-size package began to take shape.

The package appeared to be foam. That puzzled me until I began to realize that what looked like foam must be the new radiation material. It had a blue tint in the dim light within the van. Except, as my vision continued to sharpen in the dark, I could see that the blue covering was broken by a large patch of grey.

It took a few seconds before it registered. I think it was the slow beeping from the radiation detector I was wearing that gave me the first clue.

A large portion of the Demron shield had been ripped off, exposing the side of the bomb. Pieces of the shield material were scattered on the floor.

Tae-hyun was sitting crossed legged beside the shield, his right arm extending inside. He had to know I was close by, but he was concentrating instead on the bomb.

I slowly moved closer and as I did so two facts became apparent. First, the pitch of my sensor was increasing. It was now almost constant. Second, a portion of the grey inside the shield was missing and his hand was twisting something unseen within the bomb itself.

Then a third fact.

A small object sat on top of the shield, just in front of Tae-hyun's head. From the shape of it I recognized the key from Angella's purse.

So far, Tae-hyun was ignoring the sound from my sensor as well as my movement as he continued to concentrate on the bomb. That could only mean that he was close to setting it off.

He shifted his body, moving to his knees. The air in my lungs evaporated when he reached his left arm up toward the key.

"Don't," I said as calmly as I could, but I think the words came out as a sharp command. My sensor began sounding a steady shrill tone that became louder every few seconds.

Tiny, reacting to the deafening sound from my sensor, jumped into the trailer and began crawling toward me. His silhouette against the afternoon sun was that of a great grizzly bear.

The sound caused Tae-hyun to look toward me. He again wore the same bemused expression as he had all the other times I had seen him. Only this time he seemed to want to say something.

I said, "Tae-hyun, come out of here. Killing people is not a good thing." I knew I sounded foolish, but I didn't know what else to say to him. I didn't even know for certain if he understood English.

Slowly he withdrew his arm from the shield. His eyes held a self-satisfied glow, as if nothing could be done to stop what was about to happen. He had the look of a terrorist about to destroy himself and everyone around him, after having made peace with his maker.

He started to stand up. I moved toward him. My intention being to push him out of the trailer away from the lethal package.

Pain shot across my right hand and up my arm as I reached forward. I involuntarily yanked my arm back.

Seeing my distraction, Tae-hyun immediately thrust his arm back into the bomb housing. His whole body twisted with the force that he applied to something hidden from view.

I could hear something snap inside. It sounded like a match-stick, but louder. Then he again reached for the key, this time retrieving it. His arm again disappeared inside the housing and I mentally prepared myself for an explosion. Instead, all I heard was a series of clicks, reminding me of an igniter on a grill or the starter on a gas stove.

I assumed he had just lighted a fuse. How long it would burn I had no idea. The only thing I could focus on was to get Tae-hyun out of the van so that the detonation experts could come in and defuse this puppy—assuming it was not already too late. And assuming it was even possible to deactivate a fifty-year old A-bomb once its fuse had been lighted.

I again started for him, but he rolled into a tight ball, leaving nothing to grab.

My right hand was numb, so I wrapped my left arm around him and pulled him toward the open back door. At first his body didn't budge. It was as though he was glued to the floor.

With my elbow, I hit him in the spine several times, and then aimed at the base of his neck. His feet shot out. I don't know if that had been a voluntary movement aimed at me, or the result of the blow to the neck.

I landed another blow, and this time his right leg hooked mine and I fell onto my face. Tae-hyun then dove past my sprawled body, jumped to his feet and ran toward the open door and directly into Tiny.

Tiny tried to contain the Korean, but received a knee to the chin for his efforts. Tae-hyun got between Tiny and the wall and slid toward the back door.

Tiny threw out his leg in time to knock Tae-hyun off balance. The Korean then plunged headfirst off the back of the transport.

Bullets from several assault rifles, led by our young Marine guard, caught him in mid-air. His body spun from the impact.

Tae-hyun was dead before he landed on the Texas ground.

SIXTY-SIX

Tiny carried me out of the trailer. My head was pressed against his sensor, and it also was beeping.

He carried me several feet away from the transport and placed me gently on the ground. The young Marine guard retrieved my boot and replaced it on my foot.

"The key's in there," I said. "I think he's set off a fuse."

Tiny, running faster than I thought a man his size could run, leaped onto the truck bed and disappeared inside. A moment later he reappeared, holding the key.

Our guard exclaimed, "What the hell's an Evenrude motor key doing in this van?"

Tiny and I turned to face him. "What is that you just said?" Tiny demanded. "An Evenrude what?"

"Key. That key belongs to a sport fishing boat," the guard responded, puzzled at Tiny's question. "I mean, nobody uses that kind any longer. They're old."

"Are you positive it's a boat key?" I asked.

"Absolutely!" the guard replied. "My old man owns a repair yard, and that key was only used for a few years in the mid-eighties. They're hard to find now."

"So Angella was right after all!" Tiny said.

A human form, I couldn't determine if it was male or female, dressed in a white hazmat suit with a dark tinted helmet, walked slowly down the steps from the transport. I hadn't seen him—or her—go in. A mechanical voice then announced, "It's secure. Korean was attempting to set it off manually. It appears as if the manual control had been inactivated. He busted the lock mechanism, but we caught the electronic timer in time. Thank God. I've replaced the shield. Radiation won't be a problem now."

I called Jamison and told him about Tae-hyun.

"I'll let the President know," were his only words before the line went dead.

A few minutes later the guard said, "I was just instructed to move the guy, you know, the one got shot, from the interrogation room out to hanger Baker Six. Want to go?" He then noticed my sensor. It had stopped making noise, but its color had permanently changed to blue. I didn't know what that meant—and frankly I didn't want to know. Not yet anyway. Bad news travels fast enough. "You need to get the radiation looked after. Blue's not good. Lucky it's not red. We wouldn't be able to come near you."

I glanced at Tiny's sensor. It held a tinge of blue, but not as vivid as mine. Tiny and I joined the guards as they moved to take Burner into custody. Both of them had their weapons out when they opened the inner door to where Burner had last been seen. It would be a long time before I'd be able to use my right hand to hold a weapon. That is, assuming the radiation didn't take me out.

I unsnapped the detector and turned it so I could read the face

"Don't bother," Tiny said. "If your friend Cindy is right, then you're fix'n to be real sick for a while. But unless you plan to have children, you should recover. But I'll tell you this, your baby-producing days are over."

"Hate to break it to you big guy, but we may be in this together."

Tiny was reaching for his sensor when the guards returned from the building. They need not have bothered with the guns. Burner was long dead.

My military phone buzzed. "Cowboy," the voice said, "thought you'd want to know. The President aborted the Korean mission."

"Thanks for telling me," I replied into a dead phone.

My Christmas present to Cindy McNaughton and her lover, General Maxwell Jamison, was going to be a book on telephone etiquette with emphasis on *hello* and *goodbye*.

I called Angella while I waited for the guards to load Burner's lifeless body into the jeep. "Buy a turkey," I said, when she answered, "I'm taking you up on the Thanksgiving dinner. And, Angella, I'm looking forward to the trimmings—all the trimmings."

"You're pumped, Jimmy, what are we celebrating?"

I gave her the short version of Woody, Burner and Tae-hyun. "Department of Energy took charge of the weapon," I concluded. "By this time tomorrow it will be dismantled and harmless."

"What about the detonator key? Did it ever show up?" I could hear the anxiety in her voice.

"What detonator key?" I responded. "Only found an old Evenrude engine key. Got to go. There's one piece of unfinished business we have to attend to. See you in a few hours. Keep a light on."

We raced across the base heading toward a small hanger tucked away at the far edge of one of the massive runways. In the air above us planes were forming into pairs in preparation for landing. Soon, those deadly predators would all be back safely on the ground.

I said a silent prayer.

Inside the hanger we found a well-traveled single-engine Cessna. Burner's body was lifted into the pilot's seat.

A few moments later another jeep raced up and Tae-hyun was deposited in the passenger seat beside Burner. Two men wearing mechanics overhauls with no military insignia maneuvered the Cessna onto the taxiway. The engine fired, the flaps moved up and down several times, and the plane began rolling forward. It turned onto a short side runway gathering speed as it went. Soon it was airborne and gaining altitude.

Tiny tapped my shoulder and pointed to a man standing off to the side holding a controller. "He's controlling it from over there."

The plane made one circle over the base and then headed northwest.

On another runway, a fighter jet revved its engines and rocketed skyward. It circled far above the Cessna and then was lost in the sky.

"There's your answer," Tiny quipped, a broad smile spreading across his face. "They're going to shoot down the *rogue* Cessna somewhere over the countryside. That'll give them cover for scrambling the planes today. And they won't have to explain any dead bodies or hold any messy trials. It'll all be self-evident. Even your pal Abigail Johnson will have a tough time with this story."

"Beautiful!" I said. "And how are they going to explain the bomb?"

"Bomb? What bomb?"

Mary

Thank you for your unwavering support. My biggest hope is that I always return the effort. Please don't ever stop being what you are; an inspiration for all of us.

Other Books by David Harry

the Padre Puzzle

Naming Rights

The following character names were suggested by fans for use in this story. I trust I have not disappointed you.

Te Burner

Abigail Johnson

Brea

McSlednehona

Anyone wishing to send in names for the next story can do so by going to www.hotray.com or by E-mail to davidharry@hotray.com

Thank You

Thank you to everyone who provided comments on the story. A very special thank you to Kathlyn Auten for her fabulous editorial accomplishments.

David Harry can be reached at davidharry@hotray.com

For information on upcoming books and other items of interest, please go to http://www.hotray.com. You can follow David Harry on Facebook: davidharry, on twitter: david1harry and on his blog : davidharry.wordpress.com

Made in the USA
Lexington, KY
20 December 2019

58651796R00280